An excerpt from *Blue Blood Meets Blue Collar* by Cynthia St. Aubin

Remy Renaud didn't remember her.

Cosima wasn't sure whether to be insulted or relieved. Both, it turned out, but at different points in their conversation.

Insulted because every detail of their original meeting remained burned in her brain.

Relieved because it had been a pretty severe gambit to assume that a one-night stand nine years ago might make him more likely to agree to her proposal.

And she needed him to agree.

"Miss Lowell?"

That voice. Haunted by just a hint of a drawl and rich as wood smoke from the bonfire at the biker rally outside Memphis where she'd first seen him. She still remembered how it had ripped through the neon-colored haze of the hole-in-the-wall bar later that same night.

"Yes?"

"I asked you what story you think is so worth telling." Time had carved deeper wedges beneath his prominent cheekbones. Chiseled his jaw into a more dangerous cliff. His hair was shorter. His chest, deeper. His hands, rougher. His stare...just as hungry.

The thought brushed ~~~~~~~~~~ butterfly wings.

An excerpt from *One Stormy Night* by Jules Bennett

Trouble in stilettos walked straight toward his door and Cruz Westbrook braced himself for the impact.

Mila Hale wrestled against the blowing wind and sheets of rain as her umbrella flipped up. A gentleman would go offer some assistance, but Mila would likely claw his eyes out if he came to her rescue. He'd met her only once in person, but he picked up pretty quick that she valued her independence and control.

When she stepped up onto the porch, Mila tossed the broken umbrella into the landscaping and swiped the thick dark strands of wet hair away from her face. Damn it. Even soaking wet, maybe especially soaking wet, the woman stirred something inside him that should most definitely not stir.

They were entering into a working relationship, nothing more. No matter how much those bold red lips called to him.

* * *

CYNTHIA ST. AUBIN

&

USA TODAY BESTSELLING AUTHOR
JULES BENNETT

BLUE BLOOD MEETS
BLUE COLLAR
&
ONE STORMY NIGHT

HARLEQUIN
DESIRE

HARLEQUIN®
DESIRE™

Recycling programs
for this product may
not exist in your area.

ISBN-13: 978-1-335-45757-8

Blue Blood Meets Blue Collar & One Stormy Night

Copyright © 2023 by by Harlequin Enterprises ULC

Blue Blood Meets Blue Collar
Copyright © 2023 by Cynthia St. Aubin

One Stormy Night
Copyright © 2023 by Jules Bennett

For questions and comments about the quality of this book, please contact us at CustomerService@Harlequin.com.

Harlequin Enterprises ULC
22 Adelaide St. West, 41st Floor
Toronto, Ontario M5H 4E3, Canada
www.Harlequin.com

Printed in U.S.A.

CONTENTS

BLUE BLOOD MEETS BLUE COLLAR 9
Cynthia St. Aubin

ONE STORMY NIGHT 247
Jules Bennett

Cynthia St. Aubin wrote her first play at age eight and made her brothers perform it for the admission price of gum wrappers. When she was tall enough to reach the top drawer of her parents' dresser, she began pilfering her mother's secret stash of romance novels and has been in love with love ever since. A confirmed cheese addict, she lives in Texas with a handsome musician.

Books by Cynthia St. Aubin

Harlequin Desire

The Kane Heirs

Corner Office Confessions
Secret Lives After Hours
Bad Boy with Benefits

The Renaud Brothers

Blue Blood Meets Blue Collar

Visit the Author Profile page
at Harlequin.com for more titles.

You can also find Cynthia St. Aubin on Facebook, along with other Harlequin Desire authors, at Facebook.com/HarlequinDesireAuthors.

Dear Reader,

When I first met Remy in Marlowe and Law's story, I found myself trespassing inside his head. It was a little scattered in there and a surprising amount of real estate had been given over to the process for perfectly smoking meat, but the secrets I found down some of the more neglected hallways convinced me he had a story to tell. I'm so glad I get the chance!

Cosima Lowell may have traded her biker boots and miniskirts for power suits and her own production company, but this blue-blooded former wild child still remembers what Remy Renaud seems to have forgotten—the wild night they spent together nearly a decade prior. For all the things that have changed, the chemistry between them is as electric as ever, and even though he's turned from a deliciously bad boy to a temptingly good man, the single father and recently minted millionaire is strictly off-limits. Now that she has a shot at a clean slate *and* a binge-worthy reality series based around the Renaud brothers, Cosima is determined to seize both...if she can keep their old spark from kindling a fire that burns both their dreams to the ground.

Happy reading!

Cynthia

BLUE BLOOD MEETS BLUE COLLAR

Cynthia St. Aubin

For crazy aunts everywhere, but especially for my aunt Patty, who laughed like a pterodactyl and who gave me "the talk" with equal parts brass tacks and beauty. Save me some peanut M&M's.

Acknowledgments

First and foremost, my undying gratitude to my husband, Ted, who puts up with the oily cave troll I become when I'm on deadline.

Huge thanks go to my amazing editor, Stacy Boyd, who makes every story better.

For Kerrigan Byrne, my critique partner, emotional support human, platonic life partner and the only other human to enthusiastically embrace the idea of slipping into an inflatable sloth suit. Me and thee.

My endless appreciation for my talented agent lady and momma pit bull, Christine Witthohn, whose pack I am ridiculously lucky to be part of.

Sincere gratitude to Eric at Lockwood Distillery, who answered all my pesky liquor-related questions and even helped me come up with a few more. Better late than never?

Finally, my heartfelt appreciation for readers everywhere who make it possible for me to do what I love. Your minds are magnificent, and your hearts are magic.

One

Rainier "Remy" Renaud had been many things in his thirty-five years.

A brother, a thief, a convict, an ex-con, a biker, an offshore oil worker, a father, a single father, co-owner of a distillery, and most recently a millionaire.

But before all of that, he'd been one of Charles "Zap" Renaud's boys.

And his father raised no fools. Fools were a considerable liability to a third-generation Louisiana moonshiner and purveyor of assorted ill-gotten gains to an ever-changing cast of shifty locals and shady passers-through. Remy knew this because, like his three brothers, he'd been part of the operation.

In the process, Zap had given him the one good

thing to come from his whole, hungry, hardscrabble youth: a no-fail, honest-to-God bullshit detector.

At present, it howled a grab-your-waders-and-a-shovel warning at a most unlikely source.

Cosima Lowell.

Television producer and trouble with a capital *T.*

Walking, talking temptation in a dove-gray power suit.

"Well? What do you think?" Full lips painted a double-dog-dare-you red twisted in a smirk that told him she already knew the answer.

He thought the woman asking him this question was a trick the whole damn universe had decided to play on him.

If someone had taken his every teenage fantasy and created a composite in female form, Cosima Lowell would be it. Smooth skin a shade that brought to his mind the buxom lifeguards forever sprinting in slow motion down the beach on the show he'd watched obsessively the summer of his fourteenth year. Curls the color of the toasted chestnuts he and his brothers had scrapped over when they could get them. Hypnotic hazel eyes as deep as the ocean he'd never seen and as wild as the waves he'd dreamed of surfing.

All of it seated across from him in an office chair that probably cost more than his first car. Haloed with light from the tall bank of windows containing a snatch of the distant Los Angeles skyline behind, she was everything he had ever wanted but could never have.

The Renaud Luck.

Zap had referred to it often and with a lot of venom. His nickname—earned after a run-in with a circuit breaker at the oil refinery—being a prime example.

As a fully grown man, Remy had come to the conclusion that almost all of their troubles had mainly been self-inflicted. Not so much bad luck as consequences of famously bad ideas and even worse decisions.

Agreeing to come to Los Angeles had been one of them.

He'd known it when, seated on the couch across from his youngest brother, Law, and Law's very pregnant and very significant other, Marlowe, Remy had watched his brother nod, smile, and lie.

Of course, a docuseries based on 4 Thieves distillery was a good idea, Law had said. Couldn't believe he hadn't thought of it first. He would just love to talk with Marlowe's producer friend from prep school to talk about it. He'd book the next flight to LA.

They hadn't booked the *very* next flight, but one still too damn soon for Remy's comfort. Then Marlowe had to go into labor with her twins seven weeks early, leaving Remy to travel from Fincastle, Virginia to face his personal adolescent fever dream solo.

"Mr. Renaud?" Cosima Lowell's question triggered an involuntary clench between his belly button and spine. She had the kind of earthy, sexy, burnt-sugar husky voice he didn't usually hear until *after*.

After whiskey.

After sex.

"Remy." He reached for the glass of water he'd accepted after being offered everything from a latte to a massage in the plant-choked waiting area of the coworking space in west LA that housed Ferro Studios. "And I what I *think*, is that I need some more information."

She pressed her lips together, the smile tightening slightly. "About the preproduction process?"

"About you."

The light in her eyes flickered like a candle flame in a sudden draft.

"What would you like to know?"

A fair question.

Marlowe had given him a basic rundown and some of the details had surprised him. Daughter of a once world-famous Italian opera-singer mother and a father from New England old money, Cosima had up and vanished her senior year of Lennox-Finch Preparatory Academy. When she'd reappeared several years later, it had been all the way across the country and in a field far distant from her family's Philadelphia connections.

Hollywood.

"How'd you end up all the way out here?" he asked.

Her eyebrows were a shade darker than her hair, and dramatic when arched. "You'd like to know the physical route I drove, or is this a personal question?"

Damn if his ears didn't burn just as they had when his freshman algebra teacher had caught him star-

ing down her blouse while she bent over to help him
with an equation.

He'd needed *a lot* of help with equations that year.

"I'm not in the habit of conducting business with
people I don't know on a personal level," he said.

"That's funny." The pointed tip of an almond-
shaped nail tapped the tiny dimple in her chin. "The
article I read about Samuel Kane's new venture capital company making an investment in 4 Thieves almost read like you two weren't acquainted at all."

It had to be some kind of progress that he could
hear a string of words like *Samuel Kane*, *venture
capital*, and *investment* without his eye starting to
tick.

Not that he wasn't grateful that Marlowe Kane's
older brother had swept in to keep the distillery expansion project afloat when Kane Foods patriarch,
and notable jack-hole, Parker Kane had washed his
hands of it. But it still chapped Remy's ass that they'd
accepted an offer from either of them in the first
place.

He took another sip of water, as if he could swallow the fact like a bitter pill.

"Samuel Kane wanted to put money into my business," he said, resisting the urge to yank at the neck
of the dress shirt Law had insisted Remy wear for
the meeting. "Not a damn camera crew into my life."

"Not into your life," she said, sliding back into
her sales-y tone. "Into your distillery."

"The distillery *is* my life."

Or had taken over most of it in the months since the investment.

He'd learned quickly what was expected of him. Present his hand for shaking and his back for slapping.

Work.

And work. And work. Put in extra hours as the orders poured in.

Sacrifice. Offer up the only thing he held sacred.

Time with Emily.

Tenderness trampled his heart like a stampede of wild horses just as it always did when his eight-year-old daughter ambled through his mind. Huge gray eyes, wind-whipped hair, limbs growing longer by the day.

By the hour, it sometimes seemed.

He was all too conscious of how many of those hours he'd lost during this process.

"My therapist would say that statement is an indication of an unhealthy work-life balance." Cosima's red mouth twisted in a wry, self-deprecating grin that eased the tightness in his chest. An admission meant to both gently rib him while hinting at her own dysfunction.

Not that any of it was visible from his vantage.

"I'm guessing your therapist never built a distillery with his bare hands."

"Her," Cosima corrected. "And, no. I think she built her practice with delicate Hollywood egos and a poorly concealed desire to judge." Mirth sparkled beneath the dark lashes of her eyes as she sat back

in the rounded cup of chair and crossed one leg over the other, the tawny curve of her calf reflected in the chair's chrome base.

I will not *think about her legs.*

A commandment he broke in the same moment it had been decreed.

Legs were, and always had been, Remy's thing. Third in birth order but dead last in height at a respectable six foot one, he'd chased and frequently caught women whose willowy limbs meant they had a couple of inches on him if they wore heels.

Cosima Lowell wore heels every bit as high as women he'd dated in the past, but if they were to stand toe-to-toe, the crown of her curly head would barely brush the tip of his nose.

Tiny. Short. Petite. Diminutive. Delicate.

None of the words frequently welded to women of her height seemed to fit.

Distilled felt much closer to the truth. Every ounce of sex and sophistication refined to its purest, most powerful form and radiating the same banty rooster energy that made Chihuahuas swagger up to pit bulls at the dog park.

The sound of a cleared throat snapped his eyes back into his head and his attention back to the present, where a whole other human had arrived in the office without his noticing.

Shit.

"Remy Renaud, this is Sarah Sharp. She's part of the 'damn camera crew' and my assistant when we're not filming."

Lean in T-shirt and skinny jeans, Sarah had hair the color of an orange rind and the coat of pale freckles that came with it. She assessed him from huge doe eyes behind chunky nerd glasses. Just a kid, really. Which, to Remy, meant anyone between the ages of three and twenty-four.

"Can we be *The Camera Crew of the Damned*?" the "kid" asked. "That sounds much cooler."

Cosima shrugged. "His distillery, his rules."

Remy folded his arms across his chest, angling a skeptical look at her. "I don't recall agreeing to let you film."

"Not yet, but you will. I'm just that good." The cocky way she said it left not one shred of doubt in his soul that that word put its fingerprints not just on her office, but every aspect of her life.

"That's factually correct," Sarah said, hoisting the silver thermal carafe in her hand. "I've witnessed. Coffee?"

"Please." Cosima leaned forward to shrug out of her blazer.

"I'm okay, thanks," Remy said, never quite rid of aligning refusal of resources with politeness.

"You're sure?" She shimmied to get the sleeves down her forearms and the motion did things that failed to aid his concentration. "This is from my personal stash. Not that weak bean-water they serve out there at the bar."

Taking this as a cue, Sarah set one of the white ceramic coffee cups on a glass-topped table at Cosima's elbow and began to pour.

When the rich aroma of roasted beans hit his nose, Remy's salivary glands clenched so hard it hurt.

Good coffee was hard to come by at 4 Thieves. Not because they didn't buy it. Because Emily insisted on making it, and he and Law didn't have the heart to tell her that the last sip shouldn't come with a bonus mouthful of grounds.

"Jamaica Blue Mountain," Cosima said, her smoky voice winging through the words like a barn swallow.

He felt like one of those hapless cartoon dogs, fingers of steam hooking him by the nostrils as she pursed her lips to blow it from the surface of her cup.

"All right."

You're an oak, Renaud.

"Told you so," Sarah murmured under her breath after filling his mug.

The coffee tasted even better than it smelled, and it was all he could to do keep himself from making sounds that had no business in a glass-walled office.

With great effort, he set his cup back down. "So, where were we?" he asked, wincing inwardly. Though he'd received the official explanation for his compulsive fidgeting and difficulty focusing on extended conversations from state-funded health professionals at Nelson Coleman Correctional Center, the symptoms had been present since his boyhood and only marginally helped by the medication he forgot to take half the time.

This morning being part of that half.

Cosima's red-lacquered fingernails clicked against

the ceramic as she lifted it to her lips for another sip. "You were staring at my legs."

There went his ears again.

"I wasn't, either," he said, hating the hint of bayou that crept into his voice when flustered. "I was just… thinking."

"Thinking about my legs?" She glanced down at them and pointed the toe of her high heel, flexing her shapely calf.

Because she looked, he felt obliged to do the same. All too easy to imagine how the backs of her thighs would feel pressed into his palms as he lifted her onto the desk.

"Are you absolutely certain you and Marlowe Kane were friends?" he asked.

The longer he spent with this firebrand of a woman, the harder it was to imagine her and the cool, reserved billionaire heiress palling around together, even as long ago as prep school.

"More like, friend-*ly*." Cosima stared into the dark pool of her black coffee. "Our circles were a Venn diagram that intersected at old money and cheerleading."

Cheerleading.

Cheerleading?

She *had* to be doing this on purpose.

"Marlowe said you transferred to another school your senior year?"

A noticeable change of topics, but it was either move this conversation to safer ground, or use one of the many plants as a lap screen and scuttle his way to the door.

The light in her eyes dimmed. "The official version, yes."

"And the unofficial version?" he asked, piqued by the admission.

She looked up from her mug, clearly weighing whether to answer. "I dropped out. Well, ran away, technically."

"And you came straight to LA, or…"

Christ, he was terrible at this.

Unlike Augustin—thief two of four—Remy hadn't inherited their father's silver-tongued smoothness when it came to business matters. Never mind that his brother had chosen to use this gift in ways destructive to their business in general, and Law's relationship with his former girlfriend in particular.

"I spent a few years knocking around. Causing good trouble for bad people but saving plenty for myself." She offered him a roguish smile. "Eventually I came down from the adrenaline and got my act together. The production company where I'd worked my college internship hired me right after graduation. The rest, as they say…" She waved a hand to paint the road to her present.

"What made you want to get into television?" He had to ask this carefully, avoiding the Luddite resentment for all things bright and beautiful that had been forged into his bones in the mud-colored shotgun house of his youth.

She took a deep breath and stared out the window, a wistful expression smoothing her face. "My older brother, Danny, and I used to watch reruns together late at night. *I Love Lucy. I Dream of Jeannie. The Brady Bunch.* That kind of thing. We used to talk about hitchhiking to Hollywood. Getting jobs at some little all-night diner where some producer would inevitably discover us and we'd both be *huge* stars."

Now that sounded vaguely familiar. Siblings sharing improbable dreams.

He couldn't help but wonder if Cosima and her brother had similar reasons for wanting to plan their escape.

"So how did you up behind the camera?" he asked.

"By being in front of it first. I did a few commercials. Even had a minor part on a soap opera once upon a time."

His antennae twitched.

An actress.

That made just a little too much sense.

"It was the stories, when I think about it," she said. "That's what it was really about. Not the movie stars or the red carpets or the chance at fame." When she looked at him again, her eyes were alight with conviction. "That's why I reached out to Marlowe if you want to know the truth of it. I think 4 Thieves has a story worth telling and that I'm the right person to tell it."

Damn.

She really *was* good.

Almost good enough to drown out the tornado siren of his bullshit detector firing off once again.

Not because of what she'd said.

Because of what she *didn't* say. What she *wouldn't* say.

Remy should know, after all. Secrets were his specialty.

And he intended to find out Cosima Lowell's if it took him all night.

Two

Remy Renaud didn't remember her.

Cosima wasn't sure whether to be insulted or relieved.

Both, it had turned out, but at different points in their conversation.

Insulted because every detail of their original meeting remained burned in her brain.

Relieved because it had been a pretty severe gambit to assume that a one-night stand nine years ago might make him more likely to agree to her proposal.

And she needed him to agree.

Having spent her very last cent buying her ex-fiancé out of Ferro Studios—the production company she had founded and foolishly made him a partner in—she hadn't so much as file cabinet to store the settlement agreement in, or a pen to sign it with in the aftermath.

"Miss Lowell?"

That voice. Haunted by just a hint of a drawl and rich as the woodsmoke from the bonfire at the biker rally outside Memphis, where she'd first seen him. She still remembered how it had ripped through the neon-colored haze of the hole-in-the-wall bar later that same night.

"Yes?" she said, having learned long ago that *sorry* was not a word to be used casually in negotiations.

"I asked you what story 4 Thieves has that you think is so worth telling." He slouched in his chair, an irritatingly amused smirk notched into one corner of his mouth. Time had carved deeper wedges beneath his prominent cheekbones. Chiseled his jaw into a more dangerous cliff. His hair was shorter. His chest, deeper. His hands, rougher. His stare… just as hungry.

Eyes doing all the work as his mind worked behind them, already tasting the thing he wanted.

At twenty-one, it had made her knees weak.

At twenty-nine, it made her desperate. She was so close.

And Remy Renaud could be all the separated her from the reality she'd worked for since she'd fled her parents' Long Island estate and never looked back.

"Right," she said, recrossing her legs. Her coffee had cooled, but she sipped it, anyway, to give her hands something to do. "The story of brothers who forged a shared dream with grit, determination, and the skills gleaned from their hardscrabble youth."

The furrows branching out from the corners of his eyes deepened. "And how would you know anything about our youth?"

Crossroads.

There was more than one way to answer this question. She chose the simplest.

"Because it's referenced in the section entitled 'About the Bad Boys of Booze' on your website."

Remy heaved a disgusted sigh and muttered something under his breath that might have been *goddamn marketing punks,* but she couldn't be sure.

His fingers flexed against the arm of the white leather club chairs Cosima hated with a deep and abiding passion. Like the rest of the furnishings, they had come as part of the office package that she had rented specifically for this project. She wasn't certain she could pay the second half until VidFlix came through with the advance production fees for the show she'd pitched.

A show the Renaud brothers hadn't *technically* signed off on.

Yet.

Risky? Yes.

Necessary? Also, yes.

She needed a win.

When a familiar pair of brooding eyes peered out from the screen of her iPad above an article in the *Los Angeles Times* salaciously titled Bad Boys Make Good, she knew she'd found it.

And the idea for *Bad Boys of Booze* was born.

Four Thieves distillery was docu-reality gold. An idyllic setting, a colorful cast of characters, an irresistible rags-to-riches hook, and above all…drama.

Drama she'd learned about under cheap motel sheets, her ear pressed to his chest after an hours-long marathon of back-bending, wall-thumping, going-to-feel-this-tomorrow sex.

She'd had to throw a mental fire blanket over this part of her memory when he'd stepped over the threshold of her office, and it all came rushing back.

His scent. His sarcasm.

His sexy scowl.

"*If* we agree to move forward with the show, there would need to be some ground rules in terms of filming at 4 Thieves," he said.

Her pulse picked up to a trot at his use of the conditional. "Such as?"

"We're not doing any bullshit story lines or scripted scenes for emotional conflict. I hate it when they do that shit."

Busted.

"And which reality TV show have you watched where this was a problem for you?" she asked.

The tips of his ears crimsoned once again.

"*Kardashians*, but only one seasons because I was at the mercy of the hospital's cable after surgery."

"Before or after Kim announced she was studying to become a lawyer?" she asked, tickled by the revelation.

"Can you believe that? She can't even keep track

of a seventy-five-thousand-dollar earring, and we're supposed to believe she can handle law school?" His hands launched into flight, illustrating his apparent exasperation.

Cosima remembered the way those work-roughened palms and scar-latticed fingers cushioned, sliced, and stabbed at the air to emphasize a point.

Sometimes, mere words didn't seem sufficient to express the full force of his thoughts.

Sometimes, his hands had made thoughts and words unnecessary.

"One season, did you say?" She raised an eyebrow at him. "I'm pretty sure Kim lost that earring in season six. Which any self-respecting reality TV junkie knows happened over a decade ago."

The flush bled from his ears into his cheeks. "They ran repeats late at night. The pain meds made it hard to sleep."

"No judgment." She held up her own hands in a deflective gesture. "What other conditions do I need to be aware of?"

Remy cleared his throat and all traces of levity evaporated. "Under no circumstances will my father or the Renaud brothers other than Law be mentioned or asked about."

Cosima quickly fixed a curious expression to her face and asked a question she already knew the answer to. "May I ask why?"

His broad shoulders stiffened. "I'd rather not get into it."

This stonewalling answered a question she knew

she couldn't ask outright: whether Remy was still sitting on the secret he'd been keeping from his brothers for over a decade.

Excitement simmered in her belly, effervescent as champagne.

Truth had a way of bubbling to the surface no matter how tightly it was bottled or how deep it was buried.

She had learned that the hard way.

"So, no fake storylines, dad and brothers aside from Law are out," she said, ticking the items off on her fingers. "Is that all?"

Those iron eyes bored into hers with the same feral intensity she'd seen when he'd stopped her from being crushed beneath six and a half feet of drunk biker when a fight had broken out at the bar.

"Under no circumstance is my daughter to appear on camera."

Moisture bloomed between her shoulder blades and under her breasts. The cheerful background hum of the office died away as the rushing sound of her pulse filled her ears.

A daughter.

Remy Renaud had a daughter.

Did she have a mop of curly hair? A crooked grin? *Not now. Don't think about that now.*

"Warm-up for anyone?" Alarmingly prescient as ever, Sarah hovered in the office door, carafe in hand.

"Please," they said in unison.

A sly little smile played about Sarah's lips as she quickly refilled both mugs and made herself scarce.

Just one of the many qualities that had made her an indispensable resource since their unlikely meeting in an all-night coffee shop several years back. Cosima had taken one look at the prickly, pissed-off young thing perched at the counter and seen her entire life.

The chipped nail polish. The ragged fishnets. The raccoon eyes smudged with liner and shadowed by worry.

A girl she knew. A girl she had been. A girl she couldn't let down.

"Provided I work all those stipulations into the contract, do we have a deal?" Holding her breath was one of those habits her acting coaches had warned her about. But as she looked at Remy's rugged profile, she couldn't help herself.

She wanted this.

Wanted it so badly, her chest ached.

He set aside his mug and scooted forward in his seat. "I'll need to let Law look over the contract, of course."

Adrenaline punched her fast and hard.

"Of course," she agreed, hoping she didn't sound as pathetically overeager as she felt.

"And we'd need to find a when Samuel Kane's team isn't on site," he added. "Those weeks tend to be…busier."

She suspected that *busier* was a political choice in words judging by the grimace rolling across his face like dank fog.

"Absolutely," she agreed.

"I su-u-po-o-ose," he drawled, clearly drawing it out to torture her at this point, "we might be able to work something out."

Iron will alone prevented her from rocketing out of her chair, pulling him up by his lapels, and planting a kiss straight on his lips. Not that she hadn't thought about it for reasons entirely unrelated to a victory lap.

She'd become so jaded by living in the land of prenups that at first she didn't realize why he had risen or was holding out his hand.

This, not the paperwork or lawyer-reviewed contracts, was the sealing of their deal for Remy Renaud. They'd both spoken their piece. Agreed to help one another.

A vein of fear streaked through her elation.

The gesture was so heart-shreddingly earnest.

And incredibly naive.

Their handshake when he'd arrived at her office had been a brief, gentle, perfunctory squeeze.

But now.

But *now*.

An electrical current leaped from his palm to hers, tingling all the way up her arm and grounding itself with a surge of warmth in her chest. They stood there facing each other, neither of them releasing the hold.

He looked at her so intently, she half expected a "hey, wait a minute…" To fall from his lips.

"Any chance you're free to have dinner with me tonight?" A sheepish smile softened the stony expanse of his jaw. "Purely to celebrate our joint venture."

Interesting.

She angled her chin to look up at him from beneath her lashes. "Is that what you did when Samuel Kane wanted to invest in 4 Thieves? Ask him to dinner to celebrate your joint venture?"

The comment had been meant to provoke him, but he resisted the bait. Mostly.

"He's not my type," he said, his left eyelid ticking ever so slightly.

Cosima's heart froze in her chest as the scraps of their first conversation drifted back to her, nostalgic as gilded leaves on the first stiff wind of autumn.

You're not my type, he'd said.

Single?

Short.

His rebuff had stung at the time. Now, it was fuel.

"Rich?" she challenged.

He cleared his throat and shifted on the soles of his battered work boots. Paint-flecked and totally at odds with his pressed slacks, they had been the second thing she noticed when he stepped over the threshold of the office.

His dress shirt had been the first. At least two inches too small in the collar and arms. Faded from too many washings. Court hearings and funerals.

He'd had plenty of both.

Remy leaned in, stirring a warm current of air that smelled of fabric softener and clean skin. "Maybe I just enjoy your company and want a little more of it before I head back."

Cosima straightened the gold-lion pin on his probably borrowed tie. "Or maybe you want more time to study me?"

From the second he'd arrived, his eyes had been all over her hands, her face, her legs. The last, he had in common with his younger self. It amazed her that men considered these kinds of assessments subtle.

"Can't think of a nicer subject," he said, not missing a beat.

"Then I accept. As long as I get to pick the place."

His dark eyebrows shot up.

"And don't you worry your pretty little head," she said, noting the lines bracketing his mouth. "It won't be somewhere the words *sprout* and *tofu* are featured prominently on the menu."

He treated her to the full width of his smile. "It's like you know me."

Isn't it, though?

Glancing at her phone, she did some quick math. "If you don't mind, I just need to wrap a few things up. I could be ready by seven?"

"Perfect," he said.

She glanced toward her office door in a subtle invitation.

"Should I get your number?" he asked at last. "Just so we can coordinate?"

"How about you give me yours and I'll shoot you a text?"

He rattled off the string of numbers. Seconds later, his pocket pinged.

A familiar sound effect.

The descending whistle that typically announced a large object falling toward an animated character.

He gave her a self-effacing grin as he pulled out the phone and swiped his thumb over the screen. "Emily's choice. I've been introducing her to vintage cartoons."

Emily.

Why did knowing his daughter's name make her feel like she'd been mule-kicked in the chest?

"A vastly undervalued cultural artifact," she said breezily. "Speaking of dinner spots, where are you staying? I can pick something nearby."

Remy rocked forward on his boots, thumbs hooked in his pockets. "The thing is, I was kind of hoping this meeting would be over early enough that I could just hop an earlier flight home."

She cocked her head. "You didn't book a hotel?"

He gave her a dazzling smile. "I figured I'd find a spot if I decided to stay."

"And?"

"Seeing as I have dinner plans, I guess I better get looking."

"Hold, please." She glanced back down at her phone and tapped out a quick message to Sarah, receiving a reply almost immediately.

Done.

"Sarah has a reservation for you at the Proper on

Broadway," Cosima said. "How about I just pick you up there? Say, seven thirty?"

His stiff nod was adorably unconvincing. "Even better, why don't I meet you at the restaurant at eight? That will give me time to check in with home first."

With his manners, she knew this most likely had more to do with his discomfort at the idea of having *her* come to collect *him* than it did needing the extra thirty minutes, but decided to let it slide.

"Alrighty," she said. "I'll text you the address."

"See you then." He gave her a nod, then made his way through the maze of trendy tables and booths from which kids barely into their twenties would launch their million-dollar start-ups. Disastrously young as they all appeared to her, several sets of eyes covertly tracked him as he stalked toward the elevator.

Cosima lingered in the doorway, pondering the broad expanse of his back.

He looked so solid.

Like the kind of structure she could huddle under or near in a hurricane.

Which is exactly what her life had felt like as of late.

Caught in the middle of gale-force winds, watching pieces of herself flying away. Picking through the rubble. Trying to decide what, if anything, she should keep. Finding little that actually resembled her in the life she'd worked so strenuously to assemble.

Irritated at herself for these useless thoughts, she sat down at her desk, fired up her laptop, and composed the email to the contact who had been not-so-patiently awaiting the results of today's meeting.

A sharp rap on the door made her jump as she stared at the screen, desperately trying to think of a way to buy herself more time.

Sarah's eager face floated in the doorway.

Cosima had deliberately ignored the last response in their text thread.

Hotel…good sign?

"Well?" she asked, chewing the ragged cuticle of a nail.

Cosima closed her laptop. "I'm at least eighty-three percent sure we have a green light. I'm meeting him for dinner tonight, so I should have a better idea after that."

Sarah leaned a narrow hip on the doorframe, eyebrows raised on her freckle-dappled forehead. "Oh, *really*?"

Rolling her eyes, Cosima stood and began tucking her things into her bag. "Don't get any ideas."

"I get ideas all the time," Sarah said. "I'm getting one right now, in fact."

"Seriously. I'm pretty sure he just wants to drill me for details about Samuel Kane."

At least, that was one theory.

The ferocity of Remy's reaction both times Cosima had mentioned the Kane Foods CEO's name had surprised her. From what she could remember, it had always been Parker Kane, not his quiet, bookish eldest son, who had tended to produce such vibrant dislike.

Her own parents, ambitious as they were, had bulldozed her into asking him to a Sadie Hawkins once upon a time. It had been a painfully awkward evening marked by her occasional attempts to engage him in conversation and Samuel's mumbled replies as he pretended not to be staring at Arlie Banks—now Arlie Banks-Kane—across the gymnasium.

She took strange comfort in this thought.

Some things really were meant to be.

"Well," Sarah said, picking at the chipped nail polish. "Keep me posted."

Cosima shrugged her bag onto her shoulder and met her assistant in the doorway, gently guiding her hands back to her sides. "We're not picking, remember?"

Sarah blew a strand of strawberry-blond hair away from her face. "Sorry. It's just… Work has been really stressful for Justin lately and—"

"I know," Cosima interrupted, saving her the trouble of finishing the excuse.

And, anyway, she *did* know.

In addition to rough edges and a fondness for riding life's rails, Cosima had recognized another glaring similarity between them almost immediately.

Terrible taste in men.

Overhearing Sarah's half of the conversation that night at the café and the few times they'd traveled together for a film project had been like watching reruns of her own life.

Which is why she had offered her a job with Ferro Studios. She was hoping that financial stability might empower her protégé to realize that Justin was a narcissistic leech in need of a swift kick to the curb.

The full width and breadth of the irony hadn't emerged until Cosima's own relationship had spectacularly imploded, placing *both* of their livelihoods in jeopardy.

Guilt.

Always, it nipped at her heels like a mangy dog.

It had been the reason she spent the years following her dropout from high school bouncing from town to town, from bar to bar, job to job, trouble to trouble.

The one time she had stopped, Remy Renaud had found her.

Now, she might have a chance to leverage that past devastation to repair her present.

If she could keep history from repeating itself.

Three

Cosima told herself it was the heavenly aroma of smoked meat, not the sight of his sculpted torso in a pectoral-hugging black T-shirt that caused her salivary glands to contract when she spotted Remy in the waiting area of the restaurant she'd chosen for their celebratory dinner.

"You clean up nice." His eyes lingered on the clingy nude cocktail dress she'd selected during her rushed postwork ritual, which had involved fifteen minutes of trying on, and flinging off, fourth fifths of her wardrobe. All of which seemed to draw attention to the pallid hue that long hours indoors staring at legalese during the year-long battle for control of Ferro Studios had left her with. Robbed of the summery glow she typically managed to hang on to well into winter because of her Nona Ferro's side of the family.

As soon as the second half of the preproduction check was on its way, she intended to remedy that situation.

"And you…" she began, searching for but not finding the linguistic equivalent for a man who was at his most powerfully attractive when *not* cleaned up. "Look…relaxed."

"This old thing?" he said, tucking a thumb in his jeans pocket.

Cosima was familiar with the expression "the clothes make the man," but with Remy, it seemed to be the exact opposite. Even a plain black T-shirt and well-worn jeans took on the look of something too permanent, too classical, to be affected by considerations as ephemeral as style.

"Your choice of venue is a little surprising," he said, glancing around the entryway.

She understood what he meant.

One of the better-kept secrets in Los Angeles, Ruby Que couldn't be classified as a hole-in-the-wall or dive.

More like, a homey but completely unpretentious backyard barbecue moved indoors.

"You'd expected somewhere with six courses and name-dropping waitstaff?" she asked, shifting her weight to plant a hand on her hip.

"Four, maybe," he said. "And at least a name-dropping maître d'."

"Sorry to disappoint," she said.

"You don't disappoint me in the least." Heat flared in his quicksilver irises as they landed briefly on her mouth.

"Well, hey there, Miss Lowell!" A perky blond Tinker Bell of a server came bouncing over to them, menus in hand. "I haven't seen you in forever. How have you been?"

"Great," Cosima said a little too quickly, desperately trying to communicate with her eyes what she couldn't with her lips. Going so far as running her conspicuously ringless left hand through her hair. "Really great."

When Greta motioned for them to follow her, Cosima mistakenly thought she was home free.

"And how are the wedding plans coming?" she added, glancing over her shoulder.

No such luck.

"They're not, actually," Cosima said.

Greta faltered, nearly running into the giant barrel of salted peanuts that were doled out to each table in tin pails. "I'm so sorry to hear that," she said, thankfully leaving it at that.

"It's all good." A weightless lie to cover a heavy truth.

"Will this be okay?" Greta asked, pulling up at a booth several spaces down from her—*their*—usual one.

"This is perfect," she lied.

Greta set down the menus and scurried off with a promise of returning with water to flee the scene of her social faux pas.

Cosima wished she could do the same. Somehow, the booth felt five times smaller with Remy filling the other side of it.

"So," he said, cracking open one of the menus and examining the laminated page. "What's good?"

"Everything," she said. "Just depends how hungry you are."

"So hungry my stomach thinks my throat's been cut." He flashed her a sheepish smile.

"Oh, wow." Cosima shook her head fondly. "I'd heard about those but never seen one in the wild."

"One of what?" he asked.

"A dad joke." She could imagine him saying it as he sat across a cozy kitchen table from his daughter, delaying the punch line until he had her attention. Receiving an eye roll and a '*Dad,*' for his trouble.

Because she had no doubt that's what he was.

A dad. Not a *father*, like Daniel Alcott Lowell had been to Cosima and her brother. Or an *estranged* one.

Even now, that term felt altogether insufficient for capturing the resounding familial lack she often felt.

"I'll warn you," he said. "I'm somewhat of a barbecue snob."

"Is that right?" She already knew this, because barbecue, or the promise of it, had been the reason they'd met. The reason why she'd pointed her Mustang off the exit ramp just outside of Memphis when a local had told her where to find the best burnt ends in the state of Tennessee. *If* she could get the sour-faced monolith of a bartender to part with a plate.

"Yes, ma'am." He folded the menu and set it aside,

leaning back in his bench seat. I do all the smoking for the Blackpot. My brisket—"

"'Takes on its signature flavor from being smoked with the distillery's own recycled bourbon barrels,'" she said, reciting some ad copy.

Remy rested his forearms on the table, laced his thick fingers and studied her with an intensity that was mostly harmless.

Mostly.

"Seeing as you seem to know so much about me, don't you think it would be fair if I knew a little more about you?"

His request had more merit than he even realized.

She knew that he liked to drink his bourbon neat. That he talked in his sleep. That he was good with his hands and even better with his mouth.

Luckily, Greta arrived with their water. Cosima gulped at hers, hoping it might ice her revving libido from the inside out.

After ordering drinks, she pretended to be enthralled with her menu once more, half praying he'd forget what he'd asked her.

Memory didn't seem to be his strong suit, after all.

"I don't know if you're a pulled-pork guy," Cosima said, not looking up, "but theirs is first-rate."

He cleared his throat.

"I mean, a lot of places overcook theirs and it basically shreds into pulp, which totally defeats the purpose, if you ask me," she continued.

Remy drummed his fingers on the tabletop. She could *feel* his eyes boring through her skull.

"But that's not as bad as when it's oversmoked. There's nothing more disappointing than pulled pork that's like a mouthful of mesquite chips." Turning to the menu's back page, she ran a nail along the meat plates. "But if pulled pork isn't your thing, their spareribs are also amazing."

"Cosima."

The sound of her name uttered in that deep, raspy voice sent warmth rippling through her.

"Hmm?"

"You never answered my question."

"About?" she asked.

"Getting to know you better." He folded his menu closed and set it aside.

Begrudgingly, she did the same. "I gave at the office, remember?"

"You really expect to get through a whole meal without telling me anything else about yourself?" He lifted a dark eyebrow at her.

Inclining her head, she mimicked the placid plaster saints who had creeped her out as a kid. Always glaring down at her from the walls of St. Joseph's with their painted eyes and frozen smiles.

"What are we supposed to talk about then?" he asked.

She shrugged. "Sports. The weather. The merits of cold smoking versus hot smoking."

"Now you're just trying to distract me," he accused, the corners of his mouth curling upward.

"Is it working?" she asked, nodding her thanks

as Greta set a generously poured glass of cabernet before her.

"Like a charm." Remy lifted his frosted mug in a toast.

"Do you guys know what you want, or do you need a need another few minutes with the menu?" Greta asked, not so subtly eying Remy's flexed bicep when he brought the mug to his lips.

"I'm going to let her order for the both of us."

"Such trust," Cosima marveled. "You're sure about that?"

"Anyone who has such great taste in cars can pick my dinner anytime."

She snorted. He must have been watching when she whipped around the corner, sailing into the parking lot on two wheels. An impressive feat for a 1978 Mustang King Cobra.

"The three-meat plate with brisket, burnt ends, and the spareribs."

"Sides?" Greta asked.

"Let's do the loaded potato salad, coleslaw, and, oh, do you have any of the jalapeño cheese cornbread?"

"You bet," Greta said.

"That oughta do it." Cosima gathered both their menus, handed them off, and turned back to Remy. "Where were we?"

He folded his arms across his chest and sat back in the booth. "In danger of falling madly in love."

Cosima laughed as she reached for her wine, relishing the silky flavor of dark fruit as she sipped, already anticipating how it would mingle with the smoke and spice. "Pretty shallow method of choosing a partner, don't you think?"

"I can think of shallower ones," he said.

"Touché." She felt uncharacteristically awkward, her head empty of words. Generally, she experienced quite the opposite problem.

Chiachierrona.

That had been her Nona's nickname for her.

Chatterbox.

Always spoken fondly and typically in concert with her hair being ruffled. She could feel the ghost weight and warmth of her grandmother's hand perched atop her head like a hat.

Greta returned with a basket of corn muffins and two small plates. Remy automatically reached for them, dealing a plate to her before folding away the tea towel and sliding it across the table.

This small act of care pierced her.

He waited until she had selected one to add one to his own, then broke it open in a puff of steam to add a pat of butter. His eyes widened as he chewed.

"Good, right?" she asked.

"Better than mine." He grunted appreciatively. "How'd you find this place?"

Ugh. No way around this topic, she supposed.

"My ex-fiancé. He worked here part-time before he got cast in the TV role that launched his career."

His jaw flexed. "So he's an actor?"

Cosima didn't think she was imagining the flicker of a chill in his tone.

"He is."

"Have I heard of him?"

This was always the first question anyone asked after discovering this fact. It had been much easier when she could say "probably not" and mean it honestly.

Because truly, he wasn't just an actor, he was a movie star.

Releasing a heavy sigh, Cosima flipped over her phone on the table and did a quick Google search before sliding it across the table to Remy.

He stared at it, disbelief stripping about ten years from his face. "Michael Cooper?"

The man who had broken her heart and her spirit.

Hearing his name conjured him as he'd been the day they'd met. Both crammed into a tiny waiting room at one of the endless rounds of casting calls she'd gone to shortly after her arrival in LA. This one, for a minivan commercial. She'd taken one look at him sitting there among the other hopefuls and had to grab the doorframe so as not to swoon.

Sandy hair that fell perfectly across his smooth, tanned forehead. Eyes the sparkling blue of tropical waters. Killer smile. All wrapped up with a shy Midwestern farm boy's unassuming politeness. Her diamond in the rough, now honed to brilliance by a publicist, stylist, and talent agent. A realization that had gouged her just as deeply as when he'd shown up with an equally dazzling starlet on his arm the day they'd met for the last time in her lawyer's office. Three months ago.

"Yep," she said, taking a much healthier swallow of her wine.

"You were engaged to Michael Cooper?"

She'd developed a defensive streak a mile wide at this brand of smug surprise mixed with patronizing disbelief. She'd heard it at red carpet events, after-parties, restaurant openings, movie screenings.

This *is your fiancé?*

You're just not what I'd pictured.

Or her personal favorite: *I guess opposites really do attract.*

Scraping away little bits of her confidence, comment by comment. An old wound that felt like a fresh bruise for Remy's having poked at it.

"Still yep," she said tightly. The base of her wine glass clinked as she set it down just a hair too hard.

"I didn't mean that like it sounded. He's just not who—"

"Quit while you're ahead," she interrupted.

He aimed a disarming grin at her. "I have a feeling that would be never, where you're concerned."

"Smart man." She pressed a finger to a tender muffin crumb and dropped it back onto her plate.

"Michael Cooper sure isn't."

Cosima nearly choked on her wine, coughing into her curled first and desperately trying to recover her composure.

"Excuse me?" She blinked watering eyes and reached for her water glass instead.

"Look, I know it isn't my place and that we don't know each other very well, but if you're telling me he had you and now he's settling for that Ashley Mc-whoever girl, I'm telling you the man's a fool."

She blinked at him, wholly thunderstruck and with her heart suddenly galloping in her chest. Michael and his new arm decor hadn't even made themselves red-carpet official yet. The only way he could know that was if...

"Rainier Renaud," she said, crossing her arms and leaning back against her bench. "Are you telling me you read *gossip blogs*?"

Glancing at his reddening ears, she couldn't help but smile. With his upbringing, having such an obvious external barometer of his inner thoughts must have been a significant liability.

"I might have become familiar with one or two of them over the years. Purely to stay informed about the legal proceedings between Khloe and Lamar, you understand."

"Naturally," she said.

"Anyway." He cleared his throat. "All I meant to say was, he downgraded by an order of magnitude."

Beneath the table, Cosima gripped the edge of her bench seat to keep from floating away. "It wasn't all his fault. I'm not exactly the easiest person to live with."

Remy took another sip of his beer. "And what makes you so intolerable?"

"How long have you got?" she laughed.

The beer mug clunked down onto the wood tabletop as he leaned in, sending a fresh wave of his heady, dizzying scent washing over her. "I've got all night."

Her mouth went suddenly dry as the moisture relocated itself much farther south.

"I'm bossy," she said.

"I believe you mean *motivated* and *direct*, but go on," he insisted.

She thought for a moment. "I like things my own way."

"It's a shame you're the only human being in history afflicted with *that* condition," he said drolly.

Cosima rolled her eyes at him. "I'm also incredibly impatient and always right."

"Yes, ma'am," he said. "Sure would be a terrible thing if every girl grew up to be enthusiastic and self-assured like you."

"I'm too loud," she said, hoping to stay ahead of the feelings welling up inside her.

He raised an eyebrow at her. "And who told you that?"

"Actually, a lot of people." She swirled the stem of her wineglass between her thumb and forefinger. "My mother, my father, my teachers, the priest—"

"Michael?" he interrupted.

Her throat caught.

No stranger to the entertainment industry, Cosima knew how she stuck out among Hollywood's golden ones. The heartbreaking part had been watching Michael realize it. Lamenting that she always had to pass when designers sent couture gowns designed for the tall and leggy. Teasing about how easy she was to lose in a crowd. Joking that her slightly nasal laugh always seemed to carry a second too far into sudden lulls in the conversation.

"Maybe." She shrugged.

His smile flattened. "Did he cheat?"

It was the perfect question, really.

Just personal enough that she had full license to shut down this conversation. Seal away that part of her life and return them to any number of mundane and inconsequential topics.

So when her answer came, it surprised her.

"Yes." The word hung suspended on air warmed by the pendant light overhead, until he spoke.

"You want to know what I think the shittiest part about being cheated on is?" He stared at his hands, wrapped around the bottom of the condensation-fogged beer mug.

"What's that?"

"It's not that they slept with someone else, or that they lied to you. It's that now, you have go back over everything. Every conversation. Every smile. Every kiss. You doubt every memory."

Cosima tasted metal beneath her tongue as guilt crept in like an undertow, making her hands and feet feel cold and heavy.

"Emily's mother?" she guessed.

He nodded.

"Met at the tail end of a wild streak. We were dumb, she got pregnant, we got married in a hurry and regretted it just as quickly."

"You have a picture?" She molded her lips into

what she hoped was at least a reasonably convincing smile. "Of Emily," she clarified.

"If you insist." He shifted in his seat, then brought out his phone, swiped the screen, and slid it over to her.

The device was still warm from his pocket and felt strangely alive and intimate in her hand.

His whole life was on here.

Beginning with the girl grinning up at her from the screen.

Cosima's hand floated to her mouth, but not in time to stop a small bleat of surprise from escaping.

Huge gray eyes, a wild cascade of chestnut-colored curls, lips stained cherry-red and in the perfect *O* of a singing Christmas-card angel as she pointed up at a lotus of fireworks.

A girl just like the one she'd imagined when she'd learned she was pregnant after their one-night stand.

Four

The shock and dismay frozen on Cosima's face brushed the primal part of Remy's brain that had always launched him straight into panic when confronted with female distress.

Unlike Law, he hadn't taken a backhoe to his own subconscious.

Mostly because he knew on some elemental level that his wasn't a hard-packed pile of resentment for Zap and his assorted neglect and cruelty.

It was as spongy and treacherous as the marshlands he and his brothers had often escaped to on a commandeered pontoon. Pits that could swallow up not just a stone or a stick, but an entire vehicle if you didn't keep it moving at a steady clip.

His memory—such as it was—felt like that, too.

Places that his recollection had painted prettier than they actually were. Corners where shadows turned regular branches into gnarled fingers reaching for him in dreams. Spots where the ground fell away into a blank void.

Holes.

Better not to stand on the edge of this one for too long.

"You okay?" he asked.

She blinked her dampened eyes and handed the phone back to him. "Can I say yes and you pretend like you believe me?"

"Sure," he agreed.

First, her ex-fiancé, and now this.

He was on a roll, all right.

His mind swam, desperately casting about for something that would banish the gut-shot hurt from her eyes. Or better yet, restore that cocky pirate smirk that could probably steal his heart along with his wallet if he'd a mind to let it.

"Any other incredibly painful memories I can dredge up for you?" he offered. "Seeing as the brisket isn't here yet and I still have a little room after swallowing my foot?"

Shoulders rounding, she set her elbows on the table. Her lips pillowed as she blew out an exhale. "My brother died in a car accident while I was in high school, if we want to get that out of the way."

Remy's hand moved to cover hers without him thinking about it. "I'm sorry," he said.

She sat up and tucked a curl behind her ear. By the

time she met his eyes, he could see she'd capped off whatever well he'd accidentally backed into.

"Who doesn't have a sad story, right?"

He couldn't argue with that.

Greta chose that exact minute to arrive with a giant aluminum cookie sheet bearing various bowls and baskets, the pride on her face striking a discordant note with the moment. It faltered slightly as she set down the tray.

"Can I bring you anything else to drink?" Her eyes flicked to their half-empty glasses.

"Bourbon," they said in unison.

"Any preference?" Greta asked.

Remy glanced across the table. "What are my options?"

"Oh." The girl flipped her blond ponytail over one shoulder. "We have Southern Comfort, Evan Williams…or if you want something local we have Film Noir, Angel's Aid—"

"Angel's Aid will be fine," he said.

"Snob," Cosima accused once their server had disappeared again.

He shrugged helplessly. "Is it a sin to like the finer things in life?"

Where he'd come from, the answer had been a resounding *yes*. Scorning anyone else who had them had been the most effective way of smearing lipstick on a very obvious pig's snout.

Lipstick on a pig. Not a bad name for a drink.

He made a mental note of it for Grant, general manager of the bar and Blackpot's resident mixologist. Law frequently fussed at him for his ever-more elaborate and nuanced concoctions, but there was something about the ambitious, unpretentious, burly, redheaded former inmate that Remy had liked right off. His stupid party trick of telling each of the bar's patrons which liqueur they resembled notwithstanding.

Remy wondered which comparison Cosima Lowell would garner.

Campari. Bittersweet and red as a cardinal's wing, like the lipstick she favored.

Or sambuca, maybe. Silky and dark as her hair, full of earthy depth.

It made him some kind of bastard, having these thoughts while the last of her awkwardness burned away like fog.

But the fact remained that he *was* having them.

And mentally comparing the woman seated across from him to things he dearly loved the taste of was about as bad of an idea as he could think of.

The dress wasn't helping.

It fit her like skin on a peach, clinging to breasts even fuller than he'd imagined—and he'd imagined hard. While in the shower, he'd quickly had to turn to cold water before quickly scrubbing up.

Following her to the booth, he'd realized how lucky he'd been that pencil skirt had concealed just as much about her generously rounded posterior or he might *still* be in that shower. Because the hint of its hills moving beneath the gently swaying fabric had just about run him into the peanut barrel.

"You keep eating it with your eyes and there won't be any left for your mouth."

The sentiment and the curiously musical way Cosima had pronounced it had the feel of a well-loved adage.

That it applied just as well to the image in his mind as it did the carnivore's feast before him would have to remain his secret. Noticing she'd already served herself a plate, he set about hastily constructing his own.

"Where'd you hear that?" Forking up a slice of brisket, he forbade himself from commenting on the smoke ring—or what passed for one here—and why trimming was such a vital part of the process.

"My Nona Ferro."

He watched as she tore one of the slices of pillowy white bread in half, piled it with pulled pork, and hosed it with barbecue sauce from a plastic squirt bottle.

The corners of his eyes began to tug.

You will not explain why vinegar-based sauces are inherently superior for pork.

"You're not going to have any ribs?" he asked, noting the untouched slab.

She dabbed the corner of her mouth with a paper towel from the roll provided near the condiments. "There are certain things a woman needs to do in the privacy of her own home."

And certain things a man would pay to see.

"Nona Ferro," Remy said, picking up the thread of their conversation. "Your father's mother?" he asked.

"Mother's," she said, spearing a bite of macaroni and swiping it through the puddle of sauce.

Eyes on your own plate.

"Nona. That's Italian?" he asked.

"It is," Cosima said. "She was an opera singer, actually. Traveled all over Europe. Just like my mother."

"And do you sing?" he asked.

"Not unless bribed," she said.

Remy watched in rapt fascination as her fork scooped up some coleslaw, then some macaroni and cheese, and then, to his horror, traveled toward the one item on her plate that approached being decent.

The brisket.

"The starch will completely overpower the flavor of the smoke."

It shot out of his mouth despite his best efforts to keep his teeth welded together.

Irritation creased her features.

"If we're going to work together, there's something we need to get straight right now." She aimed the pointed tip of her red-lacquered nail at him. "I eat what I want, drink what I want, and do what I want. Your opinions, instructions, and/or approval are not required for any of those items. Got that, Renaud?"

He raised his hand as if on the witness stand. Palm turned toward her.

"You have my sincerest apologies and my word that never again will I weigh in on any of the above."

The tension in her face eased incrementally. "Good. Now, open wide."

He studied the fork now poised in the air between them, not quite believing what she was asking of him.

"I—I don't think I could." Already, his heart had begun to beat a little faster at the prospect of the mishmash of textures. The muddying of flavors.

"I'm quite certain you can. Seeing as the personal questions that tap-danced all over my psyche seem to be issuing from that general vicinity." She wiggled the bite at him.

Remy swallowed the dry lump at the base of his throat.

"It's this or you're paying for my next therapy session."

"How much does your therapist charge?" he asked.

"Two hundred dollars per hour. Per forty-five minutes technically."

"God damn," he said. "You ever consider just breaking things?"

"Things, yes," she said. "People, no."

That proved the pole he needed to knock loose the buzzing hive of his panic. His jaw creaked open.

He felt the cool, smooth metal tines on his lower lip as she withdrew the fork, leaving its burden behind.

"You're going to have to chew eventually, as much as you like to talk."

He chewed.

And damn if, once he pushed past the knee-jerk revulsion, he didn't start to see her point. The complimentary combination of textures. The layered flavors.

"Well?" Cosima leaned forward in her seat.

"Well," he said, "I lied. I am going to offer you an opinion."

"About?"

"I could have used a little more coleslaw on the finish."

She made a rude noise and lobbed a balled-up paper towel that bounced off his sternum.

"Don't start something you're not ready to finish," he warned. "I'll have you know that I was a remarkably mediocre pitcher for the South Terrebonne High Gators when I wasn't out committing minor felonies."

Remy reached for his drink but was thwarted by Cosima's warm but surprisingly firm grip on his wrist. The sensation did absolutely nothing to assist with the blood rushing to a very particular part of his anatomy below the table.

"I'm beginning to suspect there's not a single mediocre thing about you, sir."

As if summoned by the offensive honorific, Greta arrived with their second round.

"I appreciate the sentiment, but can we leave the sir out of it?" Remy asked when she'd departed.

"Mr. Renaud?"

He winced.

"Worse?" she asked.

He nodded. Not because of any associations with

his father. Zap wasn't a man who people troubled themselves with titles for.

It had been the appellation of choice for the iron-faced judge who'd taken one look at a scruffy boy barely out of high school and decided to throw not just the book at him, but the entire shelf.

Because wearing the name *Renaud* in a community where gossip bred like mosquitos in the stagnant puddles of rumor had proved to be an uphill battle on an almost daily basis.

"My point," she said, "is that you don't do anyone any favors by selling yourself short. Least of all you."

He tried to let this sit for a moment, but it refused to stay put.

Was this some kind of preemptive buttering? An attempt to stroke his ego?

"From what I can tell," he said, "your therapist is worth every penny."

"Smart-ass," she grumbled under her breath. Phantom fingers remained on his wrist as he sampled the bourbon.

"The verdict?" she asked, lifting her own drink.

Despite trying to keep his face neutral, he found himself pressing his lips together and sniffing hard through his sinuses to land on the specific notes. "I can't say I've ever had a particular hankering to eat rotting peanuts out of a leather pouch before, but if I do, I certainly know what to reach for." He put down his glass and turned his attention to his food.

She only shrugged. "Tastes fine to me."

Remy leaned forward. "Tell me one scent you get from that."

Cosima rolled her eyes at him. "Aren't you at all concerned that I won't be eating my brisket at the optimal temperature?"

"Humor me."

"Haven't I been doing that all evening?" she asked archly.

Had she?

The thought coated his insides in oil as she held the drink below her nose, delicate nostrils flaring.

"Nu-u-u-tmeg?"

"You asking or telling?"

"Guessing," she said.

"You know you're actively terrible at this, right?" he teased.

"I guess ignorance really is bliss."

He placed his palm over the rim of the glass when she attempted to take another sip. "I'm sorry. I cannot in good conscience allow you to drink bourbon that looks and tastes like it's been filtered through a lumberjack's sock. Not in my presence, at least."

"Then I guess it's a good thing you're not going to be at my condo at one o'clock in the morning." She turned her attention back to her plate. "Because I plan to eat these leftover ribs right out of the fridge while slurping rotgut through a bendy straw completely in the nude."

Jesus.

Already the image had begun to unfold itself in his mind in vivid detail. Down to the rounded curves of her ass rinsed in in the refrigerator's light blue glow.

"Best that way," he insisted. "No shirt to stain."

"I'll have her bring us two boxes so you can take some with you to the hotel," she offered.

"I appreciate the thought," Remy said. "But after how early I was up today, I'm likely to face-plant straight into the sheets and stay there until my alarm goes off."

"Suit yourself." She motioned to Greta, who brought over a box and helpfully packed up the ribs before promising to return with the check.

"But, if the minibar doesn't have anything that passes muster," she continued, "I'm just a few short miles away and I get gifted bottles all the time. I'm sure to have something you at least mildly detest."

Remy felt the tips of his ears going warm again. He studied her face for any sign that she'd meant it as an invitation and not just an after-hours alcohol-delivery service. He got nothing. His bullshit detector seemed to be shorting out in direct proportion to the tightening in his crotch.

"Very kind of you," he said. "But I also have a flight at eight thirty and I'm actually not much of a drinker these days."

Her mouth curved into a sly smirk. "Neither am I."

Oh.

Remy did some very quick math.

Eleven months.

That's how long it had been since he'd been with a woman.

So long that it took a message this overt to draw his awareness to her body language.

The way her breasts rested on her arms, her cleavage mounding above them. The way she looked at him—not straight on, but from beneath her lowered lashes. The tilt of her head.

He glanced down at his phone.

No messages from Law. He'd already called to wish Emily a good-night and to make up a story for her via phone. She would be tucked into bed now, fast asleep and clutching her weathered unicorn stuffed animal to her chest, kicking the covers off her long, skinny grasshopper's legs.

He didn't have to be a brother, or a father, or part owner of a distillery also partially owned by Samuel Kane.

Just for this moment, he could just be him.

Did *he* want this?

Want wasn't even the word.

What he felt was more akin to hunger. To thirst.

The overwhelming imperative fired up from every cell in his body at once.

"Say I wanted to wash the taste of that liquid chaw from my palate?" he began.

"You're wondering if it might be convenient to just go to my place now?" She paired the question with the toe of her high heel nudging the outside of his boot. Then he felt warmth probing beneath the cuff of his jeans and realized it was her foot.

Her bare foot grazed his calf, then his knee, sliding against the inside of his thigh as it came to rest on the bench between his legs, mere inches from his rapidly thickening cock.

Remy reached beneath the table. Her instep fit against his palm as precisely as Cinderella's glass slipper. He squeezed gently, feeling the delicate bones of her toes.

Her good, hard ankles.

Wrapping his fingers over the top of her foot, he began to knead her high-arched foot with the pad of his thumb.

"You know high heels are terrible for your posture." He shifted positions so he could access her with both hands, gently rolling the under pads of each toe. "They put way too much pressure on your lower back."

Her head dropped back against the bench as her lashes lowered. "Guess you'll need to rub that, too."

Sliding down on the bench, she flexed her toe to press the ball of her foot against his now rock-hard erection.

He hissed out a breath.

"Ready to get out of here?" she asked, sliding up his length.

Remy glanced out at the dining room, as much to look for Greta as to see if anyone had noticed there might be a foot job in progress.

Predictably, everyone remained tunnel-vision focused on their own tables. Their meals. Theirs lives.

"Ten minutes?" he asked, giving her foot a

squeeze and setting it aside. "Unless you want me to scandalize the staff."

"Speaking of," Cosima said through one side of her mouth. "Incoming."

Remy quickly dropped a cloth napkin in his lap and reached for the small black leather folder.

Cosima batted his hand away, pinning it to the table. "This is on me."

Generations of male pride rose up in him. Demanding that he argue. Demanding he stop her.

"I'm the producer. You're the client. Which means when you're in LA, you're on my dime."

He relinquished his hold and allowed her to slide in her credit card and pass the folder to Greta.

"And being on my dime means I'm in charge," she said in a much silkier tone. Her foot was moving, finding him again, renewing the gentle pressure.

"You keep this up, and you're going to need a pitcher of ice water to drop in my lap before we can leave."

"Unless…" She trailed off, raising an eyebrow at him.

All at once, he understood.

"On the count of four."

Her lips remained sealed, but the hand resting on the table raised an index finger, then a middle finger, then…

Then a sound more beautiful than anything he'd ever heard filled his ears and goose bumps rose on his scalp and spilled down his body in prickling waves.

His mouth dropped open. His breath caught in his chest. For a moment, he was paralyzed. Cosima's eyes widened at him even as her red lips moved, shaping the sound as a sculptor shapes clay.

She was singing. Something Italian that made him feel lighter than air.

This was the diversion.

At last, he came unstuck. After a quick glance at the path between him and the restaurant exit, he found it clear and made a beeline for the door.

Once out in the parking lot, he located her cherry-red Mustang and took his time strolling to it, then circling it. Years spent in the company of bikers rendered him physiologically incapable of placing a hand on it, however tempting the prospect might be. These were prized possessions, dearly bought, and often the symbol of money and sacrifice beyond what its owner had to give.

When he neared the passenger door, he caught a whiff of acrid smoke, and smiled.

Life seldom offered clear delineation, such as pinpointing the exact moment when love turned to hatred, or grief to nostalgia.

But on this night in early spring, Remy could identify the exact second when his casual curiosity about Cosima Lowell had turned into infatuation.

And it had come with the screech of tires.

The sound that made him look out the restaurant window at the precise moment she'd taken a sharp turn into the parking at a speed far greater than most union stuntmen would perform.

His eyes had lifted from the smoke of burned rubber to find her face…caught in a moment of pure, potent joy.

It had almost made him feel like a voyeur, having this stolen image burned in his brain. A vision of her that he alone could keep tucked into his pocket like a lucky stone.

He steered his thoughts from it, not wanting to rub the shine from sharp chrome and her ecstatic smile.

She emerged from the restaurant and strode toward her car at a quick clip, cheeks as red as candy apples and eyes sparkling with mischief.

Remy turned toward the door as she approached, not entirely free of his very obvious arousal.

He'd thought himself long past the days of such uncontrollably enthusiastic biological responses.

He'd been wrong.

He just hadn't met Cosima Lowell yet.

Remy didn't recognize it at first.

It had been so long since he'd felt it that he'd all but lost his ability to recognize the symptoms. The thunderous applause of his heart. The lightning branching in his veins. The antigravity stomach flip. The tunneling of his vision down to one, single human. His entire life altered in one instant and eternal moment.

Mortal terror.

The engine of Cosima's Mustang roared as the slim white needle barged its way between the deceptively mundane tick marks separating 115 from 120 miles per hour.

In his peripheral vision, the city lights smeared into iridescent caterpillars.

With the top down, the night air blasted their faces, whipping her hair into a tornado of silk that fluttered skyward.

His fist ached from white-knuckle clutching the door handle. When he glanced in the side mirror, he half expected his teeth to be peppered with insects.

"Think we could slow down a little?" Words he'd spoken at what seemed like an unreasonable decibel were stolen by the wind.

"What?" she shouted back, hair flying into her mouth and being blown back out again.

"Can we slow down?" he asked, enunciating every word.

She glanced at the speedometer, gave a little *O* of surprise and let up on the gas.

"Sorry," she said, once the roar had died away. "This thing just makes it a little too easy to go fast." Reaching out a hand, she patted the tawny leather of the dashboard.

Remy wasn't sure what scared him more—that she hadn't realized how fast she was going, or the indication that this happened on a regular basis.

He bit back the need to make some sort of joke that might plant the idea of caution in her head. Since the threat of immediate danger had passed, he was able to appreciate the sight of her hand on the ball of the stick shift, expertly gearing down as she exited the freeway.

"Almost there." She slowed before a sleek granite building crosshatched by glass balconies, then turned into a parking garage. There, she pulled up to a valet station and put the car in Park.

A man in a light gray button-up shirt and black pants opened the door for her as Remy levered himself out.

"Out causing trouble again I see," he said, winking at her.

The *again* stuck in Remy's craw.

"Don't you worry, Ralph," Cosima said, leaning in to grab her purse and the container of leftovers. "I left plenty for you."

The man chuckled and waved a fatherly hand at her. "You have a good night, Miss Lowell."

"Only if you do the same."

Remy quick-stepped to beat her to the glass door so he could hold it open for her.

"You really don't need to do that." She punched the button for the elevator. "I manage this myself every night."

It pinged almost immediately, and he hung back when the doors opened. "After you."

She rolled her eyes at him and shook her head in apparent exasperation as she hit the button for the eleventh floor.

"Just because can't teach an old dog new tricks doesn't mean he forgets the one's already learned," Remy said as the elevator doors closed.

The car surged upward.

The air in it seemed to thicken.

"You know this one?" In a quick flash, she swiped her fist sideways to hit the red stop button. The car halted abruptly, giving Remy's stomach a roller-coaster lift.

She turned to face him.

"I *invented* this one." He took a step toward her and, with his eyes on hers, took the leftovers container, and set it on the floor at their feet.

"How very practical of you," she teased.

"I have a feeling we're going to be hungry later." The control he'd had a stranglehold on dissolved through his fingers like sand and he couldn't keep himself from touching her a single second longer.

One single fingertip traced the downy curve of her jaw, slipped down the elegant curve of her neck, and across her collarbone.

They reached for each other at the exact same moment.

Her, winding one arm around his waist and pressing a palm against the back of his neck. Him, by-passing her face to fill his hands with the luscious curve of her ass.

Her moan began in her throat but ended in his as their mouths met in a wet, hungry clash. No hesitance or tenuous exploration. No time spent in coy flirtation or polite invitation.

They got right down to the business of mastery from the start.

She opened to him and immediately demanded

the same, her honey-sweet tongue sweeping over his in a call that he immediately answered. A dance of velvet. Stroking and curling and sucking their way through this final introduction.

Remy had long ago given up the idea of an afterlife and only in this present moment did he understand why.

He had no taste for heaven.

His paradise was here. Warm and real. Solid and alive.

He believed in what he could touch, and what could touch him.

Cosima did.

Her hands molding him like living clay. Fisting in his hair. Cupping his jaw. His neck. Rounding over his shoulders, his biceps, his forearms.

Finding the aching arousal straining against jeans and growling her delight like a lioness.

He wrenched his mouth from hers to drag in a breath as she pressed the tips of her fingers against his swollen head through the denim, thumbing the sensitive ridge.

"*Christ,*" he hissed.

"Let's keep religion out of this," she whispered. Her warm breath tickled his ear, moist lips brushing the cartilage. The soft tip flicked into the hollow as she gently sucked in a breath, making him break out in a full-body shudder.

Remy moved her hand away from his cock, backing her into the elevator's chrome.

Cosima grabbed his hips and undulated against him.

He grunted at the increased friction, quickly jerking back his hips before he wandered anywhere near losing himself.

Since when had it taken so little to whip him into a lather?

Since her was the immediate response.

"Might we continue this conversation five floors up?" he asked, panting.

"Why don't we finish it here?" Nimble fingers slipped beneath the waistband of his boxer-briefs. "I think we'll have plenty more to talk about when we get there?"

"Impatient?"

"I like to think of myself as *eager.*" She smiled against the base of his neck. Planting kisses there, letting him feel the ridge of her teeth as she sucked before following it with her tongue.

"Easy," he said. "Or I'll have some explaining to do when Samuel Kane arrives at the distillery tomorrow."

He glanced down at her and, seeing how his censure had dimmed her fire, pulled her closer.

"How about you do the talking and I keep my damn mouth shut?" Remy slipped a hand beneath her dress, riding the curve of her hip.

"That sounds like an excellent idea." Her head lolled backward to rest against the panel when he located scrap of lace at the apex of her thighs, already damp with her need.

"God *damn*," he rasped.

"What did I say?" Her hand covered his, arresting his movement.

"My apologies." He slid the soaked fabric to the side and began to explore each ridge and ripple of her slippery folds. Trying to memorize with his fingertips what he couldn't see with his eyes. She jerked when he grazed the swollen bud, lower lip caught between her teeth. "I won't let it happen again."

"Damn right, you won't." Looking at him from beneath heavy-lidded eyes, she punched the red button and rearranged her clothes as the elevator lurched to life. "I think I'm ready for that back rub now."

Remy bent to grab the leftovers as the elevator slowed to stop on her floor. The doors opened, but she stayed put, smiling sweetly at him.

"You first," she invited.

"I'm not... I can't... You have to—"

"Only one way out of here," she said with a shrug.

A gust of frustration blew through him as he stepped into the hallway and waited for her lead. She exited, stopped about halfway down the corridor, unlocked the door, and held it open for him once again.

He didn't know what the point of these little tests was, but his mood was beginning to tank. And fast.

Purely for the sake of avoiding argument, he complied.

What he saw as soon as he stepped inside brought him up short. Huge windows with a view of west Los Angeles took up one entire wall. To his left, a set of spiral stairs led up to a loft opposite the view. To his right, an open-concept kitchen with a gleaming black granite countertop, white cupboards, and a kitchen island.

Straight ahead of him was a bed.

No couches. No rugs. No TV. Not so much as a picture on the wall.

His whistle echoed.

"I hate to tell you this," he said, "but I think you've been robbed."

Cosima clicked passed him into the kitchen, where she set down her purse on the countertop. "Decorating hasn't exactly been high on my priority list."

The long shadow of a bad break-up was implied in her statement.

"I have to admit, the proximity of the bed to the kitchen is a stroke of pure genius."

"All the easier to eat ribs at midnight," she said, disappearing into the pantry.

When Remy noticed that she'd gone in with her heels on and come back without them, he followed her to take a peek.

Sure enough.

There, neatly lined up on the walk-in pantry shelves, was an extensive collection of shoes. Though he knew nothing about brands, he could tell by looking that, like the Mustang, these had been ceremonial objects. A piece of herself she was unwilling to yield.

Cosima caught him peering at her and instantly assumed what he'd already come to identify as her defensive posture. Weight on one foot, hand on her opposite hip. "I hardly ever cook and the closet in the loft is barely more than a cupboard."

He suspected this might be a bit of hyperbole but decided to keep his thoughts on the matter strictly to himself.

"No judgment," he said.

She padded over to the cabinet and opened it, taking down two glasses from the bottom shelf. The only shelf, Remy noticed, that had anything on it.

All the ways he'd thought himself at a disadvantage when it came to his brothers, he'd never once considered the predicament of someone whose height made standard cabinetry a challenge.

He leaned against the kitchen island and made a show of watching as she opened the freezer.

"What?" she asked, dropping a large ice cube into each glass.

"Just making sure it's not being used as an entertainment center."

"You certainly seem entertained," she quipped. She bent at the waist and opened a lower cupboard, coming back with a bottle that she set on the counter.

"Eats barbecue, *and* likes scotch," he said. "If you're trying to put me under some kind of spell so I'll sign contract before I leave LA, you've certainly got the right ingredients."

Remy hated knowing that what he said in jest, he'd been told in earnest from the time he was a boy.

An old, ugly refrain sung by a man who both feared and mistrusted women as a general principle. A man who taught his sons to sleep with one eye open because women always had one foot out the door. A philosophy he'd no doubt inherited from his own patriarch.

Generational trauma, as he'd learned from Law, on whose therapeutic journey Remy had been a supportive, if not always reliable, copilot.

Cosima slid the bottle over for him to pour. "The Mustang doesn't get me anything?"

The cork squeaked as he withdrew it and poured them each a finger of the deep amber liquid. "Speeding tickets, I'd wager."

She crossed her arms below her breasts. "Speaking of the contract, I guess we'd better get our terms straight."

"About the filming?" he asked.

"About this," she said, motioning between them.

"So this is a business proposition?" Saying the words aloud made his rib cage felt a size too small to contain all his vital organs.

"Let's say, a proposition I don't want to affect our business." She accepted the glass Remy held out for her and sipped.

Remy followed suit, imagining fire scalding the central channel he'd always pictured filled with mud.

"What terms would you like to suggest?" he asked.

"One night only," she said. "When you leave here, I'm the producer, you're the show participant, and nothing more. That that's all. When we see each other again, this never happened. It's erased from your memory."

"Like that's going to happen," he said.

"Something tells me you'll manage." Her gently patronizing tone failed to set him at ease.

"Do I get to add any terms of my own?" He hated how needy his question sounded. Spoken by that same, awkward tongue-tied boy not quite trusting his luck.

Her eyes narrowed. "Go on."

"If I'm able to get Law to sign the contract, you owe me one motorcycle ride to a location of my choice once you're on site at the distillery. Subject to twenty-four hours' notice, of course."

"Seventy-two hours' notice," she said.

"Forty-eight," he countered.

"Done."

Just as he had earlier in the office, she held out her hand.

Remy took it and shook before shooting his scotch and walking into her pantry.

"What do you think you're doing?" she asked.

Browsing among the rows, his eyes fixed on a pair stiletto heels the exact shade of her Mustang. "Choosing the shoes it will be the most fun to try and make myself forget."

Five

"Those don't even match my dress," she pointed out.

"Good thing you won't be wearing it for long." His eyes blazed like banked coals as he wrapped his hands around her waist and lifted her onto the counter.

Her mouth dropped open and stayed that way for a good thirty seconds.

Among the other indignities her height had inflicted was a tendency to trick men into thinking that being shorter also made her lighter, and therefore a natural choice for all their unfulfilled romantic-hero moments.

It was all fun and games until someone—Michael—

had slipped a disk trying to carry her over the threshold of their first apartment together.

The apartment she had feathered like a nest. Laboring for months on end to pick out the perfect classic leather sofa. The correct texture and variety of throw pillows. Lamps that created the proper ambiance.

A home.

Their home.

Or it had been, until she'd come home early after landing a meeting with a nature documentarian she'd chased for months and found her fiancé with another woman on the sofa she'd spent an entire month visiting before buying.

It was as if the entire apartment and everything in it had been stained by that moment.

When she'd left, she couldn't bear the thought of taking a single thing with her.

She watched Remy walk back into the closet and return with the bright red Louboutin Torrida silk-bow platform sandals she'd unwisely splurged on for her first red-carpet event, post-Michael.

The salesclerk had attempted to politely talk her out of them, specifically citing the exact feature she'd instantly fallen in love with. A wide cuff with a length of silky red ribbon tied at the ankle that the clerk helpfully pointed tended to *shorten the leg*.

Her stubborn streak demanded that she buy them immediately, putting a meager 1,300 dollars on her American Express card already so near its limit that that the Roman centurion's eyes had started to bulge.

The decision had earned her a jab from the local fashion police about one of the munchkins making off with Dorothy's ruby slippers.

She hadn't worn them since.

Remy, dark and sleek as a panther, prowled around the kitchen island.

A warm current of air stirred as he leaned in, caressing her nostrils with the subtle scent of his cologne and warm, clean skin. She rested her hands on the smooth, cool countertop to keep from reeling.

The same scent she had inhaled from the T-shirt he'd left behind, sheepishly tucking it into her duffel bag.

She brought her glass of scotch to her lips, letting the smoky liquid carry her backward in time on a river of peat smoke and heat.

His hands were warm on her ankles as he slipped the sandals onto her feet, carefully tying the bow at each ankle.

He did this with such effortless gentleness that it made her want to cry.

This was a man used to seeing to the needs of another human on a daily basis.

She couldn't remember the last time she'd felt cared for.

He took several steps backward, admiring his handiwork like an art gallery patron.

"You're right," he said, eyes on hers. "The dress doesn't match."

Taking her cue, she pulled the stretchy fabric up and over her head, and tossed it at him.

"Better?" she asked. She watched him eat her with his eyes the same way he'd had their meal, his gaze moving over her black lace bra, the matching thong.

"Much."

A little shiver of anticipation rippled through her middle as he took two steps toward her. His hands were warm on her knees as they pushed them apart to make room for his hips.

Remy leaned in, and Cosima measured time not in days or hours, but in the endless, uncountable span separating past and present. In the infinitesimal degrees he traversed to release her from the purgatory of all the years between then and now.

His kiss had aged like the scotch mingling on their tongues. Deeper and more intoxicating than anything preserved in her memory. He cupped the backs of her knees, dragging her forward until his lean hips pressed the insides of her thighs. Remy's fingertips dimpled her backside and she felt herself being lifted.

His erection branded her stomach, notching itself against her as she wrapped her legs around his waist. His dark groan rumbled through her as he walked them toward the bed.

Falling through time and space, they found themselves on another set of cool sheets.

Hands planted on either side of her, his mouth moved down her throat, lighting up her senses with the delicious rasp of a day's stubble. Friction. One body moving against another, opposing surfaces kindling heat. And that's precisely what he did.

Everywhere his lips landed, he started a new

blaze. In a small smooth spot below her ear. In the dip of her collarbone. At the base of her throat. On the swell of her breasts.

As his mouth worked downward, his hands worked upward. Tracing a line up the inside of her thigh, skimming over her stomach.

"I need to see you," he mumbled against her skin.

She felt a knuckle against her sternum and the cups of her bra fell away.

"You're so beautiful," he murmured. Reverence lit his features from within as he stroked the curve of each breast, his thumb rolling one nipple, then the other, before he lowered his mouth to her.

Exquisite torture.

His tongue finding that hard bud, flicking across it with quick feather-light strokes, sucking it, teasing it.

Cosima threaded her fingers through his hair, black as a raven's wing, as she arched into him. The hand on her thigh began to move again. Fingers gliding up and down her soaked panties, pressing against the spot, spiraling with sensation with the heel of his palm.

Her hips bucked and she bit back a cry.

Remy planted a kiss on her sternum. The plane of her stomach.

Lower.

He woke every area with his lips, then followed with his tongue, increasing until Cosima was a wriggling, impatient wanton thing.

It seemed to take forever for her panties to make

the short journey from her hips to the floor. Even longer for his mouth to make its way to her bared skin. When, at last, he parted her with the flat of his tongue, she buried her face in a pillow to keep her scream from echoing off the loft's ceiling.

A habit she had developed under Michael's tenure.

You want the neighbors to call the cops?

Sometimes, she had thought, but didn't say.

Remy raised his head and looked at her from beneath hooded lids. Intent. Determined. Angry.

"Don't," he said.

"Don't what?"

His fingers released their possessive grip on her hips and glided down her inner thigh.

Then he was *there*. Cupping her. Slipping inside her. Showing her just how wet she was. Kindling heat and a pressure so delicious, Cosima was in danger of biting through her lip.

She relaxed her jaw with a deep breath, releasing a soft, sultry sigh.

"That's it," he said. "That belongs to me. Give me what's mine."

He *wanted* to hear her. The unfathomable thought remained pinned in her mind as he rose to his feet.

"What are you doing?" she asked.

That damnable grin lifted one corner of his reddened lips. "Gonna open a window."

"Remy," she stage-whispered. "No!"

"I'm sorry?" He dramatically cupped a hand to his ear as he walked backward toward her uncurtained window. "I'm around a lot of machinery at the distillery. I'm afraid I'm going to need you to speak up."

She blinked at him, dumbfounded. She couldn't believe what she was hearing.

Always, she had been told she was too loud. Too blunt. Too short. Too hungry. Too passionate. Too needy. Too intense.

Too everything, basically.

And here Remy Renaud was, inviting her to be more. To be her *most*.

Kneeling down before her, Remy lifted her ankle, setting it back down on the edge of the bed with her knees bent. Repeating the process with the other. Curating the view for his own delectation. He kissed her everywhere. Lighting up all her sensitive spots and inventing a few new ones.

Then his mouth was on her again and her back bowed off the bed of its own accord. He supported her hips, moving with her, but never stopping the onslaught.

He took to the task like a composer, coordinating his hands and his mouth to coax out of her ragged cries, her desperate gasps.

Her fists knotted in his silky hair as her hips undulated in time with his relentless rhythm. She clenched around his fingers—random, furious pulses that seemed to begin behind her belly button and unfurl endlessly outward. Her legs began to shake and she careened over the edge while pleasure pinwheeled through her on a cry that only faintly resembled anything human.

A gentle tap on her knee lowered her out of the stratosphere, and Cosima became aware she had his head pinned there.

"Sorry," she breathed, willing her knees to relax.

"Don't you ever be sorry for that, cher." Remy gave her a wry smile as he sat back on his heels. "I can think of far worse ways to go."

He reached for the bottom of his shirt, but halted when a tinkling sound took on the notes of a recognizable song.

"My Girl" by the Temptations, low but unmistakable, emanating from the kitchen counter.

Remy sprang away with catlike grace, an impressive string of curses trailing him like smoke.

"Hey, Bug." The instant infusion of warmth and enthusiasm in his voice told Cosima everything she needed to know.

His daughter.

"What are you doing up so—" He stopped in mid-sentence, listening.

Even in the dim light spilling in from the hallway, she could see his brow furrow. The corners of his mouth turned down. "Okay, okay. Take a breath."

"I'm so sorry, Bug." A pause. "I'll be on that plane first thing tomorrow and I'll be right back home with my girl."

Her chest caught so hard she thought it might crush her heart flat. Ridiculous biological hardwiring designed to release an oxytocin dump at the tiniest hint of protective behavior in a male of the species. Cosima folded the blanket over herself and sat up, feeling exposed and tawdry in the face of such a tender scene.

"All right, honey," he said. "You get back to sleep and no more of those bad dreams. I'll be home before you know it." The corners of his eyes crinkled as his grin widened. "No, I love you more." Another pause. "I guess we'll just have to arm-wrestle about it when I get home. *Bonne nuit, cher fille*," he said, making the words into a singsong rhyme. He disconnected, but didn't set down his phone, fingers working over the keyboard.

"Everything okay?" she asked.

"Yeah," he said without looking up. "Just had a bad dream and woke up scared because she didn't remember I was out of town."

Cosima already knew the flat, slightly cool tone of his voice brooked trouble.

Quickly tugging at the ribbons, she untied the shoes and let them fall to the floor next to the bed.

"Is there anything I can do to help? I can look at an earlier flight, or—"

"I've got one here," he said.

Cosima slipped out of the bed and retrieved her dress. Driven by an insistent need to be less vulnerable in the wake of this abrupt shift in temperature.

"Do you want me to drive you to the airport? I'd be happy to swing you by your hotel so you can grab your stuff."

"It's okay. I'll just grab a cab." The hollow echo of those words confirmed it.

This had become her fault.

Whether he knew it or not, he had already decided.

For being the reason he needed to come to LA and leave his daughter.

For asking him to come back to her place. For making him want something that now made him feel guilt.

She knew the matrix well.

"Hey," she said, placing a hand on his bicep. "Look at me."

On a short, sharp exhale, he tore his attention away from the phone.

"You didn't do anything wrong, Remy. You know that, right? You're allowed to take time for yourself." Cosima pulled her hand away as he stiffened beneath her palm.

"I sure appreciate you pointing that out to me," he said, shoving his phone in his pocket and crossing his arms over his chest. "Any other parenting tips you'd like to share? Seeing as you have so much experience."

She sucked in a breath, startled by the sharpness of his remark.

"Maybe don't be an asshole?" She turned on her heel and stalked to the bathroom, where she slammed the door.

Hands planted on the cool granite countertop, she made herself meet her own eye in the mirror. Tears blurred her vision, obliterating the fine details separating her from the scared, sad girl who had made such a thorough mess of her life following her brother's death. She saw only the passion-tangled hair. The kiss-swollen lips. The smudged, smoky eyes.

A mess.

Then, and now.

Cosima turned on the faucet and splashed her face with cold water, elbows on the countertop as she patted her cheeks with a towel.

She heard footsteps and felt him hesitating on the other side of the door. Try as she might, she couldn't make herself reach for the handle.

Another eternity of minutes elapsed before she heard his boots shift and then clomp away. Her front door opened and closed.

When she emerged, she found that history had indeed repeated itself.

Remy Renaud had walked out on her for the second time.

Six

Remy felt like a first-class asshole.

Staring at the phone in his palm while he waited at the airport, he had willed Cosima's number to appear on the screen. A call to bawl him out. A text to inform him he was a bastard.

Because he had been.

Despite years spent unlearning the behavior, he had taken the coward's way out and slid a pair of wheels under his feet at the first sign of trouble.

Trouble that hadn't even been her fault. Unless she could be blamed for being too tempting to pass up, however idiotic his reasoning in accepting her invitation.

All the way home, he'd replayed the scenario in his mind, putting different words in his mouth.

Swapping out the look of irritation on her face for one of satiated languor.

What had he accomplished by hightailing it out of there, anyhow? The earlier flight had been delayed, landing him in Roanoke only an hour earlier than he would have been had he taken the original. In the process, he had managed to deny himself something he wanted so badly, his gut still ached.

When he found Emily curled like a cat on the porch swing outside of Law's house on the distillery property, his heart nearly tore itself in two.

"You didn't have to wait out here for me, Bug." He slung down his bag on the front porch before plopping on the swing beside her.

"I didn't," she said, rubbing sleep from her eyes with the palm of one hand.

"Gee, thanks," he said, feigning offense.

"I just mean I came out here because it's really loud in there."

As if on cue, a thin, reedy sound rose from inside the house and quickly became a duet.

The twins.

"Shit—er, shoot," he corrected before Emily had the chance. "I completely forgot grab flowers."

"Dad," she said, the way she always did when exasperated by something he'd forgotten to do.

"Guess I better get my hide in there and apologize." He slapped his thighs and rose from the bench.

Emily hadn't been kidding. Scarcely had the front door creaked open, when Remy was plunged into a hive of activity. He had a vague recollection of Law mentioning Kane family reinforcements coming to help once the twins were born, but hadn't held onto the particulars if they'd been given to him.

Taking a bracing breath, he crossed from the foyer into the kitchen.

There, a woman in yoga pants and an oversize sweater popped a metallic capsule into a machine that looked like something off a spaceship. Reaching a hand up to tuck a dark red tendril back into the pile atop her head, she turned and jumped as she saw him standing in the doorway. Her face struck him as vaguely familiar, but nowhere in his sleep-deprived brain could he land on a name.

"Charlotte Westbrook," she stated. She wiped a hand on the dish towel and reached out to him. "I'm the one who always sends you those irritating meeting reminders."

"That's right," Remy said. "Nice to meet you in person, finally."

"If you'll excuse, me, I'm just going to take this up to Law." She lifted a steaming mug from the counter. "The capsules are in the cabinet next to the sink," she said. "If you want some coffee."

Remy didn't just want it. He needed it like a brushfire needs a crop duster. He eyed the gleaming black-and-chrome machine with mistrust.

Much as he didn't like to admit it about himself, he was aware of his tendency to balk at change of any kind.

He was squinting at the text on one of the boxes of capsules when a blond woman whose face and name he'd never be able to forget breezed out of the laundry room.

Arlie Banks-Kane.

Samuel Kane's wife.

Whose lap he'd accidentally dropped a plate of lobster étouffée into when Samuel had first come to review the operations. She'd been nothing but gracious about the accident.

Her husband, less so.

"Remy," she said, offering him a smile that seemed genuinely warm. "So good to see you again."

"You as well."

"Mind if I jump in there and make myself some coffee?"

"Not a bit." He stepped out of her way, covertly making note of the procedure.

"How have you been?" After loading a capsule, she pressed a button that made the machine hum to life.

"Oh, you know. Pretty busy. How about yourself?"

"Just about the same," she said. When the hissing and spitting had finished, she set her mug on the counter and added a splash of cream from the fridge. "I heard you guys might be going through a rebrand. That's got to be exciting."

A high-pitched buzzing invaded his ears.

News to him.

"Definitely." He felt ape-like and stupid, imitating what she'd done in hopes of producing the same result.

"Is it just the name you're changing, or totally starting from scratch?" she asked.

"I'm not too sure about that."

Because no one had bothered to discuss it with him.

He felt prouder than he had a right to be when the machine began to dispense the steaming liquid.

It was nowhere near Cosima's coffee, but certainly better than Emily's muddy brew. As if summoned by the thought, Emily chose that minute to come bouncing into the kitchen with a giant grin on her face.

"Aunt Arlie, will you make me your cheesy eggs again?"

Aunt Arlie?

He'd been gone one day, and the entire family structure had shifted?

Arlie smiled and turned to Remy. "If it's all right with your dad."

Her asking felt like token effort. A bone tossed in his direction.

"Not at all," he said through a tight smile.

"You know the drill, sous chef," Arlie said, tying an apron around Emily's narrow hips.

Remy abandoned the kitchen to them and pointed his boots toward the stairs.

The syncopated wailing swelled as he climbed, and he noted the new pictures sprouting on the wall like spring tulips.

Memories Law and Marlowe had begun to make together.

Family.

He stepped hard on the pang of loneliness he felt as he rapped on the half-closed door.

"Come in," a voice called.

The scene he witnessed when he stepped inside hit him like a freight train.

His youngest brother, backlit by the light of the window, looking equal parts awestruck and terrified as he swayed from side to side with a pink-faced bundle tucked protectively in his arms.

Remy remembered.

Emily's birth. Holding her for the first time. That moment had become the axis of his entire world, wiping away swaths of his experience. Scrubbing out everything but her. Those sleepless, endless nights and the grave, overwhelming sense of responsibility he'd felt knowing it was his job to stand between her and the rest of the world. The first late-night feedings when he was paranoid he would break her just by picking her up from the crib. How strange it had been to hold her tiny fist with a hand that had gripped prison meal trays, and the handles of oil derricks, and the handlebars of motorcycles and pool cues.

"Hey there, Uncle Remy." Marlowe's voice snapped him out of the reverie. She sat bathed in the light of the window, gliding back and forward in a rocking chair, the other twin resting against her chest.

Remy lifted a hand in greeting and crossed the room to get a better look at the tiny thing cradled in his brother's giant arms. He'd known that twins would be smaller, but the little face staring up at him seemed unreal.

"I don't know," Remy said, catching Law's eye. "You sure these two are big enough to keep?"

"They're actually in the ninetieth percentile by birth weight."

This information came to him unsolicited courtesy of Samuel Kane, who Remy had failed to notice in the brand-new leather chair in the corner.

The stab of annoyance he felt was instant and intense.

Samuel was the kind of man who changed the air of any room he walked into. The kind of man who knew the right bottle of wine to order and the history of the vineyard it came from. The kind of man whose shirts refused to wrinkle and who probably never spilled anything on anyone in his entire life.

The kind of man who could operate seamlessly in the social circles Cosima hailed from.

"Especially in identical twins born in the thirty-third week," Samuel continued.

Not for the first time, it occurred to Remy just how satisfying it would be to jam a pie straight into Samuel's patrician-featured face.

Instead, he broke for bait just as predictable and problematic.

"That's the Renaud genes for you. What we lack in brains, we make up for in brawn."

Law cut him a sharp look and shifted to reach for the steaming mug in the windowsill.

"You should let Remy hold him," Marlowe suggested gently.

"Are you sure that's a good idea?" Samuel asked. "He did just make a joke comparing infants to sport fish."

That he knew he was being teased did absolutely nothing to stop the sweat that had broken out between his shoulder blades.

"Seeing as he has an eight-year-old daughter, I bet we can trust him just this once," Marlowe replied dryly.

After an awkward shuffle, the small bundle was transferred successfully.

"What's your name, young man?" Remy gazed down into eyes the amorphous gray-blue of all new infants.

"Franklin Kane," Marlowe answered. "And this distinguished gentleman is Joseph Kane."

Remy felt a quick burst of defensive pride.

He didn't know Law and Marlowe's plans where marriage was concerned, but it was foolish of him to assume that his nephews would share his last name when the Kane legacy was available.

It shouldn't sting as much as it did.

He looked at Law, coffee in hand, standing next to Marlowe's rocker, not an ounce of contention visible on his face.

"They're named after—" Samuel began.

"The Hardy boys," Remy said, finishing for him.

He'd been the only one of the Renaud boys who enjoyed disappearing between the pages of a book as much as he did working on go-carts that never seemed to go.

"How was the meeting with Cosima?" Marlowe asked in a deliberate bid to steer the conversation back onto safer ground.

"Cosima Lowell?" Samuel asked before Remy could answer. "I haven't seen her in ages. What she's up to these days?"

Irrational jealousy crept in sleek as a mink, and he found himself wondering what the specific circumstances of the event in question was. Until he saw Samuel's eyes light up and his face soften when Arlie appeared in the doorway with a stack of folded receiving blankets.

"She's a television producer in LA," Marlowe reported. "She reached out to me when she saw the article on 4 Thieves in the *Los Angeles Times*."

"For what purpose?" Samuel asked.

"She wants to film a docuseries about the distillery." Remy winced inwardly at how boastful his tone sounded.

"A *docuseries*?" Samuel pronounced with skeptical mirth. "You know that's code for reality TV, correct?"

Correct.

One of the flag words in the Samuel Kane lexicon that Remy had come to associate with something he was about to be taught. Usually followed by another term that he'd not had occasion to make part of his own regular usage. Such as *meeting cadence* or *company culture* or *long-term incentive plan*.

Franklin began to fuss as Remy's bouncing motion had become a hair too frenetic.

"May I?" Arlie asked, setting down the blankets on the bench at the end of the bed.

"Of course." He handed off the baby with far more grace than he'd received him, glad to be relieved of the delicate burden.

The room's temperature seemed to rise with all the bodies in it. Remy's shirt stuck to his back, the travel and the company making him long desperately for a shower.

Samuel, who looked like he could walk through a volcano and not darken the pits of his light blue dress shirt, gazed at Arlie as the baby quickly hushed in her arms. "You told Cosima we're not interested, I hope."

We.

What used to represent all four Renaud brothers, then just Law and Remy, had been shoehorned to include a third.

"Why would I do that?" Remy asked, folding his arms across his chest.

Samuel scooted forward in his chair.

"In the first place, with the aggressive road map we've set for the 4 Thieves expansion, having a camera crew on site would represent a significant disruption to production. In the second, that kind of publicity would undermine our rebranding efforts."

"Right," Remy said. "Seeing as I learned that those were happening all of five minutes ago, I'd appreciate any additional information you'd like to share about that."

Unfolding himself from the chair, Samuel assumed the posture Remy had come to think of as *visionary monologue*, and typically associated with ten-minute speeches five minutes before the meeting was supposed to end.

"If we have any hope of making 4 Thieves a globally recognized brand, our energy is best spent aligning it with class and sophistication. Mastery of craft. Essentially, having the distillery aligned with a reality TV show would be directly counterproductive to our efforts at rehabilitation."

That word.

It had been condescendingly explained to him by his court-appointed lawyer. It had been preached to him by the judge who looked at his 18-year-old self and seen nothing worth his mercy. It had been dangled in front of him like a carrot by the parole board year after year and it had been handed to him like a trophy he hadn't really won. Now, he was having his face rubbed in it by a man who hadn't just been born with a silver spoon in his mouth but an entire goddamn drawer.

Red edged Remy's vision as his heart sped in his chest. His teeth clenched so hard that his head ached.

"I guess it's too bad I already agreed then." He threw it into the center of the floor like a gauntlet.

"Agreed?" Samuel asked. "Or *signed*?

"I gave her my word."

The Kane CEO's lips pressed together, his jaw

flexing as he thought. When he spoke, it wasn't to Remy, but to Law.

"Why don't we table this discussion for now? We have a steering-committee meeting in a week. We can run it by Angela Cheng. She's had some experience with visual media and—"

Joseph broke out in a sudden voluminous wail that effectively cut off Samuel.

Law leveraged the opportunity.

"Would you mind if we revert offline?" he said, proving his superior acuity with this new language. "There's a couple things I need to check on down at the granary."

"Of course," Samuel said.

"Remy, can you give me a hand?" The look in Law's eye left no doubt that this was not a request.

Everyone in the room knew exactly what this was.

He was being escorted out.

Law bent to kiss the top of Marlowe's head. "Back in a bit."

They climbed down the stairs and through the kitchen, where Emily sat across from Charlotte at the table, her knobby elbows on the table, chin sitting in her cupped hand, eyes glued to the cascade of glorious auburn hair being woven into a French braid.

Law opened the back door and stepped out onto the porch, eyes scanning the distant tree line.

"I know this has been a lot," he said. "The investment. The twins. But agreeing to film this show without even discussing it with me? Since when is that something we do?"

Remy turned to face him, acid eating away at his insides. "Since when do you and Samuel have discussions about *rehabilitating* 4 Thieves?"

"You've told me on numerous occasions just how much you hate anything related to sales or marketing."

He did. With a bright and abiding passion.

"That doesn't mean I don't want to be involved when we're discussing changing the name of the company that you and I have been dreaming of since we were boys.

"But we're not boys anymore." Law turned his stony profile to look Remy in the eye. "And 4 Thieves isn't just some backwoods bootlegger."

"So that's what this is really about," Remy said. "You want to use the Kane money to erase the Renaud name."

Law's posture stiffened. "That's not what I'm doing."

"Really?" Remy demanded. "Is that why you don't even want your own sons to have it?"

"You're going to want to watch yourself there, brother." Danger flashed in Law's eyes, but Remy couldn't stop himself.

"You want me to change Emily's last name, too? God forbid she would want to have part of the business someday."

Law loomed over him in a way he hadn't since they were teenagers, full of toughness and testosterone. "You're out of line, Remy. Why don't you get some sleep and we can talk about this later?"

Remy refused to grant him any quarter. "Sleep isn't the problem. The *problem* is sitting upstairs in his custom-tailored slacks talking to me like I'm some slack-jawed idiot while you stand there and let it happen."

He watched his brother wrestle for control of his temper, nostrils flaring, deep chest inflating on quick sharp inhales. "Maybe if you paid less attention to his clothes and more attention to his ideas, you'd see that he's trying to help us."

"You," Remy said. "He's trying to help *you*. And I just come with the package. Everyone knows that 4 Thieves was your idea. Hell, it's right there on the website."

Three hours delayed from the flight he'd spent eight hundred dollars to switch to, Remy had forced himself to visit the About Us page that Cosima had referenced in the story-worth-telling part of her pitch.

He'd sat there while fellow travelers ate their over-priced airport-food breakfast and seen exactly how his role in all of this had been framed.

Law opened his mouth to speak, but the front door swung open and Emily stepped out holding the backpack Remy had dropped near the front door. Her eyes had the feverish look they usually took on when showing him some YouTube video demonstrating a new gadget she absolutely had to have.

"Aunt Charlotte was just telling me that there's a camp for kids who get to be in plays and she knows one of the directors and that I can go if you say it's okay."

Remy and Law exchanged a look, simultaneously catching on that this *aunt* business had likely been Emily's doing.

"It's supposed to be a really good program." Law shrugged, both offering this olive branch and communicating that he didn't care if Remy took it.

"It's two weeks from now when I'm on spring break," she added, clearly trying to sweeten the deal.

"I'll need to talk to *Aunt* Charlotte a little more about the details," Remy said, "but I think it should be alright."

"So I can go?" Her small hands laced together and she clasped them to her chest.

"It's a conditional *yes*."

She leaped forward, arms winding around his waist as she grabbed him in a fierce hug that stole his breath. Every day it seemed the crown of her head rose a little higher on his sternum. Soon he'd no longer be able to pick her up and somersault her onto his shoulders. He did it now to her whooping delight.

When he recovered his equilibrium, he saw that Law had already turned to go back into the house.

The unfinished conversation throbbed in his consciousness like an open wound.

Left untreated, it was deep enough to scar.

Seven

She had broken one of her own cardinal rules.

Never be the first to text when he did the walking out. Her reasons for doing so justified the infraction. Unable to sleep after his abrupt departure, she had cracked open her laptop to discover a very enthusiastic email from her VidFlix contact asking if there was any way they could expedite the pilot timeline to hit the summer sweeps.

She'd done some creative cursing while staring at her cell phone and figuring out what combination of words would get a man who hadn't even signed a contract yet excited about the idea of her crew coming pretty much yesterday.

After typing out and deleting several long explanatory messages, she'd reverted back to a principle she'd learned in the television-commercials unit of her filmmaking class.

Consider your audience.

She opted for a simple: Well? Do I owe you a ride? To reopen the lines of communication.

The message she received back was promising, if odd.

Do you ever.

Cosima felt a flutter in her stomach followed by an instant stab of annoyance. Even now, after he had run out of her apartment like someone had lit his ass on fire, she found herself excited by the prospect of seeing him again.

What followed was a rapid-fire back-and-forth that left her jittery with endorphins.

Cosima: How soon can we take it?

Remy: Is this a hypothetical question?

Cosima: Is that a hypothetical answer?

She almost dropped her phone when it instantly began to ring in her hand. Shaking her head, she answered it.

"See, the way this works is, you're supposed to give me some times that might work for you, and then I choose one and then we talk."

"How about now?"

As a trained singer, she was conceptually aware that vocal cords thicken overnight, then loosen as they're used throughout the day. In actual practice, all she heard was what he might sound like when she woke up in bed next to him.

Not that she'd ever had the chance.

"You're talking to me, aren't you?" She heard a crunching sound in the background and imagined him walking up one of the many gravel paths she'd seen in the pictures run with the article about Samuel Kane's investment. When thinking about shooting locations, she had already been identifying areas of the distillery they would want to avoid. Spaces between buildings or areas where extra equipment had piled up on the warehouse dock.

"Is that an actual rooster I just heard?" she asked.

"Foghorn," he said.

"This is going to come as a shock to you, but even though I was raised in Philadelphia, I recognize the difference between poultry vocalizations and warning sirens."

"Foghorn is the rooster's name," he said. "Like Foghorn Leghorn?"

She slapped her a hand over her face out of reflex, immediately hoping he couldn't identify it by the sound.

"Yeah," she said. "That's a bit before my time."

The crunching ceased and was replaced by the sound of footsteps on something wooden and hollow. A door squeaked, then closed. "You know how to hurt a guy, don't you?"

Look who's talking.

"We'll have to save that topic for a future discussion." She pushed herself up from the bed he'd set ablaze and began to pace. "But Law signed off?"

His pause lasted a hair too long. "He's on board."

"You're sure?" she asked.

"You'll have the contract back within the hour."

Hurdle one cleared.

"The thing is, I heard back from the network executives, and they wanted to know if there's any way we could move up the production schedule. I told them that you were very adverse to—"

"No problem."

Cosima felt like a carp. Her mouth opened and closed without the arrival of any words to justify the action. This was nothing like the response she had expected. She had a little speech prepared. Note cards of possible rebuttals to the refusals she expected. It had long been a habit of hers in situations where she expected to receive the answer she didn't want.

With an east coast trial lawyer for a father, arguing had been both a sport and a rite of passage. Mealtimes, especially, were dedicated to an extended game of *can you guess what I already know*?

And with the father who'd been a prosecutor and then a judge, winning had been a near impossibility. No matter the topic.

"Really?" she asked.

"Really," he said. "When would you want to come?"

Drawing in a deep breath, Cosima scribbled on the notepad near her to release her nervous energy.

"A week from now?" She braced herself for an exclamation of dismay from his end of the phone.

"Fine. Anything I need to do for my end?"

Cosima's eyebrows scrunched together in the expression her mother always warned her would create permanent grooves in her forehead.

Why was he making this so easy?

"Not yet. I'll get my crew together and make travel arrangements. I was thinking Roanoke for the hotel. That would probably make the most sense in terms of getting back and forth?" She hovered at the kitchen counter, phone sandwiched between her ear and shoulder as she began typing in the search engine on her laptop.

"Or you could stay here," he suggested. "Seems like that would save you a lot of time and trouble."

Time, yes.

Trouble, no.

Trouble she intended to avoid by sticking to a new cardinal rule.

Never be alone with Remy Renaud.

"I'm not sure that's such a good idea, given our history."

"Don't think you can keep your hands off me?" A lightness had crept into his voice that hadn't been there until that point.

She fought a solar flare of temper.

"My hands are making a very particular gesture right now," she said, stopping to sip her mug of lukewarm coffee. "Feel free to use your imagination."

His chuckle was rich, warm, and genuine.

"Your hands and the rest of you wouldn't be staying anywhere near me," he explained. "When we built out the distillery, we added a section of staff cabins to the property. Marlowe just finished having them redone, so I can vouch for the quality."

She couldn't pretend it wouldn't shave a nice chunk off their budget for lodgings, in addition to allowing her crew to catch footage they might otherwise miss.

"We'll take you up on that then." Cosima set down her mug on the counter and wandered over to the window. "I'll call you when I have a more definite ETA."

"No text first?"

She sighed loud enough to let it be heard through the phone before disconnecting. Staring out over a city famously slow to rise, she hugged her robe tighter around her.

She'd gotten exactly what she wanted.

So why was her stomach a knot of dread and elation?

The Mercedes cargo van slowed to a roll as it turned onto the mouth of a tree-lined drive. Thick, beautifully gnarled wood polls rose at least sixteen feet on either side. Connecting them was a large copper plate with the words *4 Thieves* cut out of the metal. The elements had aged it with the beautiful green patina she had seen on the copper accents of French chateaus.

Chateaus like the one in the Berkshires, where her parents summered.

Times like this, she felt ridiculous coming from the kind of family that used seasons as verbs.

"Hello, trailer fodder." Roosevelt Toussaint looked more like a club bouncer or NFL linebacker than a seasoned camera operator. Tall and solid, he had russet-brown skin and a closely shaved head perpetually kissed with sweat.

Always their default driver, he craned to see out the windshield.

"That's way too obvious for an opener." The predictable reply came from Matthew Lee, Roosevelt's right-hand man and self-appointed hype guy. A closet film nerd, wiry, and virtually tireless, he had proven to be an asset on some of their most grueling shoots.

"It's way too early for you two to start bickering." This observation was Sarah's contribution. Curled onto the van's back bench, where she had been sleeping, she hauled herself upright and pushed her large dark sunglasses onto the top of her head. "Please tell me they have Wi-Fi out here."

Cosima had to laugh.

Though Sarah had been with her only a couple of years, she'd quickly become accustomed to a lifestyle that didn't involve the application of mosquito repellent. An item she groused about roundly when she saw it listed on their preproduction shopping list.

"They have Wi-Fi," Cosima said. "Running water, too, I think."

Two weeks.

She had repeated this phrase to herself over and over as she made preparations for the trip. She could do anything for two weeks if it meant getting what she needed for a company-launching series of her very own. Especially if it meant showing the network executives who had dropped their interest when Michael Cooper's name was no longer attached to the company that they'd made a huge mistake.

Even if that anything was keeping her distance from a man who had proved to be damn near irresistible both times she'd been anywhere near his physical proximity.

The van continued down the lane, which was shaded by oak trees already beginning to slip on their green-studded spring jackets. At the end of the tree line, they came face-to-face with a beautiful quilt of sprawling green dotted with buildings that housed the distillery's various operations.

When they reached the last leg of Remy's comically descriptive instructions, she shot him a text.

Almost to the office.

The answer came immediately.

I'll be waiting.

And he was.

He wore a white T-shirt this time, but the rest of what she'd come to think of as his standard uniform was present. The jeans. The boots. The stomach-flipping smirk.

Cosima often heard the expression "heart skipped a beat" but had never experienced it until now.

He stood beneath yet another large wooden arch on the part of the distillery she knew had been partially converted from an old barn on the property.

"Holy shit," Matt whispered under his breath.

"Told you so," Sarah hummed from the back seat.

"You said he looked like a lumberjack," Matt argued. "Not a goddamn Spartan."

"Are you two going to be able to keep it together?" Cosima asked. "Or do Roosevelt and I need to do all the talking?"

"Don't volunteer me for that job," Roosevelt said, glancing over his shoulder at her. "That man looks three parts mean and one part crazy."

Seeing him standing there on the stoop, arms crossed over his broad chest, she could understand his concern.

If men were dogs, Remy would be a rottweiler. A big, beautiful beast whose bark and bite both promised trouble.

"All right, kids," she announced. "Go time." Pulling a deep breath into her lungs, she scooted across the middle seat and pushed the button to open the sliding door.

Dressed for scouting in a pair of designer joggers, hiking shoes, and a plain white T-shirt, she became very conscious of the way the fabric clung to her breasts and butt as Remy's eyes roamed freely over both areas.

His dark hair looked shower-damp and was combed back from his face but brushed the nape of his neck. He hadn't shaved since their meeting in LA and her skin lit up in the places where it held the tactile memory of that dark stubble grazing against her.

Lips that had been on hers curled up into a mischievous smile. He held out his hand as if they were meeting for the very first time.

"Miss Lowell." Her name was honey dripped from his tongue. When his hand closed over hers, that same pop of electricity shot up her arm and her entire body filled with a silky liquid warmth. Gazing into the gunmetal-gray depths of his hooded eyes, she read there what lived in her own head.

Desire.

Awake, alive, and ready.

Exactly who the hell had she been kidding?

Keep her hands off Remy Renaud for two weeks?

She wasn't going to last ten hours.

"Morning," he said.

"Morning," her entire crew chimed in enthusiastically as if he was a teacher they wanted to impress. Cosima went through the introductions, giving a brief bio for each of the three people who had become absolutely invaluable to her. Remy greeted them each with a nod and some variation of "pleased to meet you" that sounded welcoming and warm.

"I'm sorry my brother Law couldn't be here,"

Remy said. "His wife just had twins, and between that and the distillery, things have been a bit hectic for him of late."

Cosima had been so distracted by the morning light playing off the planes of Remy's T-shirt that it took her a moment to catch the unfamiliar word in the sentence.

"Wife?" she asked. "Since when?"

"Since they filed the paperwork at the county courthouse," Remy said. "Marlowe said it was the most efficient use of their time and resources."

"That's the most Marlowe thing I've ever heard in my life," Cosima replied, stealing a glance at the back of those well-worn jeans as he propped open the distillery door for them.

A guest at Marlowe's sweet-sixteen birthday party, she'd heard a different version of the same logic. But back then the argument had been pointed against marriage. Why it was always a great deal for the man and a terrible deal for the woman. And if you were foolish enough to cave to societal expectations, why spend all that money on a ceremony that lasts half a day when it could be invested in a tech stock and potentially double in minutes? Even then, she had been a far more practical creature then Cosima.

Like all other fanciful things about her, her imaging of a fairy-tale wedding was solidly her Nona's fault. Cosima had sat for hours staring at the pictures taken of her Nona in her wedding gown. Acres of handmade Italian lace, waterfalls of creamy silk, a high collar above which floated her grandmother's face, complete with dark, heavy-lidded eyes, and dreamy smile.

Her parents' wedding pictures had looked so different. Her father handsome and his Navy dress uniform. Her mother in a couture gown like something from a French bakery. Lots of billowing taffeta with a cathedral length train. Theirs had been a society match. Beautiful, famed opera singer marries young maverick from old money.

What they lacked in genuine love and affection, they made up for in pomp and circumstance.

A theme that carried over into all aspects of their life.

And Cosima's.

"So how do you want to do this?" Remy asked as they filed into a vestibule leading to a second set of doors.

"It would be great if we could get a tour of the distillery itself, and then just the general grounds for shot-scouting purposes," Roosevelt said. "Once we have that planned out, we can do a little storyboarding?" he added, glancing over his shoulder Cosima.

"Okay," Remy said. "Do you want to start here?"

What she wanted was to go back in time and slap her hand away from her laptop when she'd composed the email to Marlowe Kane. Or better yet, to drop her laptop off the balcony from her fourth story apartment to prevent her from reading the article that had put this idea in her head in the first place.

"Sounds great," she said.

They stepped into a whoosh of cool air, thick with

smells. Some of them pleasant—grain and wood. Some of them not—alcohol, nail-polish remover. Down the center of the vaulted building, a row of gleaming copper pot stills perched, sentinel-like, an array of various pipes running back and forth between them. For the first time, it occurred to her to wonder where they'd gotten the seed money for the initial build-out.

With Sarah busy making notes on her phone and Matt and Roosevelt already plotting out camera angles, Cosima was free to feel Remy's eyes on the side of her face. Heat seemed to vent from the neckline of her T-shirt and she suddenly became very grateful she'd worn her good bra with both lift and padding.

"Doing all right?" he asked in that deep, resonant purr that so moved her. "You look a little rattled."

She swallowed hard and lifted her chin, refusing to look at him. "We should keep moving," she announced.

He obliged.

For a solid hour, he paraded them through the operation. The granary. The bottling and temperature-controlled storage area. Finally, they trooped through the warehouse and down to a long room where rows of stout barrels stretched down a corridor with a central walkway.

"Oh, man," Roosevelt said, an excited light brightening his eyes, "this would be a perfect spot for the OFT station." He turned to Remy, ready to explain. "An OFT is—"

"On the fly," Remy said, finishing for him. "Interviews usually done minutes or hours after action happens to capture immediate reactions."

Remy tapped his head when Cosima blinked in surprise. "Been studying up."

His wink softened her knees in the most annoying way possible.

"Oh, man." Matt's cheeks were a glowing pink. "If the main areas are this amazing, I can't wait to see the rest of the property."

"Tell you what," Remy said. "I've got an ATV outside. Why don't you guys take it out and look around yourselves?"

"That sounds perfect." Cosima said.

Remy grimaced. "I'm afraid it only seats three."

"Weren't you saying you wanted to see the smoke-house setup?" Sarah asked helpfully. "You and Mr. Renaud could go look at that while the three of us scout the rest of the property." Mischief sparkled in her green eyes.

Cosima had the feeling that no matter what she proposed, it would be countered. And, it was ridiculous of her to think she could spend the next two weeks having absolutely no one-on-one contact with the head of operations for the entire distillery.

"Sounds like a plan," she said.

"Keys are in it," Remy said, turning to Roosevelt.

The cool, damp, humidity-controlled air was heavy with wood and smoke. Cosima imagined this must be what the hull of a pirate ship smelled like. It was a fantasy all too easy to extend to who the captain might be. Remy's face was just the kind of brutal and charismatic one that inspired fear and loyalty in his crew.

"So," Cosima said as soon as they were out of earshot. "Which way is the smokehouse?"

He grinned at her.

Grinned.

"In a hurry?"

"Actually, yes. Our schedule is incredibly packed today. If you don't mind—"

"But you got here a full two hours ahead of schedule. Surely you could spare a few minutes of conversation?"

She crossed her arms over her breasts and glared up at him, waiting for whatever it was he had wanted to get her alone to say.

"The way I left things—"

"We don't need to do this. You don't owe me an apology. We're two grown adults. We tried to scratch an itch. It didn't work out. End of story."

"Who said anything about apologizing?" He took a step toward her, flooding her senses with that intoxicating scent. Soap, laundry detergent, and warm clean skin mingled with the oak barrels.

"Then what are you saying?" She held her ground, a skill she had honed early and out of necessity. Women of her size were frequently loomed over, talked over, and passed over. A state of affairs that bothered her to no end.

"I'm saying that I wish I would have stayed."

He spoke these words with no idea what they would mean to her in a different context. What a balm they would be if they could apply to both situations.

Though she knew she should shut down this conversation immediately, she couldn't resist the peek inside his head. Starved to know what it had been like for him in the week since their encounter.

"Why is that?" she asked.

"Because for the last seven days, I haven't been able to get you off my mind for a single second. Because I go to sleep thinking about how good you feel." His heated gaze fixed first on her mouth, then traveled lower. "And wake up thinking about how good you taste."

The air refused to be drawn into Cosima's lungs. Heavy with tension that seemed to find its way into her pores. Gathering in the creases where her hips met her thighs, drawing her stomach muscles down where a clench tightened everything between her belly button and spine.

She clutched at the fraying threads of her irritation in a desperate bid to hold on to her resolve. "Is that why you were so in favor of our coming out early? You want to finish what you started?"

He inched closer still. "Technically, I believe you were the one who started it."

And he was right about that, too, damn him.

"I did," she admitted. "But as I recall, you were the one who ended it."

"Didn't, either," he said, his voice going husky. "I just pressed Pause."

Her body moved toward his as if someone had

planted a magnet behind her sternum. His hand anchored in the hair at the base of her skull and angled her face upward. It felt electric and a little terrifying to be on the receiving end of his undivided attention. It reminded her of an odd impression she'd had the first night they met. That there wasn't one Remy Renaud, but many, and now they were all united in wanting her.

Within seconds of their lips grazing, they shot straight to the same fever pitch they'd had in the elevator.

Zero to fifty in point-two seconds.

He kissed the way an animal ate when it was unsure of its next meal. The hunger winning over the urge to slow down and savor.

She was starving, too.

Minutes, hours, entire evenings of fantasizing about touching him the way he had touched her. Of seeing him. Feeling him.

Her hands slid under the soft edge of his T-shirt, playing over the hard wash of muscle she found there.

Remy's rough, low grunt tingled up the lifeline of palm as her fingers found the tracks of his ribs. All the while his tongue tangled with hers, seducing and sparring until she was too dizzy to stand on her own.

She clung to him, encouraged to rest her weight against him by strong hands beneath the curve of her behind. He walked them backward between two of the barrels, where they were no longer visible to anyone who might happen to glance down the aisle.

In that cool pocket of shadow, he lifted her against

the curve of a barrel to align their bodies. She wound her arms around his neck for better leverage. Angling her hips to grind the waking part of her against the hard heat growing behind the zipper of his jeans.

He gasped air from her mouth and wrenched his lips from hers.

"God, do I want you," he growled, grinding his hips against her. "But, I don't have anything with me."

"Want to go back to high school?" she asked, rocking against him.

"Even though this happens to be the one subject I was good at, you're about to get me for as long as I would have lasted then if we don't slow down."

"Been a minute?" she asked, nipping at his earlobe, where a tiny hole in the lobe reminded her of the silver hoop he had worn there when they'd met all those years ago.

"Been forever."

Then they were devouring each other again.

Remy cupped her breast through her shirt and bra, kneading her, thumbing her nipple through the layers.

"…said they were down here?" A voice both familiar and authoritative echoed down the aisle.

They froze, ready to leap apart just like guilty teenagers.

"Actually, I thought they said they were moving onto the smokehouse." Sarah's hasty and somewhat panicked reply had no effect on the strident footfalls proceeding toward them at an alarmingly quick clip.

Remy swore beneath his breath as he eased her back to her feet.

"Who is that?" Cosima asked, quickly running a hand through her hair and adjusting her shirt.

"Samuel Kane," he muttered.

"What's Samuel Kane doing down here?" Pulling a tissue from her pocket, she dabbed at her kiss-swollen lips. No time to powder or reapply lipstick. Maybe, coming from LA, he'd assume she'd just had a disastrous collagen treatment.

"Beside ruining a good time and shining a flashlight up the distillery's collective hindquarters?"

She scooted as close to the main walkway as she could without being seen.

Remy moved to follow her, but she planted a hand squarely in the center of his chest. She widened her eyes and cut them toward his crotch, where a very significant problem bulged beneath the denim.

"Shit." Turning his torso away from her, he thumped his forehead on the rounded wood.

"Just stay here and be quiet. I'll take care of it."

His brow furrowed. "What are you going to do?"

Cosima offered him a smile as she pulled a set of earbuds from her pockets and wedged them in her ear canals. "What I'm best at."

Remy's amused grin began to slip from its moorings when Samuel was almost on them and she'd yet to move.

When she could see the mirror-polished tip of an expensive Italian loafer, she whipped herself around the barrel and straight into Samuel's path.

Eight

Remy smiled to himself at Samuel Kane's startled curse.

Apparently, there was a human being beneath that unflappable calm. He stopped himself from peeking out between the barrels when he heard the scuffling of shoes and a masculine grunt of displeasure. His fear that Cosima might have been hurt was as great as his desire to see whether or not the Kane Foods CEO might have eaten some concrete.

No such luck.

"Oh, my goodness, I am so sorry," Cosima gushed.

"It's fine. Just make sure you—" The bristling irritation died a sudden death, and when Samuel spoke again his tone was considerably softer. "Cosima?

What a pleasant surprise. I had heard you might be on-site at some point but had no idea it would be so soon."

And damn if he hadn't said that exactly like he knew Remy would overhear.

"Yes, well, Remy was kind enough to rearrange his busy schedule at my request," Cosima said.

This, he had *definitely* been meant to overhear. Had she picked up on his irritation? Made the connection that agreeing to the expedited timeline was just a convenient way to irk Samuel Kane?

"What a guy," Samuel said with no enthusiasm.

Remy's jaw ached as his molars ground together. He loosened his jaw, remembering how his dentist had commented that if he kept it up, he'd have nothing but nubs back there soon. He had half a mind to send Kane Foods International the bill.

"Congratulations on your wedding, by the way," Cosima said. "I'm so sorry I wasn't able to make it. I was filming in Italy at the time."

"Thank you," Samuel said. "It was a wonderful day. Your parents looked well."

"They always do." Some of the daylight had gone out of her voice.

Samuel must have heard it, too, but unlike Remy, he was able to smoothly steer the conversation away from a potentially painful area with the ease of a naval captain. "Speaking of filming, tell me about this 4 Thieves project."

"It's a docuseries, actually," she said. "About the

distillery, its operations, its history. But I promise, we'll do our best not to get in the way."

"Oh, I wasn't worried about that at all," Samuel said. "I was just hoping to get a better understanding around the approach."

A pause. Remy would have paid a hefty sum to see Cosima's face in that moment.

"Approach?" The sweetness in her voice sent up red flags of warning, and though Remy had no particular love for the man who had interrupted them, he found himself silently telegraphing *don't do it, man* to Samuel from his hiding spot.

"Your take on the story, so to speak," he clarified.

"You're suggesting I have an angle?"

A familiar feeling of unease began to creep into Remy's gut, dissolving the residual heat of their encounter like so much dish suds.

"The Cosima I knew wouldn't leave her desk without an angle, much less travel all the way across the country."

There was no heat in Samuel's statement. Not even a hint of suggestion, but he definitely had a point, and he was getting at it.

"I'm not exactly sure what you're implying," Cosima said.

"I'm implying that you've always been excellent at assembling a narrative. I have a stake in what that narrative will be where 4 Thieves is concerned."

Splinters dug into Remy's knuckles as he ground a fist against the barrel.

"Maybe the Renaud brothers would like to shape their own narrative," Cosima suggested.

"Which I have no objection to," Samuel said. "I just feel that there are elements of it that might best be left out of frame, if you take my meaning."

"Such as?"

"Forgive me," Samuel said. "I'm just remembering a recent project of yours where the participants seemed to have a very differing version of events from what made it to the final cut?"

Remy felt a twitch of annoyance. While he'd thought to do research on the filming process itself, looking up the specific projects Cosima had been associated with hadn't occurred to him.

"Isn't it funny how different people will have different recollections of the exact same memory? For instance, the graduation party I threw at my house. I seem to remember it was you who slipped me fifty to draw Mason's name from a hat when it was Arlie's turn for seven minutes of heaven. But you kept telling everyone Mason had done it. It seems I remember several occasions of strange things happening on debate-team trips that mysteriously ended up being blamed on Mason. Isn't that odd?"

Now, Remy couldn't help himself. Slowly, carefully, and as quietly as he could, he slipped down to the end of the row and leaned forward to peek through the tiny gap. The barest sliver of Samuel's face was visible.

His coloring had miraculously changed from a healthy glow to something resembling a late-summer beet. Refreshing, not to be the only one whose body parts glowed with embarrassment.

Samuel cleared his throat. "Well, it's been pleasant catching up with you. Please let me know if there's anything you need from me or the distillery staff in terms of filming."

"You, as well," Cosima said. "And I appreciate that."

Remy waited until the sound of footfalls faded into faint echoes before stepping out.

"All right, spill it. What kind of dirt do you have on him? Jaywalking? Did he run a stop sign? Fail to help an old lady cross the street?"

She angled her face up at him. "More like a lifelong subversive campaign to supplant Mason Kane as their father's favorite. Which, if you knew their father, wouldn't surprise you."

"Oh, I know their father, alright. His backing out of an investment in 4 Thieves is the whole reason Samuel Kane has crawled all the way up into our business."

"In that case, Parker Kane did you a huge favor," Cosima said, beginning to walk toward the stairs. "However much you dislike dealing with Samuel, take that and multiply times a billion."

Remy fell into step beside her. "If you're trying to make me like the guy, it won't work."

"Wouldn't dream of it," Cosima said. "But it would be in your best interests to make him like you."

Remy's throat felt hot and sour.

This sounded a little too much like a threat.

* * *

When they walked into the restaurant, Remy felt a swell of pride.

Gleaming floors and cathedral ceilings built from wood they had salvaged from old churches in the hulls of decommissioned ships. But perhaps Remy's favorite feature was what they called the Boxcar Bar.

In the distillery's earliest days, when Bastien had been around, he and Remy had stumbled across an estate sale where the family of the recently deceased was trying to off-load an old dining car from the Atlantic Coast Line. It had been in pretty bad shape, but then so were most of the things the Renaud boys had inherited. From well-meaning church ladies, teachers, and distant cousins. They had taken one look at the moth-eaten seat cushions and long, gleaming rosewood bar top, and made an instant offer.

These days, it was most frequently manned by Grant, who was currently stocking the backlit shelves with clean glasses, while Law sat at the counter with his laptop and a mug of coffee.

Given his bloodshot eyes and the grim set of his jaw, this conversation wasn't destined to go well.

They'd been doing a pretty good job of avoiding each other since the other morning, and over the years, had figured out a pretty solid system for never talking about uncomfortable things when possible.

These days, they'd just about run out of track.

Law stood at their approach.

Even with her rugged-soled hiking shoes, he would have guessed Cosima topped out at about five-two, whereas Law, a solid six-five with an added inch of workboot, had more than a foot on her. If Cosima noticed the inequity in their height as Remy made the introductions, she gave no visual cues.

"Any chance I could get one of what he has?" Cosima asked Grant as she hopped onto a stool.

"Would you like the bourbon-infused vanilla syrup in your latte as well?" he asked, nearly tripping over his shoes in his excitement to retrieve a mug.

Remy raised an eyebrow at Law, who, like himself, had always taken his coffee black.

"It has a really smooth finish," Grant said.

"You talked me into it." She swung her knees toward Law and crossed one leg over the other.

A wave of déjà vu swept over him, and in a flash, he saw her smooth tanned legs with their curving muscles against the edge of a denim skirt.

Wishful thinking.

"I really appreciate you letting me come on such short notice," Cosima said to Law. "My network contact is hot to trot, and I know you have plenty going on, but Remy has been so accommodating."

Law gave her a tight smile, then shot a sideways look at Remy. "He certainly has." Closing the lid on his laptop, he turned to Cosima. "*So* accommodating, he entirely forgot to tell me you were coming."

As gifted a communicator as Cosima had proven to be, Remy was sure she didn't miss the filament of frustration in Law's outwardly teasing statement.

"Well, I'd say you'll barely know that we're here, but that would be a lie." She accepted her steaming mug from Grant with a smile that caused his ginger freckled cheeks to flush atomic pink at the edge of his russet beard. "We've tried to stay out of the way of operations as much as possible, but I'm afraid that, as one of the show's principals, I will need you for at least a couple hours of day for the next two weeks."

A crease dug in the center of Law's dark eyebrows as he scowled. "A couple hours a day? Seriously?"

As if Remy hadn't been required to sacrifice so much more than that with his own daughter in order to accommodate Law and Samuel's plans for the business. As if this TV show, just like Remy going to Los Angeles to speak with a television producer, hadn't been Law's idea in the first place.

"Not all at once," Cosima reassured him. "We'll need to do a little storyboarding up front so that we know which shots we need to get, but after that, we'll mostly just be following you through a typical day. With a few separate on-the-fly interviews, of course."

Having observed his youngest brother in a variety of stressful contacts, Remy felt his own blood pressure rising when he spotted the vein becoming a fat worm beneath the skin of Law's temple. He tried to catch his brother's eye to signal that they could talk about this later. Law refused to look at him.

"You've got to be kidding me," he grumbled under his breath.

The gentle curve of Cosima's lower back flattened as she sat up straighter. Her posture was instantly recognizable. Defensive.

"I seem to remember us reviewing this process when we had our initial discovery call. In fact, I believe your words were something like 'that sounds fun.'"

Remy remembered it, too.

Whether he'd said it just to please Marlowe, or because he assumed that Remy would turn her down flat once he'd flown out, didn't matter. Lots of things sounded fun before you were running on little sleep and had a near constant soundtrack of stereo screaming from two tiny infants.

Even with a household of help. Which was a hell of a lot more than Remy'd had when Emily was first born.

He flicked away the nib of resentment. It would do nothing to help the situation.

"We'll find a way to make it work. When did you want to hold this storyboarding session?" After draining the last of his coffee, Law slid a class to Grant, who had been hovering nearby. "We have state inspectors coming today, a call this afternoon with a potential brewery affiliate, and video session with the Kane Foods marketing team."

None of which Remy knew about.

Grant cleared his throat.

"I'd be happy to meet with the state inspector. I shadowed Remy last time he was here, and I've already been filling out the inspection checklists."

Having begun his career at the distillery in the granary, Grant had slowly found ways to make himself indispensable in other areas. Like Mira, the restaurant manager, and a good deal of the warehouse staff, Grant had come to them by way of a prison bus. Law had been initially dubious about the prospect of taking on ex-cons.

Something Remy was still working on trying to forgive his brother for.

He remembered all too well the hell that was job hunting after his own release. The gnawing worry as he sat across from employers with the power to turn him away. Waiting as they silently read through his application. Anticipating the moment when they get to that most terrible of checked boxes.

Watching as their faces changed. From surprise, to dismay, to disgust. And even worse than the disgust was the pity.

The invisible dismissal. *I'm afraid we don't have anything for you here, but I might be able to come up with something in a different department.*

That *something* almost always required heavy lifting for light pay.

Remy had told himself that if he was ever in a position to provide opportunities to people feeling that same pain while trying to rebuild their lives, he would stop at nothing to do it. Which is why when they finally decided to get serious about the distillery, contacting the local prisons to build a work-release program had been on Remy's list of nonnegotiables.

"I suppose that would be alright," Law said.

Grant beamed a slightly gap-toothed grin that

both Remy and Law returned despite the simmering tension between them.

"You could just let me sit in on the storyboarding once the crew gets back," Remy suggested. "Since you and Samuel have such a busy day."

He knew he should have left off the second sentence, but he couldn't quite help himself.

He could see his brother grappling with the same temper he'd been wrestling with on an increasing basis. As had been the case when they were younger, they saved their worst fights for private.

"Works for me." Law pushed himself up from the stool and glanced down at his phone. "Looks like I better head back. Good to meet you," he said, nodding toward Cosima and tucking his laptop under his arm.

To Remy, he said nothing.

"I'll catch you up later, brother," Remy called after him. The hand Law held up in acknowledgement as he walked away might as well have been a middle finger.

When Grant disappeared into the kitchen with Law's mug, Cosima wheeled on him.

"What the hell was that?"

"Exhaustion would be my guess," Remy said.

Cosima snatched away her coffee when he reached for it. "I meant what the hell was that with *you*."

He shifted on his feet, not at all comfortable with this turn in the conversation. "With me?" he asked dumbly.

Cosima was one of those women who ripened

with anger the same way fruit ripened in the summer sun. Her cheeks flushed. Her lips reddened. Her eyes sparkled. He wondered if this is what male praying mantises saw right before they were relieved of their heads. So fascinated with the magnificent creature in front of them, they lacked the good sense to be afraid.

"First Samuel Kane, then your brother," she said. "I know memory isn't your strong suit, but I don't believe it just slipped your mind that we'd be arriving today."

"It didn't," he admitted.

"Which means you chose not to tell them despite knowing how they'd react."

"Correct."

She arched a dark eyebrow. "Well?"

Remy couldn't think of a single thing to say.

"Let me guess. You thought it would be a fun way to jam your thumb into Samuel Kane's eye, right? Show him he's *not the boss of you*?" She coated the saying with sarcasm.

"No, I just thought—"

"I'm gonna stop here right there, because if you took the time to think about anything, you would know what a monumentally stupid idea pissing off a man like Samuel Kane really is."

Remy's heart hammered in his ears, a deafening throb that threatened to split his skull.

"You think I don't know that?" The question scorched the back of his throat like battery acid. "You think I haven't been reminded my entire goddamn life what men like Samuel Kane could do to me?"

Cosima hopped down from her stool to face him, hands firmly planted on her hips.

Despite the animosity whipping between them like a downed power line, he felt an affectionate respect for her need to fight from her feet.

"Look, if you're determined to commit career suicide, that's your business. Next time, find a different vehicle."

The sole of her shoe squeaked as she spun and stomped off.

The rest of the day passed with a maddening sluggishness. Like the hands of a clock moving through cold molasses. Stationed at his desk in the loft office above the distillery's main floor, Remy did his best to focus, as elsewhere in the property, Samuel and Law held their meetings and made their plans while Cosima's crew scouted for locations and unloaded their equipment.

That afternoon, he managed to get through three hours of storyboarding. A process he decided had been invented to personally vex him. An entire hour would be broken down into twenty-minute segments. And then the twenty-minute segments broken into five-minute segments. And then the five-minute seconds broken into individual shots. He was considering breaking his own finger in order to have an excuse to leave when at last he heard the blessed words.

"Let's take a break." Any hopes he had of them

ducking off to a quiet place so he could apologize to Cosima were promptly dashed when her phone rang.

She glanced down at it, smiled, swiped her thumb over the screen, and answered. She wasn't quite out of the room when he heard her greet the person on the other line.

Michael.

Remembering the blond god whom he absolutely had not Google stalked after the fact, his jaw tightened.

Was her ex-fiancé making some sort of reconciliation attempt?

The thought did little to improve his mood.

Glancing down at his own phone, he felt an intense burst of gratitude when he realized a task was available to him. A task that would take him out of this room, out of this building, and down the gravel road.

He breathed easier the second he was outdoors. After sliding behind the wheel of his ATV, he sent gravel flying as he took off.

Emily's joy at having him meet her where the bus dropped them off was tempered with her embarrassment that the Varmint was parked within view of her classmates.

The promise of being allowed cookies for an afternoon snack instead of the usual healthy options smoothed the matter considerably. A bribe. He had been hoping she might agree to simply go back to their home on the property and forgo their usual routine.

Foolish of him.

"Dad," she said with apparent exasperation. "You know I need to take the mail up to the shipping office. And then I always help Mira roll silverware for the dinner shift. And I haven't even checked on the twins yet."

He felt a pinprick of guilt at the insistence in her tone. She'd grown up mirroring him out of necessity. When they had a staff of less than ten, it was just easier to take her with him. First strapped in a carrier across his chest, then in a backpack, then in a wagon, and then under her own steam. Her mind had seemed to have grown twice as fast as her body. Learning first by simian mimicry, stunning him with her unabashed delight when she figured out how to do a task by herself. She had officially reached the phase where she knew how to do things so well, the idea of him helping her was an insult instead of an aid.

He sometimes wondered if he let her do too much. If, instead of letting her become their self-appointed mail carrier, he should have insisted she go play.

They entered the warehouse, where, just as she always did, Emily followed the safety path marked with a little white shoe prints of the kind people used to use for instructional dance illustrations. As they turned down the hall that led up to the shipping office, they nearly collided with Cosima, earbuds firmly wedged in her ears, her phone held out in front of her.

What she'd done to Samuel Kane earlier hadn't just been an act, but a consequence of habit.

Her face cycled quickly through several expressions. Irritation came first. Then recognition, then, when her eyes landed on Emily, disbelief tinged with fear.

For the second time since they'd met, she looked like she'd seen a ghost.

Nine

The small girl standing before her had stolen the breath from Cosima's lungs. The blood from her cheeks. The heart from her chest.

"You must be Emily," she said, stooping to pick up the stack of talent release forms that had flown out of her hands when she'd almost collided with Remy's chest. "It's very nice to meet you."

"You're not allowed to wear those in the warehouse." The girl tapped her ear, which was absent the earbuds that were wedged into Cosima's.

"Emily," Remy warned. "That wasn't a very polite thing to say to Miss Lowell."

"It's okay." Cosima managed a smile even though her knees threatened to abandon her as she tried to rise. "She's just following protocol. Isn't that right?"

She winked in what she hoped was a disarming manner.

Emily remained armed.

Her gorgeously snobby, freckled face was completely implacable.

Remy angled an apologetic look at her that Cosima batted away with a harried grimace.

"Well," she said, holding up her hastily gathered stack. "I better get these taken care of."

She stalked off without a follow-up, willing her feet to carry her around the corner before the tears blurring her vision could spill down her cheeks.

Unfinished business.

Isn't that what all ghosts had in common?

In Emily Renaud, Cosima hadn't just seen one. She'd *felt* one.

Her calves and thighs burned as her heart rushed in her ears and she sidestepped into a small meeting room just in time.

Windowless and blessedly dim, the unoccupied space held her as she let herself collapse backward against the wall and slide down until her bottom hit the floor.

A tide of memory rose.

Too tired to fight against the current, she let herself sink.

In film, she could show the aftermath of their one-night stand in less than five minutes.

Bird's-eye view. Human puzzle pieces on a disheveled mattress. Her back fitted perfectly against his bare chest, their legs a calibrated chevron pointed east, where gray dawn spills through the window.

Fade to daylight.

She is there; he is missing.

Full shot. The woman from behind, sheet wound around her body as she parts the curtain. A motorcycle's ripping engine fades into a distant rumble.

Neon tears streak her face.

Cut scene.

Three weeks later. The girl in an old-fashioned pink waitress's uniform. Wide lapels, black apron and all. She's carrying a tray of chicken-fried steak toward a table of truck drivers in the corner when it hits her. Her face goes deathly pale, the skin at the corners of her mouth darkening to a gray-green. She shoves the tray into the closest set of hands and bolts for the bathroom, where she heaves until her stomach is empty and sore. She begs a coworker to cover for her, and heads straight to the nearest drugstore, where the clerk takes one look at her in the feminine-needs aisle and gives her a pitying frown.

Pregnant.

She receives this life-changing news while seated in a stall covered with numbers to call for a good time. A dirty limerick featuring a man from Nantucket. A heart containing the initials of a couple who felt their love at least worth memorializing in this most uninspiring of venues.

Pregnant.

Cut scene.

She counts an envelope of dwindling cash in her

hotel room. Searching GED programs on her phone. Emailing instructors at Lennox-Finch Preparatory Academy. Night classes at a community college to finish her high school classes.

An acceptance letter to UCLA.

The old Mustang pointed west.

Bridging shot of a map—a line as red as the Mustang tunneling through it. Her waitress notepad on the seat next to her. All through Arkansas, she writes down boy names. Through Oklahoma, it's girls.

Outside of Amarillo, she starts to cramp.

A kind doctor confirms what she already knows.

A miscarriage.

She keeps driving.

She sees the road through sheets of tears, then sheets of rain that look like tears. And sometimes a combined veil of both.

No official tests had confirmed this, but Cosima knew.

A girl. It would have been a girl.

Had Cosima not miscarried, the girl would have been Emily's half sister.

Had she not reached out to Marlowe Kane, the one-night stand, like the pregnancy it caused, would have remained a singular event.

A thing that had happened to her.

But now, it was history. *Their* history.

History that Remy didn't know they shared.

What exactly did she owe a man who had been gone before she'd woken up? How hard was she supposed to try to find him? They'd both been irresponsible. He'd assumed she was either prepared to deal with the consequences, or didn't care about them any more than he did.

It was hard to reckon that careless version of the careful man he'd become. The patient, affectionate father raising a daughter on his own.

Given a hundred years and the worst possible intersection of experiences, she couldn't imagine Remy reacting to Emily the way her father had when she'd called him in a moment of desperation after her miscarriage.

You made your bed.

He hadn't been wrong about that.

Even from her present vantage, she couldn't fault him. Cosima had made her parents' lives a special kind of hell in the days of their deepest grief following her brother's death. Expecting them to turn around and bail her out of the misery she'd created for herself with her staggering irresponsibility had been both naïve and entitled.

She knew this, and here she was, hurling herself headlong into another risky venture, hoping the cost would be worth it when the dust cleared.

All because she'd given her body, her money, and her livelihood to another man.

Michael, this time.

Cosima hugged her knees to her chest, holding herself together. She was so damn tired. Of the fear. Of the pain. Of the shame.

Of the hope that this time would somehow be different. That she'd finally found someone who understood.

Once the pilot episode was off her desk, she would find a way to tell Remy everything.

After that, she would have her answer.

Remy looked on as Emily watched Cosima go, completely agog.

"She was rude."

"Not everyone likes to be corrected like that, Bug. People around the distillery are used to you reminding them of things. But for people like Miss Lowell, it's kind to be a little more patient while they learn."

She considered this, still clearly not pleased with this interaction.

"Maybe you could give her another chance at dinner tonight," he suggested.

Despite her lukewarm acceptance of this idea, their evening meal with Cosima and her crew proved to be just as adversarial.

Emily corrected her about the year the distillery had been founded. About which kind of grain was used for which kind of liquor. About which side the little fork went on in a place setting.

For her part, Cosima bore it patiently, though Remy could see her tolerance was growing threadbare.

Hoping for a ceasefire, he announced Emily's impending bedtime, reminding her that she only had one more day before spring break and would be able to stay up later. Her expression of abject pleasure melted into such a look of horror that for a moment Remy thought she might've seen a grizzly bear standing behind him.

"My spring project. It's due tomorrow. I thought I had two more days."

Remy took a deep breath against the instant spike of irritation that always came in the wake of these last-minute revelations. This was just as much his fault. He had a vague memory of her mentioning it, but he had been so stuck in work that he'd completely forgotten to follow up.

"What spring project is this?" he asked.

"We're supposed to do a presentation or demonstration on what we want to be when we're grown up."

Glancing down at his phone, he felt a wave of exhaustion roll over him. They had a long night ahead.

"And what would you like to be when you grow up?" This question came from Roosevelt, who sat at the end of the table, scraping the last bites of banana pudding from an old-fashioned parfait glass.

Remy had to smile at this question despite his flagging energy. The answer changed rapidly, and usually every week. He had heard everything from flight attendant to monster-truck driver within the last several months.

"I want to be a personal chef, like Aunt Arlie's mom."

Figured.

"How about we film a cooking show?" The sound

of Cosima's voice caused a ripple of movement as everyone seated at the table turned to look at her.

She'd been uncharacteristically quiet throughout the meal, her eyes a little forlorn every time Remy stole a glance at her.

Emily's face brightened, then darkened as quickly as clouds blown across the sun. "That would take way too long," she said, her longing evident by the regret weighing her words.

Cosima cleared her throat and leaned forward in her seat so she could catch Emily's eye.

"You seem like a girl who knows an awful lot about an awful lot of things. But I bet you this is one of those things where I might know just a little bit more than you do."

The softness and lightly teasing cadence of her words struck him as incredibly generous in the face of Emily's constant provocation. She had absolutely no reason to offer up help.

"She's right," Roosevelt chimed in, pushing aside his glass. "We could set up a camera in the kitchen back there quick enough. We'd need maybe one umbrella light."

"Easy," Matt confirmed. "I could have that up in fifteen.

Emily aimed her freckled face up at Remy, seeking either approval or permission. He knew the days were waning when she would want either.

"Sounds like a pretty fantastic idea to me," he said, lifting his eyes to find Cosima.

"Roosevelt, you know the drill. Remy, you're on props. Sarah, you want to be in charge of wardrobe?"

"I'm on it," Sarah said, winking at Emily.

Cosima clapped her hands like the director's placard and her crew launched into motion.

Within twenty minutes, they had everything set up to film the impromptu episode of *Bug's Bistro*.

Its star was receiving her final touches from Sarah, who bent to powder her delicate button of a nose, and Cosima, who loosed her braids from their characteristic pigtails.

Watching these women tend to his daughter, Remy felt a sick ache deep in his gut.

Emily deserved this.

She had from the beginning. It was a pain he knew despite trying to convince himself that it didn't exist. Remy hadn't decided which he thought worse. To have, then lose, a nurturing maternal presence, or to never have experienced one at all.

He shook his head as if to clear away the thought, not wanting to hold the bitter memory in his mind while watching the sweetness of the scene before him.

When everything had been arranged, Cosima stepped back and gave Emily a thumbs-up. Emily returned it confidently with a decisive nod.

It took her a few tries, but using the hastily drawn-up cue cards, she was able to talk the audience through the construction of the perfect grilled cheese sandwich. Complete with an ad-lib anecdote about how it was her go-to snack after school.

"That's a wrap," Roosevelt said, after the last run was finished. "I think we have everything we need. I'll get this edited and then share it with you guys via dropbox."

The crew began packing up their cameras while Grant and the kitchen staff took over the cleanup. Emily came out from behind the kitchen worktable like she might be offering autographs at any moment.

"You, young lady, are a pro," Cosima said.

"I kept messing up the introduction," Emily said, staring down at one sparkly purple sneaker.

"I was nowhere as good at that when I was your age."

"Really?"

"True story," Cosima said. "I even got kicked out of a play once."

Emily's eyes peeled open, such an affront unimaginable to her. "You got kicked out of play?"

"Yep. I got the part of Little Red Riding Hood, but on opening night, when the wolf jumped out from grandmother's bed, I punched him right in the snout instead of screaming and running like I was supposed to."

A peel of laughter escaped through the fingers Emily clapped to her mouth. "You did?"

"Of course, the boy in the wolf suit used to pick on me for being short, so that might have had something to do with it," Cosima said.

Emily nodded sagely, "He sounds like Jackson Myers."

Remy almost ran into a door. "How come I've never heard of Jackson Myers?"

"Because if I told you about him you would come to school and scare him, and he'd make fun of me even more."

Cosima looked over her shoulder at Remy with eyebrows raised.

Remy shrugged with a guilty-as-charged look on his face.

"I think I could give you a few pointers to take care of old Jackson," Sarah said. "It just so happens scaring bullies is my specialty."

They spoke in hushed whispers as they all made their way up to the Varmint, where Matt and Roosevelt were already loading their equipment into the back.

"Can Sarah take me back to the house?" Emily asked. "I was going to show her my Roblox."

"It is *so* past your bedtime, Bug," Remy reminded her.

Her small shoulders slumped.

"I can get her tucked in," Sarah offered. "I have a little sister her age. I miss her a lot."

Cosima and Remy exchanged a look.

"Alright," Remy said, relenting. "But no more within half an hour. If you're not in bed by the time I get home—"

"I have to scrub the goat trough with my toothbrush," she recited.

"For the record, she's never had to do that," Remy

said when he received horrified looks from both of the cameramen.

Somewhat relieved, they, along with Sarah and Emily, bundled into the ATV and rumbled off into the night.

Remy filled his lungs with a long, slow breath and turned to Cosima. "Long day."

"It was," she agreed.

"Walk you to your quarters?" he offered.

"If you like."

"What's on the agenda for tomorrow?" he asked, beginning to amble down the path.

She fell into step beside him.

"We're going to shoot some B-roll around the property. Get some one-off interviews with the staff." Already, she'd begun to outpace him and was half a step ahead.

An effective metaphor for their dynamic in almost every regard.

"I believe I offered to *walk* you to your quarters?" he said, jogging to catch up.

"Exactly," she said. "This is me walking."

"Like you're trying to get away from the scene of a crime."

She gave him a sidelong glance. "What's wrong with getting from point A to point B efficiently?"

Remy slowed in the center of the path, the sound of the gravel crunching dying away to reveal the faint cry of a loon in the distance. "You would have missed that."

Cosima shook her head, her wild curls blowing in the breeze.

"Next you'll be hitting me with platitudes about life being a journey and not a destination," she grumbled.

"Furthest thing from my mind," he said.

"What's the closest?" She glanced at him from beneath a fringe of lashes.

"Nothing it's proper for a gentleman to talk about while he's alone with a lady."

She made a disbelieving sound. "I don't know which is funnier. You comparing yourself to a gentleman, or me to a lady."

Only to Remy, she would have been. Anyone in the rural area he grew in could spot the difference between someone with money and someone without as easily as they could tell a cupcake from a carburetor.

What someone with Cosima's upbringing might have experienced, he couldn't begin to guess and she didn't seem inclined to tell him.

"You going to tell me what's wrong?" he asked.

The smile she gave him was tight and completely unconvincing. "What makes you think anything is wrong?"

"Maybe the fact that you ate next to nothing at dinner, but now you're trying to eat your lip for dessert," he said.

She shrugged. "Nervous habit, I guess."

Remy shoved his hands in his pockets and slowed abruptly. "What's to be nervous about?"

Stopping several paces away, she huffed air through her nostrils like a frustrated filly, irritated at having her canter slowed. "The production schedule, the fact that neither your brother nor Samuel particularly wants us on-site. I can't say that makes me especially excited about the filming process."

Just as he had that day in her office, Remy felt something beneath her words. Deeper, and older, and heavier. Something she didn't yet want to share.

He took a couple steps toward her and slipped his fingers through her belt loop, tugging her into a pocket of shadow just off the path.

She let him walk her backward until her back met the bark of a cottonwood tree.

Even in the dim light, he could see her narrowed eyes. "Remy, I'm fine. I don't need to be coddled."

He didn't answer. Only stood there, waiting.

She heaved a disgusted sigh. "I mean it. I don't need you to fix things for me, or hold open doors, or make sure I'm driving safely. I don't need you to worry if there's food in my fridge or shoes in my pantry. Just because you're a father doesn't mean that I need one."

Remy took a step closer to her. "Have you ever considered that maybe this is about what *I* need? That maybe being near you makes wrong things seem right and the world feels a little steadier under my feet? That after what has been a colossally shitty day, I might find it just the least but helpful to have you in my arms?"

Cosima shifted on her hiking shoes, looking equal parts shocked and surprised. "Actually…no."

"Well, it's true." He himself hadn't considered this until he'd spoken it.

"When you put it like that…"

"Would you just get your stubborn ass over here and let me hold you?"

Then, wonder of wonders, she did as he'd requested, letting her arms encircle his waist and her ear rest against his sternum. Her body was stiff at first, but by degrees, began to melt into him. Remy held her there. Letting his arms encircle her shoulders, his chin rest on top of her head.

What followed felt like the longest exhale of his entire life.

They stayed in exactly that position for a span of time he'd never be able to calculate.

She moved against him, releasing his waist to mold her soft hands to his rough jaw.

He let himself be drawn down, his mouth lowering to meet hers. For the first time in his life, Remy let himself be kissed. Gave himself over entirely to whatever it was she wanted to take.

Her lips brushed over his, sweet and faintly scented of wine from dinner.

Nectar he was powerless to resist any more than bees could resist Technicolor flowers when buds began to open.

Spring fever.

That was about right.

The first taste of sunlight on skin after a long,

cold, lonely winter. That extra hour of daylight rinsing dark, dusty corners. Waking up the world.

He was waking up, too. Coming alive from scalp to soles.

He pressed his lips to her temple. Her cheekbone. The curve of her jawline.

Then he kissed her back.

Cosima opened to him, granting him access to the source of words that drove him half-mad. Source of pleasure that drove him the rest of the way.

Remy plumbed those velvet depths with thorough, languid strokes, holding his breath until his lungs burned with the effort of drinking every last drop of her throaty moan. Touching her, tasting her, filling his senses now for all the times he'd gone without.

As a boy.

As a man.

As a human.

Only in allowing himself this luxury did he realize how empty he'd been.

Existing on fumes. Praying that it would be enough to get him over the next hill. Through the next day. Last the next year.

She caught his hand as it moved beneath the hem of her shirt, guiding it downward instead, beneath the band of her pants. To silk panties already damp with need.

"God damn." Pleasure bordering on pain knotted at the base of his spine. "Already?"

He felt her smile against his lips.

"You kidding me?" Nimble fingers made short

work of his belt buckle, button, and zipper. "I've been wet since I set foot on your property."

An answering growl rumbled from his chest when her warm fingers wrapped around his cock and began to glide up and down its length.

He lost his breath again. Or found too much of it and couldn't seem to remember how to fix that. Gasping inhales and ragged exhales in time with her ministrations.

Tree bark branded his forehead as he leaned into the pleasure, the feeling of her hot, wet mouth sucking and sampling the skin at the base of his neck a maddening accompaniment to the increasing friction below.

The ridge of her teeth sank gently into his shoulder when he slid aside the small scrap of fabric to find the silken petals of her sex, coating the small, taut bud with slick strokes.

She quickly matched, then exceeded his pace once again.

A race.

Each trying to get the other there first.

Cosima bucked against his hand, sending a muffled cry into the wall of his chest a precious half second before Remy lost himself in endless, rhythmic pulses.

And still, he was starving.

Ravenous with the need to be inside her.

With nearly Herculean effort, he dragged his mouth free. He gazed down into eyes the gold-green of a meadow in late summer.

"You have no idea how bad I want you right now."

Her fingers flexed against his still-stony length. "I think I can make a reasonable deduction."

He brushed a damp lock away from her face. "Know what I want even more?"

"A cigar and bottle of Macallan eighteen-year?"

That wave of déjà vu surged through him once again, blurring reality like a watercolor.

Her face became his anchor. The pad of his thumb found a soft damp swell of her lower lip. "I want you all to myself."

"What do you call this?" Warm lips planted small kisses around the spot she'd bitten.

"For a whole night," he added, notching a finger under her chin to tip her face up to his. "In a place where only the stars get to watch."

Cosima began restoring her clothing to its rightful arrangement. "Do I get to know where this place is?"

He followed suit, tugging up the band of his boxers and closing his fly. "Nope."

She rolled her eyes as if amused by his need for subterfuge. "When?"

"This Sunday."

He'd given it considerable thought. Or at least as much thought as he was capable of in the last five minutes with minimal blood supply above waist level.

Emily would be safely installed at camp. Samuel Kane would be back in Philadelphia. And maybe he and Law would have a chance to smooth things over. All of which felt like it needed to happen before he could devote his complete and undivided attention to an event that surely required it.

Cosima pinned him with her cocky grin. "What should I wear?"

Remy reached out and plucked a leaf from her hair. "Something easy to get off."

Ten

For the days that followed, Cosima lived in a state of near-constant state of arousal.

Watching Remy around other people, knowing she couldn't have him, left her swooning in her beautifully appointed cabin. In the warehouse. In the distillery.

There had been some near misses, of course.

When they ran into each other in the barn.

When she'd caught him alone in the shipping office.

When they'd met in the hallway after the grueling hour she'd spent coaching Law through his first confessional segment in the axe-throwing gallery.

Each of these times involved an inevitable fusion that left them both raw-mouthed and panting, frequently rearranging their clothes mere seconds from getting caught.

It was a dangerous game they were playing.

And that danger proved to be the most potent aphrodisiac of them all.

Tempering this ardor was what Cosima had come to think of as The Emily Situation.

Namely, that the more time she spent with the girl who had once been her self-appointed safety supervisor, the more she found herself developing wildly protective feelings for her.

In their early collisions, she'd begun to recognize a common theme.

She and Emily had butted heads because were so much alike. Bold, bossy, and absolutely convinced they alone were responsible for making sure the earth remained fixed on its axis.

This realization had finally crystalized on Saturday afternoon during the preparations for a group dinner Emily had insisted was necessary before she departed for camp the following morning. When Emily learned Cosima would be cooking her Nona Ferro's manicotti she had asked if she could "help."

See: supervise.

They'd spent the next several hours in the kitchen together, hand-crushing San Marzano tomatoes. Picking fresh basil from the distillery's herb garden.

Talking. Laughing. Flicking each other with suds when they did the first round of dishes.

When Emily checked the oven temperature for the third time, it finally clicked.

We control what we don't trust. This truism floated through Cosima's head as she observed the relief on Emily's face when she'd confirmed that all was right with the world.

It wasn't the oven or the temperature Cosima had provided that Emily didn't trust.

It was herself.

That she had remembered to do what she was supposed to do, or that she'd done it correctly.

Cosima had been surprised by the intensity of her longing to sit the girl down at the table and share something, anything, that would help.

But she didn't, knowing it wasn't her place.

The thought pierced her as the afternoon began to drain away.

Later, Law and Marlowe arrived, each with a twin strapped to their chest, followed by her crew, followed, at last, by Remy.

Turning with a pan of manicotti held in two oven-mitt-covered hands, she spotted him leaning in the doorway with a strange little smile on his face.

Family.

He'd never had much of one.

What she'd known of hers, she'd lost.

A grandmother. A brother. A mother who had tried. A father who didn't know how to.

She hadn't realized until that moment exactly how much she missed it.

The following morning, Remy saw Emily off to camp—a scene that left even stoic Sarah dabbing her kohl-rimmed eyes.

And then there was nothing to do but wait.

Which Cosima was exceptionally terrible at. She spent the day returning emails and catching up on various administrative tasks she'd allowed to fall behind while they were filming. After the two hours that ate up, she migrated to Sarah's cabin only to find her still asleep.

Her crew and the distillery staff, including Grant the Viking, stayed up a little too late sampling their own wares. More than once over the last couple of days, Cosima had caught what she had hoped might be a flicker of mutual interest between the gentle giant and her scrappy, thick-skinned assistant.

Unable to further her cause as matchmaker, Cosima took herself on a walk to the part of the property containing the sprawling Craftsman home Marlowe and Law shared. With her sister-in-law and soon-to-be sister-in-law back in Philadelphia for a couple days and the twins down for a nap, Marlowe gratefully accepted Cosima's offer of company.

They sat down at the kitchen table together with coffee and slices of the cake Marlowe had begged her to help eat.

"This is a trip, right?" Marlowe said, acknowledging the massive elephant in the room while simultaneously leaning down to stroke the ear of the brown-and-white mutt of a dog she'd seen patrolling the property on occasion.

"I mean, raising twins isn't exactly a promenade through Hyde Park," Cosima said.

They shared a conspiratorial smile at the mention of their sophomore-year, debate-club summer trip to London.

Cosima and Marlowe had met two adorable Irishman at a nearby pub and ended up on the back of their scooters, missing curfew entirely and sitting together on a bench in Hyde Park as the sun came up.

"You really were a terrible influence." Marlowe smiled fondly.

"You needed one."

"No argument there," she agreed.

"I have to say, out of all of us, you would have been the last that I picked to end up married," Cosima said.

Marlowe chuckled softly to herself. "Getting pregnant with twins after a three-day fling with Law Renaud wasn't exactly a part of my life plan."

Cosima felt a little start of surprise. She had known the relationship advanced quickly, but had no idea of the circumstances surrounding the pregnancy.

"When did you find out?" Cosima asked, knowing she was being deliberately nosy but unable to help herself.

"At Samuel's reception—wait, no. That's when everyone *else* found out. *I* found out in the bridal suite before the ceremony," Marlowe said.

"Holy shit." Cosima clapped a hand to her mouth, imagining Marlowe and the various immediate family members receiving that news in environs as luxurious as they would be for any Kane wedding. "You and Law weren't even together?"

Midsip of her coffee, Marlowe coughed, and for

a terrifying moment, Cosima thought she was going to be treated to a spray of atomized caffeine.

Marlowe dabbed at her mouth, then her eyes, with a clean spit-up rag draped over the back of her chair. When she had recovered control of herself, she set aside the cloth.

"We were about as *not* together as you can be. We slept together while I was there to conduct an audit and hadn't even spoken to each other in two months."

Cosima blinked at her, thunderstruck.

All this time she'd assumed Marlowe was gliding along like a swan, having no idea how furiously she'd been paddling below the surface.

"How did you two decide that you wanted to…" She trailed off, not sure how to categorize their union in light of this new information.

"Have a shotgun wedding?"

"I didn't say that."

"But you were thinking it." Marlowe tucked a stray strand behind her ear.

"Maybe a little," Cosima admitted, tracing the smooth of the mug's handle with her thumb.

"I went through the normal stages of emotion associated with an unexpected pregnancy."

"Shock, denial, more shock, existential dread, more denial, acceptance?"

Only when Marlowe's shrewd gaze lingered a beat too long on Cosima's face did she realize what she might have given away by pegging it so precisely. "Exactly. Anyway, after I made my way through all of that, I actually started to get…"

"Excited," Cosima said, finishing for her. *In for a penny.*

"Of course, my father was furious when I told him."

Just that sentence alone demonstrated how far Marlowe had come.

The prim, somewhat prudish young woman she'd been when they were in prep school had always sat up a little bit straighter when Parker Kane walked into the room. She'd missed out on parties and trips for her polo matches. Even after the accident that ended her polo career, she hadn't said a single word when her father sold off her beloved horse.

Cosima had never mastered this skill. She seemed to be categorically incapable of hiding emotion. Positive or negative.

"How are things now?" she asked. "Between Law and your father?"

Marlowe flashed her a beleaguered smile. "A reasonable degree of mutual tolerance has been established. I think the fact that Law has more contact with Samuel than he does with our father helps."

"I'm sure," Cosima said, careful to keep her tone even. "And you and Law? Storybook happy?"

"If by that you mean that sometimes I'm a witch and he's an ogre, then yes."

"I'd have gone with Snow Queen. Or I *would* have, anyway." Cosima lifted her friend's wrist, lightly puffy, but still retaining its elegant lines.

"I know, right?" Marlowe rotated her arm. "How

weird is it that have an actual tan. Like, from *the sun*."

"I'll bet you garden and everything."

"It's even worse." Marlowe pushed herself up from her chair and swung open a cupboard door to reveal a legion of gleaming Mason jars. "I've discovered canning therapy."

"Eat your heart out, Martha Stewart," Cosima clucked.

"How about you? Think you'll ever pair off permanently?" Marlowe stopped at the counter to grab the French press and held it out in question. Nodding gratefully, Cosima held out her mug for a top-up.

The thinking she could do. It was the implementation phase where everything always seemed to go awry. Her roots never sank deep enough before the next storm came along.

Cosima shrugged. "If my history is any indication, finding men who are willing to put up with my schedule are hard to find."

They exchanged a meaningful look, held in the spell of silence created by a chain saw dying away.

"It's a tradeoff," Marlowe said. Following her eyeline out the window, Cosima spotted Law, barechested and sweaty, grinning as he raised a hand in greeting. Marlowe waved in return, love falling across her features like a veil. "Especially with a man like Law."

"How so?" Cosima asked.

Marlowe studied the beautifully burnished surface of the farmhouse table.

"Have you ever watched wood being stained?" The heiress's voice took on a soft, dreamy quality.

"I can't say that I have."

The slim tip of Marlowe's fingernail followed the maze of knotholes. "It brings out the wood's natural beauty. The grain. The striations." She lifted her winter-sky eyes to meet Cosima's. "It also brings out the flaws. You can't see one without seeing the other. Being in a relationship with someone like Law or Remy who had such a traumatic upbringing is a little like that. It's going to take you closer to the beauty and the pain."

She paused, allowing time to absorb the metaphor.

"Am I making any sense?" Marlowe dropped her elbows to the table, massaging the dark circles beneath her eyes. "I'm so tired."

Cosima drained the last of her coffee. "Here you have a chance to nap while the twins are sleeping and I'm here drinking all your caffeine and yapping your ear off."

As if on cue, a green light blinked from a futuristic baby monitor on the table before it begun to emit a wail.

Marlowe offered up harried half-grin. "That will be my manager," she said, rising.

No sooner had she gained her feet when the front door swung open, and Law, wearing a concerned expression and fine coat of sawdust, appeared in the foyer.

"Is that Frank?" he asked. "That's Frank, right?"

"He keeps one of the monitors clipped to his belt," Marlowe explained.

Cosima experienced a sympathetic surge of oxytocin. "That's the cutest damn thing I've ever heard."

"Right?" They both glanced in the direction of the stairs as Law took them two at a time.

"What was it?" Cosima asked. "What made you decide you wanted to build a family with Law?" she quickly added, realizing the question followed not their conversation, but her own thoughts.

"Remy, actually." Marlowe flipped a switch on the monitor when the bass rumble of Law's voice became audible.

"Remy?" Cosima asked, irritated at herself for the instant heat flushing her cheeks.

Marlowe nodded.

"Seeing how he and Law were with each other and with Emily. That fierce loyalty. How protective they are of each other. How hard they've worked to get past the pain they came from."

Guilt lanced the warmth in Cosima's chest.

Marlowe reached down and squeezed Cosima's hand, communicating some essential truth through that touch. "It's worth it," she said. "Love is always worth it."

As a button to their conversation, it solidified Cosima's resolve.

She had to tell Remy tonight.

Eleven

At exactly ten o'clock, there came a tap at her window.

Her stomach flipped as she crossed to it and pried up the painted frame.

Remy stood in the golden square of light painted on the grass below, a helmet in his hand and a smile on his face. He wore a slight variation on his standard attire. Worn jeans, a ribbed sleeveless undershirt, and battered black leather motorcycle jacket.

Cosima, on the other hand, had prepared herself for their meeting with an almost bride-like devotion to ceremony.

Something old: a long bath in the old-fashioned clawfoot tub.

Something new: the beautiful cream silk bra-and-panty set she'd treated herself to before the trip.

Something borrowed: this simple white sundress Marlowe had loaned her with eyebrows raised when she'd asked for something light and breezy. Because *easy to get off* would have shot her eyebrows straight into the stratosphere.

Something blue: the pall of worry cast over what had been pure excitement only a day earlier.

"This place comes with a door, you know," she said gazing down like Juliet from her balcony.

Moonlight and mischief colored his eyes a more ghostly version of their typical iron-gray. "Where's the fun in that?"

"Speaking of," she said, hands on the sill, "I have a question."

"I can try to have an answer."

"What kind of footwear would you recommend for the evening's festivities?"

Remy sucked at the inside of his cheek for a moment. "Don't suppose you have any boots? Leather, preferably. Something that covers your calves."

"This is part of your shoe thing, isn't?" Cosima teased.

"Hell no," he replied. "I mean, yeah. But this time it just happens to be practical as well as personally beneficial." He gave her the full wattage of his dazzling smile.

"Just so happens we're both in luck then." Padding away from the window in her socked feet, Cosima sat on the battered steamer trunk at the end of the bed and zipped herself into a pair of stiff, custom-made leather riding boots she'd had to dust off before packing for the trip. Luckily, her shoe size hadn't changed since her own disastrous foray into women's polo at age sixteen.

She grabbed a denim jacket from her bedpost and shrugged into on the way back to the window, where she would apparently be making her exit.

Though she could have easily stuck the landing without his help, she planted her hands on Remy's broad shoulders and allowed him to hold her hips as she came down.

He surprised her by lacing his hand with hers on the way to his motorcycle.

Classic lines. Well-maintained. Gleaming chrome showing its age in a way that seemed dignified and proud and quietly powerful.

Bikes that look like their owners.

Remy mounted first. A gentleman even now, he turned his face away while she stepped on the pedal provided and swung her leg over.

Unlike the first time they'd ridden together, they both slipped on helmets.

A stark reminder of the lessons life had brought them both since that night.

Now, they both had something to lose.

The bike came to life beneath her with a deep, throaty growl that vibrated through the insides of her thighs into the creases of her hips.

Remy handled the machine like an extension of his own body, expertly shifting his weight to round corners. As he did, she melted against his broad, muscular back. Arms like vines creeping around his waist. Abdominal muscles flexing against the insides of her wrists through the soft fabric of his T-shirt.

They had the country road entirely to themselves, winding upward for what felt like an eternity, but what she logically knew had been less than ten minutes.

The motorcycle quieted as he slowed to turn off just after a sign advertising a scenic overlook. Balmy night air felt deliciously sweet on skin dampened slightly by the helmet's close interior.

"'Fraid we have a bit of walking to do," Remy said, hanging his helmet off one of the handlebars.

They climbed over a short wall of crumbling stone and followed an unofficial path clearly worn by people with the same idea in mind. Tall grass already gathering condensation kissed her kneecaps as they stepped into a small clearing.

From this vantage, they had an unobstructed view of the valley below. Rendered in shades of gray and midnight blue with a glittering constellation of lights gathered in their throughout.

Four Thieves sat apart. A diamond solitaire set in the velvet hillside.

"Wow," she breathed, so mesmerized by the sight that she didn't see the blanket until the yellow glow of a camping lantern—LED but engineered to mimic flame—began to flicker in her peripheral vision.

Additional details arrived as her eyes adjusted to the darkness. The vintage picnic basket. A cozy heap of throw pillows. The light gray dome of a tent back in the shadows.

"You didn't have to go to all this trouble," she said.

Remy scuffed his feet in the grass like a teenage boy caught caring about something that his friends would later mock him for. "I figured it's easier to watch the stars without rocks poking you in the ass."

"That may be the most romantic thing anyone has ever said to me." She knelt at the edge of the blanket and rested her rear end on the heels of her boots, watching as he set out a handful of small, round plastic disks.

She wasn't sure what they were until he turned one over and flipped the little black tab on the bottom. A flickering orange obelisk appeared above it surface.

Flameless candles.

"Courtesy of Emily. Because having an open flame *is so incredibly dangerous*," he said, affectionately channeling his daughter's lecturing tone as he crawled around the blanket's perimeter to set out the lights.

As he crouched there, Cosima *knew*.

She could love this man.

This man who quoted his daughter's words and borrowed her flameless tea-lights.

This man who opened the lid of a wicker picnic basket with hands that held babies, and fixed motors, and shaped wood.

This man whose smile she could erase by letting seven words fall from her lips.

There's something I need to tell you...

Many somethings, beginning with all the tiny untruths designed to plumb his memory. The coffee. The barbecue. The blues record. The scotch.

Clues.

To see whether a fresh start might truly be possible.

She should have known better.

It never was.

These thoughts left her feeling empty. Hollow. Purged of any hope. Resigned to whatever fate this night brought her.

Remy set out a plastic-wrapped charcuterie board she recognized from the Blackpot's Heads section— named after the term for the first draw of liquor following the distillation process.

Rocks glasses followed.

Then a glass bottle whose blue-and-gold label froze her heart in her chest.

Macallan scotch whiskey, aged 18 years.

"Is this okay?" he asked, clearly concerned by the expression on her face. "I just thought, since that's what we were having when——"

"It's perfect," she said, infusing her features with as much gratitude as she could. "Really."

He opened the bottle and poured them each a finger's worth.

The scent of peat smoke rose from amber liquid as Cosima consulted her glass. If she held it still enough, she could see the night sky reflected in its surface. As if constellations, not barley, had been distilled for her consumption.

Star-crossed.

She remembered how disappointed she had been when her eighth-grade honors drama teacher explained that this was a *bad* thing.

Ill-fated.

Later, after Danny's death, she'd found the hard kernel of truth at the center of her resistance to the term. She'd seen herself in it. The same way she had seen it in Remy when he'd sat down on the barstool next to hers.

Broken people, recognizing shared fault lines.

Tears crowded her throat and a single, warm drop slipped down her cheek.

Remy spotted it immediately, of course.

"Hey," he said, putting down his glass. "What's the matter?"

She shook her head, knowing that that second she opened her mouth, more would come.

Do it. Do it before you lose your nerve.

Drawing in a shaky breath, she turned her torso to face him.

"You know the other night, when we were walking back to my cabin, and you asked me what was wrong?"

"Oh, I remember," he said, a wicked glint in his eye.

"I wasn't entirely honest with you."

Remy was silent for a moment, his smile fading

to something more poignant. "I know," he said, surprising her to her very core.

Her cheeks began to tingle as all the blood drained from her face. "You do?"

He nodded. "The way you looked when you saw Emily's picture for the first time at the restaurant. The same way you looked when we ran into you in the hallway in person."

Her vision blurred.

"And then, there was the dinner," he said.

"The dinner?" she asked.

"The way you were with the twins," he explained. "I don't think anyone would pay me two hundred dollars an hour, but I can make an educated guess as to why someone might have that reaction when around babies or kids."

Cosima set down her glass and hugged her knees.

Now was the moment. She could feel it right there at the base of her throat.

We've met before, Remy.

"I had a miscarriage." Not the words that she had intended to say, but now they were out, and she had to continue. "A couple years after I left home, when I'd turned self-destruction into an art, I wasn't being careful, and got pregnant." She glanced at his face to see how this information had been received before continuing. "I...wasn't in a relationship with the father, but I had this ridiculous idea that I was going to raise her myself."

"It was a girl?" he asked quietly.

"I wasn't quite far enough along to say for sure,

but I think so." Reaching for her drink, she took a fortifying sip. "It had been such a dark time. I felt like maybe this was a light at the end of the tunnel. My wake-up call."

Remy took a long, slow breath. "I know that feeling, alright."

"I had just learned that I'd been accepted into UCLA. I had packed the little I owned into my Mustang and was on my way to Los Angeles when it happened."

Her voice broke, and she felt Remy's warm hand land between her shoulder blades.

"Nona had died only a couple months before, and I was such a mess." A bitter laugh escaped her. "Who am I kidding? I still am."

She dropped her face into the hollow of her arms, her forehead resting on her knees.

Literal navel gazing.

Remy shifted to crouch before her, taking her by the wrists to peel them away from her face.

"You are *not* a mess," he insisted.

"Right," she agreed sarcastically.

"I mean, Jesus. Just look what you've been able to accomplish. And all by pulling yourself up by the bootstraps."

"A broken engagement, a barely furnished loft, and a production company that's going to tank if this series flops?" Cosima said, dabbing her nose with a wadded tissue she found in the pocket of her denim jacket.

"It's not going to flop." He said it with such conviction that for a moment, Cosima was tempted to believe him. "I'll make sure of it."

"How do you plan to do that?" she asked.

"I'll take my shirt off in every episode."

"Remy," she said, shaking her head.

"My pants?" he suggested.

"Wrong channel."

"I'd be willing to clock Samuel," Remy said. "Or back over him with the Varmint? Whichever you think would be better for ratings."

Her laugh sounded more like a honk through a nose swollen by crying. "I thought you said you were against scripted scenes."

"Depends on the storyline." Plopping down onto the blanket next her, Remy wrapped his arms around her and maneuvered her onto his lap.

She came to rest with her behind on the ground and her back against his chest, her legs stretched out between his much longer ones. His chin gently rested atop her head.

Together, they gazed down into the silent valley below.

The steady rhythm of his heart against her felt like a song from an instrument she'd stolen.

"Is it stupid of me to want this?" he asked.

"No," she said. Because she wanted it too. Even if this night was all they would ever have, she needed them to have it.

Cosima turned in his arms and, like hawks, they grappled as they sank earthward.

At last, they came to rest, facing each other side

by side, blanket below and stars above. Bodies knitting themselves together in a configuration that was all their own. Her breasts against the bottom of his rib cage, legs tangled like vines.

Desperate to feel every part of him she'd not yet touched, Cosima ran her hands over the wide, muscled wings of his back.

At first, she thought he must have been leaning up against something with a pattern when she felt the smooth, raised web of skin beneath her fingertips.

Then recognition hit.

Scars.

"Oh, Remy," she breathed. "What happened to you?"

"A truck," he said, pushing himself up on an elbow. Using one hand and moving awkwardly, Remy pulled his T-shirt over his head and rolled onto his side.

The small exclamation of surprise escaped her before she could stop it.

From the top of his left shoulder down to the bottom of his rib cage, his skin was several shades lighter and marked by the telltale repeating diamond-shaped pattern of a healed skin graft.

"According to witnesses, anyway," he continued. "Seems getting clipped by a farm truck and sliding under a semi left me kind of foggy on the details."

"What's the last thing you remember?" she asked.

He was quiet as he sifted through his thoughts. "I was supposed to meet up with some of my riding

buddies, but I got caught in a huge storm just outside of Memphis."

A sick twist gripped Cosima's gut and she reached
for her scotch to wet her suddenly dry mouth.

Her pulse had begun to rush her ears, drowning
out the soundtrack of night birds. "How long ago?"

She already knew.

She knew, but she needed to hear him say it.

Remy rolled over to face her. "About nine years
back."

An accident.

He'd been in a horrific, life-altering accident. She
had no way of knowing whether he had any intention
of returning to her room before he'd been clipped by
the truck and slid under a semi. But she did know
that this was the reason he had no memory of her.
Not because she'd been so inconsequential that she'd
fallen straight out of his mind the second the door
had closed behind him. Not because he had so many
one-night stands that she blurred into the vast quilt
of his conquests.

Because he'd been hurt.

Badly.

She felt the scaffolding of her plans crumbling
beneath her.

Remy Renaud had suffered a tragic childhood and
a heartbreaking adolescence, followed by a string of
misfortunate that would have driven a lesser man
into the bottle or the grave.

And she had leveraged all of it for her own gain.

Twelve

Remy experienced a physical pain in the center of his chest when he saw the expression on Cosima's face.

Stricken.

God, but he was an asshole.

The accident. Her brother. Of course.

He had been so mesmerized by her warm, light, feathery touch that he hadn't even paused to think whether he should share this story. The fact that he could feel her fingers at all was miraculous. Even now, half the time he registered sensations as either pressure or tingling. He felt like the worst kind of starry-eyed fool, imagining her as some sort of princess capable of turning his toadlike bumpy skin into something smooth and normal.

What he had, he'd earned after months of a painfully slow recovery, and in the parade of nurses, doctors, surgeons, and a very persistent ambulance chaser of a lawyer. He never could get past the irony that it had been the settlement he'd received from the trucker's employer that provided the seed money to start 4 Thieves.

Other people liked to say they poured their blood, sweat, and tears into a project. But he actually had.

Law seemed to have forgotten this fact and Remy had chased away.

"I'm so sorry." Cosima's hand moved from the ruin on his back to his chest, pressing firmly against his heart. "I'm so sorry, Remy—"

He stopped her words with his mouth, tasting the tears on her lips as their kiss morphed from tender to tempestuous.

Remy pulled her back onto his lap, facing him, this time. She whimpered when he thumbed down the straps of her sundress, baring her breasts.

He wanted to put his mouth on her more than he wanted air, but the last shreds of his self-control howled at him to slow down. To drink in her elegant shoulders juxtaposed against the valley where the distillery slumbered quietly beneath the blanket of stars.

To burn this into his memory if it took all night.

For once in his life, he had to savor instead of devouring. To take his time, and believe he had time for the taking. To fight the urge to consume as quickly as possible for fear that this one good thing he wanted would inevitably be taken away.

It began with her legs.

He let his hands move up her thighs, the smooth, hard muscles gliding beneath his palm. He felt the power in them, the years it had taken to tone them, the effort it took to maintain. Their role in the purposeful stride that had carried her through life, and for much of it at a pace everyone around her had to scramble to keep up with.

A pace he apparently failed to match now.

Cosima captured his hand and guided it to the soaked lace of her panties. "That's what you do to me, Remy. Now let me feel what I do to you."

She molded her hand to the erection straining against the denim and scooted backward on her knees to grant herself better access to his belt and zipper. "Lose the pants."

He did as ordered.

A smug smile curved her lips as she picked up the accordion fold of several condoms that had fallen from his jeans pocket when he'd worked them over his hips.

"Four?" She lifted an eyebrow at him.

"A lot of hours in one night." Remy's cheeks warmed as he reached for the packet, but she dropped them just out of his reach.

"You won't be needing those just yet."

She sank to her elbows, and seconds later, he felt warm breath against the skin of his stomach followed by the silky sweep of her hair as she freed him from his boxers. Looking at him from beneath her lashes, she planted kisses to the left and right of his twitching cock, and brushed her velvety cheek against its marble-hard shaft.

The blanket bunched where Remy wadded fistfuls in anticipation, not realizing he'd been holding his breath until his chest began to burn. Then her capable hand wrapped around his base and her lips closed over his throbbing head, and he thought he might lose his mind.

That smart mouth. Tasting and teasing him. Sucking and swirling. Sliding up and down his length in concert with her fingers.

Unable to sit still, Remy he leaned forward to gather her dress up to her waist, tracing her thong where it met the downy dip in her lower back, filling his hands with the rounded globes of her ass before venturing lower. He curled his fingers into her silken folds from behind, relishing the slick warmth he discovered there.

Her moan vibrated all the way to his root and he sucked in a breath, arresting her movement with a hand on hers.

"Wait," he groaned, grappling for control.

For once, she complied, waiting until he had released her hand before lifting a foil packet to her mouth. After tearing it with her teeth, she carefully sheathed him, kneeling while he slipped her panties down her thighs.

Her hand rested on his shoulder, and at last, Cosima lowered herself onto him, inch by glorious inch.

Remy lost his ability to speak. Not that any of the words he knew could adequately describe the perfection of being inside her.

Peace such as he had never known kept him still at first. Exchanging exhales and inhales as they adjusted to this new thing between them. Innumerable living creatures had and would do exactly this thing in the spring darkness. Theirs was only one joining in an endless cycle, but somehow the center of the universe at the same time.

Then the need took him and he began to move. They rocked together for what might have been an eternity, slowly kindling the blaze that would incinerate them both.

"We should have done this a hell of a lot sooner," he said, tilting his pelvis to angle himself deeper against her core.

Cosima's eyelids fell closed, the dark fringe of lashes fanning against her cheeks as she let out a sigh. "I agree."

"There's a first time for everything," he chuckled.

There was also a last.

He swatted the thought away, not wanting it to pull him out of the moment.

"Are you suggesting…that's my fault?" she purred.

Leaning forward, she rested her elbows on his shoulders, and for a moment he was so distracted by the proximity of her naked breasts that he failed to notice she had wrested control of the pace, her undulations speeding it ever so slightly.

Endearingly impatient as ever.

He might have been tempted to slow it down again if it didn't feel so damn good.

"Wouldn't dream of it," he said.

"What *do* you dream of?" she asked in the breathless, throaty voice he'd come to crave.

His hands wandered up her rib cage, testing the weight and supple softness of her breasts, running the pads of his thumbs over her hardened nipples.

"Other than this, you mean?"

She laced her fingers at the back of his neck. "Other than this."

The truth was, he didn't know.

He'd been working to make the distillery a reality for so long that it had never occurred to him to stop and think whether it was what he truly wanted.

"Gonna have to get back to you on that." Remy lowered his mouth to her breast, painting her rosy areola with lazy strokes of his tongue before sucking its pearly peak.

"You're trying to distract me." Her fingernails dug into his shoulders.

"Is it working?" Parting her sex with his thumb, he found her swollen clit and coated it with the slippery warmth, teasing her nipple with the edge of his teeth at the same time.

Her fingers threaded through his hair as she gasped. "Like a charm."

He smiled against her skin. "Good."

She was panting now. Short, sharp bursts of breath carrying equally urgent cries of pleasure.

"Please." The plaintive note in her voice nearly pitched him over the cliff then and there. All uncharacteristic softness. Desperate, soul-deep need as she fluttered and contracted around him. Dancing the edge of oblivion.

Cosima tugged at his hair, lifting his mouth from her breast so they were eye-to-eye. And he knew it was because she wanted him to see her face. To read the pleasure he had created there.

He had meant to hold himself back. To let this first time be about her and her alone. But hearing his name erupting from her lips while she tightened around him detonated his own end with startling force.

His hips jerked and he thrust upward on a growl as he lost himself in hot, rhythmic pulses.

She collapsed forward against him, cheek on his shoulder, limbs as heavy as sand. He held her until their breaths began to slow. She lifted her head to look at him and panic leaped into his heart when he saw the silvery sheen glazing her eyes.

"You okay?" he asked, pushing sweat-damp hair away from her face.

"Yeah." Blinking rapidly, she shook her head, sending the curls bouncing back against her cheekbone. "Just wishing we'd met under different circumstances."

A chill crept into Remy's chest. "You're afraid this is going to ruin your show."

Her gaze shifted from his face and she looked downward. "It's not quite that simple."

He was silent for a moment, feeling the words at the back of his throat like lead fishing weights, knowing he shouldn't say them. "What ever is?"

She blinked at him. "I'm just saying that there's a lot at stake here. For both of us."

This information was no revelation. But his heart sank all the same.

Glancing around him at the candles, the basket, the scotch, and the view he felt an old hurt waking in a small, cramped part of his psyche. In elaborate mating dance for a mate who had no intention of setting up shop.

Trying too hard.

"You think I don't know that?" he asked, hastily pulling his boxers back into place. "I'm not stupid, alright? You're in LA, and I'm here, and I have a daughter that will always come first. Believe me, I'm very aware of the factors that make me a less than desirable choice for a woman like you."

Cosima tugged the straps of her dress back up and pushed herself to her knees. "Remy, I'm not saying that at all—"

"What *are* you saying?"

Her gasp wrenched him abruptly out of the quicksand of his memory.

His heart sped when he saw one of her hands fly to her mouth and the other point down at the valley.

Fire.

A small column of flickering orange feeding on the converted barn housing the Blackpot.

Remy let fly a string of curses as he jammed himself back into his jeans, fumbling with the blanket to find his cell phone.

With shaking hands, he punched 911 into the keypad and hit Send only to hear the distinctive beeping of his call failing. No cell reception.

"Come on," he shouted, already jogging toward the motorcycle as he shrugged his shirt over his head.

Cosima scrambled to grab her jacket and sprinted after him. They thundered through the brush and breathlessly mounted his bike after buckling themselves into their helmets.

His motorcycle felt like it was flying. The ground was scarcely present beneath the wide tires as he cornered, accelerating into turns and pushing the engine to its very capacity.

As they completed the homestretch, a glow rose like an artificial sunrise and true metallic panic began to set in.

He should have been there.

It was all Remy could think about as the motorcycle's engine ripped in his ears and vibrated through his body.

If he lived a hundred years, he would never forget the fear etched into faces glazed the color of lava by the roaring blaze. Grant, Mira, and the restaurant staff. Warehouse and distillery workers who lived in the staff quarters on site. Cosima's crew.

With dawning horror, he saw the scene unfolding.

Law, charging like an enraged bull, looking like he'd tear straight through anyone idiotic enough to set foot in his path. Roosevelt with his camera aimed at the towering inferno and Matt with a boom mic held near the staff.

Remy sprinted to head him off, shoving Law hard by the shoulder to set him off course before he could slap the expensive machinery out of the cameraman's hands.

Law stumbled, caught himself, and wheeled on Remy.

"Where *the fuck* were you? I've been calling you for *twenty* minutes. Why didn't you answer?"

The instant rush of defensiveness added to the deadly cocktail of adrenaline and guilt boiling in his gut. "I took my bike out for a ride up the canyon and I didn't answer because I didn't have cell reception."

Law's eyes moved from Remy's face and focused over his shoulder. He didn't have to follow them to know what he saw.

"You were with her, weren't you?" The question came with an arctic chill.

"What business of that is yours?" he growled back. "I'm allowed to have a life outside of the distillery, remember?"

"Not when that life is a direct threat to my livelihood and legacy."

He knew now was not the time to have this conversation. Not while sirens wailed, and firehoses roared, and chaos ruled. Not while Law, sleep-deprived and gripped by the fiercely protective aggression of new fatherhood, could see flames less than half a mile from where his twins slept. In cooler, more logical sections of his brain, Remy knew this.

But he did not live in those regions at present.

"*Your* livelihood," Remy replied, incredulous. "Get the fuck over yourself, Law. Samuel Kane may have sheared off a pretty minor chunk of his multi-billion-dollar inheritance to grow the business, but I gave you every damn dime of my accident settlement to help start it. I helped you build this place from the ground up. And whether you like it or not, Bastien and Augustin did, too. So stow the shit about *your* legacy. Because the fact is, if I hadn't taken the fall for the Robichaud scrapyard job, if we *all* hadn't pulled your ass out of the fire time after time, you'd still be *rehabilitating* your name just like the rest of us."

Law's hands bunched into fists at his sides.

Remy lifted his chin, daring his younger brother to take a swing. To answer a question they'd both been dancing around for months now.

Did 4 Thieves belong to the Renaud brothers?

Or did it belong to Kane Foods International?

For Remy, it was a one-or-the-other proposition.

Bitter thoughts crowded his chest, pushing against his ribs and filling his throat with cement. All his resentment for Samuel Kane's interference. The long hours he'd had to work. His irritation with Law. All of it had obscured one vital fact.

Four Thieves had been their dream.

That dream was burning.

Thirteen

Cosima watched as Remy and Law faced off in glowering opposition, wanting to intervene, knowing her interference would only make things worse.

Small snatches of the screaming match that ensued were audible over the wailing of sirens, rush of water from the fire hoses, and the roar of the blaze itself.

Glancing through the crush of firefighters and huddled staff, Cosima saw Roosevelt motion to Matt, who nonchalantly aimed a small handheld camera they often used for diary-entry-type cuts and aim it at the wrangling Renaud brothers.

She hated herself a little for the conditioned twitch of excitement she felt picturing the teaser for this part of the pilot.

This hadn't been part of their storyboarding, but she'd have to be insane to leave it out.

Just when she was sure they were destined to come to blows, Grant rode to the rescue, placing a hand on each of their chests and urging them to step away from each other.

At last, she could exhale. She flexed her fingers to stretch knuckles aching from death-clutching Remy on the ride back to the distillery.

Shivering from the mix of adrenaline and terror from the bike ride, Cosima didn't even notice Sarah until a silvery foil blanket landed around her shoulders.

They blinked at each other, then clutched in a spontaneous hug. Sarah's lithe, thin form shook just as hard as her own.

"You okay?" Cosima asked, pulling back to examine her assistant.

Black charcoal tears streaked down Sarah's cheeks. "I don't know what happened. We were all just sitting around, throwing axes and shooting the shit, when all of a sudden the smoke alarms went off. We thought it was just a drill. Then we saw smoke, and…"

Her voice thickened at this, her eyes sinking toward her boots.

Cosima fanned out the blanket like a cape and wrapped them both in it. They stood side by side, holding each other and shivering as the flames eventually gave way to plumes of steam.

While none of the staff had been hurt, the entire

kitchen and half of the dining room had been eaten away, along with the beautiful Boxcar Bar.

Watching as Remy and Law spoke first with police, then a fire marshal, had left her feeling brittle and hollow.

When the last emergency vehicle had pulled away, Remy made his way over to them.

"You guys all right to get back to your cabins? I have some things to finish up here."

"I'll walk them back." Grant's booming voice echoed in Cosima's ringing ears. "There was a leak in the sink of Sarah's cabin I was going to look at, anyway," he said.

Glancing at Sarah's face, the correct answer came to Cosima immediately.

She turned toward her protégé and squeezed her in another hug. Then, very quietly asked, "You're sure you're okay?"

Sarah nodded, her cheek brushing past Cosima's.

"Be careful," she said, sotto voce, as she pecked her assistant's cheek.

"You, too," Sarah whispered back.

Cosima ducked from under the blanket and secured it around Sarah's shoulders, squeezing her elbows before she walked away.

Then, she was alone.

A thousand different times during the course of this evening, she'd meant to tell him. She had rehearsed the words in her head at least twice that much.

How could she tell Remy now?

In the wake of such a horrific loss, what was the proper way to inform him that she knew exactly how much this evening had cost him?

He stood in front of the smoldering ruins of the restaurant that had been his passion project. Arms folded across his chest.

With soot staining the creases at the corners of his eyes and etching brackets around his mouth, he looked carved from stone. Permanent in a way she didn't understand and couldn't pretend to.

For the first time in her life, she couldn't think of a single thing to say.

Grass baked by flames crunched under her boots as she came up behind him and wrapped her arms around his waist.

She felt the breath go out of his lungs. His shoulders slumped and he rested his weight against her. A hard knot in his spine met her cheekbone as she pressed her face between his shoulder blades, buttressing him.

Her hands slid up the ridge of his stomach and layered themselves over his heart.

They didn't speak. They didn't have to.

She released his body and took him by the hand instead. "Come on," she said. "Let's get you home."

Once there, they removed their boots on the front porch and she led him to the master bathroom, where she turned on the shower and helped him out of his smoke-stained clothes before stripping off her own.

Even here, his handiwork was evident.

The doors swung smoothly outward on hinges

she knew he had installed himself. The spray she nudged him into fell from an upgraded showerhead he had chosen and screwed in with his own hands.

She lifted a chunk of rustic soap and glided it over the taut muscles of his neck and back, loosening ashes that peppered the common stream winding toward the drain.

When his body was clean, she sat him on the bench and washed his hair, working her fingertips against his scalp. His big body shuddered, releasing tension.

This completed, she quickly washed and rinsed herself, then turned off the shower spray. After swathing herself in one of the clean, fluffy towels hanging from the back of the door, Cosima used the other to dry Remy off.

She caught herself being gentle over the scars long healed as she steered him toward the bedroom. Treating them as if they might still pain him. An external symbol of internal hurt she couldn't help.

Peeling back the bed covers, she guided him into it, and then slid in beside him. Remy melted into her, lying with his head on her chest, his arms winding around her rib cage like great vines.

"Anything you want to tell me about it?" she asked.

"Not tonight," he mumbled sleepily.

As if he, too, understood that the problems would still be there to solve tomorrow.

Just as dawn began to crawl through the blinds, Cosima woke to the feeling of him hard against the small of her back. Her hips arched backward, instinctively seeking his heat.

His sexy, sleepy mumble curled her toes as his hands found her hips. That contact alone was enough to release a rush of moisture at the juncture of her thighs.

Remy nuzzled her neck, his jaw deliciously abrading the spot below her ear as beneath the covers, he discovered how ready she was for him.

Sliding his length against her, the blunt silky head of his cock teased the taut bundle of nerves while his fingers found her nipples. Lightly pinching and rolling as his wicked mouth sampled the sensitive skin of her neck and earlobe.

"Should I make you come like this first, *cher*?"

The tide of memory rolled in, dragging her into its undertow.

Cher.

That's what he'd called her. This man who had made her feel alive for the first time in years.

"I think," she sighed, head already swimming in sensations, "I'm pretty damn close already."

Remy shifted, rolling her beneath him.

"I lied," he said, kneeling between her legs. "I need to taste you first."

I lied.

The words landed in her stomach like a lead weight. She evicted them from her head and forced herself to focus on Remy's face in the silvery light.

He crawled down her body, planting kisses on

her collarbone, her sternum, each of her breasts. Her stomach. Her thighs.

Then his mouth was on her and she was grateful to be relieved of all thought. Feather-light strokes teased her open, lighting up her nerves just so he could intensify this feeling by circling and flicking the aching nub between her folds.

"Remy," she panted, gripping his hair and arching her hips toward the source of the pleasure electrifying her body.

"That's right," he murmured against her. "Say it."

He paired the order with fingers slipped inside her, their tips curling against a spot that made her stomach shudder.

Cosima didn't just say his name, she chanted it like a prayer as she felt the first quakes of the shockwave threatening to turn her inside out. Helpless, she contracted around his fingers as he sucked and tongued every last spasm out of her.

She lay there in the aftermath, utterly slack and dazed.

Remy tasted of the earth and rain when he kissed her.

"Roll over." His command further contracted her already pearly nipples.

Despite feeling mostly boneless, she managed to roll onto her stomach. Cheek in the snowdrift of a pillow that smelled like his clean skin, she breathed him into her lungs. She heard a drawer open and close. The metallic tearing of the foil packet.

Time had taught him to be careful.

His hair-roughened knee slipped between her thighs, guiding them apart.

And then he was there. A hot, silky presence nudging at her most sensitive flesh. One hand planted on the bed by her ribcage and she felt his fingers trailing down her spine.

"You're the most beautiful thing I've ever seen." He murmured this almost as if not saying it to her.

Cosima stifled a snort in the pillow.

"No," he corrected. "That's not what I meant. You're the most beautiful person I've ever known."

Her throat tightened. "Don't say that," she said.

Strong hands tucked under her hips, drawing her pelvis upward. "Why not?"

She hugged the pillow to her chest and pushed up on her forearms. "Because it's not true."

He teased her opening, barely breeching her before pulling back again. "How would you know?"

Cosima gripped handfuls of the pillowcase to keep from wriggling. "I just do."

He advanced again, delving deeper this time. "You know everything, don't you?"

How she wished that was true. Wished that she had even a scrap of that eerie prescience that Nona had always used to tell her what she was feeling before Cosima herself even knew half the time.

More than that, she wished she knew what she could say, what she could do to bring them all out of this unhurt.

"I know I want this." She waited until he pushed forward again to arc her hips back to bury him to the hilt.

Remy sucked in a breath that escaped with a curse Cosima recognized through a common Latin base.

Merde.

He lowered to his elbows, gluing his stomach to her back, his pectoral muscles to her shoulders. His fingers laced with hers as he curled his hips forward in a slow, undulating wave that sank him deeper still. Stretching her. Filling her with a perfection she had experienced only once before, all those years ago.

"God, I love being inside you." His mouth was wet and warm on her shoulder.

Cosima tightened her grip on his fingers. "I love it too, *caro.*"

He stilled.

Shit.

The endearment had been a slip. An orgasm-induced misfire in the primordial part of her brain where memory and language overlapped. A portal between past and present.

He had called her *cher.* She had called him *caro.* Traded endearments from dramatically different upbringings.

"Say that again," he whispered against her ear.

Relief, thick and sweet as warm honey, spilled through her, quickly tinged with sadness.

"I love the way you feel, *caro.*"

Remy rewarded her with another slow, deep thrust.

And another, and another. Speeding his strokes as he set them on a breakneck course with oblivion.

Remy wanted to forget.

It seemed an absurd thing to long for, famously faulty as his memory was.

Now that the horrific details had been burned into his brain, he realized for the first time just how much he'd taken this gift for granted.

The flames glazing Grant's eyes. Emily's half-burned drawing clinging to what remained of the hostess stand. Tough-as-nails Mira, silent tears streaking her face as she lifted the remains of a wooden butcher's block he'd helped her seal.

All there, every time his eyelids closed.

Two hours of this hellish cycle, and he had reached for Cosima again.

Losing himself in her for the third time since last night.

It had been their most frantic by far. Dreaded daylight crawled across the floor an inch at a time, dragging consequences in its wake.

Cosima gripped the headboard, her hair a passion-tangled squall as she rode him hard. Remy used the leverage of his superior strength to roll her beneath him, pinning her hands to the mattress only to have her swing her legs up and clutch his rib cage in the viselike grip of her thighs.

They had given up the ruse that this was anything but an out-and-out battle for control. A mutually agreed-upon contest of wills ending in a long, explosive draw.

Their sweat-slicked limbs tangling in ever-changing configurations aimed at exhausting their bodies, if not their minds.

Relinquishing her wrists, Remy anchored his arms beneath her, cupping her shoulders to anchor himselfl.

Claiming her. Marking her as his, if only until they faded.

Sooner than he would have liked.

She clutched the damp hair at the nape of his neck and brought his mouth to breasts already swollen and mottled with pink from his mouth and unshaven jaw.

Hooking her ankles behind his back, Cosima bucked against him, spurring him toward a final, frantic finish.

If he could just stay inside her longer, maybe he could make it all go away.

If he could keep his face buried in this sweet-smelling crown of Cosima's hair, he could chase the ghost of smoke from his lungs. If he could taste the sweetness of her tongue, he could rid his mouth of ash.

Startled by the gentle warmth of her palm against his cheek, Remy looked down to see Cosima's gold-green eyes aimed up at him, full of a poignant tenderness that was almost worse than the pain.

Tethering him to this moment.

To the gift of her coming undone beneath him,

fusing around him in clenches that lit the fuse of his own explosive climax.

They collapsed together in an exhausted heap.

On the nightstand, several empty water bottles and a graveyard of foil wrappers were evidence of their foolhardy quest to outrun the inevitable. Cosima reached for the one bottle with a few sips left and took a swallow before offering it to Remy.

He held up a hand. "All yours."

She raised an eyebrow at him, still managing to look sophisticated even with her face scrubbed bare of designer cosmetics.

"Don't get all noble on me, Renaud. If you don't get some hydration in you, you're going to pass out before you make it downstairs to drink some of my amazing coffee."

Remy took the bottle and drained the remaining swallows before reaching across her bare breasts to set it among its fallen comrades. "Kind of you to offer, but I'm afraid I just have your standard top-shelf, grocery-store fare on hand."

Dragging a sheet up to cover her chest, Cosima gave him a saucy smile as she swung her legs over the side of the bed. "Shows what you know."

He tried to sit up but was met with a stiff finger to the chest. "Stay."

Too tired to argue, he sank back against the pillows. There he stayed, until the intoxicating aroma of coffee crept from the air-conditioning vent.

Remy stepped into a pair of boxer briefs and athletic shorts, and shuffled down the hallway, mouth open to call downstairs when a sound snapped his mouth shut.

Voices.

One male. Low, rumbling, accusatory.

One female. Loud, earthy, agitated.

Remy ran a hand through his hair and thundered down the stairs to fling open the front door. The sight that met him proved just as shocking as the fire had the night before.

Cosima Lowell, standing there in nothing but his T-shirt, hands on her hips, eyes blazing at an opponent who towered over her by at least a foot and a half.

His brother. Bastien.

It had been over three years since Remy had seen him last and very little had changed, save for a few more silvery hairs sprinkled among the coal-black beard obscuring his upper lip and most of his jaw. His eyes were as serious as ever, pale blue and intense beneath dark eyebrows. A few more creases had gathered at their corners. They deepened as he studied Cosima, arms folded across his flannel shirt.

"Well, hey, brother," Remy said. "Nice of you to drop by. Coffee's brewing if you'd are to come in."

Normally, this sort of sarcasm had earned Remy a bicep punch when they'd been growing up and he found himself almost flinching out of reflex even after all this time.

"Pass." Bastien's voice had grown even deeper and more gravelly, rusty with disuse.

"Then maybe you'd like to tell me what the hell you're doing here?" Remy asked.

"Been wondering the same about her." His brother jerked his woolly chin at the woman standing opposite him.

Remy cleared his throat. "Bastien, this is Cosima Lowell, a television producer. Cosima, this is Bastien, my oldest brother."

Cosima's kiss-swollen mouth twisted into a tight line. "Such a pleasure to meet you," she said, her voice dripping with saccharine sarcasm. "Glad you decided to come around to the porch instead of just staring in the window like a creeper."

Bastien's eyes flicked down to a finger being pointed at his chest like a bayonet.

"I see," he said. "We're pretending like you don't already know who I am."

The rosy flush all but disappeared from Cosima's cheeks.

"What are you talking about, Bastien?" Remy stared at his brother, awash in a brain-blunting blend of confusion, irritation, and, below it all, a hard knot of stubborn gladness at seeing him again.

"I've been monitoring web searches for anything related to the Renaud name for years. When I saw a bunch of hits recently, I tracked them to an IP address in Los Angeles registered to her name," he said, glancing at Remy. "That name suddenly pops up on local surveillance-equipment rentals, and naturally, I get a little curious. When I learn there's been a fire, I get a lot curious."

"*Camera* equipment rentals," Cosima clarified with no small amount of frustration. "For the specific purpose of filming a docuseries about 4 Thieves distillery."

"You mean you actually signed on to do this voluntarily?" Bastien asked incredulously.

A burst of defensive anger chased away a measure of the irritation. "What difference does it make to you? We haven't even heard from you in three years. Not one damn word. Not to me. Not to Law. Not to your niece."

Remy felt a stab of satisfaction when he saw the jab land home, but Bastien's face hardened again just as quickly.

"I left to keep our family safe, and here you are planning to air our dirty laundry for every troglodyte with a TV—"

"Excuse me," Cosima interrupted. "That is not the kind of show I'm making here."

Bastien's voice dropped to a register that had the power to send the average Terrebonne Parish resident running for the hills.

"Then why is it that you've been searching for our mother?"

The bottom fell out of Remy stomach. He looked at Cosima, whose face had gone bone-white.

"Cosima?"

She looked at him, blinking a little too much, talking a little too fast. "Even if it's a topic you don't plan on discussing on film, doing background research is a completely normal part of the pre-production process."

"That's where I'm a little confused," Bastien said, eying her warily. "The first search you did for our mother was nine years ago."

Fourteen

The stone porch went spongy under Cosima's bare feet, and for a moment she wished it would just open up and swallow her whole.

"That can't be right," Remy said. "It couldn't have been nine years ago. Four Thieves hadn't even been founded yet."

As soon as the words were out of his mouth, he turned to look at her, and she knew.

His eyes hardened into flints. His mouth tightened into a line.

"How?"

"Can we please talk about this privately?" Her voice sounded strained and thin.

Remy took a small step closer to his brother. "I

think we've done all the talking in private we're going to do."

"Remy, *please*." It was the last of what she had to offer. The only plea her guilt would allow her to make. She could have—should have—found a way to tell him before now, she knew, but Remy's deliberate show of masculine solidarity with a man he hadn't even spoken to in years woke an old grudge.

"Fine," she said, grateful for the ice water that had invaded her veins. Cooling her head. Numbing the ache in her heart. She yanked opened his front door and stalked inside to gather her things. She needed to get out of here.

Now.

At the moment, she didn't care if she lost her office, her company, her entire world, as long as she didn't have to stand and face their scrutiny.

Remy followed after her, catching up to her on the stairs.

"How?" he asked again.

"Oh, so you *do* want to talk in private?" Breezing into the bedroom, she stripped off his T-shirt and grabbed her discarded dress from the foot of the bed.

Of all the times for her father's voice to come rising up in her. The how-dare-you hauteur overriding the part of her brain that knew she was at least partially in the wrong.

Remy stood in the doorway, arms folded and face grave. He didn't look at her when he spoke. "How did you know enough about our family to look up my mother nine years ago?"

She supposed there was no way around it. Never had been, really.

Sinking down on the edge of the bed they had so thoroughly rumpled, she scrubbed her face with her hands before beginning.

"Nine years ago, we met at a biker bar. We slept together, you left the following morning, and I didn't see you again until your face was in the *Los Angeles Times*."

It felt completely irrational that the trouble should summarize so neatly when it had made such a thorough mess of her life.

Remy planted a hand on the wall to steady himself. "We...*slept* together?"

"Yes," she said, bending to jam her feet into her discarded riding boots.

"And I told you about my family?" he asked.

"Yes," she said again.

He blew out a breath and began to pace. "We slept together nine years ago, I told you all about my family, and you sat there in that office and pretended like we've never met?"

"I didn't *pretend* anything. I sat there in that office waiting for you to remember and completely ready to talk about it. When you didn't, I just assumed it hadn't been particularly memorable for you, so it didn't need to be particularly memorable for me. Until last night I had no idea you'd been in an accident."

He stood there in the doorway, staring at her like she'd just stepped off a UFO.

"I just don't understand how you could sit there and act like you hadn't—that we hadn't—"

"You have one-night stands all the time Remy. You told me so yourself. Exactly how much weight and space do you give those women in your future decision making?"

"That's not the same situation and you know it." He pushed himself off the wall and stabbed a finger at her.

Cosima forced herself to stop and take a breath before continuing.

"I offered you the same kind of contract I would offer anyone I was planning on engaging for a series. During the discovery process, I would find out as much as I can about them and decide what my angle would be. Exactly the way we did when we were storyboarding. If you and I had never met before, I would have framed your back story exactly the same."

The summary sounded far more simplistic and dismissive than she had wanted it to. But when backed into a corner, the lines she drew were sharper and always farther from the center than she would have liked.

"It didn't matter," he said quietly.

"What's that?" she asked.

For the first time since he'd come downstairs and found her face-to-face with his estranged brother, Remy looked her straight in the eye.

"Before you knew about the accident, when you

thought that I'd just slept with so many people that I didn't remember you. It didn't matter."

Cosima was silent.

"I was an asshole, right?" he accused. "I slept with you and left before you woke up and so you were perfectly justified in doing whatever you needed to get your hit show. Better that than Ferro Studios going belly up?"

Resisting the urge to bite back with something twice as scorching proved a significant difficulty.

"I genuinely thought this could be a good thing for both of us. That may be with my help you could get out from under Samuel Kane's thumb. That you would have more control over your life and the operation."

He took a step closer. She could tell from his stiff posture that it wasn't to increase the intimacy of the moment.

"But you still didn't tell me, even though you were willing to sleep with me. And what's the harm? You get your show. I get a paycheck. Does that sound about right?"

She shot up from the bed. "Remy, I *wanted* to tell you. I was *going* to tell you."

"I'm supposed to believe that right? Gullible, simple guy like me. Perfect mark, basically." His mouth twisted into an ugly smile. "That's why you were so upset last night when I showed you my scar. Here I was feeling bad for bringing it up because it probably reminded you of your brother. When really, it just made it so you couldn't feel okay about taking advantage of our family.

"Now that we're discussing it, exactly how far do we need to walk this back?" He closed the small space separating them, his eyes as empty as a shark's. "Your brother's death. Is that just part of your backstory? Something you thought might increase your chances?"

Furious tears blurred her vision. "Is that Zap talking, Remy?"

He paled.

"You told me all about him, you know. How he was a misogynist who bullied your mother. How he—"

"Stop," he barked.

"Told you never to believe a limping dog or the tears of a woman." She swiped one from her cheek and held her shining finger out for him to see. "See how good I am at manipulation?"

He took a step backward and she ducked around him, flying down the stairs and out the front door, where she found a bonus Renaud on the porch. Law and Bastien standing there like towering bookends.

She stalked past them without a word.

The acreage looked too much like heaven for what had unfolded in the past twenty-four hours. Rolling hills muted by a coat of morning dew. Tender leaves barely committing themselves to life.

"Cosima."

The urgent sound of her name on air still clinging to last night's smoke brought her up short.

Remy stood on the opposite side of the porch as his brothers, one hand gripping the railing, the other holding out a fluttering white paper singed black at the edges.

Her feet felt rooted to the spot.

Just walk away.

But she didn't.

Where Remy Renaud was concerned, this had always been her problem.

Crown of her head high, chin raised, she marched back to the porch and snatched the paper from him.

And immediately wished she hadn't.

It was a drawing.

Showing a sophistication that a casual observer might mistake as ignorance of proportion. The gamine sprite of a girl standing next to a woman only half a head taller. Both their hair a teddy-bear-brown. One bound into braids. The other a riot of curls. Both figures aproned and standing behind a counter.

Like the hosts of a cooking show.

At the bottom, leggy cursive letters already beginning to show a distinctive style spelled out two lines followed by an exclamation point whose dot had been replaced by a hasty little heart.

Thank you, Cosima,
Love Emily!

Damn him.

She couldn't bear to ball it up and pitch it back in Remy's face, so she flung words instead.

"I imagined a girl who would draw things like this for me once." She placed the paper back on the railing and drilled the full force of her teary gaze into him. "It felt like a miracle. Like despite everything that had happened, everything I'd done, I could bring this perfect life into the world. I always wondered if your mother felt the same. Wondered why she chose what she chose." She swiped the wet tracks from her cheeks with a knuckle and looked from Remy to his brothers. "All those years, you hated them for hating her."

She pronounced the sentence just like he had that night when telling her about his brothers. He had made those words seem like a gift. In fact, they'd been a millstone. A piece of his truth she had carried for years.

"Don't you think it's time they knew?" she asked.

Remy flinched, flanked on either side by the men whose reputations had loomed large enough to keep him in the dark.

This time, she didn't look back.

Lies hide behind pretty eyes. You remember that, Remy.

Zap's mocking voice paraded through his head, dragging a train of nasty words in its wake.

Dupe. Sucker. Fool.

Of all the details for his colander of a brain to hold on to with perfect clarity, it had to be the one thing he swore he'd take to his grave. The thing he'd never tell another living soul.

But he had.

He'd told Cosima Lowell.

Don't you think it's time they knew?

Remy stared long after she disappeared around the side of the barn, this phrase looping through his head like a melody. Maddeningly familiar but unplaceable.

Impossible to think that she'd held his secret in her head from the second he had set foot in her office.

He thought back to their first meeting. The way his bullshit detector had fired four alarms when she told him the story about the article in the *Los Angeles Times*.

He'd been right after all. She *had* been hiding something.

Small comfort against the flashes of past and present trying to assemble themselves like puzzle pieces in his head.

A different porch.

A different time.

Another woman departing his life, leaving him with a heart full of lead and a head full of questions.

Déjà vu.

Already seen. Already lived. Just like the moment he found himself in now.

How many times had he pictured it? Standing here with his brothers. Only, in those scenarios, it had been all four of the thieves present when he finally let the words roll off his tongue.

"This a kitchen discussion?" Law asked.

"Yep," Remy answered.

"My place?"

"Yep."

This was all the discussion required.

Bastien trailed them down the front steps and out to Law's brand-new—and much more spacious—ATV parked at the bottom of the drive.

Law took the back road from Remy's section of the property to his own, avoiding the scorched wreckage down the hill. The journey was short and silent, and then they were back in the kitchen, where Law had all but begged him to go to Los Angeles and at least *talk* to Cosima Lowell.

On a gut level, he had known it was a terrible idea.

But he had flicked the voice of self-preservation Jiminy Cricketing from his shoulder, stomped it flat beneath his work boot, and agreed.

The reason he'd ignored his own better instincts goaded and gutted him in this sunny kitchen.

Because Marlowe had asked them to, and Remy knew what it was like to sit beside a woman with your child in her belly and want to bring her the world and build her a cabinet to keep it in.

Only, his brother succeeded where Remy had failed.

As usual.

"I'm going to check on Marlowe and the twins," Law said, toeing out of his boots in the mudroom. "Coffee's on the counter."

Bastien glanced around after his departure and located the coffee maker, quickly loading a pod and starting the cycle with no apparent consternation whatsoever.

"Don't tell me you have one of those, too," Remy scoffed, leaning back against the counter.

"Hell no." When the machine had finished its hissing, his brother carried the mug to the table and pushed it toward Remy. "I imported a *Marzocco Linea* from Italy," he said, effectively ending the short-lived feelings of solidarity.

Figured.

He thought of the French press of coffee sitting on his counter. This simple gesture of kindness growing cold.

Only one set of footfalls came down the back stairs.

Until that moment, Remy hadn't realized he'd been hoping Marlowe would join them. That he'd have the benefit of her cool, level-headed counsel.

Though he doubted even she could untangle the knot of dread tightening in his chest.

Law appeared in the doorway, the thunderheads in his eyes having lightened to a drizzle after seeing his wife and sons. He picked up the mug on the counter and put it in the microwave before setting it on the table along with the baby monitor he unclipped from his belt.

The sound of their chairs scraping back was the gavel calling the court to order.

"Let me see if I'm all caught up here." Law pinched the bridge of his nose, cupping his elbow with his opposite hand. "You and Cosima…" He trailed off.

"Yeah," Remy said.

"But nine years ago you also…" Law held out a palm as if to receive a word.

"Yeah," Remy repeated.

"But you didn't remember because…"

"What the hell is this?" Bastien growled. "Amnesiac ad-libs?"

"The accident," Remy said, ignoring his eldest brother. "It was just the one night."

"Once is all it takes," Bastien pointed out. One of Zap's favorite decrees, often repeated.

That both he and Law had lived long enough to inadvertently prove their father right was perhaps the most painful irony of all.

"That's not what we came here to talk about," Remy said.

Where to begin?

The same place they all had. Their mother.

"You remember how I used climb up on the roof when I had trouble sleeping?" he asked.

"The wolf dreams," Bastien said, surprising him.

"Right." Wrapping his hands around the mug his brother had pushed at him, Remy sat back in his chair. "I was up on the roof the night mom left."

Silence thick as concrete poured into the room. Even the birds, lunatic with spring mating songs, fell quiet.

A deep trench appeared between Law's eyebrows. "You saw her leave?"

Remy had been expecting this.

As the youngest, Law had taken her departure the hardest. The only fistfight the two of them had ever had had been as a direct result.

"It was the week before Thanksgiving," he continued. "Zap was doing overnights at the refinery, and when I saw her hauling a suitcase out of the house, I climbed down to help."

Glancing up from his coffee cup, he found his brothers wearing twin expressions of resignation.

They'd long ago hardened themselves against her absence.

They'd had to.

Remy didn't enjoy that luxury.

He could still see the expression of fear on her face when he'd tapped her shoulder.

"She told me that she was leaving, but that as soon as she found a job somewhere and made some money, she'd find a way to come back for us."

Human lie detector that his father had made him, that younger version of Remy had looked his mother in the eye and known she was telling the truth.

Or believed that she was at the time.

Remy had offered to go with her. He could work, too, he had insisted. He was good at fixing things.

She had hugged him then. One of her tears fell on his shoulder. He could still remember that. How he could feel the cool night breeze on the small damp spot as he watched her taillights grow smaller and smaller.

"Looks like she forgot." Bastien's voice was flat as he picked at a gouge in the table.

Once upon a time, he would have argued that point. *Had* argued that point until right after he'd been released from prison, when he'd been assigned a mental health liaison to make sure he was adjusting to life on the outside. At the center of the wild centrifuge of his pleasure-seeking, he'd found a mother-shaped oubliette of bottomless rage.

He'd gone looking for her in the big cities she used to tell him about. Charlotte. Savannah.

Turned out, he didn't need to go far.

"She was killed in a car accident outside Shreveport less than a week after she left," Remy said. "Zap knew about it. He admitted as much right before he punched his ticket."

Amelia Evelyn Renaud.

He'd always felt like a coward for choosing a name for his daughter that combined his mother's first and middle names instead of directly and obviously paying homage. A secret tribute. An apologetic afterthought.

Black coffee splashed onto the table as Law set down his mug hard. "She was dead, and all that time, Zap didn't tell us?"

Bastien, who had displayed no reaction to this point, lifted his gaze from the glossy wood. "It was easier for him to make us resent her for leaving if we didn't know she couldn't come back."

Law shoved back in his chair. "But *you've* known this for the past eight years," he said, pointing at Remy. "How could you not say anything to me about it?"

It was Bastien who answered for him. Quietly, and with a pain that made Remy's throat ache.

"Neither of us went looking, Law."

Law shook his head, not satisfied with this explanation. "But Cosima knew?"

It appeared his brothers had been comparing notes while he was verbally duking it out with the woman in question.

"It would appear so."

The baby monitor squawked and Law lunged for it, grateful for a task that would take him out of this room. "Coming," he said after pressing the button.

"Actually…" said a slightly furred, mechanized version of Marlowe's voice. "Can you send Remy up?"

His brother narrowed his eyes at the small, gray speaker. "Remy?" he repeated.

"Remy," Marlowe confirmed.

A fine film of sweat broke out on the back of his neck.

Like a kid summoned to the principal's office, he rose from his chair, crossed through the living room, and climbed the stairs, each one seeming taller than the last.

He cleared his throat to announce himself before tapping on the doorframe, ever on guard against interrupting her while she was nursing.

"Come in," she called.

Remy nudged open the door and found Marlowe seated in the gliding recliner, a small, round bundle strapped to her chest and a lap desk propped on the chair arms.

She glanced at him over the screen and pushed a pair of reading glasses onto her head.

"Please," she said, indicating the cushioned window seat opposite her.

Because he made a point of never disagreeing with women wearing infants, he obliged.

"Technically I wasn't eavesdropping," she explained, keeping her voice quiet and even. "Law always forgets to put it the monitor in one-way mode."

Not knowing exactly what she'd heard, Remy thought it prudent to let her lead the discussion.

"You remember when you ambushed me on that porch down there?" she asked, glancing out the window over his shoulder.

Shit.

The film of perspiration stuck his shirt to his shoulder blades.

"Vaguely," he admitted.

"Then I'm hoping you'll also remember us walking out to the horse corral and you telling me that you were going to ask me an honest question, and you wanted an honest answer."

"I recall something of that nature being said." A single bead of sweat crawled down his ribs.

"Well, it's officially your turn to do the answering."

He swallowed a throatful of sand. "I'm listening."

She reached out and flipped the laptop screen closed before rocking the recliner into its forward-most position. Her glacier-blue eyes fixed on his, pinning him to the spot.

"Did Cosima tell you about the night her brother died?"

Remy's mouth opened. Closed. Opened again. This was not at all the line of questioning he had expected as he'd taken his death-row walk up the stairs. "I'm sorry?"

"Did Cosima tell you about the night her brother died?" she repeated.

"I'm not seeing how this relevant to the discussion we were having downstairs," he said.

"Just answer the question, Renaud."

He sagged against the wall as a wave of exhaustion swept over him. "Just that he was killed in a car accident."

"He was on his way to pick her up from a party."

A swarm of bees had taken up residence in his skull, drowning out all logic with their numbing drone. "What?"

Marlowe nodded. "Her mother didn't leave her room for weeks afterward. Her father wouldn't even look at her. I think that's why she really ran away. They made her believe it was her fault."

Remy's throat felt hot and dry. "Why are you telling me this?"

The bundle at her chest cooed and Marlowe smiled down at it.

"Maybe the reason she didn't bring up what had happened between the two of you when you didn't seem to remember is because she thought you, of all people, could look beyond a past, to see a future."

In the wake of those words, several pieces of information assembled themselves into an order that made his pulse thunder in his ears. Cosima's miscarriage. The girl she'd dreamed of. Her reaction to Emily. Their one-night stand.

Remy pushed himself up from his seat, unable to stay still for a second longer.

He had to know.

He found Law and Bastien at the table, just where he'd left them, and only half heard the question called after him on his way out the door.

"—think you're doing?"

Flinging himself into Law's ATV, he was forced to admit that it *might* in fact be just the tiniest bit faster than the Varmint. That it didn't belch out black smoke that smelled like burning tar was an added bonus.

His heart dropped into his guts as he rounded the side of the barn and saw the gravel parking area in front of the cabins.

Their van was gone.

Only in that moment were Remy's true feelings on the subject of Cosima Lowell made clear to him.

He missed her.

"Would you just call her?" Law aimed the slim black remote at the wide-screen television to pause the show that he and Marlowe had been watching and Remy had been mostly ignoring.

They'd taken pity on him.

With Emily still at camp and the Blackpot out of commission for the next month, Marlowe had insisted he spend his evenings with them.

Which, unfortunately, looked mostly like his third-wheeling a dinner eaten in shifts according to the twins' current demands, followed by hours of his watching them adore each other on the large leather sofa.

Even monolithic Bastien would have been a welcome addition. But, ever the agent of chaos, he had disappeared back to the wilds of Maine and his off-the-grid shipping container shortly after frag-bombing Remy with unsolicited information. His promises to return once they'd received the permits from the city to begin rebuilding the restaurant were met with a stiff—but affectionate—middle finger from Remy.

"Law's right," Marlowe added, shifting the bowl of kettle corn to the cushion beside her. "It's been four days. She's got to talk to you sometime, right? I mean, they need to come back to continue with filming."

Remy dragged himself off the couch in favor of raiding the liquor cabinet. "She's sending a sub agent."

"What?" Marlowe asked, her voice laced with concern. "How do you know that?"

His shoulders jerked upward in a shrug. "Basically, her email stated that with the many project bids she'd been receiving, she would be far too busy to be onsite supervising the filming of my big, stupid face."

"She used those exact words?" Law took a healthy pull on his bottle of beer.

"Hers were much less complimentary," Remy said, bypassing the bottle of scotch and opting for cognac instead.

Law whistled under his breath, earning him Marlowe's elbow when she thought Remy couldn't see.

"Emily gets back tomorrow, right?" she asked brightly. A clear bid to change the subject.

"Saturday," Remy corrected, tipping amber liquid into a rocks glass.

"That reminds me," she said. "I saw that 4 Thieves has been selected as one of the 'top tastes of ten states' by *Travel* magazine."

"I'm sure Samuel will be excited to hear that," Remy said sourly.

"That's it—" Law set his beer aside and scooted to the edge of the couch. "Either you lighten up or I'm throwing your ass out of here."

"Law," Marlowe scolded. "It's been a rough week for him."

Her attempt to sound concerned was seriously compromised by the last few words being eaten up by a yawn.

"Let me help you upstairs," Law offered.

"I can see the stairs *and* climb them now, remember?" She patted her shrinking midsection.

"It's let me help you or be carried," he said, covering her hand with his. "Those are your options, woman."

Witnessing this affectionate exchange produced a familiar knife twist of envy in Remy's guts.

Law steered her toward the stairs, casting a look over his shoulder to let Remy know that he was expected to hang back.

Hearing the boards squeak overhead, he tracked their progress down the hall and into the bedroom, where the faint murmurs of their conversation sank through the ceiling. In the meantime, Remy rinsed his glass and placed it in the dishwasher, pausing to look down at his hands as he dried them on the dishtowel.

What a story they told.

Wind-chapped and weathered, often etched with some kind of grit or engine oil.

Empty.

Just like he felt.

Every time he dragged the swamp of his memory for any detail about his one-night stand with Cosima. Every time he thought about her waking up alone the following morning. Every time he imagined himself immobile in a hospital bed while she carried, then lost, a life he'd irresponsibly helped create.

Having witnessed the early months of a pregnancy firsthand, the thought of Cosima enduring them alone and scared filled him with a crushing sense of regret.

Hearing heavy footsteps on the stairs, he steeled himself, drawing in a deep breath as he shuffled to the fridge. If he was going to be verbally backed into a corner, he could at least do it with a cold beer in his hand. His brother's silhouette filled the doorway in the reflection of the kitchen window, superimposed on early spring dark.

So this was to be a another kitchen talk.

Retrieving a second beer, Remy placed it in front of his brother, as required by the rules of engagement. How many problems had they solved this way? Hundreds? Thousands, maybe.

"It's partly my fault you've been miserable lately, brother."

Remy's ears pricked. *Brother* was a term of honor reserved for only the most sincere of requests.

"And I know you're sick of hearing Samuel's name, but there's an idea he wanted me to run by you and I think it's worth your time." Law lifted his beer and set it back down on a coaster, dealing one out to Remy as well.

Remy sipped his beer, keeping his mouth occupied as was dancing right on the edge of saying something dangerous.

Law twirled the neck of his beer bottle, spinning the coaster with it. "Samuel has offered to buy you out."

Remy was silent for a moment. He couldn't pretend to be entirely surprised by this news. "And what do you want?"

Leaning forward in his chair, Law waited until he had Remy's attention. "For my brother to be happy again."

Well, shit.

He really hated it when genuine emotion got in the way of a good mad.

Sighing, he picked at the damp label on the brown bottle's condensation-misted surface. "Brother," Remy sighed. "I don't have the first clue how to get there anymore."

Law met his weary smile with one far more mischievous. "I do."

Fifteen

"You have to answer him sometime, you know." Sarah's manicured nail tapped the screen of Cosima's phone before she could swipe it into the tiny, beaded clutch next to her on the seat of the limousine.

"Says who?" Lifting the glass of champagne to her lips, Cosima took a healthy swallow and tried not to cough. It had been a minute since she'd had the good stuff.

Not that it hadn't been offered.

By network executives.

By bankers.

By her parents.

All of whom had come crawling out of the woodwork since the first round of trailers for *Bad Boys of Booze* went live a month ago.

Tonight was the red-carpet event for season one, filming well underway for a second season with the help of the production company she had engaged to keep her as far away from Remy Renaud as possible.

Because…

Well, *because*.

Keeping a clear head was essential now that opportunities were flooding her inbox. Already, she'd been contacted about a potential series following a celebrity who discovered recent familial roots in Tuscany. Another about the oldest bordello in Provence. And another still about a woman in London who ran a bridal boutique specifically for brides over sixty-five.

And Cosima couldn't make herself be interested in any of them.

Instead, she'd spent and embarrassing number of hours re-reading the multitude of text messages and emails Remy had sent. First, the apologies. Then, the questions about the night they'd spent together. Whether he'd been the cause of her accidental pregnancy.

So why hadn't she answered any of his calls when he was practically begging to help carry the secret that had sat so heavily on her soul?

For the same reason she hadn't answered when she saw her father's number on the screen of her cell phone for the first time in almost ten years.

She wasn't sure her heart could handle it.

"Holy shit." Sarah's face was damn near glued to the window. "Do you see that crowd?"

She had.

First glimpsed it earlier while they sat in side-by-side pedicure chairs while *Access Hollywood* aired on the salon's flat-screen TVs.

"And this just in from an anonymous source," a perky blonde announced in conspiratorial tones. "Reality-television star and first-class hunk Remy Renaud was recently spotted in Los Angeles for the premier of *Bad Boys of Booze*, and with a very special lady."

Cosima's nail technician had yelped when she'd accidentally dropped the wineglass into the foot-spa, splashing them both with the pinkish liquid as Remy's face had appeared on screen.

Nausea had gripped her stomach until the angle pulled back and the "special lady" became visible.

Emily, freckle-cheeked and beaming, an iconic cap bearing two round mouse ears perched atop her head as her father shepherded her toward an equally iconic teacup ride.

The scene buried a hatchet in her heart before the story flashed to the venue for tonight's red-carpet premiere, already beginning to glitter with paparazzi staking out their territory.

And why wouldn't they?

Bad Boys of Booze had made Remy a star.

Or rather, YouTube had.

Someone—and she felt reasonably certain she knew exactly who this someone might be—had leaked advance clips from the third episode in the series where Remy had been "caught" skinny-dipping at the pond on the property by an ATV containing none other than Samuel Kane and a handful of investors.

The comments had been enough to make Cosima spit nails.

Should I call him father, or daddy?

They need to change the distillery name from 4 Thieves to 1 DILF alert!

Cosima drank the rest of her champagne as flash-bulbs began to strobe the limousine's tinted windows.

"You ready for this?" Sarah asked as the car began to slow.

"Of course," she lied, nodding eagerly.

Her assistant scooted across the leather seat, popped open Cosima's clutch, and tucked in a small fold of extra tissues. "Well, you look hot at least."

Damn right she did.

She'd spent a goodly chunk of season two's advance on a Jezebel-red classic couture gown that worshipped her every curve and created a few new ones. With a deeply décolleté halter neckline in front, brazenly baring from behind and a generous slit revealing her tanned leg almost to the hip, she was ready for Remy Renaud from any angle.

Only, he didn't show.

Not at the celebratory cocktail reception, not at the dinner, and not even for the red-carpet march itself.

Where was he?

By the time everyone had made their way into the

theater for the preview and the velvet curtain had risen, Cosima had chewed off two coats of candy-apple-red lipstick.

The audience sat in rapt fascination during the pilot's concluding scene, their eyes glazed molten by the flames, immersed in chaos that took Cosima's breath away even though she'd been there.

Stunned silence gave way to thunderous applause when the lights came back up.

One by one, bodies began to rise all around her in a standing ovation.

Sarah clasped Cosima's hand and squeezed so hard she thought her knuckles might pop.

There was a smattering of confused laughter when the house lights dimmed and Remy's torso filled the screen just before his voice filled the theater.

"Well, damn. I think this thing is working after all."

As he backed away, the distillery's barrel room became visible behind him, complete with the single stool they'd set up for the solo off-the-cuff interviews.

"What the hell?" Cosima wondered aloud. This hadn't been part of the final cut of the first episode.

"I hope you don't mind if I keep you for just a second longer." He grinned into the camera. "I never like to stand between a person and their after-party."

Uproarious laughter, hoots, and catcalls filled the hall.

Cosima turned to Sarah and caught her a split

second before she could arrange her face into an appropriate expression of shock.

"What's going on?" she asked in a harsh whisper, only to be met with an infuriatingly unconvincing facsimile of innocence.

"Come to think of it, there's really only one person I need to talk to, and I'm pretty sure she knows who she is, so the rest of y'all can leave if you have a mind to."

He was playing up the low country twang in his voice just as he had during the episode, turning the crowd to putty in his hands.

"No?" He cocked his dark head, a smirk twisting lips she could remember all too easily. "Ain't you a nosy bunch. All right then, Miss Cosima Lowell—" the hooting reached fever pitch at the mention of her name "—I guess they're all just going to have to hear what I've got to say."

Her cheeks stung as heat flooded her face. Cosima was positive that, if she looked in a mirror, she'd be hard-pressed to tell where her dress ended, and she began.

"I've been a lot of things in my thirty-five years."

Miraculously, the audience picked up the audio from the show's trailer, reciting the list right along with him. "A brother, a thief, a convict, an ex-con, a biker, an off-shore oil worker, a single father, co-owner of distillery, and most recently a millionaire."

More applause.

"In addition to all that, I'm also sorry. Which you'd know, if you'd answer your damn phone."

Another swell of laughter.

"But it's not like you're perfect, either," he added, to the chorus of an anticipatory *oooohh*.

"You're stubborn, impatient, and possibly the most terrifying driver I've ever met in my life." He paused, and his expression shifted from mock seriousness to his cat-that-ate-the-canary grin. "But you're also the most passionate, loyal, brilliant, brave, and beautiful woman I've ever known."

The entire auditorium combined in a collective gasp as everyone realized the sound was no longer coming from the speakers.

It was coming from the stage.

There stood Remy in his trademark white tank-top and jeans, beautiful biceps on display and dark hair gleaming beneath the stage lights. He looked right at her and Cosima knew at once he'd been there all along, watching her from some out-of-the-way pocket usually only reserved for the crew.

"I, on the other hand, am a suspicious, accusatory, taciturn asshole. But it just so happens that I'm also crazy about you."

The audience erupted once again, and that uncontrollable roar turned into white noise, blurring out everyone and everything, save for the two of them.

Cosima became aware she was standing, then walking, then sprinting to him, her four-inch heels discarded somewhere along the way.

Remy tossed his microphone at one of the stage-hands before leaping off the edge and into the aisle.

His arms flung wide just in time for her to leap into them as the crowd collectively lost its mind.

The momentum turned into a spin, her dress flying out behind in a perfect arc that would make the front page of half the entertainment sections across the country.

She let herself dissolve into him for the perfect happily-ever-after movie kiss.

As the soles of her feet again touched the ground, Remy leaned down and whispered in her ear. "You think that will get us to season three?"

He glanced to the side of the aisle, where one of the main cameras dedicated to filming the premiere was aimed squarely at them.

And that's when she understood.

The ridiculously scripted episodes that had created the manic fervor. The on-stage stunt. His in-person appearance.

He hadn't done any of it to get her attention. He'd done it to ensure the continuity of the project that had become Ferro Studios's bread and butter.

Cosima looked up at him, feeling like her heart might punch its way out of her chest at any moment. "I'm still pissed at you, you know."

"Oh, baby," he said, his hand gripping her hip through her gown. "I'm counting on it."

Remy laced his fingers through hers as they walked up the aisle, heads bent toward one another to talk above the din.

"Just so happens I have a Harley-Davidson Knucklehead parked outside. How do you feel about riding off into the sunset?" His gaze shifted from her eyes to his lips. "Or at least until we're out of frame and can go somewhere to talk."

Cosima glanced down at her complicated couture gown with its yards of crimson taffeta. "This dress isn't exactly motorcycle-friendly."

Remy only smiled and leaned close to her ear. "But it's sure camera friendly."

Like a pair of newlyweds, they ran up the aisle and out of the venue to where his motorcycle was parked conspicuously at the curb. He hopped on and turned the engine over, waiting until she gathered her dress and straddled the bike behind him. The valet attendant brought them their helmets.

"Do you have any idea how much this hairstyle cost me?" she asked, carefully snugging the helmet over her updo.

"No, but I know how much I'm gonna enjoy messing it up."

"That's pretty presumptive of you," she said, an atom bomb of heat already detonating in her middle.

"Is it?" he asked.

"Shut up and drive, Renaud."

He did. To the Los Angeles Mandarin, where they rode in a gilded elevator up to his suite.

She couldn't help but marvel at the contrast between this room, with its decadent fabrics and beautiful furniture, and the sad little motel she'd called home on their first night together so long ago.

What had changed between the last time she had seen him and now, she wasn't sure. But Remy looked…comfortable. With the luxurious surroundings. With himself. With life.

She perched at the end of the bed, her stomach floating and her head dizzy. Remy dragged a chair opposite her and seated himself in it.

"I let Samuel buy me out," he announced.

Cosima felt like she'd been hit with a bucket of ice water. "What?"

"Don't worry," he said. "I'm going to stay on at this distillery. At least until they finish season three. But it's high time I started figuring out what I want to do. What I want my legacy to be. What I want my *life* to be." He looked up from his hands, and his eyes lit with the fire from within. "All I know is, I want you in it."

She searched his face, eyes already beginning to well.

"That morning, after the fire," he continued, "all I could think about is what I'd lost. Everything I've ever tried to build blowing up in my face. Sometimes literally," he added with a sheepish smile. "I was looking for a reason not to trust what I knew was a good thing. Because good things always go away. It was easier to lose you if I convinced myself I'd never really had you in the first place."

"I know," Cosima said after a beat.

"You do?" An endearingly boyish expression lifted his features.

She took a deep breath, knowing she had to say what came next if there was any way forward for them. "It's the same reason I didn't try to find you when I learned I was pregnant after our night together in Memphis."

She watched the realization solidify in his eyes, confirming his suspicion.

Remy stood, stalking over to the window.

Cosima rose as well, but let him keep his distance.

"You brought me back to life that night, Remy."

His broad back expanded on a breath.

"I'd spent years just trying to numb or outrun the pain of losing my brother. My Nona. My parents. You listened to me. You made me feel…safe," she said, her throat tightening over the word. "For the first time in so long. I'd never experience that kind of connection with anyone. When you were gone the next morning, I convinced myself that it had all been in my head. And then I found you again, and everything came flooding back, but you didn't remember. I thought that maybe we *could* start from scratch. That the past didn't matter. That maybe this show was a way for some kind of good to come from all of it."

Her passionate plea seemed to hang on the air between them for an eternity.

"If I could live my life all over again," he said, finally turning around to face her, "I would stay. I would stay right there and hold you until you woke up, then put you on the back of my bike and never let you out of my sight."

Cosima hugged her arms around her torso, feeling an emotion too large for her body to hold. "But then you wouldn't have had Emily."

His eyes misted and his voice was gravelly when

he spoke. "I don't know how well fate worked in her favor on that score."

"Are you kidding me?" Cosima asked. "Do you know how lucky she is that instead of allowing all the pain and trauma of your upbringing to continue, you dedicated your life to making sure she never had to suffer like you did?"

She took a step toward him when he didn't answer. "When I look at Emily, I see a girl who she *knows* she's loved. Unconditionally. Not just by you, or Law, but by a whole family that you've built from people who society had thrown away. *That* is your legacy, Remy. And I'm already part of it."

She saw his jaw flex as he swallowed. When he looked at her, it was with a longing so poignant that she felt it to her very bones.

"Would you just get your stubborn ass over here and let me hold you?"

She did, letting herself melt against a man more solid and real and alive than anyone she'd ever known.

"Speaking of Emily," Cosima said, looking up at him. "Where is she?"

"In the presidential suite, helping Law and Marlowe with the twins," he said. "Now that she's discovered what a jetted tub does to bubble bath, she may up and turn amphibious."

Cosima's heart gave a painful squeeze. "In that case, I don't suppose I could interest the two of you in a trip to SeaWorld? I hear it's where all the amphibious cool kids hang out."

Remy gazed down at her, and a million questions boiled away.

"There's nothing I'd love more," he said, his voice hoarse as he wrapped even tighter.

"*Nothing*?" She let a suggestive hint dance through the word.

He drew back from her, eyes hooded with desire. "Aside from seeing what you've got beneath this revenge dress."

She batted her lashes in exaggerated innocence. "Revenge?"

"Mmhmm," he said. "But if you really wanted to make me suffer, you should have worn the shoes."

"The ones I left sitting somewhere in the aisle of the Village Theatre?"

Remy pulled her into him once more, lowering his mouth until his lips barely grazed hers. "The ones even another truck couldn't erase from my memory."

With his kiss, Cosima came to the end of a long, lonely journey, finding in Remy Renaud the only thing she'd ever been searching for over those many miles.

Home.

* * * * *

Look for the next Renaud Brothers novel,
Bastien's story!
Available June 2023.

USA TODAY bestselling author **Jules Bennett** has published over sixty books and never tires of writing happy endings. Writing strong heroines and alpha heroes is Jules's favorite way to spend her workdays. Jules hosts weekly contests on her Facebook fan page and loves chatting with readers on Twitter, Facebook and via email through her website. Stay up-to-date by signing up for her newsletter at julesbennett.com.

Books by Jules Bennett

Harlequin Desire

The Rancher's Heirs

Twin Secrets
Claimed by the Rancher
Taming the Texan
A Texan for Christmas

Angel's Share

When the Lights Go Out...
Second Chance Vows
Snowed In Secrets

Business and Babies

Friends...with Consequences
One Stormy Night

Visit the Author Profile page
at Harlequin.com for more titles.

You can also find Jules Bennett on Facebook, along with other Harlequin Desire authors, at Facebook.com/HarlequinDesireAuthors.

Dear Reader,

Are you ready for Cruz's story? If you read *Friends... with Consequences*, you already know Cruz is perfect hero material and deserves his own happily-ever-after! I couldn't wait to get to his story and there is no better shero to challenge him than Mila. I mean...I can't let him find love the easy way, right?

Mila wants nothing to do with any type of commitment, while on the flip side, Cruz built a palatial estate to fill with a family. They might be total opposites, but when they're stranded in his home during a storm, they realize maybe they have more in common than they first thought—namely chemistry.

But when the storm passes, they're left to face their true feelings and decide if their fling is something that could last. Will Mila overcome her past and take a chance with Cruz? Or will she move on with her growing career just like she'd always planned?

I hope you love Cruz and Mila's story and enjoy seeing Zane and Nora again. Now grab your drink of choice and head to your favorite cozy, quiet spot!

Happy reading!

Jules

ONE STORMY NIGHT

Jules Bennett

Stacy, Alisha, Stephanie and Kristie—
thanks for all the laughs! Love you all!

One

Trouble in stilettos walked straight toward his door and Cruz Westbrook braced himself for the impact.

Mila Hale wrestled against the blowing wind and sheets of rain as her umbrella flipped up. A gentleman would go offer some assistance, but Mila would likely claw his eyes out if he came to her rescue. He'd only met her once in person, but he'd picked up pretty quick that she valued her independence and control.

When she stepped up onto the porch, Mila tossed the broken umbrella into the landscaping and swiped the thick, dark strands of wet hair away from her face.

Damn it. Even soaking wet—maybe especially soaking wet—the woman stirred something inside him that should most definitely not stir.

They were entering into a working relationship, nothing more. No matter how much those bold red lips called to him.

"Beautiful day, isn't it?" he offered, as he rocked back on his heels and slid his hands into the pockets of his jeans. "Flight okay?"

Those wide, bright green eyes landed on him, and he couldn't be certain, but he got the impression she might be a bit cranky.

"The flight was fine. It was the rental car nightmare and then the two-hour drive here that got me." She glanced at the rain and the blowing wind, then back to him. "You live in the middle of nowhere."

Yes, he did, and that's exactly how he enjoyed his life. Since becoming co-owner of the successful, world-renowned magazine *Opulence* with his twin brother, Zane, their lives had become a bit chaotic. When Cruz had decided to build on his own little slice of Northern California heaven, he'd purposely gone off the grid by choosing a little valley tucked in the bend of a river. While Zane had built on a hill overlooking the valley about thirty minutes away, Cruz liked being nestled in nature. He'd been living with his brother temporarily and, now that his home was complete, was happy to finally be in his own space.

"We've taken some great shots here for the magazine," he informed her, then kept going. "You know our art director, Maddie? She had the idea for the project in my wildflower field and the board is all in agreement that you'd be perfect."

Cruz had never had a model come to his estate without other staff around, but Maddie hadn't returned his texts or calls over the past couple of hours, and Mila had actually made it in thirty minutes early.

"This is quite a storm," Mila stated. "I don't know how we're going to be able to start in the morning, let alone see the property today."

Yeah, there was a legit concern about using the property for a shoot right now and this freak storm didn't seem to be getting any better.

Mila had flown in from Miami a day earlier than the shoot was scheduled for with the intention of checking out the project first. She wasn't the first model he'd worked with who'd had demands, but she was the first one who had starred in his dreams in the most intimate, erotic type of way.

Those red lips…

He clearly needed a social life. He'd been working too damn hard over the past couple of months, ever since Zane got engaged to Cruz's best friend, Nora. Between their upcoming wedding and the baby on the way, Cruz had tried to take some of the heavier workloads.

Which was why he found himself staring at those wet clothes plastered to each one of Mila's sweet curves.

Focus, damn it. You're a professional.

Thunder rolled in the distance, but enough that the ground seemed to shake. Mila jumped and put a hand to her chest.

"Not a fan of storms?" he asked.

She straightened and faced him fully. "I'm fine. Just ready to get this project started."

"Mother Nature has other plans, but hopefully this will pass soon. You never know in the spring."

Northern California was known for its temperamental weather... Mila should feel right at home.

When he'd met her in Miami a couple months ago, she'd been a bit standoffish, but the majority of the models he'd worked with were. She'd been reserved, yet bold. Most people jumped at the opportunity to work with *Opulence,* but she never showed her emotions.

The magazine had started small, using unknown photographers, art designers, models, and more, and since their meteoric rise—expanding to include a jewelry arm, travel arm, and hotel arm—they'd kept the same concept. Seeking out unseen talent had been their ticket to unmatched success.

"I lived in an area like this once, but we had snow. I couldn't wait to leave."

Cruz chuckled, unsure if she just wanted to share a personal story or if she associated her short time here with wanting to exit. He couldn't get a grasp on her. They'd extended the invitation for her to work with them, but he couldn't tell if she was just nervous or too much of a diva to act like she cared.

He had to assume the latter. Models, no matter their status in the industry, had egos. He didn't care about any of that. What he cared about was his magazine's empire and remaining at the top of their game.

"Are we at least going to go inside?" she asked.

Cruz shifted his attention from his thoughts to her question as another round of thunder rumbled. Flashes of lightning lit up the sky. He didn't know what was more dangerous—remaining outside in the storm or going inside alone with temptation.

"If you're comfortable with that," he offered. "I don't typically bring subjects into my home without other members of my staff on hand."

More thunder boomed, this time with lightning striking something close, based on the echo of the crack.

Mila didn't ask again, and she didn't wait on an invitation. She skirted him toward the door, but he was faster. He might not like her attitude, but he could sense her fear and he was still a gentleman. And he didn't necessarily want to get struck by lightning, either.

The moment they stepped into the foyer, Mila shifted to the side and started to slip off her black heels. His eyes immediately landed on her perfectly polished red toes, and he instantly realized red might be his favorite color.

"I'm dripping."

Right. Manners. He needed them instead of letting wayward thoughts cloud his judgment and common sense.

"Let me get you a towel."

He headed toward his first-floor bedroom and grabbed a plush towel from his en suite, then made his way back down the hall toward her. She'd turned toward the large oval mirror above the accent table that he'd built years ago. She attempted to smooth her hair and twist it up into some knot.

"Here you go."

He stood behind her and reached around, catching her reflection in the mirror. Her eyes locked onto his, and for half a second, he wondered what she was thinking. Likely, she already wished she were back in Miami with warmth and sunshine instead of a freak spring storm in the woods. He'd take this over humidity and hurricanes any day.

"Thank you."

He nodded and stepped back just as his cell vibrated in his pocket. Another flash of lightning and boom of thunder had Mila jumping as the windows rattled.

"You okay?" he asked, searching her reflection.

Her chin tipped up. "Perfectly fine."

The rapid pulse at the base of her throat proved otherwise, but he wasn't about to call her out on that. Everyone had their fears, and clearly, hers happened to be intense storms—or being alone in a virtual stranger's home during such a storm.

Not wanting to pry anymore into her personal life, Cruz pulled his phone out and glanced at the text from Maddie.

Flight rerouted due to storms. See if Mila can meet us there tomorrow.

"Problem?"

Cruz glanced back up as Mila dabbed her neck.

She turned to face him, her eyes darting down to his cell. This was certainly not a position he wanted to find himself in, and he sure as hell didn't want to have Mila feeling uncomfortable or stuck with nobody else around and the weather raging outside.

"Your assistant canceled, didn't she?"

He pocketed his phone and nodded. "She's not my assistant—she oversees our art department. Her flight was rerouted because of the storms, so no, she can't make it today."

Mila blinked. Cruz didn't know if she was going to cry or throw something. She was emotionally guarded, and she couldn't stay here. That much was evident.

"Where are you staying?" he asked. Even though his company made the arrangements, that wasn't his department.

"Golden Valley Bed and Breakfast." She made very precise motions in refolding his towel before her eyes sought his once again. "How far is that from here?"

"Too far to be driving in this storm. It's about twenty minutes on a sunny day."

The roads were curvy and she'd have to go over a mountain to get to the other side and into the next valley. Unfamiliar roads and these conditions did not make for a smart combination to be out in.

"Well, I can't stay here." She let out a humorless laugh and handed his towel back. "I guess this was all in vain, since I'm heading back out."

"Why don't you wait until this passes?" he sug-

gested. "I know we only met once before, but I promise I'm not a creeper, and you're safer here than out
there on roads where you have no experience."

Mila held his gaze for another moment. "I should
try to get to my room. I'll go slow and pull over if
need be."

Cruz had a feeling she would want to stand her
ground on this matter. He wanted her to be safe, but
she clearly had her mind set. Likely, the more he
pushed, the more she'd push back and be even more
set in her decision.

"Send me a text when you get there so I know you
made it safely," he told her.

Mila jerked slightly. "You want me to check in
with you?"

"You're technically my guest and here for my
magazine, so yes. I'd like you to let me know you
are safe."

Mila pursed her lips and ultimately nodded. "Fine.
I'm sure I'll be there in no time."

He doubted it but held the door open for her to
head back out into the harsh elements. Crazy woman.
Why was he even attracted to someone so hard-
headed and stubborn?

Good thing she wasn't staying in town long and
that she showed no interest in him, because there
was no way he could avoid temptation. Plus, nothing good would come from trying a relationship with
someone with her attitude anyway.

Cruz stood on the porch and watched as she

slowly pulled down the drive. The torrential rain came down in sheets, and he knew without a doubt that she wouldn't get far.

Well, damn.

Mila made her way back up the drive toward Cruz's house. She wasn't going anywhere anytime soon, not with the bridge that led to the main road of the estate washed out.

She hated—absolutely hated—being at the mercy of anything else. The storm, the man…her desires. It had been quite a long time since someone had captured her interest the way Cruz had, which was ridiculous since he annoyed the hell out of her.

But she had caught him staring at her mouth earlier, which had only brought more desire to the surface than she could allow. This arrangement had to be all about business. Her entire life could be nothing beyond work and dedication. She'd come too far to lose sight of her ultimate goal- to become a fashion designer and make beautiful clothes available to women of all shapes and sizes.

Mila squinted and willed her wipers to go faster. She'd been foolish to think she could leave. Storms were never good for her nerves, but neither was staying in that house alone with a man who had awakened every one of her fantasies. "Tall, dark, and handsome" wasn't just a cute saying. Cruz Westbrook embodied each and every adjective.

She pulled as close to the front steps as possible

and didn't even bother with her purse or the luggage in the trunk. She grabbed her cell and jerked open the door and made a mad dash for the shelter of the porch.

The second she stood beneath the safety of the porch roof and somewhat out of the elements, she swiped the rain and hair from her face and blinked.

Cruz stood before her extending the same towel she'd used earlier. "Figured you'd need this."

Damn it. He knew she'd be back, and that smirk of his irritated the hell out of her. She hated predictability and she hated that sexy grin on his face. Mila took the towel and muttered a thanks as she followed him back inside. Just like before, she toed off her shoes and started the drying process once again.

"The bridge is out, by the way," she informed him.

"Is there a tree over it?"

Mila shook her head and patted her neck and chest with the towel. "No. It's literally out. As in, washed away."

Cruz muttered a curse and sighed. "Well, damn. I'll have to go down there once the storm passes. Nothing I can do right now."

"Is there another way off the property?"

"Helicopter."

She narrowed her eyes at his grin. The man had the audacity to *smile*. How could he smile at a time like this? Being stuck did not sit well with her, and he'd just lost access to civilization. How the hell was he so calm?

"Do you have a suitcase in the car?" he asked. "I'm sure you want dry clothes."

Mila patted her face and eyed him over the terry-cloth. "You seriously want to go out in that?"

Cruz shrugged. "It's just water. If you want your things, I'll get them."

She did want her things. She wanted to be dry and comfortable, but in her own room at the B and B that had been booked. She wanted her sketch pads and pencils, and a retreat to hide away in and do what she secretly loved. She also wanted to hear back from the two prospects she had for upcoming projects. Being self-employed really was a struggle at times, but she'd be damned if she'd ever go back to Montana just to hear her father say, "I told you so."

"I'm already wet," she countered. "I'll get them."

Cruz held up his hands. "You've been through enough. It's no trouble."

Before she could argue further, he headed out the door and off the porch. Maybe a true gentleman lay beneath that snarky exterior. She'd take a smirk and sarcasm if that also meant he had a tender side.

What the hell was she thinking? This wasn't a date or some relationship interview. She was only here for a few days to do a job. The end. Period.

With the double doors wide open, Mila couldn't tear her gaze from his broad, masculine form. The rain pelted him, immediately molding his shirt to his body.

Damn. Who knew this CEO billionaire had such excellent muscle tone? The moment he popped the hatch on the small SUV, he paused, clearly taking in all of her belongings. So what? She liked to be prepared. He was the one who volunteered.

Mila watched in awe as Cruz managed to get all of her belongings, including the purse in the front seat, and bring them back inside. She stepped out of his way and closed the set of doors, shutting out the sound of the pounding rain.

"Impressive," she murmured.

Cruz set her makeup case on top of her large suitcase, then piled her toiletry bag and purse onto it. There was another bag he'd put up on his shoulder and he set it down by his feet.

"How long were you planning on staying?" he asked.

"Just a couple days."

"Not a month?" he asked, again with that smirk. "I can show you to a guest room if you'd like to change and freshen up."

Of course he thought she was some high-maintenance model. If he only knew the truth, he'd feel like a fool for his assumption. But whatever. He wasn't the first and he wouldn't be the last. She knew what she had to do in order to survive each day and work toward her goals. The opinions of others didn't matter…if they did, her father would have ruined her long ago just as he had done to her mother.

"That would be great."

When she started to reach for her bag down by his feet, Mila's bare foot slid in the puddle on the hardwood floor, and she tumbled forward. Strong arms banded around her, but the impact sent them both to the floor. Cruz broke her fall, but she landed directly on top of him.

Every delicious, hard plane seemed to mold perfectly against her.

"Gracious sakes."

Mortified, she scrambled to move away, but those thick arms didn't budge.

"Are you all right?" he asked, his dark eyes holding her in place. "Are you hurt?"

"Am I hurt? I landed on you."

Could this whole situation be any more humiliating? She looked like a drowned rat, with her hair flattened to her face and her clothing plastered to her curves. Not the glamorous impression she wanted to portray.

Thankfully, they'd met before and he'd seen some of her still shots and work or this would be even more of a disaster.

"Are *you* hurt?" she countered.

"I'm perfectly fine."

Cruz released her and helped her up as he came to his feet as well. He kept a watchful eye on her, as if he didn't believe she was okay. She truly wished she'd stayed in Miami. Being trapped in this home, for who knew how long, and having a ridiculous crush on the man who could launch her to stardom, would not do well for her psyche. But she desperately needed this gig and hoped *Opulence* could get her over the slump her career had settled into.

"How about that room?" she said, nodding in the direction of an open door.

Mila lifted the bag containing her sketchbook and hoped it wasn't ruined from the rain. Some of her favorite pieces were in there. When she attempted to reach for her larger suitcase, Cruz held up a hand.

"We're going upstairs," he informed her. "I'll get it."

"Do you think I can't?"

"Not at all, but I'm trying to be helpful."

"I can get my things. I'm sure you want to go dry off as well and get changed."

The mental image of him peeling that shirt off gave her pause and she stilled, her eyes landing on his chest.

"My eyes are up here."

Busted.

And what she thought might be a smirk was actually a naughty grin. She didn't know which was worse.

"And my room? Where is that?" she asked, not addressing his comment.

Why did he have to be so adorable and frustrating…and sexy? This storm had come at the worst possible time and things wouldn't have been nearly as bad if that art director had shown up. At least they would have all been trapped together and Mila's attention could be elsewhere instead of on Cruz Westbrook and all of his appealing, irritating traits.

Cruz pointed up the steps. "Any room up there," he replied. "Mine is down here."

He walked away, leaving her to get her luggage just as she'd requested. But damn the man, whose carefree whistling echoed from the hallway and mocked her as she wrestled with her things and wondered how she'd lost control so fast.

Two

Cruz had never had a woman in his house...at least not as an overnight guest in another room, and his best friend Nora didn't count. He had no idea what the protocol was, but maybe if he just treated her like one of the guys, then he could maintain professionalism.

Things would be quite different if they were on location with his staff, but the fact that he and Mila were alone together under his roof already made this a unique situation.

Cruz changed from his wet clothes and threw on a pair of jeans and plain gray tee. The storm continued to rage outside, and he just knew that when all was said and done, there would be a mess on his property. He'd have to get his grounds crew in to clean up, but that bridge issue had to be addressed first.

Cruz headed from his bedroom back down the hall to the living area. He figured Mila would come down eventually and they could discuss necessities such as dinner and sleeping and how they could make this not so awkward. Professionally, they had to be able to find some common ground. They were both adults, so this shouldn't be too difficult...he just hadn't factored in those red lips and this sexual tension. Nor had he factored in being under the scrutiny of those vibrant green eyes.

If he could look at her like every other model he'd worked with and not a challenging, sexy vixen, that would go a long way in making this situation a bit easier.

Cruz pulled his cell from his pocket to send his brother a text about the bridge. He didn't expect Zane or Nora to come by, but he wanted to update them just in case. He typed out the message, but it failed to send. Confused, he tried again.

Nothing.

The lights flickered once, twice, but ultimately remained on.

This could be a very long night if this storm didn't pass soon. Having grown up on a working farm, Cruz knew how to be prepared for many situations. He headed to the utility room off one of his garages and gathered flashlights, candles, and a lighter. After lighting a candle in the kitchen and another on the table near the base of the steps, he went back to the living room.

Mila stood near the fireplace, glancing over the photos he had on display.

"That's my brother."

Mila glanced over her shoulder. "I'm aware."

Yeah, he didn't know why he felt the need to point that out. Everyone knew who the Westbrook twins were. Considering the fact that they looked exactly alike, there really was no need for him to explain.

But he'd stepped back in and been distracted by the sight of her all dried off. Her hair was back to the state he remembered from their meeting. Big, curly, hanging down her back and almost touching her backside. She'd put on a pair of body-hugging jeans, black heeled booties, and a red sweater with a deep vee in the front and back, and had a full face of makeup.

Sometimes, these models took things a bit too far. He highly doubted she'd gotten all dressed up for him, and they sure as hell weren't going anywhere anytime soon.

Mila's eyes darted to the flashlights in his hands. "Expecting the power to go?"

"It's a possibility. I have a generator, but I'd need to see to get there, plus I wanted you to have one."

The lights flickered again but still remained on. He knew if the power went, the whole house would plunge into darkness, and a storm combined with Mila Hale would only lead to trouble.

He set the lights on the table and crossed to stand

beside her. She'd not only gotten into high-octane diva mode, she smelled way too damn good. Something fruity and floral all at the same time.

"Your parents?" Mila asked, pointing to an old photo.

Cruz nodded as he recalled the day the image had been captured at an amusement park. They'd all had their faces painted and his mother had had hers done like a butterfly. Cruz and Zane had each chosen action heroes and their father had picked a scarecrow. He'd kept this picture of a reminder of how good his childhood had been. They'd had it all… until they didn't.

"Yeah. I think I was about five here." Just before his world fell apart.

"You guys look like your dad."

They did, which pissed Zane off. After their mother passed, their father spiraled downhill fast. He lost their ranch, gambled and drank himself nearly to death, and gave up on parenting to wallow in self-pity. Now he wanted to work on their relationships, and while Cruz had been open to that, Zane had been a tougher nut to crack. But he was coming around.

"They must be proud of what you guys have done," she went on.

Cruz didn't like to talk about his past or his parents much, and the last thing he wanted to do was get too vulnerable with a subject. He had to keep that at the forefront of his mind.

He checked his cell once again and his message to Zane still hadn't gone through.

"There's no service right now," she offered. "I've tried, too."

As if they needed to be even more isolated and pushed together.

The next clap of thunder and flash of lightning came simultaneously, and Mila jumped as she let out a sharp squeal.

Cruz reached out and placed a hand on her arm. "It's okay. Everything is out there and you're safe here."

Her wide eyes landed on the floor-to-ceiling front windows for a second, then back to him. She blinked as her body relaxed beneath his touch.

"I'm good." She presented a wide smile that didn't quite reach her eyes. "Just startled me. That's all."

Yeah, well, she'd been *startled* since she got here and he'd bet that if he mentioned the phobia, she'd argue and get defensive.

"How about something to eat?" he suggested. "You traveled a long way and I'm sure you would be getting dinner by now if you'd gotten to your lodging."

Since that part of the magazine wasn't his area, he wasn't sure what all had been lined up for her. He also wasn't positive what food he had in his house, considering that he paid someone else to do his grocery shopping. He never cared what they got, as long as his favorite coffee blend always remained stocked.

"I could eat," she admitted. "But don't go to any trouble. Point me toward the kitchen and I can get something for myself."

"Follow me."

He wasn't about to just turn her lose to fend for herself. Not because he didn't trust her, but because he figured she must be exhausted emotionally from the situation and physically from a day of traveling. Yet she still managed to be "on" with her appearance now that she'd dried off. He wanted to ask her if she always felt the need to be made up or if she thought she had to do all of that because she would be working for him for a short time.

Cruz stopped under the wide arched doorway that led to the kitchen and turned to face her. He needed to make something perfectly clear and hopefully put her at ease. He couldn't imagine how she must feel being in a stranger's home, a man's no less, with no one around.

"You can be comfortable here," he started.

Mila stared back at him, her brows drawing in. "Do I look uncomfortable?"

"Actually, yes." He chuckled, deciding to stick with honesty as often as possible. "I'm sure you packed something more casual, and I didn't want you to think you had to be all together all the time. We're not working right now, and you already have the job."

Those painted lips thinned as her brows relaxed. "I realize being the CEO is a different position than what I do, but I assure you, I have also have an image that always has to be presented. I'm quite comfortable because this is how I've always been."

Clearly, he'd struck a nerve. He wondered if she

was always this defensive or simply felt the need to control the conversation. Either way, she obviously had a chip on her shoulder, but he assumed that came along with the industry. Again, he didn't care her about attitude, he just cared about making the next issue of his magazine better than the last.

"You also need to know you're safe here," he added. "And I'm not just talking the storm. My very best friend is a woman and I know there is always that concern about safety, especially being alone with a man. But you have nothing to worry about."

Her shoulders relaxed somewhat, and he felt that maybe he'd finally said the right thing with her.

"I appreciate that," she replied. "Your best friend has taught you well."

Cruz laughed. "Oh, Nora taught me *and* my brother. They're engaged and expecting a baby."

A stirring of unexpected jealousy slithered through him. Why was that? He couldn't be happier for Zane and Nora. Hell, he'd tried to fix them up, but they hadn't needed his help. They were well on their way to building the happiest life with their own little family…everything Cruz had always wanted and Zane had dodged.

"You seem sad now."

Mila's soft statement pulled him from his thoughts. He blew out a sigh and shook his head. He hadn't realized she was trying to read his thoughts.

"Not sad at all," he replied. "Maybe sometime I'll tell you about when I tried to hook them up."

Mila laughed and the sudden sweet sound tugged

at something inside him. He hadn't heard her laugh before. She seemed all business, all the time. When they'd met in Miami, she'd been very structured and detailed with her list of questions and requirements. She'd ticked them off without cracking a joke or even smiling at his lame ones. Then she had shaken his hand and left. He'd never met anyone more focused on work than Zane until Mila stepped into his life. But this was what she should be, right? A professional.

"You run a billion-dollar company and still have time to play matchmaker?" she asked. "Maybe if this tycoon gig doesn't work out, you can try setting up a dating site."

Cruz snorted. "A single man setting up a dating site? Not sure how well that would go over and I have no experience in serious relationships."

"Too busy working?" she asked, quirking a brow.

Zane turned back toward the kitchen and moved around the dark marble island toward the industrial refrigerator. "Too busy traveling," he told her as he surveyed the contents. "Have a seat."

He glanced over his shoulder as she slid onto one of his leather barstools. The wide window behind her provided a stunning view as the sky lit up with lightning. He didn't miss the way she tensed with each roll of thunder, but he wasn't about to bring it to her attention. He could keep her distracted, which was more than she'd have if she'd gotten to that B and B.

"Do you want a sandwich, or I can whip up some breakfast dinner," he offered.

"Breakfast dinner?" she scoffed. "That's for people too lazy to make it in the morning."

"Or for people whose stomachs don't know the time," he countered.

She rested her elbows on the counter and laced her fingers together. "Don't go to any trouble for me. A sandwich is fine. Whole-grain bread?"

"White or bagels."

She pursed her lips. "What cheese? Swiss?"

He opened one of the drawers and pulled out all the cheese, all the meat, condiments, pickles, and a tomato. He lined up everything on the island and then went to the walk-in pantry to retrieve the bread options. Once he had all of those on display as well, he held out his hands.

"What will it be?" he asked.

Mila's eyes scanned the bar, then she shot him a wry look. "I've changed my mind. If the magazine doesn't work out, you can open one of those sandwich shops."

Maybe she did have a sense of humor after all.

"I think the magazine is working out just fine," he retorted.

Mila slid off the stool and came around the counter. "I'll make it."

"I'm happy to do this for you. I mean, you are stuck in my house, so I'm pretty sure I should play the host."

She reached for the white bread but only grabbed one slice. "No offense, but you'd make it wrong."

Cruz jerked. "I am offended. How can a sandwich be made wrong? You throw the stuff on the bread and eat."

"See? Wrong. If you put your condiment or pickle directly on the bread, you get soggy bread."

Cruz watched as she assembled her half sandwich, then folded it where all the extras were, in the middle. He'd never given this much thought to how to make a sandwich, nor did he really care. He had a feeling she had a precise way to do every single thing in her life and didn't mind one bit sharing her strategies with anyone who would listen.

"I guess I eat it too fast to worry about anything going soggy," he told her.

"Well, now you know for future guests and that restaurant."

She grabbed a napkin off the counter and took a seat back at the bar. Without asking, he pulled out tea and poured her a glass.

"Does that have sugar or caffeine?" she asked, eyeing the glass.

"Both. High-octane all the way."

When she said nothing, he laughed. "Do you find fault in everything or do you just need to retain control over every aspect of life?"

Her eyes landed on his. "Oh, I always have control. In everything."

Why did that last part she'd tacked on take on a sultry tone—and why did he instantly envision her in his bed, beneath his sheets?

"Is that why this storm is bothering you so much?" he asked, though he'd told himself not to bring up that topic. The words slid out before he could stop himself.

"The storm isn't bothering me."

She took a bite of her sandwich and offered no further explanation. Clearly, she didn't want to let him in on anything personal, which was fine. He should take a page from her book, but he figured that if they were stuck, they'd at least have to have some type of small talk.

Cruz put all the items back and grabbed a bottle of water for himself. By the time he was done, Mila had finished her sandwich and drunk half her tea.

"Would you like something else?" he offered.

"I'm good, thanks. Weren't you hungry?"

He shook his head. "I ate before you got here. And since I'm not sure how long you will be staying, feel free to make yourself at home. If you want something, just ask."

"Hopefully, that helicopter will be here tomorrow to rescue me."

Cruz's lips twitched, but he held back the grin. Her dry sense of humor amused him in an unexpected way. The woman he spent the most time with, Nora, was assertive, loud at times, and sarcastic. While Mila was bold, she portrayed herself in an entirely different manner.

And he damn well liked it way too much.

The lights flickered once more…and then they were plunged into darkness.

Three

Mila really tried not to freak out. She wasn't afraid of the dark, and there was a candle burning on the island that offered a soft glow, even if minimal. No, what had her heart racing was the fact that this storm wasn't calming down, the road was washed out, and while Cruz might be a total professional, he'd looked at her as if her clothes were already off.

And that didn't help her rush of desire where this man was concerned.

She knew he'd never make a move. The Westbrook brothers had impeccable reputations. They wouldn't be the most sought-after magazine moguls if they had any blemishes. From everything she'd seen, people she'd talked to and her meeting with Cruz in advance, she knew that being associated with *Opulence* was exactly the step she needed to thrust her career into new territory. She just hadn't counted on his eyes smoldering with desire. What should she do now?

"Okay, well, this isn't a surprise," he stated. "Let me grab a flashlight and head to the garage."

He left the kitchen and came right back with both flashlights, handing one to her.

"You can stay in here or come with me," he offered.

Before she could reply, a large crash came from the front of the house. Cruz turned and ran back that way. The front door opened and he cursed. Mila wasn't sure what happened there, but she could help in another way. She headed toward the garage and swung her flashlight around the spacious five-car area until she found what she needed.

She propped her light on a shelf and, even though she hadn't done this in a while and it took a few tries, she got the generator up and running.

"What the hell?"

She turned, catching Cruz in the doorway to the garage, his eyes locked onto her.

"You've done that before," he stated, nodding toward the generator that now hummed.

Mila grabbed her flashlight and flicked it off now that the power was back up.

"I have," she confirmed. "What happened out front?"

"You don't want to know."

From the look on his face and that tone, she probably didn't, but she needed to.

"Did a tree fall on the porch?" she asked.

"Your rental car."

Mila cringed. "Glad my things were out of it."

"That damage will be on the company, so don't worry about that. We'll take care of everything."

She started back toward the doorway leading into the house, but he hadn't moved.

"Thank you," he told her. "For getting that started."

He'd gotten drenched again from going outside. Droplets clung to his fanned-out black lashes and she found herself staring, waiting for one to fall onto his dark skin. He blinked and a single bead of moisture slid down his cheek, stopping right at the corner of his mouth.

"Mila."

Her name came out in a husky tone as her eyes darted up to seek his. Merely an inch or two separated them and she didn't know if it was being strong for so long or the circumstances that made her want to ignore all the red flags waving around in her head and press her lips to his.

Cruz took a step back into the house, but not before his gaze dipped to her lips.

"Not a good idea," he murmured.

Mila squared her shoulders and gathered herself together. "No. It's not."

The muscle in his jaw clenched and Mila knew that if she wanted to make a move, he wouldn't stop her. She also knew that he was too much of a gentleman and professional to make one himself.

"If you're afraid of the storm you can—"

"I'm not afraid." She'd die before admitting such a thing. "But I'm heading to my room."

Cruz nodded and stepped aside for her to pass. As she moved around him and started toward the kitchen, his voice washed over her from behind.

"I was just going to say, my room is the first door down the hall past the steps if you need anything."

Oh, she needed something, but it wasn't anything she could take. She'd been here only a few hours and already, her desires were well beyond her control. She didn't need this trouble, and she had to remember everything at stake…her career and her freedom.

Without another word, she gripped her flashlight in her hand and went upstairs to the room she'd chosen. After she closed the door, she flicked the lock, but that was silly. Cruz had made it clear that he wouldn't make a move, so the question was, would she just lock herself in so she didn't?

How in the hell could he sleep? Rain continued to pelt the windows and flashes of lightning lit up his room every few minutes.

And a seductress slept just upstairs.

The look she'd given him earlier had been nothing short of hunger and desire. He'd seen the look before, but he'd never been so torn between right and wrong or business and pleasure. It was way too risky to take a chance on a fling, but he didn't remember a time he'd stared down temptation and walked away.

Cruz laced his fingers behind his head and stared up at the ceiling. Aside from the invisible tug of attraction pulling them together, he did worry this storm might keep her up. The last thing he wanted was for her to be alone and afraid, but going to her room was out of the question.

Above all else, he had to remain a professional. He was the CEO, damn it. He needed to get his hormones in check and act like it.

Turning away her silent request earlier had taken every bit of willpower. His hands itched to touch those curves, to peel her out of those body-hugging clothes, to taste her full lips…

Cruz tossed his covers aside and sat up on the edge of his bed. The vast array of images of Mila flashing through his mind were not helping. He'd tried a cold shower, he'd even tried going through work emails, but the damn cell wasn't working.

He stilled. Had he just heard—

Yes. There it was again. The creak on the steps. He held his breath, focusing only on the sounds coming from the other side of his door.

Cruz didn't know if she couldn't sleep, if she was worried about the storm, or if she needed a snack from the kitchen. Or perhaps she was coming to his room.

His gut tightened at the image of her moving down the hall just outside his room. Did she have her fist up to knock—or had she even thought of him since they parted ways? Maybe that invisible tug he'd experienced earlier had just been something he'd blown out of proportion in his head.

The way she'd looked at him had been nothing short of hunger, but had she just gotten caught up in the moment and their predicament? Being thrust into the situation of being stranded had a romantic element that certainly didn't belong here. Nothing about what he felt could or should be labeled with the word *romance*.

Despite how most billionaire bachelors lived their lives, Cruz wasn't a player or a playboy. Yes, he traveled most of the time for work, meeting up with potential clients or partners. But he wanted a family. He'd always wanted the lifestyle he'd grown up with before his mother passed.

True, he was young when she died, but he remembered that feeling, that sense of belonging and stability and pure happiness. He wanted nothing less for his future.

But until that woman who shared his vision came along, he could entertain a fling here and there.

Not with someone he worked with, though. If Mila were here under any other circumstance, he might take that hunger in her eyes and act upon it. But he'd never want to make a woman feel like she had to sleep with him for a job, and he sure as hell wouldn't put one in an uncomfortable position. This industry produced enough slimy assholes who took advantage of vulnerable people and he'd be damned if he'd ever put his morals aside for some selfish desire.

No. If something happened between him and Mila, that move would have to be all her.

Cruz listened, but hadn't heard anything for a couple minutes. He'd been foolish and arrogant to think she'd come to his door in the middle of the night. They barely knew each other, and she clearly struggled with her surroundings. He needed to get that nonsense out of his head.

But he did wonder if she needed something or if she was afraid.

Cruz eased his door open to find the hallway empty. He stepped out and headed toward the front of the house. When he reached the entryway, he glanced toward the kitchen, which was empty. To the right, in the living area, Mila had curled up on the sofa with a pad of paper and pencil. She'd flicked on the small accent lamp on the end table and seemed to be lost in whatever she was working on.

She had piled her hair on top of her head, with only a few tendrils caressing her neck. She had on a pair of fuzzy socks, black leggings, and an oversize tee that draped off one delicate shoulder. She didn't seem to be upset or needing him for anything, and standing in the hall like some creeper wouldn't match well with his affirmation that she'd be safe here.

Cruz started to turn when she glanced up and caught his gaze.

"Sorry." He offered a smile and remained in place

so as not to spook her. "I thought I heard you earlier and wanted to make sure you were okay."

Her eyes drifted downward toward his bare chest, and he realized too late that he should have at least thrown a shirt on. But here he stood, in his shorts and nothing else. At least he'd kept a good distance between them.

"I hope I didn't wake you." She laid her pencil on the pad and tipped her head. "I couldn't sleep."

Yeah, he knew the feeling. But he didn't know if her insomnia stemmed from the storm of sexual tension or the storm raging outside.

"Is there anything I can get you?" he offered, hating how he had to continue to play the dutiful host and pretend like he didn't want to kiss her and thrust his hands into that mass of hair.

"More paper?" she joked.

He found himself taking a step forward, then another, until he stood at the opposite end of the sofa where she sat. Mila quickly flipped over her pad and tapped her pencil on the cover.

"No peeking."

Cruz held up his hands. "Mysterious and beautiful." He laughed. "I respect that need for privacy."

"I didn't mean to be rude," she offered. "I've just been working on something and I'd like to keep it in my own world for now."

"I understand." He gestured toward the fireplace. "Do you want me to light that for you?"

"Oh, no. It's late and you should be in bed."

Her eyes traveled once again, but she jerked her

attention back to his face as if she'd caught herself. Clearly, that episode earlier wasn't a fluke or just their circumstances forcing them together. The sexual tension seemed to be growing and enveloping them. He wanted to know what she'd been working on; he wanted to sit here and talk at the very least. But he only had on a pair of shorts and she looked too damn adorable.

Plus, she was pinning him with those eyes. It was a recipe for a mistake they wouldn't be able to undo. He'd never had self-control issues with anyone he'd worked with at the magazine before. Professionalism had always been a nonissue.

Mila pulled something out of him that both surprised and intrigued him. He never thought someone so high-maintenance would turn him on, but this woman had very specific ways of approaching and doing things.

Maybe that was the whole reason for the attraction. Her confidence might be even sexier than her curves.

"I'll let you get back to your project," he told her. "You know where I am if you need anything."

"Which is why I'm avoiding your room."

Cruz's breath caught in his throat as he remained still. Mila tapped her pencil against the sketch pad cover.

Tap, tap, tap.

The rain hit the windows and thunder rolled in the distance now—but her eyes never wavered.

"You have to know what you look like," she stated.

Cruz stared at the creamy shoulder on display and nearly laughed. "Says the model."

"Trying to be a model," she corrected. "That's why I'm here."

"You're here because you're damn good at what you do. You're not trying," he corrected. "You're succeeding."

Her eyes flared, her lips parted just a little, but enough that he heard her soft gasp. He wanted to cross the room, flip that sketch pad off her lap, and cover her mouth, her *body*, with his.

Mila continued to stare at him as she set her stuff aside and came to her feet. The silence surrounding them pounded in his ears, and he knew that if he took that first step, she'd be his.

But at what cost?

Cruz fisted his hands at his sides and fought against the rush of arousal and need within him... and those same things staring back at him. He had to do the right thing for both of them.

He took a step back.

"Good night, Mila."

And mustering every ounce of resolve he had, he turned and headed back to his room, cursing himself the entire way.

Four

Mila checked her cell once again and…nothing. She didn't want to miss a call or an email from her next possible opportunity. She couldn't afford to.

She touched up her gloss and gave her hair one last spray. She debated changing, but the green wrap sweater and her favorite dark jeans seemed appropriate for being stuck inside. She moved from her en suite bathroom to her spacious guest room and slid on a pair of booties. Her eyes went to the sketch pad on her bed. She'd spent hours last night designing. She hadn't planned on losing sleep over fashion, but between the storm and Cruz wearing very little, her mind simply hadn't been able to shut down.

Designing wasn't just her ultimate goal; the basics of sketching served as an emotional outlet, which she had started and become dependent on when she'd been younger. She still fell back on her drawings, no matter her moods. If she had spare time, she had a pencil in her hand.

Mila tried to mentally prepare herself for the simple act of going downstairs for coffee, but she'd quickly learned that there was nothing simple about being under the same roof as Cruz Westbrook.

She couldn't hide in here forever, and quite frankly, she didn't want to. As much as she knew she was playing with fire, she couldn't stay away.

Last night, when Cruz had stood in the living area and she'd struggled not to stare at all of that excellent muscle tone on display, she'd thought for sure he was going to make a move. She'd been aching, ready, and likely would have ignored all the warning bells going off in her head.

Clearly, Cruz had meant it when he'd said he would be respectful and professional. She wholeheartedly believed he would never make a move on her, but the look in his eyes said he definitely wanted to.

At least they had a mutual need and the sexual attraction wasn't one-sided.

So where did that leave them? Because if she made a move first, then she'd be the one putting her career on the line. She'd be the one taking more of a gamble. Cruz had billions and owned the company, while she scraped for everything she had, determined to keep her head above water and fulfill her dream.

She'd captured the attention of the most coveted magazine in the world, so she couldn't blow her chance over a temporary fling...no matter how much she wanted to.

There was no way she'd prove her father right or ever give him the satisfaction of seeing her come back home. She was on her own, just like she had been for years, which gave her all the motivation she needed to keep moving forward.

The moment Mila stepped into the hallway, the aromas of coffee, bacon, and something sweet wafted up from the first floor. Cruz could cook breakfast? As if she needed another reason to find him attractive. Her stomach growled and she hadn't even realized she was hungry until the tempting smells surrounded her.

Mila pulled in a deep breath and slid her hand along the glossy banister as she padded down the stairs. The faint sound of Frank Sinatra's crooning filtered through from the kitchen and she couldn't help but smile. Who knew the sexy billionaire bachelor liked the classics? Another layer she'd uncovered without trying.

"Morning."

His head whipped up from the stove as she made her way toward the island.

"Morning," he offered with that toe-curling smile. "I hope you're hungry. I had no idea what you wanted, so I made a little of everything."

Her eyes scanned the bar top and she laughed. "You're not kidding. How long have you been awake?"

"A while." Cruz slid two over-easy eggs from the pan onto a plate. "I didn't want to be accused of being lazy if I made this meal tonight."

She couldn't help but smile as he tossed her words back at her. "Then I'm glad you woke early."

"There's still a cell issue," he informed her. "But at least we're just getting rain now and the storm has passed. After breakfast, I need to go out and check the property for damage."

"The car and the bridge are bad enough. Hopefully, nothing else took a hit."

He bustled around, getting two coffee mugs and a couple of plates. Mila would have jumped in and helped, but he seemed to have a system and she took a few moments to admire the view and the man. Today he'd thrown on another simple gray T-shirt with a pair of jeans.

For a man of his position and power, there seemed to be something so humble about him. If she'd just met him at a bar or online, she'd never know he'd had so much success. She'd worked with people who flaunted their achievements and used their positions to take advantage. Not Cruz.

She decided that she wouldn't mind if Cruz decided to take advantage of this situation.

"Do you always put cheese in your eggs?" she asked, scooping up a pile next to a waffle she'd grabbed.

Cruz came around the bar and grabbed a handful of bacon. "Always. You can never have too much cheese."

"Interesting. I don't make mine that way. I can show you how I do them next time."

He shook his head and chuckled. "No, I imagine we don't do things the same way. I think we established yesterday that we both like control and are total opposites."

Yes, they had, but they certainly had one very strong undercurrent in common, and Mila wondered if they were headed toward the inevitable. There were only two solutions for this longing pulling them toward each other. Either they should act on it or she had to get the hell out of there.

"I can help you outside if you want," she offered, sipping her coffee. "Oh, that's a good brew."

Cruz shot her a wink. "The best."

That wink sent another tingle through her that she didn't need. Why couldn't he be a jerk or arrogant? She could handle the sexy if his attitude clung on to her every nerve, but the only things he clung to were her fantasies.

Cruz's focus went from his plate to her as he narrowed his gaze. "You still haven't told me how you know how to start a generator. I wouldn't think a model would be privy to such things."

"I wasn't always a model," she explained. "And a girl needs to have some secrets."

More like she didn't want to delve into her past. She never wanted to revisit that in her head, let alone out loud to a man she was attracted to and the very man who could potentially launch her career. She'd waited years to catch a big break and she wasn't about

to blow it now with the darkness of her childhood—
or worse, pity.

"Well, if you want to change your clothes and
head out with me, that's fine, but don't feel obli-
gated." He spread butter all over both of his waffles,
followed by a heavy dose of syrup. "There's no need
in both of us getting soaked."

"I don't mind helping." How much syrup did two
waffles need? "I mean, I am crashing here. It's the
least I could do."

"I can't believe you tried to drive out of here in
that weather."

Yeah, she couldn't either. But it had been try to
leave or give in to temptation.

So here she was.

"I can't believe you didn't stop me," she countered
with a laugh as she dug into her breakfast.

"I imagine trying to argue with you about anything would be the equivalent of bathing a cat."

Maybe he meant that as an insult, but a flare of
pride burst through her. She'd never felt any amount
of power before. Oh, she'd always tried to keep a
strong hold on every aspect of her life, but to hear
someone like Cruz admit she had the upper hand
came as a pleasant surprise.

"I bet a guy like you could've persuaded me to
stay."

He turned in his stool to face her fully. His dark
eyes penetrated her deep into her soul and she could
easily envision herself staring into those eyes in a
much more intimate setting.

"Not without crossing boundaries."

Mila's breath caught in her throat at his bold reply. There was no mistaking his meaning and he didn't seem a bit apologetic about what he wanted.

He did, however, have an overwhelming amount of self-control.

"And do you think we can stay on our own sides of that line the whole time I'm here?" she asked.

His lips thinned, and the muscle in his jaw clenched. "We have to. I can't get involved with a subject, no matter how much I want you."

Well, there it was. The unflinching admission that she already knew, but the words hadn't slid through his lips—until now.

"I can't lose this opportunity." She had to make that clear, not to mention the fact that she felt the same way. Though he likely already knew. "I have everything to lose if we... You know."

"Have sex? I'm aware."

Yeah, well. She didn't even want that word landing between them because she'd worried that would just open another door toward the inevitable, but he'd laid it right there anyway.

"Okay, well." She cleared her throat and curled her hands around her mug. "So, how about we go check out the damage? Because if we keep talking about this, it's only going to make things worse."

"They can get worse without us talking at all."

Mila swallowed hard and set her mug back on the counter. That invisible line had to remain firmly between them, no matter what. She didn't know how long she would be stuck there, and each passing moment only added to their verbal foreplay.

She slid off her seat and tucked her hair behind her ears. Before she could say anything, he pointed at her outfit.

"Are you changing before we head out?"

Mila glanced down and ran the contents of her suitcase through her head. "I'm not sure I have anything suitable, so I'll just go in this. I'll be fine."

Cruz gave her a side-eye and snorted. "Do you ever dress down or are you always ready for a shoot?"

She knew he didn't mean anything by the question, but his words struck a nerve...a nerve her father had threaded so deeply and painfully through her years ago. She'd tried her best, through therapy and all the self-care she could manage, but those roots ran deep within her.

"Stay here."

He moved out of the kitchen before she knew what was happening. Not knowing what to do with herself, Mila opted to clean up since he'd cooked. She picked up their plates and took them to the sink, then searched through drawers for something to cover up the leftovers.

"Here you go."

Mila glanced up as Cruz came back in with a stack of clothes.

"I'm sure they'll fit weird since I'm so tall, but at least you won't ruin your own clothes." He handed the folded pieces to her. "There are plenty of old boots in the garage. What size are you?"

"Eight."

"Well, mine will be big on you, but better than what you have on."

Mila didn't want to state the obvious, but… "I appreciate this, but I'm pretty sure your clothes won't fit me at all," she started. "If you haven't noticed, I'm curvier than you are."

A naughty grin kicked up at the corner of his mouth. "I've noticed every single thing about you and those curves. Now go try these on. I'll wait down here for you."

Mila took the clothes and headed toward the stairs before she could think too much about how he'd been eyeing her shape.

"Pull that hair up, too," he called after her.

She would look like a complete mess, but she wanted to help, so she'd have to let go of her looks for a bit. She rarely let anyone see her without being all done up, but considering that she'd gotten drenched yesterday on her way in, he'd already seen her at her worst.

And she had to keep reminding herself, almost on the daily, that not all men were like her father. Not all men judged women and put them down. She was still a work in progress, but she was damn proud of how far she'd come.

Still, she hoped his things fit and she didn't make a fool of herself. The last thing she wanted was to humiliate herself in front of not only her temporary employer, but the only man who'd intrigued her in quite some time.

* * *

Cruz waited for Mila and wondered if he'd over-stepped by asking about why she always felt the need to dress up. When she'd come down with full makeup and hair and completely dressed up, he couldn't help but wonder if she felt like her career was still on the line. He'd already told her once it wasn't, but she had her reasons for wanting to keep up her appearance.

He had a strong feeling she wasn't the diva people, himself included, believed her to be. She had her secrets, which made her allure even stronger. Aside from her obvious sexual appeal, there was so much beneath the surface that he wanted to know more about. If he were to ask her what she was protecting, he didn't know that he'd get an answer. She seemed to have her reasons for keeping her personal life tucked away, and he respected her for it.

Oftentimes, because of his power and bachelor status, women were all too eager to throw everything at him to gain his attention. He'd quickly realized that Mila didn't have the same methods for gaining attention as other women…which made her even more potent and dangerous.

Movement on the steps pulled his attention from his thoughts and he turned his focus to the woman who kept taking up all the spare room in his mind.

Damn, she looked adorable in his clothes. Mila had folded up the bottoms of his black sweatpants to make them fit, and her curves filled out his white T-shirt perfectly. His body stirred with arousal that he couldn't act on or even entertain the idea of. But he'd come to realize that no matter what she wore, she would capture his attention in the most primal way.

"You look a hell of a lot better in that than I ever did," he told her as she reached the bottom. "Feel free to keep that shirt."

The vee hit just at the swell of her breasts, and he realized he should've grabbed a sweatshirt or something with a high neck to cover up that tempting skin. He'd just gotten her the first thing he'd found. He shouldn't be surprised. Mila could make anything look glamorous. Even with her hair piled on top of her head, she was striking.

"I have boots and a raincoat in the garage for you."

"Let's do it." She gestured for him to lead the way. "Hopefully, there won't be any more damage to the property."

Yeah, he hoped so, too. A damaged bridge and crushed vehicle seemed like enough to handle.

Once he had her bundled in a jacket with the hood up and a pair of rubber boots that were at least two sizes too big, Cruz pulled on the same getup. He raised one of the bay doors to the garage and motioned toward the four-wheeler parked there.

"We'll take that if you don't care."

"Fine by me."

Cruz climbed on and the moment she got on behind him, he had to concentrate on starting the engine and the reason for their trip. He hadn't thought about how amazing she'd feel pressed against him, but damn...

She circled her arms around his waist. "This okay?"

He nearly laughed. Was it okay? It was more than okay and more PG than he wanted his contact with her to be, but he'd have to settle for this innocent gesture.

The moment he backed out of the garage, the rain pummeled them. He squinted against the heavy drops and maneuvered the vehicle toward the front of his property. He wanted to see the bridge, or lack thereof, for himself.

"Over there," Mila called from behind, but pointed toward his right.

Cruz glanced at a couple of trees down along his fence. Minor issues in comparison. The bridge was the first thing that would need fixing, and he'd just have the company insurance take care of the damaged rental car. His maintenance man would handle the new fencing, but he made a mental note of it anyway. He hoped there wasn't too much more to keep track of, because he just wanted to enjoy riding around with Mila plastered against his back.

He was glad she offered to come with him despite the rain and the cool air from the storm. He never rode around with anyone on his property, let alone a beautiful woman. He never really had women there for any reason.

Cruz stopped at the end of his drive as the swollen creek, which had risen up and onto the banks, divided the road. There was no sign the bridge had ever been there, so the repairs would take more work than he first thought. He didn't care about the cost and he wouldn't wait on insurance to get the replacement started.

He killed the engine and got off the four-wheeler. Mila swung her leg over and started to hop off as well, but her foot slid in the wet grass and she went down. Cruz tried to catch her, but didn't get to her in time.

"Are you okay?" he asked, reaching down to help her back up.

Her laughter filtered up and cut through the rain. She shoved her hood back and glanced up. Water covered her face, but those bright red lips parted with her wide smile and he found himself entranced once again.

He tried to pull her up, but with as hard as she was laughing, she was no help—which was how he ended up down in the mud puddle right alongside her.

"Good thing we have on raincoats so we don't get wet," she joked.

"I assume you're not hurt?" he asked again.

Mila shook her head. "I'm good."

Cruz reached out to swipe a soaked tendril from her cheek and her smile faltered as her eyes locked with his. Rain continued to fall around them, but he didn't even care. Nor did he care about being completely soaked through.

The hunger staring back at him had gotten to the point of being impossible to ignore. What would one taste hurt? They'd both admitted their desire for each other.

But Cruz didn't know which one of them had more to lose by entering into something other than a working relationship.

"Nobody has to know," she told him, as if she knew his very thoughts. "Just us."

They were both adults who craved the same thing, and she had a very valid point. Nobody had to know. Whatever they did or didn't do was nobody's business.

She inched forward. "Cruz."

That did him in. His name on a whisper sliding through those full lips...

Cruz covered her mouth with his. Between the desire, the circumstances, and the way she looked at him with longing in those emerald eyes, his control finally snapped.

They'd been building to this inevitable moment, but he'd had no idea the fierce impact kissing Mila would have on his system.

He'd never had a woman literally come alive in his arms. She opened for him and gripped his shoulders, releasing all of that fiery passion he knew bubbled just below her carefully made-up surface. Cruz swept his tongue into her mouth as he pulled her against him. He turned, taking her body farther on top of his and away from the wet ground. She let out a groan and shifted angles, as if trying to absorb every bit of pleasure he would give her.

Damn it, he wished they were inside in a warm bed or, hell, even on the couch. Anywhere but out in the chilly rain and mud along the flooded creek bank.

His hand slid beneath her jacket and T-shirt and he nearly groaned himself when his thumb grazed the silky skin there.

The warmth of her body in juxtaposition to the elements pulled him even deeper into a fantasy where they were inside with nothing stopping them from taking that next step toward ultimate pleasure.

Mila arched against his touch and adjusted her body over his. She returned his kiss with aggressiveness that could only be described as pent-up passion. He wanted nothing more than to be the man who pulled everything out of her. The man to give her all the indulgences she desired and craved.

But not like this. Not here.

Cruz eased her aside and pulled back from her lips. He slid his hand from beneath her shirt and settled it at her hip as he stared into her bright green eyes. Droplets slid down her cheeks and clung to her long, dark lashes. The lipstick smear below her bottom lip turned him on even more. Knowing he'd been the one to undo all of that perfection because she'd gotten lost in the moment pulled something territorial out of him.

"You deserve more than this," he told her. "I'm sure this isn't what you had in mind when you decided to come with me."

A soft smile flirted around her lips. "I didn't have expectations, but I'm not complaining."

No, she didn't look the least bit upset.

"Let's finish going around the property," he suggested.

Cruz came to his feet and helped steady her in those boots that were too big. Once he got back onto the four-wheeler, he held on to her hand to assist her as well. She wrapped her arms around him a little tighter this time and rested her head near his shoulder.

They'd crossed that proverbial barrier they'd sworn they shouldn't. In the span of just a few moments, they'd reached a level of comfort he hadn't expected but didn't want to give up.

The question now was…how much further would they go?

Five

The moment they got back into the garage, Mila shivered against the cold that had penetrated her clothing and skin. Cruz closed the garage door and pulled off his jacket and boots. Mila did the same, not knowing if what they'd started outside would carry over into the house. She couldn't deny herself, not when he'd touched her, kissed her, as if she was the very breath he needed to survive.

She wanted more. Cruz had sparked something within her that she hadn't felt in so long, if ever. Maybe her curiosity for more stemmed from them being trapped together, but she had been attracted to him from the moment they'd met in Miami. Never in her life did she think he'd reciprocate her feelings or that either of them would act on the urges. She'd been attracted to plenty of people over the years, but that didn't always lead to a romantic encounter. This attraction was on a whole different level.

But there was only so much self-control a person could have, and Cruz Westbrook made her want to push past the barrier of common sense.

Thankfully, they'd snapped at the same time and given in. But had she just scratched an itch for him, or did he still have that yearning to continue what they'd started?

When Cruz turned to face her, she had her answer. The hunger in his eyes had definitely intensified from what she'd seen earlier. They'd ridden around the property another twenty minutes before coming back. She'd held on to him the entire time, relishing his strength and broad frame.

Maybe strength didn't have to be an alarming or worrisome trait. Thoughts of her father hovered on the edge of her mind, but she pushed them away.

"We should get out of these cold, wet clothes," he told her in a low, husky tone that made her shiver once more.

Why did his comment sound like a delicious invitation?

Mila didn't want to think, she just wanted to feel and forget, even if only for a short time.

She kept her eyes locked on his as she reached for the hem of the tee he'd given her. The way he watched her every move with anticipation fueled her with a power unlike one she'd ever known. She needed that strength, needed that control for reasons she never wanted to explain.

The shirt came up and over her head and she tossed it aside. His gaze traveled over her curves, and she was damn proud of each one. She loved her body or she wouldn't be in this industry. But she loved that he looked like he wanted to pounce on her even more. She'd welcome that intense passion in a heartbeat.

When her thumbs hooked in the waistband of the sweats, Mila slowly eased them down over her hips and thighs, then scissored her legs to kick them off.

Standing only in her simple pale pink bra and panties, Mila propped her hands on her hips and cocked her head. "Did you only want me out of those wet clothes or are you joining me?" she asked.

"Oh, I'm joining," he confirmed. "I'm enjoying this view first."

Shivers raced through her, and they had nothing to do with her damp, chilled skin. Did he understand her need for this moment? Did he know how his empowerment of her made him all the more appealing?

Cruz started removing his wet clothes and she summoned all of her restraint to remain still. She definitely took her chance to appreciate his body. He clearly didn't get those taut muscles from sitting behind a desk or traveling the world looking for the next big artist, model, or photographer.

"You're not done." He nodded toward her undergarments and gave her a crooked grin that curled her toes. "Those are wet, too."

Mila pulled in a deep breath as she reached around and flicked the fastener of her bra. The straps slid down her arms and she released the piece to fall silently to the floor. Once she rid herself of her bottoms, she didn't even think as she closed the distance between them and reached for his boxer briefs.

The back of her fingers grazed his lower abdomen and his muscles tightened as he sucked in a breath. She stared back at him with a smile as she carefully removed the last article of clothing that separated them.

Finally. Maybe this was a mistake, but she wasn't turning back now. She had the control; she could see it in the intensity of his stare. He enjoyed relinquishing his power to her, and that was so refreshing and surprising. She'd have to deal with that whole jumble of feelings later—much later.

She wasn't sure if she reached for him first or he grabbed her, but none of that mattered now. Mila pressed her bare body against his and had never felt anything more…well, more. She couldn't even find the thoughts to complete how unbelievably perfect this moment felt, but she was done. She wanted out of her head and into this very second.

Cruz released her long enough to open the door leading into the house, and before she knew what he was doing, he lifted her to carry her inside. As if he could get any sexier.

She looped her arms around his neck and let him lead her anywhere he wanted. She was too far gone to speak or offer any thoughts. Completely at his mercy, she trembled at the possibilities.

"You're cold," he murmured as he headed through the kitchen and down the hall toward his bedroom.

"Maybe," she agreed. "But I have a feeling you're going to remedy that."

The low growl emanating from his chest vibrated against her. Mila smiled, knowing she was the one who'd caused him to break his own rule about getting involved within a working relationship.

They could still have that…but right now, business had no space in their lives. They were secluded, cut off from the rest of the world as if it didn't even exist. And for however long she could take advantage of this moment, she damn well would. She'd never been selfish in her life. She'd been in fight-or-flight mode for as long as she could remember, working to just survive on her own.

This was her time and she was done making excuses or apologies about it.

As soon as they crossed the threshold to his room, Cruz set her down. He framed her face and claimed her mouth once again, as if he couldn't get enough. She knew the feeling.

Before she knew what he was doing, he'd released her and turned away. Confused, Mila watched as he went into his adjoining bath. The water started up and another burst of arousal spiraled through her. Oh, damn. She'd never showered with a man before, but this was the best way to get warm and continue everything they'd started.

Cruz came back to the doorway and rested his hands on the frame above his head. The way he'd displayed himself was hotter than any fantasy she'd ever had—and he knew full well what he looked like and what he was doing. As if she needed anymore coaxing at this point.

"Care to join me?" he asked.

"I like my showers scalding."

He chuckled and stepped aside for her to enter. "I can guarantee things are about to get hot."

The promise he threw down had her moving into that shower and gasping at its size. The entire bathroom was completely open, and the back wall of windows overlooked the swollen river behind the house. Rain showerheads suspended from the ceiling already created steam, inviting her in.

"The windows are one-way," he explained. "Even if someone could get onto my property, nobody can see in."

The area had an outdoor ambiance while still being very private...which made the entire atmosphere even sexier. There was something so freeing about this space, as if she could do anything she wanted and completely be herself.

Cruz stepped in behind her and wrapped his arms around her waist, pulling her back against his chiseled body and obvious arousal. Mila laid her hands over his, amazed at how he'd made her feel so comfortable while still turned on and ready for everything they were about to enter into.

"You're so damn sexy," he murmured in her ear.

She'd never felt more so than right that very moment.

Mila dropped her head back onto his shoulder as he trailed his lips over her neck and walked her toward the shower. Steam started to fill the room, making the ambiance hotter. Or maybe this could be classified as romantic.

No. There couldn't be romance between them. She never wanted to get involved with a man who would ultimately control her. Cruz had too much say on the future of her career. She'd vowed long ago not to be like her mother, not to lose herself, and to always maintain the upper hand in her own life.

This temporary fling was perfect. She could take all she wanted without losing a piece of herself to a powerful man.

"You're tensing up."

His whispered words fell on her bare skin, and she shoved her wayward thoughts into the back of her mind. She'd told herself to enjoy the moment, to get out of her own head, and that's exactly what she intended to do.

Mila turned in his arms and flattened her palms against his chest. He continued to walk her until her back hit the side tile wall right next to the windows. The warm spray consumed them, only adding to her intense pleasure and anticipation.

She thought for sure he'd kiss her again, but Cruz had other ideas. Gripping her wrists, he pulled her arms above her head. Mila sucked in a breath at the vulnerable position he'd put her in, but she definitely wasn't complaining. How could she when he took several moments to admire her on display like this?

Okay, maybe she didn't mind giving up control in certain situations.

"Perfection," he murmured before stepping forward once again, still holding her arms up.

Cruz covered her mouth with his for the briefest of kisses before he moved farther down the column of her throat to the swell of one breast. She used the wall as leverage as she pressed herself toward his touch. She wanted that mouth on her—she wanted him to do anything to bring her even more pleasure. These past couple of days had been the longest form of foreplay she'd ever had in her life, but she had a feeling that every moment leading up to the main event would be worth it.

Cruz managed to grasp both of her wrists in one hand as he covered her breast with his mouth and slid his free hand down her torso. The man offered a full-body experience and she wanted to savor every euphoric second.

Mila dropped her head back and closed her eyes. She parted her legs as Cruz's hand moved to her core. He eased one finger, then two, inside her, nearly driving her to the brink with just that simple touch. She'd been without intimacy too long, and she wanted to hold out as long as possible. It had been a while since she let a man get close to her, and she respected herself too much to just hop into bed with anyone.

Yet she knew from the moment she'd met him that

Cruz would change her life…that he was different. She just hadn't known how much so.

Mila's hips jerked against his hand as he moved his fingers within her. His mouth found the other breast and she let every delicious sensation wash over her. Now wasn't the time to be stubborn. Cruz knew what he was doing and she shouldn't try to stop him.

His thumb flicked her most sensitive area and Mila cried out, tossing her head to the side as he worked her body with his mouth and fingers. She couldn't stop the rush of the climax and she let herself go, taking every bit of pleasure he offered.

"That's it," he crooned against her damp skin. "Let go."

Before her body even calmed from the intensity, Cruz lifted her against the tiles.

"Wrap your legs around me," he demanded.

Mila instantly complied as Cruz pressed one hand next to her head and plunged into her. She cried out once again at the extreme pleasure that consumed her. Water trickled down his dark skin. Droplets clung to his lips and Mila wanted to taste him.

She gripped the back of his neck and pulled his mouth to hers. She worked the kiss while he worked their bodies. Using the word *perfect* might be premature and naive, but she couldn't recall a more perfect moment in her entire life.

Water sluiced between them, causing an even more amazing bit of friction between their bodies. Mila eased her lips from his, then stared down at the stretch of skin where they were connected. She wanted to take in every bit of this experience, to lock the moments into her memories forever.

Mila lifted her gaze and landed right on his. In that moment, she let go once again and Cruz's body tensed as he reached his climax as well. He didn't look away, didn't attempt to kiss her again. Those heavy lids with dark lashes framed his beautiful eyes and she found herself getting lost even more than she'd ever planned.

So where did that leave them once they stepped out of the shower?

Six

"Electric is back on."

Mila sat up in bed and shoved her hair away from her face. She blinked at Cruz striding through his bedroom with two cups of coffee. She hadn't meant to fall asleep in there, but after that relaxing shower, he'd conveniently coaxed her into staying in his bed.

Where he'd pleasured her all over again.

"That's great news," she stated, taking one of the mugs. "Cell service is back, I assume?"

He pulled her cell from the pocket of his shorts and tossed it onto the rumpled sheet by her hip. "Back up and running. I'm going to get on finding a crew for the bridge, but that will take a while. We can't get you across until the waters recede more, so you'll likely be here a few more days."

She pulled up her emails and took a sip of the coffee, made exactly how she liked it.

"I should be going as soon as possible," she murmured, her finger hovering over her phone but her eyes locked on his.

Cruz set his mug on the bedside table and pressed his hands on either side of her hips as he loomed above her.

"You might as well cancel that B and B," he growled. "I like you right where you are."

In his bed, no doubt. They'd moved beyond sex to a level of intimacy she hadn't intended. Her control had slipped somewhere along the way and she needed to get it back. She'd keep her booking…just in case. This bedroom situation wasn't ideal and it sure as hell wasn't permanent.

"I should get up and get ready." She reached around his arm and set her mug next to his. "I have some emails and calls to catch up on."

Before she could escape off the bed, Cruz gently tipped her chin up with his thumb and forefinger, forcing her to look him in the eyes.

"What happened?" he asked.

"Happened?"

"You've retreated into your head again and you're trying to make a quick getaway." He cupped the side of her face and stroked her cheek with his thumb. "Don't have regrets now. There's no space for that."

"I don't have regrets." And she didn't. Last night had been beyond amazing. "I just know what this is and what it isn't."

He stared another moment before releasing her and taking a step back. She didn't know why he had that look in his eye and she couldn't quite pinpoint it. Something akin to sadness or confusion, maybe even a sliver of frustration. But she couldn't get tied up with Cruz. They had different lives, different goals, and those were just added reasons for them not to get involved. The main one being that she was still holding out for this project with *Opulence* to be successful. In fact, she was desperate to make it work.

Her lease was up in Miami, her next project hadn't even been scheduled yet, and she had to get her life on track. Her time for trysts was over, and now that morning had dawned, the real world needed her attention.

Mila swung her legs over the side of the bed, adjusting the T-shirt he'd given her to sleep in. She wished she'd gotten up before him and sneaked into her own room to freshen up, but apparently, she'd been sleeping too well. She just needed to take a shower, wash her hair, and get her day going.

Once she had her own clothes and some makeup on, she'd feel better. Hopefully, she could get at least one more project scheduled and start narrowing down her housing options. All she knew at this point was that she needed to be in a city that she hadn't been in before. She wanted a fresh start and the new possibilities that came with it.

"I can make breakfast," she offered, grabbing her coffee mug. "Just let me get ready first."

Cruz nodded. "Go right ahead. Whatever you find is fine."

He left her as he went into the adjoining bath and closed the door. She clutched her cell and coffee mug as she stared at the empty space. She'd pushed him away, not really knowing how to deal with the proverbial morning-after feelings.

But if she was going to regroup and move on as they'd agreed to last night, she couldn't linger in his bed. It would be all too easy to snuggle beneath those covers and nestle right into his side. But reality beckoned. They weren't as closed off to the world as they had been last night. With cell service back, they had access to everything, and once the waters went down a bit, they would find a way for her to leave.

Mila didn't want to go, but she also couldn't live in this fantasy world, either. She'd had her fun, her night of passion with the most amazing man, and now she had to focus on getting her personal and professional life back on track.

Once she showered and fixed her hair and makeup, Mila chose a perfect outfit for the day: a simple wrap dress that accentuated her curves but stopped just at the knee. She pulled out her favorite pair of backless kitten heels and instantly had a boost in confidence. While she had no idea what to make for breakfast, she headed to the kitchen to find something to whip up.

She sincerely hoped she had good news waiting in her inbox. If she could land that next project, maybe that would give her a better direction of where she'd like to relocate. Of course, she'd been looking across the country in various places, but she hadn't quite found the right city for her. Miami had been wonderful and a nice stepping-stone, but it wasn't her forever place.

Mila set her cell on the island and pulled up one of her favorite playlists. A little bit of this and that. Her music, like everything else in her life, all depended on her mood. Right now, she had a hopeful feeling that everything was going to work out and she was well on her way to bigger things with her career.

Even if she hadn't slept with Cruz, she didn't doubt one bit that *Opulence* was the opportunity of a lifetime. Once the fall and winter ads came out with her photos, she prayed the right people would see her and get her where she needed to be. Because modeling wasn't her be-all and end-all. She had bigger plans that included designing clothes for women with all body types and maybe creating a lifestyle brand someday, and the idea scared the hell out of her. But she refused to live in fear and she refused to settle.

After taking stock of the fridge and the pantry, Mila settled for making a breakfast casserole. That way, while everything baked, she could get some work done and give Cruz time to come downstairs. She needed to say something to break that tension and make him understand that she hadn't meant to be so harsh. The last thing she wanted was for there to be anything awkward settling between them. There was so much more on the line than just hormones and needs.

Once Mila had the simple casserole assembled, she set the timer and put the pan in the oven. She grabbed her cell and turned her attention to work. She had a few emails from Realtors in LA, Dallas and Chicago. All had special listings fitting her budget and her style—she was expecting a nice payout from this particular photo shoot. But those weren't the emails she was looking for. She scrolled a bit more and there it was. From the luxury goods company doing the next photo shoot she wanted to book, Meyer and Meyer.

Life would be easier with an agent, but until she got more images in her portfolio, she'd have to settle for representing herself.

The email indicated that they had been trying to reach her and for her to call at her earliest convenience.

Mila pulled in a deep breath and dialed the number. She stared at the timer on the oven ticking down. These few moments could decide where she would head next and if she would be employed beyond *Opulence*. Her spread with them wouldn't come out until the late fall, so she needed to get something moving along until the promise of bigger things developed.

"Good morning, Meyer and Meyer. How can I direct your call?"

"Hello, this is Mila Hale. I'm returning Arthur Meyer's call."

"One moment, Ms. Hale."

The silence while being on hold only got her heart beating faster. She truly had no idea which way this would go. She'd sent in her best shots and done a video. She'd also spoken with Arthur himself on the phone just last week and she knew she'd been in the final three. But was she good enough to be the next face for the company's clothing line?

Mila had no idea if the other two models were curvy or thin, but she knew everything she'd done had been her absolute best. That's all she could do.

"Mila," Arthur finally answered. "Thank you for getting back to me. I tried calling a couple times yesterday, with no answer."

"You wouldn't believe it, but I'm in Northern California and in the middle of a storm," she explained, hating to sound like she was making excuses. "We just got cell service and power back this morning. I'm sorry I missed you yesterday."

"No worries at all. I hope you're safe."

"I'm perfectly safe. Thank you."

She really wished they could cut the small talk and just get to the yes-or-no portion of this conversation. Her nerves were already on edge from Cruz and where they stood this morning. She really didn't want to add to her anxiety.

"Good to hear." He cleared his throat. "As you know, you were in the top three for models the Meyer brand had chosen. We're looking for the long-term face of our Grace line. The team spent hours poring through all of the images and videos sent by the candidates. At this time, we've decided to go with another."

Mila's breath caught in her throat, her heart sank,

and she moved around the counter to take a seat. Arthur kept going, but she'd tuned him out at this point. What did it matter? He wasn't offering her a job or even giving her other options. This was it. He didn't want what she had to offer.

Rejections stung no matter how many times she received them. With each one, she only heard her father's negative voice echoing in her head. But she'd prove him—and the entire industry—wrong. She'd gotten jobs before, so she knew she was cut out for this, plus she had thick skin. No way could she have grown up with Russ Hale and gotten through life without developing a tough exterior.

"We will keep your images on file, and if we see an area we think you will shine in, we will definitely reach out," Arthur stated. "I'm sure this isn't the news you wanted to hear, but I hope you understand you did make it through several hundred prospects."

She might as well be number four hundred. The end result was the same. She'd failed just like ol' Russ told her she would.

"I understand and appreciate the opportunity," she told him, forcing a smile because she knew it would come through in her tone.

Despite, and aside from, last night, Mila had always maintained a high level of professionalism. She had no intention of ever burning bridges, because she never knew when she'd have to cross back over one.

"I look forward to seeing great things from you," he added. "Have a good day and stay safe with that storm."

Mila said her goodbye and disconnected the call. She laid the cell on the counter and covered her face with her hands. She just needed a minute to regroup. She deserved a little pity party, but unfortunately, she wasn't alone in the house and couldn't afford to. Literally. She had to shift her focus to lining up her next job.

Her contract with *Opulence* stated that she wasn't allowed to reveal she would be working with them. That was part of their appeal and draw. They were the company that wanted to launch the average artist to stardom, so a key part of that was doing the big reveal.

If Arthur only knew what she had coming up, she wondered if he would have chosen her as the next face of their Grace line.

Damn it, she needed an agent. She and her previous agent had parted ways when he only wanted her to focus on plus-size projects and clothing. Her weight didn't define her any more than her hair color did.

Mila was banking on the images from the shoot she was supposed to do yesterday to help pad her portfolio and her bank account. She truly wished she had a little more stability and financial balance in her life, but she could only take one step at a time to get where she needed to be.

The timer beeped, pulling her from her thoughts. Mila blew out a sigh and tucked her hair behind her ears. All she could do now was get back to the grind.

This industry didn't come knocking, so she'd have to go bulldoze down some doors.

The best thing that came from rejections was her anger. Each "no" turned into fire in her veins and she became determined not to take no for an answer next time. The next thing she set her sights on, she sure as hell intended to get.

"I'm finally able to wake up like a normal person and get to work on time. Well, before this storm came through."

Cruz held his cell out as Nora's voice came through the speaker. He stepped into the kitchen just as Mila set out two plates and two mugs of steaming coffee on the island. She didn't glance his way when he came in, but Cruz kept his conversation going.

He'd overheard Mila's talk with Arthur. Cruz had never personally cared for that man or their company, though they were known to help launch models' careers. He'd been in the hallway when he'd heard her tone and knew she'd struggled to sound positive. He'd wanted to give her a few extra minutes to herself, so he called Nora to check in.

"So you're feeling better," he said to Nora. "That's great. I know Zane was starting to really worry about the morning sickness."

"Oh, he worries about everything with me," Nora laughed. "But how are things there? Any damage to the property? Zane went to check out his property, and the gazebo where we were going to be married in a few weeks is wrecked."

"Oh, damn."

Cruz took a seat at the island and glanced at Mila, who didn't seem to be interested in eating. She was doodling something on a napkin with a pen. Whatever she needed to work through, he had to take her lead and let her process it in her own way.

"Are you postponing the wedding?" he asked.

"Are you crazy? I've waited years for this. If we have to move the ceremony closer to the pond, we will. Nothing will stop this day. But I imagine Zane will have that gazebo back and even better than before."

"I'm so happy for you guys. Getting married and having a family, it's just great." He took his coffee mug and took a sip, welcoming the warmth. "And, yeah, I had damage here. A few trees down, one of them landed on Mila Hale's rental car, plus some fencing broke, and my bridge washed away."

"Oh my word, Cruz!"

"I know," he sighed. "Mila has been stuck here for two days, and I think she's getting sick of my company."

He kept his eyes on Mila, hoping she'd react to his attempt at a joke, but she simply continued to draw. He shifted a bit to try to see what had a stronghold on her attention. Was that a dress? She didn't even look up or smile or acknowledge that he was even in the room. She'd gone so far inside her head, he hoped he could get her out.

That damn phone call this morning had clearly ruined her day, and on the coattails of the awkward morning-after encounter, he imagined every conversation with Mila today would be an uphill battle.

"I wondered if you all were able to get the shoot done before things got bad," Nora replied. "Is Maddie stuck there, too?"

"Maddie couldn't get here before the storm struck."

Silence greeted him from the other end and Cruz realized that maybe he shouldn't be on speaker with Mila within earshot right now. Nora knew him better than anyone, save for his twin brother. Not that she knew him to be a playboy or take advantage of a situation, but... Hell. He'd done just that.

But Nora had already homed in on the fact that he was alone with Mila, and he didn't want her to discuss the proverbial elephant in the room.

"Is Zane around?" he asked, moving the conversation out of dangerous territory.

"I know what you're doing, and this topic is not closed," she warned. "But yes. He's right here. I love you."

"Love you, too."

Mila's pen paused. Ah, so those words caught her attention. Interesting.

"Hey, man." Zane's voice boomed through the speaker. "Nora said your bridge washed out? You good on everything?"

"I'm good. At this point, I'm just waiting on the waters to go down so I can get a crew in here to get it repaired. And once the creek isn't so swollen and rolling, I can at least get out on the kayak and head down toward the landing about a mile down the way."

Mumbling in the background filtered through the line.

"What, Nora?" Zane murmured. "I'm not asking him that."

Cruz chuckled. "Your wife-to-be is concerned because Mila is stuck here, but I assure you both that we are fine. Hopefully, we can get this shoot in within the week or we'll be behind schedule."

"We'll get it done," Zane said, sounding almost convinced. "Hell, you started with photography. You can take some pictures."

Mila's pen stopped once again, and Cruz realized she'd moved on to another napkin. This time, she was working on a raincoat and umbrella. How the hell did her doodling look like that of a professional artist?

No wonder she'd had that sketch pad the other night. Was this her secret? Did she just love to draw or was there something more meaningful behind her talent? Maybe she had a love for fashion that she hoped to grow beyond modeling. Either way, he wanted to uncover more about her, but first, he had to help her recover from this morning's bad news. And he needed to address the fact that she tried to push him away earlier. He wouldn't let regrets linger between them after what they'd shared.

"I'll leave the picture-taking to the actual professionals," Cruz told his brother. He picked up his fork and stabbed the egg, sausage and cheese casserole.

"Besides, I only did that as a hobby years ago and to get our business started."

"You still have an eye for detail."

Mila glanced up now, catching his gaze. She blinked, then put down the pen and crumpled up her napkins. She tossed them into the trash and maneuvered around the island. She took a seat beside him, but instead of digging in, she simply started picking at her food. Cruz hated knowing that she hurt, but would she even accept any encouragement from him?

"I promise not to let us get behind schedule," Cruz assured his twin brother. "No matter what I have to do."

"Great, because I need your full focus for the wedding in a few weeks."

Cruz took a bite of the dish and nearly groaned. A talented model, an artist, and a damn good cook. How many other talents did Mila keep hidden away?

"I've never been more ready. My best friend and my brother marrying is the most amazing thing that's happened to this family. Not to mention the fact that you and Dad are on speaking terms."

"I'm actually meeting with Barrett in a few days. I asked him to come to the house."

Cruz couldn't be happier. For years, their father had abandoned them—both mentally and physically. After their mother passed, he had mentally checked out. The drinking started immediately, then gambling soon followed. They lost their working ranch, and ultimately, the boys were placed in a foster home until they were old enough to be on their own.

Zane had never forgiven their father, to the point where he only referred to the man by his first name. But since the discovery of Nora's unplanned pregnancy and Zane rolling into this new title of "father," he'd softened a little. They still weren't quite to the point of hugging it out or having deep chats, but they'd all taken a step in the right direction.

"Between the wedding and the baby, we're all turning over a new leaf for the Westbrooks," Cruz stated. "Listen, I'm going to finish my breakfast and get back to work. I need to get with you later after you check that email I sent just a bit ago. There's an opportunity in Kauai I think we should look into for next summer."

"I'll get on it. I'm sure Nora would love any chance to go to Kauai."

"Getting started on those family vacations early, huh?" Cruz laughed.

Mila sipped her coffee next to him and pushed her plate aside. The food had been shifted around, but nothing was gone. Her mood had done a complete one-eighty since last night and they needed to talk. Not that he wanted to be her counselor or therapist, but at the very least, he could be a sounding board and maybe even a friend. Granted, a friendship after sleeping together sounded like working backward, but he didn't want to see her unhappy for any reason.

No wonder Nora always called him "the peacemaker."

"It's a family business," Zane replied. "Our little one will always be with us."

"I never thought you'd be a family man," Cruz admitted. "You sound happy."

"Happier than I've ever been. Now, go, get back to work. We'll touch base later, and let me know if you need anything."

What he needed was his houseguest to talk to him, but more than anything, he had to get over what happened last night. As much as he wanted— no *craved*—a replay, he knew they couldn't. They'd agreed on the one night, and he had to respect her enough to let her take the lead on their relationship moving forward. Which was damn hard because he wanted her now more than ever.

Seven

Cruz disconnected the call and placed his cell on the counter. Mila remained at the coffeepot pouring more of the brew into her mug. Evidently, this was a two- or three-cup kind of morning.

Even after replacing the pot, she kept her back to him. He didn't want to embarrass her or let on that he'd heard her call earlier. Nobody wanted an audience to rejection. He wouldn't damage her pride further, but he wanted her to know he cared, that he didn't think of her as just some quick romp. He respected her, though his actions last night might not have reflected as much.

"This casserole is amazing."

He figured he'd start with something light, just to get her talking or at least to take her mind away from that asshole Arthur, who wouldn't know talent if it smacked him in his Botoxed face.

"I learned from my mom," she murmured, still with her back to him.

"She must be quite a woman to have such a successful daughter."

Mila's soft laugh held no humor, but rather a tone akin to regret or despair. Cruz wondered if his simple statement only added to her miserable morning. Or perhaps the memory of her mother brought up a dark time. He had no idea, but he suddenly realized he wanted to know everything. How else could he understand how to approach her or any situation involving her if he didn't learn more about her personal life and background?

"My mother could have been someone amazing," she murmured.

Cruz came to his feet and moved around the large center island toward Mila. He'd definitely touched on a nerve without meaning to.

"I'm sorry. I didn't know she had passed."

Mila turned to face him as she clutched her mug. "Oh, she's very much alive. But I haven't spoken to my parents since I left, at eighteen."

The look in her eyes and that set jaw told Cruz the topic was off-limits. For now. He wasn't done trying to figure her out and uncover those carefully guarded layers. What—or who—had made her so closed off?

"I don't have a family. Not anymore," she added. "But it sounds like you're extremely close with yours. I mean, obviously, your brother, but his fiancée, too."

"Nora has been my best friend for years. I actually tried to set the two of them up, but they had their own thing going. It's kind of a long story."

Mila took a sip of her coffee, eyeing him the entire time. She tipped her head and narrowed her gaze. "You're jealous."

Cruz jerked back. "Jealous? Of what?"

"Your brother."

"Why the hell would I be jealous of him?"

Oh, they might have always been in competition with each other, but that was just a sibling thing. Especially a twin thing. But he sure as hell wasn't jealous.

"You want what he has," Mila explained.

Cruz shook his head and laughed. "I've never been in love with Nora. She's like my sister."

"I didn't mean that, though I can tell you love her." She set her mug down and focused all of her attention on him as she leveled his gaze. "You want a family. I heard it in your voice and see it in your smile when you talk about them. You wouldn't have built this giant house with this many bedrooms if you wanted to be alone."

Cruz crossed his arms over his chest, wondering how this conversation went from him needing to console her and figure her out to Mila analyzing him just from one short phone call.

"I do want a family," he agreed. "Zane was the one who always wanted to be alone, never wanting to end up like our father. But I knew I could be a great husband and father because of what I'd been through. After my mother died, my father decided his vices were more important than his boys. He decided to drown in his own misery and loss instead of helping us through ours."

There had certainly been tough times when he'd been younger, so a little resentment still lingered. But everyone deserved a second chance, and his father was only trying to right his many years of wrongs. Cruz fully believed they were well on their way to being one unit again, just like they used to be. He knew his mother would want all of her boys to be loving and close.

"And what you heard in my tone," he went on, "wasn't jealousy. It was happiness and relief that he's able to overcome our past."

A soft, sad smile danced around her lips. "Overcoming someone's past is difficult. I'm glad he was able to do that and find the best part of his life."

He wanted to know what held her back from overcoming her past. Clearly, something happened with her parents, and Mila was still so mysterious, he'd hardly found anything on her personal life on social media outside of her modeling. He knew she'd worked as an assistant to several high-society members and even a nanny for one, all while trying to get her modeling career kicked off. She'd had several small projects over the past few years, but nothing that really boosted her to the level he believed she deserved. Her social media had a large following and interaction, which is how the talent scouts at *Opulence* had stumbled upon her. The confidence and sexy style combined with class had been the perfect combo to gain her all the attention.

Cruz honestly couldn't believe she hadn't catapulted to stardom yet, but the moment Mila completed this project for him, she'd be gone. She'd have more jobs than she could handle, and she would be able to pick and choose what she wanted between brands and companies wanting to use her as the face of their products.

Which gave him the best idea. Their shoot might be running late and off schedule, but that didn't mean he couldn't do a little work behind the scenes.

"I apologize for being rude earlier."

Mila's abrupt change in direction had him shifting his own thoughts.

"This morning," she added.

"I didn't think you were rude," he admitted, leaning his hip against the counter. "You seemed to have regrets or doubts and didn't know how to show your emotions other than to run."

Mila pursed her lips as she stared at Cruz, but ultimately shrugged. "I don't have regrets, but we can't do that again, and I don't want to give you the wrong impression of me or how I am as a professional. I won't fail at this project, Cruz. I can't."

Her voice cracked on that final word, but she blinked back those unshed tears and tipped her up chin. The woman refused to admit any vulnerability, and he couldn't understand why she thought she had to remain so strong through everything.

Who in her past made her think every moment

had to be perfect? He could understand the physical need to always be polished in her profession, but this mindset went much deeper than anything on the surface. Someone had mentally damaged her and she obviously thought she had to go through every obstacle on her own.

"I never fail, and you're with me now," he assured her. "If I thought you were a failure, we wouldn't have taken you on for one of our biggest projects of the year."

"Which is why we can't let last night happen again." She took a step back and Cruz knew she had mentally as well. "I have to move forward. My morning sort of fell apart, so I also need to get some work done. I'm sure you do, too. I can clean the kitchen—"

"I'll do the kitchen," he stated. "You cooked. That's the rule."

Her perfectly arched brows drew in. "You're going to clean all of this?"

"Why wouldn't I? It's not fair for you to cook *and* clean."

That bright green gaze continued to hold him in place. He could practically see the thoughts bumping into each other in her mind. He might not know much, if anything, about her past, but he knew hurt when it stared right back at him.

Cruz closed the distance between them and rested his hands on her delicate shoulders. She tensed beneath his touch, but he didn't move. Someone needed to be there for her. At this point in her life, she needed someone she could lean on. Not because she was weak, but because she'd been so strong on her own for too damn long.

He didn't want her to worry about anything, least of all him and her career or their intimacy. Those were two totally separate relationships, and he needed her to understand that one had nothing to do with the other.

But there was more he needed to address. The crux of her issues, from what he could see, had to be a man who had damaged a piece of her soul. Cruz wouldn't let that point go ignored another second of her life.

"I'm sorry for the bastard who gave you the wrong impression of men," he started. "Whoever he is, I hope he's out of your life, but I'm assuming it's your father."

She said nothing, she just continued to look up at him with eyes that he could get lost in if he didn't watch his step. She didn't need him to heal her, and she didn't need him to be her dragon slayer. She needed him to be her stepping-stone to the modeling world so she could crack the fashion industry wide open and really flourish. Likely, that connection was just another reason she felt the need to have such a tough exterior with him.

From a personal angle, though, she needed a friend. At the very least, he could offer that, but now that he knew how amazing they were together, he couldn't dismiss his own emotions…or hers. He knew she only wanted to distance herself because of fear.

"You are strong—you've proven that over and over," he went on, making sure to keep his eyes locked onto hers so she understood each word he said. "What happened last night has absolutely nothing to do with your work for me."

When Mila remained silent, Cruz dropped his arms and smiled. "I have an idea. You game for a surprise?"

Mila threw up her arms and sighed. "I can't keep up with you. You want a family, you'll clean the kitchen, you want to surprise me. Are you a CEO of a billion-dollar company or a housewife?"

Cruz couldn't help but laugh as he motioned for her to follow him. "I hope you have casual clothes."

"Casual by whose standards?" she asked as they reached the hallway.

He turned and pointed a finger at himself. "Mine."

She narrowed her eyes and held up a hand. "Are we going back out into the flood?"

"I have something else in mind, but if you need to borrow more of my clothes…"

An image of her in his T-shirt flashed through his mind. The way the material hugged every part of her—even before getting wet—was something he'd remember forever. Mila had created an entire bank of fantasies all just from wearing one simple shirt. He never knew a plain white tee could have so much power.

"I mean, I have something that could be deemed as casual," she admitted. "Are we staying inside?"

"Yes."

"Are we—"

"No more questions." He motioned toward the steps. "Go change and meet me right here. You have two minutes."

"Two minutes? Are you insane?"

Cruz started toward the hall leading to his room. "Better hurry."

Mila had no idea what the hell he had in mind, nor did she know what his version of casual dress meant. Did he mean jeans and nice shirt, leggings and a hoodie, or a birthday suit? She hated surprises, hated not having control in any given situation.

So she threw on what she deemed casual and rushed back downstairs fifteen minutes later.

"I changed and picked up the kitchen in the time you took to get ready."

Mila shrugged as she reached the bottom. "Good for you. I wasn't given much direction, so I had to think about my clothes."

His eyes raked over her. "And that's what you call casual?"

She glanced down to her black distressed jeans and her cream cropped sweatshirt that draped off one shoulder. She'd paired her outfit with her favorite wedge sneaker and didn't see one thing wrong with her look. Then again, Cruz only had on a white T-shirt and a pair of sweats that sat low on his narrow hips. She didn't know how the man could look like he'd stepped off the page of a catalog in this outfit, but he was just as sexy now as he was in a suit or completely naked.

"If you could see everything else I packed—yes, this is casual," she informed him. "Besides, I'm running out of clothes, because I thought I'd only be in town for two days, for the shoot."

"You don't have to wear clothes when you run out," he suggested.

His words startled her until she saw that crooked smile.

"We agreed, no more sex," she reminded him.

"You're the one threatening no clothes," he volleyed back. "And I never mentioned sex at all. You just did."

Mila couldn't help but laugh. "Stop confusing me, and tell me what this surprise is. I don't like being in the dark."

"No, you don't like the lack of power." He reached up and tapped the tip of her nose with his fingertip. "So feel free to surprise me anytime and you'll have all the control."

Cruz started to walk on the other side of the steps to a different hallway than the one leading to his bedroom. She hadn't been to this part of the house before, but she assumed she was to follow.

"Wait." She stopped and held up her hands as he turned back to look at her. "We're not doing those pictures your brother mentioned, are we? Because I'll seriously need to change and work on my hair and makeup."

Cruz quirked a dark brow. "You'll have to follow me to find out. And, damn it, relax."

He offered nothing else as they headed down the hall, then turned down another hall. The size of this place was absolutely crazy for one man, which made her wonder how big a family he wanted. Or maybe he'd built something so vast because he'd lost so much as a child.

Mila found it easier to delve into other people's issues than her own. She could dissect anyone's past and problems and come up with solutions, but in order to help herself, she'd have to face those harsh memories, and she'd much rather forget that part of her life ever happened.

Cruz stopped at the end of the hall at a set of double glass doors. The room on the other side was dark, so she couldn't make out where they were going.

"Do you have one of those home theaters?" she asked, her anxiety rolling over to anticipation. "Because I could go for a movie and some popcorn."

"Is that so?"

He pushed the doors open and the lights immediately flickered on, revealing much more than she'd imagined.

"Are you serious?" Mila slowly stepped into the room and stopped just inside the doorway as she tried to take in everything at once. "This is every kid's dream."

Cruz moved in behind her. "And some adults'."

Mila laughed as she ventured farther into the room full of games, from pinball machines to table tennis, even a bowling alley taking up one entire end. The opposite end held a big screen covering the whole wall, with three rows of cozy, oversize leather recliners lined up in front of it.

"How do you get any work done?" she asked, turning her attention back to him.

"I forget about this room, honestly. I can admit I might have gone over the top when building. I knew I wanted a family someday, and when Zane and I were younger, our mom always loved family game-and-movie night."

Mila's heart flipped in her chest. She hadn't expected her heart to get involved in this shut-in scenario, but how could she not get emotionally invested? Her heart ached for the young boy who had so much love in his home only to have it all ripped away.

Even though she'd never had love in her home, she understood that longing for more. Cruz had built his adult world around the possibility of starting his own family while she'd run fast and far from anything resembling a trapped unit. She could understand where he was coming from, wanting to make all things right in his world that he hadn't been able to control before. Maybe their lives paralleled each other more closely than she thought, and maybe that's why he seemed so hell-bent on making her happy.

"You know who is going to love this room?" she asked. "Your new niece or nephew."

Cruz seemed to consider that possibility for a moment before a wide smile spread across his face. "I can't wait to spoil her, because I can only see Nora as having a little image of herself."

Mila laughed. This man truly loved his family if he'd already had such thoughts so soon after hearing the baby news. She could easily imagine him as the doting uncle, and the little tug her heart gave made her pause. An image of Cruz with a child on his shoulders instantly sprang to mind and she had to push those warm, familial thoughts aside. She wasn't part of this strong family dynamic, which really shouldn't bother her…yet a niggle of something too close to envy speared her heart.

"I'm definitely getting birthday party vibes here." Mila focused back on this amazing room and the potential. "With balloons and streamers. Kids running everywhere. Uncle Cruz wearing one of those silly party hats."

"I can't wait," he admitted with a wide smile that lit up those gorgeous dark eyes.

Another pang of jealousy hit her. Why? She'd never even thought about kids' birthday parties before, and now she suddenly wanted to be around to see Cruz in that exact atmosphere.

Mila glanced around the room once again before heading toward the table tennis setup. "I've never played. I mean, I've seen it before, but I've never had a chance."

"This is your lucky day."

Cruz opened some floor-to-ceiling storage cabinets until he found the paddles and ball. He twirled one of the paddles in his hand and that grin of his did silly, girlish things to her nerves. She shouldn't still be excited or turned on by that playful smile, yet there she was, unable to look anywhere else.

"Don't you have work to do?" she asked. "I believe you told your brother you'd get with him."

"Later. Right now, you need a distraction and Zane isn't going anywhere."

She'd forgotten about her bad morning for a just a moment, but Cruz was putting his entire schedule on hold to bring her happiness. Damn it. Why did she have to find him so endearing? Having the hottest lover of her entire life turn into one of the sincerest men, added to the fact he was also her temporary boss…this relationship just got more and more complicated.

And she'd gone and thrown in that one-night stand to really confuse matters.

"You don't have to distract me." She took one of the paddles he offered. "But I wouldn't mind kicking your butt at this table tennis game."

He scoffed. "You said you never played."

"I'm a fast learner." She shrugged and sent him a wink. "You've been warned."

His rich laughter washed over her, filling her with a sense that things might just be okay. But she wondered just where this relationship was going, because they were far beyond anything she'd set out for. And she didn't know how much longer she could avoid the fact that Cruz Westbrook just might be perfect.

Eight

"You weren't lying about being a fast learner."

So far, she'd beaten him at table tennis, every pinball game, and bowling. But she'd beamed and laughed the entire time, and that's all he cared about.

"What's left?" she asked, looking around. "Any games hidden that I need to win?"

As much as he needed to get to work and answer the cell that had been vibrating nonstop in his pocket, he didn't want to leave this moment. They'd run through the gamut of emotions and circumstances, but throwing in something fun and light seemed to take the edge off their lives. He never took days off from work, but he couldn't think of a better reason than Mila to ditch his responsibilities for the day.

"How about that movie?" he suggested. "I can whip us up some snacks and popcorn."

"Really?" Her brows shot up as she clapped, and he didn't recall seeing her happier since she'd been here.

He didn't care what emails or voice messages waited on him. After the morning Mila had experienced, he would do anything to bring her some happy distractions. He could make her personal life a little brighter now, and he'd start working on the professional side later that afternoon. In addition to the work she did for *Opulence,* he had some ideas that could turn her career around.

"What movie?" she asked.

He mentioned a new one he had that hadn't even been released yet, but already had a media frenzy surrounding the kick-ass plot and celebrity lineup.

"How in the world did you get that?"

Cruz shrugged. "Perks of knowing the right people. Now, go have a seat and let me get everything going."

She took a step toward him and then another. Getting lost in those bright green eyes might just be his new favorite hobby. Messing up that red lipstick could also a front-runner.

Her familiar fruity scent surrounded him, and that mass of curly hair made him want to thrust his fingers in and tug just enough to tip her head back. He wanted to see that look she gave him just before he covered her lips with his. The look of longing and desire…

Damn. He needed to get his hormones under control. He'd never had that issue before.

"What can I do to help?" she offered. "How about I get the snacks and you do the movie since I have no clue how to do that."

Cruz nodded. "Deal."

Mila turned and made it to the open doorway before looking back. "If I'm not back in ten minutes, come find me. I'll probably get lost with all these hallways."

The second she was gone, Cruz pulled out his cell and typed several notes. He wanted to get the wording just right before he sent his request to the masses. He didn't typically ask for favors, especially with one of his own models, but Mila wasn't like other models—or any other woman he'd ever known, for that matter.

Cruz wondered if he'd crossed into dangerous territory with this one. Everything between them had happened so fast and with such intensity. He wasn't sorry, more like intrigued as to why her and why now? Could she actually flip that arousal switch to Off? How could she pretend that last night didn't matter? He could still taste her, still feel her body pressed against his as she lost herself in the passion.

Bringing up every intimate moment and rolling it around in his thoughts wouldn't help this situation. Mila would likely be here another few days at least, and that was before the shoot even started. He couldn't wait to see what they came up with as far as the project went. Their art director, Maddie, had some amazing ideas, and with Mila being the subject, this was shaping up to be one of their most successful seasons to date.

Cruz got the movie all set up and Mila still wasn't back. He didn't think she actually got lost, but he took those extra few minutes to fine-tune his notes and decided to go ahead and send the messages. He had a few close contacts who would get on this request immediately. He wanted to keep everything private and not clue Mila in on his idea until he formulated a solid plan.

If he focused on Mila's career, then he wouldn't have time to focus on their intimacy, because he could get lost in those thoughts. He could get lost in that woman. And that would all make for a very messy working relationship. He couldn't have both with her, because she'd made it clear that they were just a onetime thing.

"Okay, that was the best movie ever. No wonder there's so much hype around the release next weekend."

Mila shifted in her oversize recliner toward Cruz, who had taken the one right next to her. The credits rolled on the screen, providing the only light in the room, but she could still make out the smile on his handsome face.

Being attracted to Cruz Westbrook was not her smartest move. Sleeping with him had been an even bigger mistake, but she wasn't sorry. She couldn't have prevented that night from happening no matter what. The amount of want and need she'd had for him far surpassed any she'd ever known…and she still longed for him just as much.

Cruz turned in his chair, his arm brushing hers as his eyes landed on her. Every single look from him turned into a full-body experience. Somehow, the man seemed to touch her with his stare. She felt it deep in her soul. The way he observed her made her wonder if he could read her every thought. He made her think more, made her want to open up and share her past with him, but beyond that, she wanted to know everything about his.

But she couldn't ask such things. She couldn't keep him at arm's length and pull him in at the same time. She'd made up her mind to keep a safe distance and she had to maintain that vow for both their sakes.

"I thought you might like that," he told her. "It was better than working."

"True, but reality awaits, and I still have to find a place to live."

She hadn't meant to voice that part out loud, but there it was. At least he didn't know she'd been rejected earlier. That would be much too embarrassing to rehash, especially to the man who was taking a chance on her.

"You're not going back to Miami?" he asked.

She hugged a knee to her chest and faced him more squarely. Living arrangements she could discuss, but not the fact that her career hung on by a tiny thread…a thread he held. She didn't like the position this put her in. She didn't want anyone else control-

ling her career. That had been one of the big draws
to this industry. Having the say-so over work and the
direction it took had been so important.

"I'm not sure where I'm going, but my lease is
up at the end of the month in Miami and I thought
I would have some idea of where I wanted to go by
now, but nothing has hit me."

"Considering you can work from nearly anywhere
and you travel, you should choose a place that has
things that interest you."

Financial stability interested her at the moment...
so did the man before her. But she wasn't settling in
Northern California. The forest and hills didn't interest her, nor did the freak flooding. All of that seemed
much too similar to the hometown she'd worked too
damn hard to escape. She needed a city and people
and a vision for her future. She had to make her life
100 percent opposite of what it had been.

"You like art."

His words pulled her back and she jerked.

"Your drawings on the napkins earlier," he
amended. "Those weren't just random doodles. You
have a talent."

She'd been so lost in her own thoughts at that
moment that she hadn't noticed him watching her.

"Drawing has always been an escape," she admitted.

"Have you always drawn clothes?"

Damn, he really had been paying attention. She'd
been inspired by the crazy floods and all the rain.
She hadn't done a raincoat and matching umbrella

before, but the little bit she did earlier already had her mind playing with designs and patterns. She'd even thrown in a pair of adorable matching rain boots.

Nobody knew about her dream. Not one person. She lived alone and had sketches all over her condo. There was a freedom like none other when she had her pad and pencil. She could do anything she wanted, with nobody to tell her any different.

"Initially, I liked to draw people in general. When I'd go out with my mom, I always had a little notepad and I just started out with faces or hands." Mila found herself opening up when she'd had no intention of exposing any portion of her past. "Somewhere along the way, that morphed into fashion. As a teen, it wasn't always easy to find clothes to fit a curvy girl. I couldn't figure out why everything was made for petite girls. Whatever clothes I had usually had to be altered, so I started piddling with my mom's sewing machine to tailor them. Then I started drawing my dream wardrobe. Years later, I'm still sketching."

Cruz laid his hand over hers. The credits had stopped, and the screen had gone white, casting a soft glow over one side of his face. The light was enough for her to see the interest and compassion in his eyes. He made her want to reveal this secret part of her life, the areas she'd kept hidden for so long. The tiny crack she'd allowed gave him the room to wiggle deeper into her world, but she still had to remain cautious. All of this was temporary—the living arrangements and the man. So the dark part of her past would have to remain in the shadows.

"You have a talent," he insisted. "Who has seen your sketches?"

Mila laughed. "Just you, and only because I was lost in my thoughts. It was just a napkin drawing, Cruz. I hardly think that counts as talent."

"You forget the industry I'm in," he reminded her with a gentle squeeze of her hand. "I find new talent, granted not usually in fashion design, but it's literally my job to discover those special skills that make people stand out from the rest. You most definitely rise above in all ways."

He seemed so confident and sure. And while she was secure in the ability of her work, she wasn't sure what her next steps were, beyond *Opulence*. She'd wanted to launch her modeling career and then present her line. She had a long-term plan, but things were just taking longer than she'd anticipated.

"I appreciate that, but my sketches will stay a secret for now," she told him. "I have to do things that actually pay the bills."

"I could make some calls in the fashion industry—"

"No."

Hell no. The last thing she needed was him paving her way. She'd gotten this far on her own and that's precisely how she intended to keep going. The entire reason for escaping a controlling man was to have the life as she wanted. Her father had molded her mother into someone Mila vowed to never be. Letting anyone have power over her would be like looking back, and for her own mental stability, she could never allow that to happen.

"You're one of the most determined people I've ever met," he added.

"Is that your way of saying I'm stubborn?"

A wide smile spread across his face. "I think you and Nora would get along beautifully. My brother definitely met his match with her."

Mila's breath caught in her throat as her heart kicked up. "Why does this sound like you want me to meet the family?"

Cruz shrugged and curled his fingers around her hand, holding it in an even more intimate way now.

"You'll meet them anyway because of the photo shoot," he told her. "You just remind me of Nora in so many ways…except the fact that she's like my sister. I never wanted to have sex with her."

Mila couldn't help but smirk. "And you want to have sex with me."

There wasn't any question. Clearly, they'd both wanted to—and still did. But that didn't make the move a smart one.

"I'm not the one who pushed back," he replied. "There's nothing wrong with what we did, Mila. We're adult enough to separate the two aspects of our relationship. We have work, which got put on hold a bit, and we have personal. I'm not trying to merge the two, but there's no reason we can't enjoy both."

Why did he have to sound so damn logical?

"If that night was all you wanted, I respect your decision—"

Mila closed that minuscule distance between them and captured his lips. Everything he said, every move he made, stirred something new inside her and she only possessed so much self-control.

And the way he grabbed hold of her and had her straddling his lap proved that his own control had snapped as well. She'd never been the reason for anyone to lose control before and this was the second time with him. There was no doubt that he wanted her. The question was, how would all of this play out in the days and weeks to come?

Cruz gripped her backside and pulled her closer. The movement had Mila bracing her hands on the seat beside his broad shoulders. He returned her kiss as if he'd been craving her since they'd last touched. She knew the feeling. Even though she'd left his bed just this morning, her body had been tingling ever since.

Fingertips slid beneath the hem of her shirt and grazed her bare back. Even something as simple as this innocent touch pushed her body even further to a level of desire she'd never experienced.

Only Cruz…

He'd been the only man in her life to pull out a vast array of emotions and she never knew what to expect next. They'd come together as fast and fiercely as the storm that had left them with no other option.

And she might not know what the long-term future held, but she was well aware of what the next few moments were going to bring, and she couldn't wait. Even with his power and unspoken demand, Cruz gave her all the control by keeping her on top.

Mila eased back just a bit. "Can we really keep these two relationships separate?" she asked, her eyes searching his.

"You're the only woman I've ever worked with and had an intimate relationship with." His strong hands gripped her hips now. "This is all new to me, but we're both smart enough to not let personal feelings get in the way of the work we both need to do. And everything we've done and will do is nobody's business but ours."

She'd always been a private person anyway. Too many things in her life gave her little choice but to keep aspects locked inside. She didn't have friends, more just acquaintances, so it's not like she confided in people.

"And how long is this going to last between us?" she asked.

He brought a hand up to stroke along the side of her cheek, sliding her hair behind her ear. As his dark eyes followed his movements, she couldn't stop staring at his striking face.

"However long we want," he admitted. "There's no pressure here, Mila. You're a sexy woman and I want you. I'm impressed as hell with your work ethic and drive. It's impossible to ignore this pull."

Mila reached up and curled her fingers around his wrist. "How are you not married, with this entire house full of children? There are women who would beat down your door if they knew that's what you wanted, and you're such a genuine guy."

"I don't want women beating my door down," he snorted. "I want one woman. The right woman. And I'll know her when I meet her."

Something way too close to jealousy sliced through her. How absurd was that? She couldn't be jealous of a woman who wasn't even in the picture yet. And Mila wasn't the woman he'd been waiting on. She had no desires for a family or marriage... she'd run like hell from one family before. No need to drop herself right into another.

"So are we just passing the time?"

Mila reached for the hem of her shirt and pulled it up and over her head, flinging it over her shoulder. Then his hands were framing her face and he locked his eyes on hers.

"I'm not using you," he insisted. "If I haven't made it clear how much I respect you on every level, then I'm doing something wrong."

Oh, he was doing everything very, very right. Which posed a problem, because she needed to find fault so she'd have an easier time of walking away. As things stood now, she had a sinking feeling she'd never want to leave.

Nine

Cruz didn't know where Mila escaped to in that beautiful head of hers, but she had a habit of getting lost in her thoughts. The pullback when she closed in on herself wasn't noticeable physically. He couldn't explain how he knew when she'd left the moment, but he wanted to get her back to this…to them.

Securing her body against his, Cruz held on to her backside and came to his feet. He began to move from the entertainment room toward the hallway.

"You have a habit of wanting to carry me." She laughed, looping her arms around his neck. "I'm not complaining, though."

"I want you in my bed."

My life.

No. That wasn't right. Where the hell did that

thought come from? Mila wasn't the one for him. She couldn't be. When the right woman stepped into his world, he'd know it. She would instantly fit and have the same goals and ideals that he did. They'd vibe on every level and come together like a perfect union.

There was no denying the remarkable woman Mila was, so he would enjoy her company for as long as she remained in town. He traveled for work, she traveled for work...hell, she didn't even have a home yet. Besides, she'd made it clear she didn't want a relationship. Likely, because of the pain she'd dealt with from her father. Cruz hated the bastard and didn't even know his name.

"You're territorial," she murmured, her warm breath tickling his neck.

"You bet your sweet ass I am." He moved through the foyer and down the hallway leading to his suite. "As much as a quickie on the chair in the movie room sounds fun, I'd rather take my time. You deserve nothing less."

She lifted her head to look in his eyes. "How do you know what I deserve?"

"Because you're amazing and I want to give you everything."

Careful. That teetered too close to exposing feelings he couldn't have for her, much less admit. She did deserve everything, that hadn't been a lie, but at the same time, they weren't meant to be together for the long-term. He'd give all he could while they lasted, and that's all he could do.

"You thought I was a diva." She smirked. "And you're still trying to pamper me."

"You are a diva," he agreed. "But I'm starting to see there's much more to the woman beneath the makeup and hair spray."

"Don't look too close," she warned. "You might not like what you find."

Oh, he didn't know about that. He had a feeling he'd be even more intrigued and attracted. With each passing moment, Cruz learned more, and she didn't even have to tell him everything. But he would get the full story. Later.

"There's nothing I've found yet that I don't like," he countered.

He eased her body down his and set her on her feet. Without another word, he slowly started removing the rest of her clothing. She rested her delicate hands on his shoulders as he bent down to take off her shoes and remove her pants and panties.

"Are we skipping work completely today?" she asked, looking down with a smile on her face.

"Oh, I'm working."

Working on keeping her out of her clothes and in his bed for as long as possible.

As he came to his feet, Cruz took his time gliding his hands up and over each curve. Even after all they'd shared in such a short time, he still wanted more of everything. More of Mila and more of their time alone.

As much as he hated the flooding and the inconvenience of the bridge getting washed out, he wasn't sorry she'd gotten trapped here. And from the smile on her face, she wasn't sorry, either. Maybe those fleeting regrets from this morning were long gone.

Cruz reached around her back and flicked the fastener on her bra, then pulled the scraps of lace and satin away from her body. Now that she wore nothing but an aroused flush of pink, Cruz took a step back.

"You're breathtaking," he murmured. "Maybe I'll just stand here and look for a while."

Mila quirked her brow and propped her hands on her rounded hips. "Is that right? So you just want to look?"

She circled his king-size bed and went to the other side. He waited and watched, wondering what she was up to. Her naughty grin and heavy-lidded gaze had Cruz's anticipation climbing. He loved Mila's playful side, but more than that, he loved knowing she wasn't still thinking of her bad morning. He'd gladly sacrifice his own work if he could take her mind off what had happened, even for a short time.

Mila climbed onto his bed and sat on her knees, shooting him a saucy grin. She trailed a fingertip from her breasts down her abdomen and back up. Slowly up, slowly down.

"So if you're staring, what should I be doing?" she asked, her voice husky.

Each time her hand went down, it went just a bit lower. He couldn't pull his eyes away as he started shedding his clothes. Yeah, he'd say her regrets were definitely a thing of the past.

"I mean, you did get me all achy and I thought you

brought me in here and ditched work for something a little more exciting than to just be a spectator." Up… down. Her hand continued to travel over that perfect body. "I took you for more of a hands-on guy."

She eased her knees farther apart on the bed as her hand trailed lower this time. Cruz just flung his last garment aside and practically pounced onto the bed. Mila laughed as he grabbed her and rolled until she straddled him once again. He knew she had a need for control, she'd told him so, but he'd gotten the impression there was a more meaningful reason behind that than just a diva personality.

Cruz wanted her to feel safe and comfortable in every aspect of any part of their relationship. While this all started as business, the second he'd met her in Miami, the sexual attraction had hit him hard and fast. Having her in his home had only intensified those heightened emotions.

And now deeper feelings were stirring just beneath the surface and he had to figure out what the hell to do with them.

Mila smiled down as she flattened her palms on his chest. "So you didn't want to watch after all?"

Cruz slid his hand between their bodies and eased one fingertip over her core. He kept his focus locked on her and wasn't disappointed when her lids fluttered, her mouth parting in a soft gasp.

"I'm definitely more of a hands-on type of guy."

"I knew it."

Back and forth, he took his time pleasuring her before slipping one finger inside. Her hips jerked, and her short nails bit into his bare chest. Bringing Mila pleasure fulfilled a need in him he didn't even know existed. He'd never been a selfish lover, but at the same time, he never got this much gratification from simply watching. So he hadn't been lying about wanting to watch, but he also wanted to touch.

When she curled her hand around his wrist and urged him on by guiding his hand, he nearly came undone himself. She used her free hand on his chest as leverage as she rocked her body against him. The way she bit her lower lip triggered another burst of arousal, and he wanted more.

Cruz removed his hand and grabbed hold of her waist as he turned them once again. With her flushed cheeks and the soft sheen on her chest as she lay sprawled on his navy sheets, she looked so damn perfect, he never wanted her to leave.

But that unintentional thought had no place here.

Cruz gripped the backs of her thighs as he positioned himself over her. When those vibrant green eyes met his, he joined their bodies. Mila instantly cried out and he began to move—quicker than he'd intended. But those moments of watching her had pushed him to the breaking point. He'd never had such a need, such a *craving* before. Would he ever get enough?

Mila reached for him, curling her fingers around the back of his neck and urging him down. He covered her lips with his, fully submerging himself into her desire and passion. He wanted as much as she'd give…and more. That word seemed to be a theme where Mila was concerned. There never seemed to be enough.

Cruz pumped his hips faster, and within seconds, Mila tore from the kiss. She arched against him, gripped his shoulders, and tossed her head into the side of the pillow. He reached up with one hand to the plush headboard and gripped it as he continued to hold one of her thighs up and moved against her. His own release followed hers, but Cruz couldn't close his eyes. He couldn't look away from the most beautiful sight he'd ever had in his bed.

The moment he came down from his high, Cruz laid his lips on her forehead, the tip of her nose, and then her lips. Even after all they'd done and been through in just a couple of days, he wasn't ready to let her go—mentally or physically.

Now he had to face those thoughts and figure out what the hell to do, because this fling wasn't a forever thing. At some point, Mila would walk out of his life. The question was, would he be ready for that?

"The bridge is supposed to be done with a week."

Mila sat in her bedroom at the window seat, but with her door open. Cruz's voice echoed up from the first floor. She'd spent the past three nights in his bed...some days, too. They seemed to have an easy pattern down of working, taking turns making meals, and tumbling into bed. She'd come to realize that Cruz had a romantic side, with consistently wanting her in his bed, wanting to pamper her, to make sure everything in her world was going right.

Damn, he'd make someone the perfect husband someday.

"Yeah, and I just found out the shoot on the property has been pushed back a month," Cruz went on, jerking her from all her thoughts.

Mila's pencil hovered over the paper as she froze to listen. He hadn't told her that yet, so he must have just gotten a notification. A month? She couldn't stay here a month. That would mean getting even more comfortable than she already was. Northern California wasn't a place she wanted to stay permanently. There was no big city without hopping a flight or driving a few hours. She needed busywork, needed that hustle and bustle in which everyone minded their own business. Staying in a small town meant setting roots, making friends…finding love.

Her pencil fell from her hand. Cruz's voice was but a muffle now as her vision grew hazy. Her head spun and she attempted to wrap her mind around the whole *love* word that had just popped into her head without her approval.

She didn't love Cruz. That was ridiculous. She'd been playing house for five days, that's all. The sex had muddled her mind and shifted her thoughts from lust to love. She didn't know when the transition had taken place, but she knew she had to backpedal, because she could not and would not get wrapped up in any man. She had too many goals, way too much to obtain in her life before ever considering if she even wanted something long term.

Cruz was an amazing man and he'd make a wonderful father and husband one day. But she was not that woman for him.

"Thanks, Dad."

Cruz's voice grew closer as he mounted the stairs. Mila swung her legs over the side of the window seat and grabbed her pencil. She quickly closed her sketchbook and set it down with her pencil on top. Cruz might have seen her doodling on a napkin, but that was entirely different than when she left her heart and her ideas on the paper.

She couldn't wait until the day her designs came to life. She didn't want to model forever, but she did want to help curvy women feel better about their clothing choices. She wanted them to have an option from casual to work, from date night to cocktail parties. And now she could add an adorable raincoat, rain boots, and matching umbrella to the mix.

When she'd told Cruz about sewing her clothes as a teen, that had been because her hand-me-downs were all so big or simply ill-fitting. She'd never had a new thing in her life, so she'd learned to make do with what she had.

Her dreams were far bigger than her budget, but one day, she would make all of this happen. She wouldn't let that scared teen girl down. Mila also wouldn't settle for anything less than the success she'd dreamed of. After years of being told she'd never make it, she was doing just that. Maybe not as fast as she'd hoped, but the speed didn't matter as long as she could keep looking ahead.

"Great. I'll talk to you later."

Cruz stood at her door as he pocketed his phone and stared in.

"The photo shoot has been moved," she stated, crossing her arms over her chest.

"Yeah." He blew out a sigh. "The photographer we wanted to use had another job after this one, so this delay ran into his schedule. We really like this guy, so we want to wait. Does that put you in a bind? Nora just texted me right before my dad called so I didn't get a chance to tell you yet."

Put her in a bind? Physically, no. Mentally? That was a different story.

In less than a week, she'd lost a piece of herself. She never would have shared a man's bed this long under any other circumstances, but she wasn't sorry. And she didn't want to look at it as if she'd lost a piece of herself, but rather that she'd surprised herself by her actions. Cruz had never demanded she stay in there, so the choice was ultimately still up to her.

"So what am I supposed to do?" she asked. "Stay here for a month or go to my bed-and-breakfast once I can get out?"

He took a step into her room and her heart kicked up. Why did that always happen? The man got into her personal space or gave her that sexy stare and she lost all semblance of rational thought.

"Stay."

His one-word command left no question as to how he felt. Maybe that's what she wanted him to say, but she hadn't had much time to think about it.

"That might not be the smartest move," she countered. "What will everyone think if I continue to stay here once the storm threat and flooding are no longer an issue? I never want people to think I got any project because I slept my way there."

In a flash, he'd closed the gap between them and clutched her arms in his hands.

"We've been through this," he ground out. "Our personal relationship has nothing to do with the working relationship. You're here because you have a talent that I want to take to the world. I'm going to give you that boost like we've done with thousands of artists over the years. You're not here for any other reason."

"But that's not what people will think," she whispered. "There's only so much my modeling can do if my reputation is tarnished."

"I won't let that happen."

He might think he had that power, but she lived in the real world. She also didn't want to get into an argument or verbal sparring match over this when they were still days away from needing to reach an agreement over where she would stay.

"I have an idea."

She blinked at his abrupt change in topic. But with that crooked grin and that gleam in his dark eyes, she had a feeling she might not like where this was headed.

"I'm afraid to ask when you look at me like that," she admitted. "I don't know that I've seen a mischievous look from you before, but it's worrisome."

"Nothing to worry about," he assured her with

a quick peck to her forehead. "Put on your favorite outfit and meet me downstairs."

Confusion had Mila taking a step back and holding her hands up. "Is there another secret room in your house I don't know about?"

"Nothing like that. Though I do have a home gym and library you'd probably love."

Of course he did. And this place was so damn big that she'd never seen either one. She wouldn't mind taking her sketchbook to the library and relaxing, but she loved drawing in her room, where her window provided a stunning view of the back of the property and the river.

"What are we doing?" she asked.

"You'll find out. In fact, just come like you are. You look great."

Mila glanced down at her long A-line skirt and the fashion tee she'd paired with some animal-print flats.

"Let me touch up my lipstick. I haven't put any on since this morning."

Cruz took hold of her hand and started pulling her toward the door. "You're fine. Everything doesn't always have to be on and perfect. You're beautiful with or without."

She truly believed he meant that because he had no reason to just say what he thought she wanted to hear. Cruz owned a billion-dollar company, he didn't need to play nice with her. Hell, she'd already been in his bed and was here for work. He didn't need to secure her in any other aspect of his life.

She followed him down the stairs but stopped when he turned and pointed a finger.

"Wait right here," he told her. "I just need to grab a couple things."

The man was a whirlwind. For as laid-back as he always seemed, something had lit a fire under his butt. Mila waited a few minutes, but he quickly returned from one of the hallways with a black case in hand.

She knew what he had in that case. She'd been in this industry long enough.

And she knew she should have changed and touched up her lipstick.

Ten

Cruz had to get her moving and out of the house before she could rush back upstairs and fix herself up. She looked beautiful and he wouldn't change a thing.

Her eyes darted from the camera case to him and she tipped her head up.

"I thought you weren't too keen on this idea, either."

He wasn't at first, but the more he thought about the idea of shooting Mila himself, the more it had grown into a brilliant plan. Why couldn't he get back to basics? It wasn't as if they were going to use these images for the shoot. But if they were decent enough, he had every intention of slipping one in to a few people he'd already reached out to. He had several lines of communication open, and he couldn't wait for something to pan out for her.

"I used to love taking pictures," he admitted, shouldering the strap of the bag. "Why not pass the time? This way, we can see what we like and don't like when the actual photographer and the entire crew get here."

She pursed her lips, and he knew she was rolling the idea around in her head. He wasn't giving her time to say no. He had a plan for her, but he wanted everything to be a surprise. Not only that, but if by some chance his idea didn't work out, she wouldn't get hurt. So for now, he'd just keep all these thoughts to himself.

"Let's go." He moved toward the front door and opened it, gesturing for her to walk out ahead of him. "It's just us, so this is going to be relaxing."

"I should at least get my lipstick," she argued.

"Your lips are still red, your hair is still big, your clothes are perfect."

She narrowed her gaze. "Did you just knock my hair?"

Cruz chuckled. "Not at all. Now, let's move."

She muttered something about loving her teased hair as she moved past him and out onto the porch. He had every intention of getting pictures of her without all the made-up extras. She had a natural beauty he wished she could see and embrace. There was nothing wrong with makeup and going all out. There were times that called for such things, but he needed her to see that she didn't have to be all of that all the time…at least not with him.

He took her hand in his and led her down the porch and into the yard. His eyes darted to the smashed car and the tree, and he cringed again.

"Don't look at it," she warned. "It doesn't get any better."

No, but he hated that it still sat there. The road crew was scheduled to work on the bridge tomorrow, and once that was rebuilt, he could get someone to take care of this mess…and Mila would be free to go if she chose.

"So, where are you taking me?" she asked.

He really hadn't thought about that. He knew what had been on the docket for the actual shoot, but he wanted something different. Something that showcased the free spirit he knew lived inside her.

"I have a few places in mind."

He tugged on her hand and started toward the opposite side of the property, closest to the woods. Cruz glanced at Mila as she surveyed her surroundings. He couldn't pinpoint the expression on her face, but if he had to guess, he would say longing or sadness.

"Hey." He gave her hand a gentle squeeze. "You with me?"

Mila blinked and turned to meet his gaze. She stopped for a minute and simply stared at the mountains in the distance. He loved this view as well and never took his land or its beauty for granted.

"Parts of this place remind me so much of Montana. I'm just taken aback."

Montana. So that must be where she grew up. Cruz wanted to press her for more, but he also wanted her to go at her own pace. She needed to open the door to her world as slowly and as much as she wanted—he couldn't just bust it down.

"Of course, our house was nothing like yours." Her soft laugh had a hint of sorrow. "The farm took all the money, so the house wasn't much to look at. Mama would try to keep flowers planted in pots on the porch, but sometimes we couldn't even do that."

Cruz listened as she unfolded a bit of her story. He couldn't ignore the parallels of their childhoods. After his mom passed, his family lost everything. The farm, the house, every bit of stability they'd ever had.

"I don't know why she just didn't leave."

Cruz barely heard the whispered sentence as she continued to stare off into the distance. At this point, she was working through something that was all her own and his place was to lend a shoulder and an ear as a friend.

"I always wondered why she didn't." Mila pulled in a deep breath and pasted on a half-smile as she turned her attention toward him. "Sorry. I didn't mean to drag you into my memories. I just saw the mountains and fell back in time."

Cruz released her hand and settled his on her waist as he pulled her closer. He kept his eyes on hers, wanting this moment to stick in her mind. He wanted her to understand that he could be more than the guy over the course of her next project or her current lover. They'd formed a bond unlike anything he'd ever known, which made his need to figure out each step all the more important. He didn't want either of them getting hurt at the end.

The end. That wasn't a time he was ready to think about quite yet. He'd have to mentally prepare himself for a day when Mila wasn't there.

"Thank you for sharing that," he told her. "And never apologize for being you or where you came from. We have more in common than I ever thought."

"Your father mentally abused and controlled your mother, too?"

The more Cruz heard about this bastard, the more he hated him. But he simply shook his head. The last thing Mila needed in her life was an angry man.

"Never. My parents were in love."

The wind lifted Mila's strands from her shoulders. They danced in the breeze, blowing across her face. Cruz reached up and tucked the wayward hair behind her ears and slid his hand along the side of her face.

"Our lives didn't fall apart until she passed and my father stopped caring about everything else, including his children," Cruz went on. "But we're rebuilding our relationship now and it's a relief and comforting to know that better days are ahead."

Mila turned her face toward his hand, but kept her eyes locked on his. "Well, better days are ahead for me, too, but they will be alone. I haven't seen my parents since I left, at eighteen. My father swore I'd be back because I'd fail. I would sleep in my car before I ever crawled back home and admitted defeat.

In fact, I did sleep in my car for a few weeks early on when I ran out of money."

Another layer of admiration fell into place. He'd never met a more resilient, remarkable woman in his life. Each time she revealed a nugget of her past, he realized how similar they were on a deeper level. There was so much more to Mila than her striking looks, and that's the woman he wanted to know more about.

"That is why you're going to be so successful," he told her. "You haven't given up when things got hard. You have the motivation and drive that most don't have. That takes people further in this industry than almost anything else."

She laughed. "You're just saying that so I'll keep sleeping with you."

Cruz shrugged. "I definitely want you in my bed, but I wouldn't sacrifice your career for it. We've got this under our control and nobody else's. We're not worrying about the rest of the world. Got it?"

"You make things sound so simple."

"They can be if that's how we make it," he confirmed. "We don't have to let anyone into the world we've created here. So if you want to stay for the month, we'll be discreet. My brother and Nora sure as hell aren't going to sabotage your career or put a black mark over you for being here."

She studied his face a bit before leaning up and kissing him. When she stepped back, she had a genuine, soft smile on her face. His heart clenched and he knew he was in some serious trouble, but all he could do was take all of this one day at a time.

"What was that for?" he asked.

"Listening. I don't usually talk about my past and you didn't cut in or judge. I've just always worried if I talk about my childhood and bring it out in the open now, then I'll struggle with moving on. But telling you about a portion of it is really freeing."

"Imagine how you'd feel if you opened up about everything."

She continued to stare back with those mesmerizing bright eyes. He easily saw how she got her first modeling job. She had a way of holding people captive with just a glance. Aside from her sexy body, she had a naturally beautiful face and a sweet smile and subtle tilt of her head that gave her a hint of the girl next door. But he knew she was a vixen in the bedroom.

He wanted to capture every single side of her, and with nobody else around, the primal side of him had kicked into gear. This moment belonged to them, and no matter what happened, temporary or long-term, whether business or personal, he had her now.

Cruz pulled the strap from his shoulder and crouched down to assemble the proper lens.

"Are we doing a picture here?" she asked, then glanced around. "There's absolutely nothing around."

He angled the camera away from her and did a test shot for lighting.

"That's the point," he replied, remaining crouched. "I want you, the mountains, and the sky. Ready?"

From this angle, that's precisely what he got. He didn't even have to tell her to pose. The moment he said "ready," she switched to on mode and played for the camera. She fisted a handful of her skirt and did a spin, her head tilted up toward the late-afternoon sunshine. With that wide smile on her face, the camera didn't pick up that she'd been in a darker place just moments ago.

She turned her back to him and threw him a sassy look over one shrugged shoulder. Cruz got to his feet now and worked around her, coming in close to capture those striking eyes.

Bedroom eyes. That's how he saw them. From now on, that's all he would associate with that sweet gaze. Seeing her in his bed, peering up at him...

"I have an idea."

Mila continued to clutch her skirt, but she tossed him a narrow stare. "Why do you keep saying that when you know I don't like surprises?"

"I didn't say a surprise, I said an idea."

Her pursed red lips gave him a whole other idea, but right now, he needed to get some pictures. He wanted this extra bond between them for reasons he simply couldn't explain.

"There's a place I want to show you," he explained, reaching down for his camera bag. "It's not far. You good to walk a bit?"

"Sure. It's nice out."

He took her hand in his as he led her farther away from the house. The sounds of the rippling water from the river intertwined with the chirping of the birds. A stirring of desire hit him hard, but not in the intimacy type of way. It was the desire to have moments like this with the right woman.

He'd always known he wanted a family and someone to share his estate with. But there was something peaceful and intimate that he'd been missing from his life. Years of traveling and building the *Opulence* brand had consumed him. He hadn't made time for finding "the one," because he assumed she'd stumble into his life.

"What made you want to have such a huge place?" she asked as they continued toward the spot he had in mind.

Cruz had never been asked that question, but he damn well knew the answer.

"When we lost everything as kids, Zane and I swore we'd never be in that position again. We never wanted to be dependent on anyone."

Cruz pointed up ahead. "We're going there," he told her. "Anyway, we also wanted a way to remind ourselves of where we came from and how far we'd come. Zane lives on a mountain because he wants to overlook things and never be low again."

"Yet you chose a valley," she chimed in.

"Yeah." He couldn't help but smile. "I know that at any time, I can be right back where I started. I don't ever want to take for granted what I have."

Mila stopped, and the movement caused her to pull on his hand. Cruz glanced over his shoulder and the most breathtaking smile and glimmer of unshed tears in her eyes flipped his heart.

Damn it. She looked way too good here—a thought that hadn't settled into his mind until now.

But she couldn't be the one to stay. They were enjoying each other's company, but this definitely gave him a glimpse into the life he wanted and the life he'd been dreaming of. He was ready. A few years ago, he wanted to settle down, but he hadn't been mentally ready. He'd still loved the travels, the women, the passionate flings.

But seeing Nora and Zane and the way they were building a life together had only propelled Cruz into that next level of preparing for his future. He had the space for the family life. Now he just needed a woman who shared his vision.

"What?" he asked when she simply kept staring.

"You're just not what I expected when we first met in Miami." She laced their fingers together as she stepped into him. "Why are you continually surprising me?"

"I didn't mean to this time," he admitted. "I'm just answering your question. I mean, I did build a house probably bigger than I needed."

"Probably?" she laughed. "I got lost before the movie."

"I didn't want to be confined when I had a family one day. I want everyone to feel like they have space. The foster house Zane and I were put into as teens was cramped, and we shared it with other foster kids. The family was nice enough and they were at least trying to help an overpopulated system, but I never wanted my children to feel that way."

"And how many children do you have in this future plan of yours?" she asked.

Instantly, the image of her belly swollen with his baby hit him hard. He had to figure out a way to keep these mental images and desires out of his head. Mila didn't want a family- she was still running from the one she had.

"I'm flexible," he told her. "I need to find the right woman first."

Something flashed through her eyes, but before he could pinpoint the emotion, she blinked and it was gone.

"By flexible, do you mean you want one kid or eight?"

He couldn't help but chuckle at her intense stare and question that he hadn't thought about before.

"Somewhere between there," he admitted. "That's definitely a discussion to have with my wife."

"And you haven't found that perfect woman on all of your trips?"

Oh, he'd found women, but none that would fit in here on his estate or into his world.

"Not yet." *And it's not like any of them could hold a candle to Mila.* "Slip your shoes off."

"What?" Mila laughed, clearly thrown off by his sudden change in subject.

"I want a picture of you on that fallen log over there." He pointed to a tree that had been taken out by the storm. "I want you with your knee up, flat foot on the limb, with your other foot closest to me dangling off. Wrap your arms around your knee and just look straight ahead so I can get your profile."

Mila toed off her flats and lifted her skirt to walk through the grass toward the log. The entire time, Cruz snapped photos. With the quick shutter of clicks, she tossed her hair and gave him a glance over her shoulder...which caused another flurry of photos. He couldn't get enough.

Cruz had no idea how he'd choose one to send. The camera loved Mila. She didn't have a bad angle, and one flash of that smile was enough to have anyone lose touch with reality. She had a natural way of drawing someone into her world, and right now, her world was right smack in the middle of his. She'd managed to surround him to the point that every which way he turned, she was there.

Once she'd hoisted herself up onto the log, she posed the exact way he'd asked, and Cruz couldn't believe how perfect those frames were. He hadn't actually known this tree was down. They hadn't ridden to this side of the property the other day. He'd been heading toward the rocky bank back a little farther away, but this spot was even more perfect.

He paused to check the viewing screen and flicked through.

"Talk to me," he told her as he held the camera back up to his eye. "You know my goals. Tell me more about these designs of yours."

"You're just dying to know all about them, aren't you?" She tossed her hair so that the thick strands spiraled down her back as she tipped her head toward the sun. "I'm just doodling, as you put it. Nothing to get too excited about."

Yet she spent all her spare time with her sketchbook. That amount of devotion led him to believe this was much more than a hobby for her.

"But you are excited," he countered. "If you didn't love it, you wouldn't be so good at it."

She flashed him a quick glance. "You saw two napkins."

"So you've reminded me before." He moved in closer, needing to capture that flawless profile. "I want to see more."

She tipped her head but kept her gaze on the camera. "You've seen enough."

Not nearly enough. There wasn't an aspect of her life he didn't want to dive deeper into.

"You're not going to let me in there, are you?"

She shifted her body, both of her feet now swinging bare over the fallen log. Cruz let the camera hang around his neck as he stepped farther toward her.

"You've gotten further into my life than anyone I've met since leaving home," she admitted. "Be happy with that."

More. He wanted more. That one word consistently popped into his mind with her. And while he was happy with what she'd revealed, he knew that if she'd let him in this far, he'd already cracked her resolve to stay closed off. There was more to discover about Mila.

They'd far surpassed their status as a working team. They'd gone beyond just lovers.

The question was, how much further could they go before someone got hurt?

Eleven

The bridge was done.

The bridge had been done for days now.

Yet there had been no more talk of her leaving. She'd continued to stay in Cruz's bed going on two weeks, but she went back to her room during the day to get ready. She hadn't moved any of her things down to the first-floor bed and bath. That room only held intimacy of the physical kind, and crossing over into any other would be a level she could never be ready for.

Mila needed that bit of separation and control. She knew she could go to her room anytime, but when would she leave? No doubt, Cruz was under the impression she was staying the month, until the shoot fired back up.

They'd have to have that discussion, but she truly didn't know what to say because she had no idea what to do. She knew what she wanted, but was staying here the smartest move?

Mila scrolled through house listings on her laptop, but nothing really popped out. Everything was either much too pricey or in a bad neighborhood, so she closed out that tab and that city and moved to the next.

Finding a house or condo shouldn't be this difficult, not with the big advance coming from *Opulence*. Being single and fairly easy to please should help her search. She needed a couple of bedrooms, a couple of baths, good natural light for her drawing projects, and she couldn't break the bank.

Although, with her lease being up and Cruz's offer to stay here for the month, she would save her on expenses for now. But at the same time, she found that whole setup to be questionable. If she didn't have to worry about reputation or the fact that she would be freeloading off the man she was sleeping with, she wouldn't mind staying.

Of course, if she stayed, that would mess with her mind even more. He stirred way too many emotions within her—emotions she never thought she could even feel. Yet here she sat, in his living room, cozied up in the corner of his plush sectional, likely chosen by some overpriced interior designer. This lifestyle was unlike anything she'd ever experienced. She could easily be labeled as a starving artist. Each job she'd taken over the past ten years had inched her closer to her ultimate goal of becoming a fashion designer. But if she had a mega brand under her belt to increase her visibility and popularity, she could launch her designs from a better platform.

While she wished like hell she had a better plan, she knew once her actual shoot with *Opulence* hit the press, she would get calls. She was so damn proud of herself for all she'd accomplished on her own so far. And that had been the most important part. She needed to stand on her own to prove to herself that she wasn't the failure her father had made her out to be. Had made her believe she was.

Mila refused to let years of her father's negativity creep into her head. She clicked on a listing in Chicago and rotated through each picture. The tiny townhome wasn't as spacious as she'd hoped, but the budget and part of town were perfect. She sent an email to the listing agent about getting a video walk-through.

While the city certainly held more appeal to her than the country, she had to admit, Cruz's land took her breath away. The beauty simply couldn't be overlooked or ignored. And something about Cruz's estate seemed calming and peaceful—two aspects she'd never had growing up.

She always thought she'd just be a city girl, removing herself as far as possible from the rural, country lifestyle. But she couldn't deny the serenity here.

Yet this wasn't her home, and she wasn't staying with Cruz forever.

The front door opened and closed. Mila glanced at the wide, arched doorway leading to the foyer as Cruz stepped in.

No, wait. That tall, handsome man wasn't Cruz. His twin brother, Zane, and Zane's fiancée, Nora, stood in the doorway. Startled by the company, Mila hurriedly closed her laptop and came to her feet. Unexpected visitors were just one reason Mila always insisted on being ready and prepared. Considering that Zane owned the other half of the company that would help launch her career, Mila pasted on a smile and started across the room.

"Hi," she said, feeling a bit odd that Cruz wasn't around and this wasn't her home.

Should she be playing hostess? What was the right protocol here? Nerves coiled in her belly as she waited to get an idea of how she'd be received.

"You must be Mila." Nora extended her hand in a warm greeting. "I'm Nora and this is Zane. Cruz asked us to meet him here."

And hadn't told her company was coming. That was fine. Again, she wasn't the lady of the house by any means. Mila shook Nora's hand and turned to Zane to do the same.

"You are even more stunning in person," Nora went on. "I can't wait to see the images we get with you."

Mila laughed. "Have you looked in a mirror? You could be a model yourself."

Zane slid an arm around Nora's waist. "Oh, we

got her in front of the camera. That spread comes out this summer."

"First and last time I model," Nora murmured to Zane before focusing her attention back on Mila. "We're sorry to just barge in. We're used to doing that. I hope Cruz gave you a heads-up that we were coming and would likely beat him here."

Mila waved her hand. "Don't worry about it. He didn't mention it, but I was just house hunting, so you're not bothering me at all."

When they continued to stare, Mila's nerves got even worse. Should she invite them into the living area? Maybe offer a drink? This new territory confused her and made her more than a little uncomfortable. It wasn't as if guests stopped by her home when she was growing up. As an adult on her own, she hadn't made many friends or acquaintances who had reason to pop in unannounced.

"I'm sure you guys know I'm staying here for a while." Might as well slice right through this tension, get it out of the way and pretend she had confidence in this awkward situation. "I don't know what Cruz has told either of you, but we—"

"It's none of our business." Zane held up a hand to stop her. "Nora and I are certainly not judging and nobody else knows where you are."

A wave of relief swept through her, because she really didn't know how to justify the fact that she was still here. The great sex? The company of a man she considered to land somewhere between friend, lover, and... Hell, she didn't even know. *Boyfriend* seemed to be such a juvenile term and they weren't looking to become long-term anyway. *Fling* seemed crass, because even she had to admit that they had more than just sex.

"You should hear the story of how we got together." Nora laughed as she motioned between her and Zane. "We had to sneak around, and all the while, Cruz was trying to fix us up. It's funny looking back, but so stressful at the time."

Cruz had touched a little on the topic. Nora and Zane clearly had an undeniable chemistry, something Mila hadn't even known she wanted. But the stirring deep in her belly could only be labeled as jealousy.

Damn it. She'd done so well at dodging that emotion. She'd recognized it a few times over the past couple weeks, but managed to shut it down. Now, here she stood, unable to hide from the heavy pain of envy.

"I'm not good at playing hostess, especially in someone else's house." Mila laughed. "But come on in."

"You don't have to play host to us," Nora stated. "We're all family."

Mila nearly stumbled over her own heels at that statement. Maybe the three of them were family, but Mila was nothing but an outsider passing through.

A niggle of regret settled into the pit of her stomach. She clearly hadn't planned on staying, but suddenly, the thought of never returning left a yawning hole in her soul.

How could that be? How could she already miss a place, a *man*, when she hadn't even left yet?

Mila scooped up her laptop and set it on the edge of the table before sitting on one end of the sectional.

Nora started to take a seat, but grabbed her stomach. "Oh my word."

"What is it?" Zane immediately came to her side, placing his hand over hers. "The baby?"

Mila stilled, her eyes locked on the couple. She knew absolutely nothing about pregnancies or children. She'd thought and discussed more about babies today than in the past several years combined.

"I think I just felt her move." Nora's eyes went to Zane as she let out a soft laugh. "Oh my word. I knew the doctor said any day, but I hadn't felt anything until now. I mean, I'm pretty sure that's what happened."

As if she didn't already feel like an outsider looking in, Mila wondered if she should leave the happy couple alone in their private moment. The two obviously shared a tight bond, just another relationship facet she knew nothing about.

Another wave of unexpected longing hit her. Mila had never wanted her own family. What did she know about a solid, happy relationship? Or proper parenting, for that matter? She'd never gotten that firsthand account of how people in love could be. Yet there was absolutely no denying the adoration between Zane and Nora as they started their life and family together.

"What's going on?"

Mila turned her attention to the doorway once again as Cruz came through. She'd been so caught up in the moment and her own thoughts that she hadn't heard him come in.

"The baby moved." Nora beamed with emotion. "We're a little excited."

"I can't feel a damn thing," Zane grumbled, his hand moving all around Nora's slightly swollen belly. "The doctor said I would feel her first and it would be a few weeks before anyone else could."

"Wait." Cruz came to stand by Zane. "Did Nora say 'her,' as in, you're having a girl?"

Nora and Zane both looked at Cruz, but Nora replied, "Surprise. We just came from our doctor's appointment and found out."

"I knew it." Cruz immediately crossed to Nora and gathered her in an embrace, then pumped his fist in the air. "I just knew you would have a little girl."

Nora laughed as Cruz swept her off her feet and spun her in a quick circle.

"Zane thought a girl, too," she admitted as Cruz set her back down. "I went back and forth, but now that we know, it's time to start on a nursery."

"My credit card will never be the same," Zane muttered.

Cruz propped his hands on his narrow hips and shook his head. "Nah. I'll be spoiling my niece, so my card is the one that will get hit."

"Do you want to hear some names we talked about?" Nora asked, a wide grin spreading across her face.

Mila listened as Nora discussed baby girl names that she'd had in her mind for weeks now. Cruz weighed in on his favorites and Mila couldn't help but get that tug once again as her heart edged closer to dangerous territory. Cruz didn't just talk about families, he thrived in the concept. He truly was a hands-on type of guy, which was something she'd never experienced before in her life.

But there was another side to this entire situation she also couldn't ignore. The dynamic power and overwhelming presence of the twins standing side by side. Of course, Mila had seen photos of Zane and Cruz together. The billionaire moguls had taken social media and the print magazine world by storm years ago and hadn't slowed down since.

Seeing them in their own atmosphere and not at some glamorous gala really gave Mila a different perspective. While they obviously shared an identical-twin physicality, Mila could easily tell difference.

For one, she had zero attraction to Zane, which seemed odd considering that they looked so similar. But Cruz had this head tilt, a softer laugh, a broader frame. He'd just captured her attention and desires unlike any other.

Nora's comment from earlier came back to Mila. The whole family vibe was more evident now than ever. Images online were nothing in comparison to what was happening in person.

And Mila felt like an intruder.

She came to her feet and grabbed her laptop. "Excuse me," she chimed in. "I have a few calls I need make."

Cruz tossed her a glance with his brows drawn in as if he didn't believe her. But Nora flashed her a megawatt smile.

"It was so great to meet you," Nora told her. "Maybe we can get together without the guys sometime while you're in town."

Without the guys. That implied that Nora thought they were all something more than they actually were. As though they were the Westbrook women or something.

Another reason for Mila to step away from this familial situation and head to her room.

She cast a smile to the group before heading toward the steps. It wasn't until she was upstairs with her door securely closed that Mila breathed a sigh of relief.

What was going on with her roller coaster of emotions? She'd been fine since leaving home. Oh, she'd struggled financially, but always landed on her feet, determined to pave her own way. Now that she'd gotten swept up in this life here with Cruz, he seemed to be in no hurry to bring their tryst to an end.

The fear of turning into her mother, of having a man control her, weighed heavily on Mila's heart. Of course, she hadn't seen signs of control from Cruz, but a powerful man like that was used to getting what he wanted, when he wanted it. They hadn't had an argument yet, and that's when someone's true colors always came out.

How would Cruz act if he didn't get his way? Would he become pushy or angry? She honestly didn't want to ever see those sides to him. The fun-loving, romantic guy she'd spent her days and nights with seemed too perfect...but nobody carried that title.

Mila set her laptop down on the bed and went to the window seat. She needed to relax, to settle her nerves, and keep her eye on her goal. She grabbed her sketch pad and flipped to a fresh page, trying to ignore her curiosity of what was happening downstairs with the others.

Because they were family, and she...well, she was simply a houseguest.

Twelve

Something obviously had upset Mila. Cruz replayed the few minutes he'd been here with her and his brother and Nora, but nothing sprang to mind. She'd been quiet and then she'd made some lame excuse to leave.

He'd called his brother and Nora over here to discuss a different angle for the photo shoot, but he hadn't filled them in on contacting other companies for potential modeling campaigns on Mila's behalf. That last part he wanted to keep to himself for now. He was in a position to open doors for her, so why shouldn't he? Though there were many great prospects, he wanted to wait until something official happened.

"So, Mila is a stunner," Nora told him as she wiggled her perfectly arched brows. "I didn't think she could be more impressive in person, but damn."

Cruz couldn't help but laugh. "She is quite beautiful, which is why she's going to explode onto the scene once we get her image out there."

"Yes, yes, yes." Nora nodded and eased forward on the sofa as she met his stare. "I'm talking personally. You two seemed to have some silent communication, which means—"

"They were in the room together for two minutes," Zane scoffed. "How could you possibly come to that conclusion?"

Nora shrugged. "A woman knows these things. Just like I know she is uncomfortable right now and that's why she made a hasty exit."

Yeah, he could definitely agree with that assessment. But Nora didn't know Mila like he did. His Mila had never backed down from anyone or anything. She held her ground with grit and determination at all times. Yet something at his home had gotten under her skin.

"She's afraid of what people think with her here," he admitted, though he had a feeling her hasty escape went well beyond that.

"But she hasn't left to stay anywhere else, so that should tell you more than what she's actually saying," Nora added, wagging a finger his way as if she'd just made a valid point.

"As weird as that sounded, that makes sense," he replied.

With the bridge fixed, a new rental car in the

driveway, and a way out anytime she wanted, Cruz didn't know why Mila hadn't left…but he wasn't sorry she'd decided to stay. He wasn't ready for her to go, and obviously, she hadn't gotten to that point, either.

So what did that mean? He hadn't asked, because he just wanted to ride this out and not bring awareness to the glaring constant between them.

"I assume you called us over to discuss business and not your roommate," Zane stated, turning his attention from Nora to Cruz.

That summed up his brother. Always business, all the time. Except now that Nora had slid into his personal life, Zane had calmed down and actually had a life outside the office. And that life was about to get a hell of a lot busier once the baby came.

A niece. Just like he'd thought. He couldn't wait.

"I took some random photos of Mila about a week and a half ago," Cruz started. "And I'm seeing a different vision for our shoot."

Nora's wide smile mocked him. "I knew you wouldn't be able to stop yourself."

"Let's move beyond the 'I told you so' and focus," he said, chuckling. "I haven't run this by Maddie yet, but instead of the wildflowers in that back field on my property, I'm thinking something more raw and authentic, yet with just a slight touch of glam."

With Mila always shown in that light of perfection and glam in all the ads she'd done in her past, he wanted to show a different side. The images he had were breathtaking—and that had nothing to do with his ability as a photographer.

Cruz pulled out his cell and procured just one of the still shots he'd taken. He passed his phone across to Zane. He said nothing as they looked over the image; he didn't need to. And from the look on their faces, they saw exactly what he had captured.

And that's the vision he wanted to show all of their clients who were looking for their next break-through model.

"Why aren't we just using these?" Zane asked, handing the phone back. "Why get an outsider when you clearly captured everything perfectly?"

"Because we hired a photographer who will be here in a few weeks."

Nora laid a hand on Zane's thigh. "We have plenty of other shoots coming up. Just transition him to one of those," she suggested.

Cruz bounced the idea around in his head. Maybe they could use his images, even though Mila hadn't been a fan of her look that day. The flowy skirt and simple graphic tee while she sat barefoot on a log with the river and mountains behind her had been absolutely perfect. The rugged, yet beautiful angles would appeal to several brands for a variety of reasons. Perhaps this would open even more doors for her than he'd originally planned.

"That's a solid idea," he agreed.

"I'm full of brilliance." Nora batted her lashes and flicked her hair over her shoulder. "Now, would you like to hear what I have to say on your personal life?"

"No," Cruz and Zane both answered, shaking their heads. Nora glanced between the two and shrugged.

"Fine," she stated. "But look how well we turned out. I know you want the same, and Mila is adorable."

Adorable hadn't been a word he'd used to describe her, and she'd likely claw his eyes out if he said that to her face. *Sexy, driven, independent*—those were all terms and labels he'd give the woman sharing his bed.

"I know that look."

Nora's mocking tone shifted his focus, and he found her smirking back at him.

"It's the only look I have," he insisted, wondering what she'd seen. "And I'm thinking of work."

"We've been best friends for years," Nora volleyed back. "Don't try lying to me. But let me tell you that if you have feelings for that woman upstairs, you need to tell her before she leaves."

Nora came to her feet and stared down at him. "And before the rest of the world gets a piece of her."

Cruz tapped his fingers on the edge of the doorframe and waited. They might be sharing a bed every night, but when Mila's door was closed, he still valued and respected her privacy.

Zane and Nora had left a while ago and he'd been mulling over so many things. Nora's words played over and over.

The whole point of Mila working with them was for the world to see her, and that's what Cruz wanted for her. At the same time, he wanted her here with him. Not to possess her, but to cherish each moment they shared. Hell, he didn't want to leave, either. In all the days it had just been the two of them, Cruz could look back and say those were some of the happiest of his life.

The door swung open, and Mila stood there in a strapless terry cloth wrap with her hair piled on top of her head. She didn't have a stitch of makeup on and Cruz realized this was the first time he'd seen her in such an authentic manner.

He'd never seen her look more beautiful and wished like hell he'd brought his camera, though she'd most definitely balk at the idea of a natural shoot.

"I was just about to grab a shower." She fidgeted with her hair and ran a hand over the side of her face. "I didn't expect to see you for a while. I thought you were still visiting, and I removed my makeup to try a new face mask, I—"

"Look perfect."

Her hand stilled before slowly falling to her side.

Cruz took a step in and held up the gift he'd picked up while out earlier. The wrapped box seemed silly, but he wanted to show her that he valued her and her dreams. Everyone had goals, but having a support system made all the difference. He couldn't help but wonder if she had anyone in her corner.

Mila's eyes dropped to the package. "What's this?"

"This is why I went out earlier," he explained. "Open it."

Mila's confused stare went from the box to him before she ultimately took the present to her bed. She set the package on the edge of the mattress and slid the large red ribbon apart before lifting the white lid.

She gasped. "What did you do?"

"Well, I had to rely on the sales associate and some random customer who helped me," he explained. "Art supplies are definitely out of my element, so I bought a little of everything."

Mila pulled out a variety of pencils and various sizes of sketch pads. She displayed everything on the bed before turning back to him. Moisture gathered in her eyes before one lone tear slid down her cheek.

"Are those happy tears because you're excited or sad tears because I got the wrong things?" he asked, moving farther into her room.

When she dropped her face into her hands, Cruz wrapped his arms around her and pulled her into his chest. Her shoulders shook as she sniffed, so he tightened his arms and rubbed a hand up and down her back.

"I've never had such a strong reaction to a gift I've given before," he murmured.

Mila eased back and stared up with watery eyes as another tear, then another, slid down her cheek. "I've never had a gift given to me."

Cruz's hand stilled on her back as her statement sank in. He searched her face for any sign of what she must be feeling. Definitely surprise and happiness, but sorrow mingled in the mix, too, and he never wanted her to feel anything but joy. He wanted to be the one to bring all of those good, positive emotions into her life, to erase all that her bastard father had imprinted onto her.

More and more, he realized that she had to force the determination she felt because life had given her no other choice. She'd clawed her way out of her past just as he had done.

Damn it. They were so much alike, so how could their journey toward their ultimate goals be taking them in totally opposite directions?

"I'm sure you had birthday presents," he finally stated, but she was already shaking her head.

"Nothing. My father always told my mother that I didn't need anything else because they already provided a place for me to live, food, and clothes. Granted, all of my clothes were given to us or Mom got them from thrift stores. I would have to make do with what she found, so oftentimes, I would sew different pieces together or have to alter something that was too big. Mom had to stick to a strict budget, so she could only spend a few bucks on each piece."

Mila swiped at her damp cheeks and tipped her head up. Right before him, Cruz watched as she continued to push away the demons of her past. He'd never met a more remarkably strong woman.

"I heard them arguing one time," Mila went on. "My mom wanted to get me this outfit she'd seen on sale in the window of a little boutique in town and my dad said we didn't have the money and, with as fast as I was growing, there was no need. And when he said I was growing, he meant gaining weight. He never missed the chance to bring that up. Being an only child really sucked sometimes because he had nowhere else to focus his attention."

Yeah, Cruz assumed the bastard would have no concern over his child's feelings or well-being.

"I'm not addressing the growth or weight," Cruz told her. "You're well aware that I think you're stunning and beautiful. Not only that, you literally make a living with exactly what he criticized about you. You have to be proud of yourself for giving him the middle finger from afar."

A soft smile spread across her flawless face. "I am. I'm not even sure if he's seen any of the work I've done, but with each project, I like to think he's fuming that I'm not under his thumb like my mother is and that I'm succeeding in life. Granted, not to the level I want, but—"

"That's only a matter of time. You'll be a household name."

He fully believed that the world was going to love her and embrace her. She would finally be treated the way she deserved and make a living not only fulfilling her dream, but paving the way for so many others who were trying to break free of stigmas and stereotypes.

"I'm not sure about that, but each step I get toward my ultimate goal is a step away from my past," she admitted.

"And your goal is to go into the fashion design industry."

He didn't ask, as he already knew the answer.

But when she looped her arms around his neck and nodded, he had his affirmation. She'd opened up to him. Finally.

"It's all I've ever wanted," she confessed. "To make women of all sizes feel special and beautiful and not ashamed of themselves."

"You know what makes women beautiful?" he asked. "Their soul. And you have one of the most incredible ones I've ever seen."

She blinked and more moisture gathered on her dark lashes. Even crying and vulnerable, she held him captive with her beauty and strength. Maybe *especially* during this time. Having an open window into her heart had changed something inside his own.

"Thank you for the gift. Truly. I don't really know what to say because I'm still so thrown off." She let out a soft laugh and tapped her lips to his. "I'll never forget this moment or this gift."

"Or me?" he asked. Maybe that was being too hopeful or showing too much of those feelings he didn't quite know what to do with.

Mila reached between them and tugged on the snap of her wrap. She took a step back, sending the terry cloth silently to the floor.

"You don't have any work you need to get to right now, do you?" she asked as she stood before him wearing nothing but a smile.

"Even if I did, nothing is more important than you."

Careful. There go more of those feelings slipping out.

"You put me first and buy me gifts?" She reached up and pulled the pins from her hair, dropping them to the floor at her feet. "Sounds like the perfect guy."

The perfect guy, maybe. But her perfect guy? Doubtful.

She wasn't staying, he knew that. But he would value and appreciate every single moment while she was here.

"I'm far from perfect." Cruz started stripping out of his jeans and tee, loving how her eyes watched every frantic movement. "But I'd do anything to see that smile on your face."

She held up her hands. "No more talk. I don't want to get emotional again."

"Fine by me."

He grabbed her by the waist and spun her around before walking her backward and out of her room. Arousal pumped through him, and anticipation motivated him.

"I have a perfectly good bed in there," she informed him, clutching his shoulders.

"That's the guest room." He maneuvered her to the hallway and stopped. "You're not a guest anymore."

Smiling, she lifted one perfectly arched brow. "Then what am I?"

"Mine."

He crushed his lips to hers with every intention of leading her down to the first floor to his room, but the second her hands started roaming over his body, he lost all control. They weren't going to make it.

Cruz backed her against the wall and braced one hand beside her head, taking his free hand and lifting her leg to his thigh. Mila's grip came back to his shoulders as she used him for leverage and wrapped her other leg around his waist, locking her ankles behind his back.

Her eyes landed on his and that smile remained in place. This playful side of her, devoid of all the fuss of hair and makeup, only added to all the layers he'd been uncovering and enjoying.

"I like you just like this," he murmured, leaning in to trail his lips over the side of her neck.

"Naked?" She laughed.

"Absolutely." He brought his eyes up to lock onto hers. "But I meant authentic and natural."

That smile faltered as her eyes widened. "Cruz…"

"I like my name sliding through your lips, too."

He covered her mouth with his once again as he joined their bodies. He swallowed Mila's moan as he worked his body with hers. The heels of her feet dug into his back as if she were locking him into place.

Cruz pulled his lips from hers and roamed over her jawline and down the column of her throat. He held on to her thigh with one hand and palmed her breast with the other, drawing out another heavy pant from Mila. All of those moans and sighs were so raw and gave him an even deeper insight into her passion. She had so much inside her and to be the one to pull all of that out only aroused him even further.

She'd let him in, little by little. Maybe she wanted

more, maybe they needed to have a serious talk…but right now, she didn't want to talk and neither did he.

Cruz jerked her leg up just a bit higher, intensifying the pleasure for both of them just a bit more. Mila cried out his name, pumping her hips even faster. He didn't hesitate to meet her frenzied pace. His own climax loomed and he tried like hell to hold back, to draw out the pleasure, but having her come undone all around him ruined him.

Cruz let go, giving in to the primal indulgence he could only get from Mila. Her tight hold on his shoulders eased, as did her locked ankles behind his back. Cruz laid his lips on the pulse at the base of her neck, wanting to be as close to her heart as possible.

He knew he was in a hell of a lot of trouble here, but being with Mila far outweighed the risk of pain down the road. He had to capture everything now—tomorrow would worry about itself.

Thirteen

"Come to the wedding with me."

Mila slid her pencil over the fresh sheet of paper from the pad Cruz had bought her. After their quickie in the upstairs hallway, they'd come down to his room and made excellent use of his wide, open shower. She sat on his window seat now wearing one of his T-shirts and nothing else. He stood at the doorway to his walk-in closet in nothing but a pair of black boxer briefs as he stared at her waiting on an answer. But he hadn't phrased his request in the form of a question.

"Why would I come to your brother and best friend's wedding?" she asked, not bothering to look up from her sketch.

She arched the shading, already seeing the elegant gown on the sheet—strapless with an hourglass shape and a delicate train. This would also make a gorgeous wedding dress, but maybe she just had weddings on her mind right now.

"Why wouldn't you?" he countered. "Nora loved you."

And Cruz? What were his feelings? Part of her wanted to know what was in his head, but the other part worried about what he might actually say. Would he admit to having stronger feelings than she was ready for? He had no qualms about wanting a family, and she certainly wasn't there in her life—honestly, she doubted she ever would be.

But she had to admit, seeing Nora and Zane so happy and expecting a child had stirred something inside her she'd never expected and still didn't quite know how to deal with.

"It just seems like a family affair and a small, intimate ceremony from what I've heard." Mila pulled her pencil back, examining the progress so far. She looked up. "I don't even know how to handle things like that, Cruz."

He stared across the room for a moment before closing the distance between them. Mila kept her gaze steady as he continued to study her. She didn't know what he was thinking, but she figured he was about to clue her in.

"You don't have to keep living in the past."

Okay. Definitely not where she thought this conversation was headed. With his dark brows drawn inward in concern, Mila swallowed past the lump of emotion in her throat.

"I'm not living in the past," she murmured.

Cruz squatted down and rested a hand on her thigh. "You are so focused on your career and proving your father wrong that you're missing out on the life around you."

Mila opened her mouth, but Cruz went on. "You didn't see your face light up when we were outside doing pictures, but I captured each moment. You love this place and it's not the same as your childhood home."

It's as if the man could read her thoughts.

"But then you looked sad and a little lost when Nora and Zane were here," he added. "Almost like you had a longing."

What the hell had he seen in her eyes earlier? Had there been stirrings of longing she hadn't recognized in herself? Did Cruz already know her well enough to read her thoughts?

"I'm not sure what you saw, but I'll tell you what I saw," she countered. "An extremely happy family celebrating the luckiest baby."

His thumb slid back and forth across her bare thigh as he continued to hold her stare. "You're trying to deflect, but you're right. This baby is lucky and we are a happy family. Not all families are broken, and if yours is, then end the negative cycle. Don't keep letting your dad run your life. He already damaged your childhood. You have the power to rise above all of that."

Mila's heart leaped. Each word he said penetrated the defensive wall she'd always protected herself with. Nobody had been able to break through, and she hadn't necessarily wanted them to because then she'd have to face her fears, face her past.

But Cruz was unlike anyone she'd ever met.

"Come to the wedding with me," he urged.

"I wouldn't have anything to wear," she confessed. "It's not like I packed for a wedding."

"You didn't pack for a flood and freak storm, but we made it work."

She should be annoyed with his smirk, but how could she when he clearly wanted to be with her? Plus, he was so damn sexy.

"I can't just show up to a wedding I wasn't invited to," she informed him before turning her attention back to her work.

Her emotions were too high and the exposure to her heart all too real. She needed to get back to something she could control.

Cruz came to his feet but said nothing else. She really hadn't expected the conversation to die so quickly. Cruz Westbrook admitting defeat and backing down? Something must be off today.

When he left the room without another word, she concentrated on the image in her mind and let the pencil flow over the paper. She hadn't drawn a ball gown for a while, but she loved the sparkle and the idea of something grand or a reason to celebrate. Maybe one day she could wear her own designs to galas or parties. She hoped she kept dreaming big and chasing those goals. The further she got from Montana mentally, the better....

From the corner of her eye, she caught Cruz with an armful of...

Wait a minute.

"What are you doing with my things?" she asked.

He stopped mid-stride as he headed toward the adjoining bath. "Moving you into my room. It's silly for us to keep going up and down the stairs when you spend your time in here now."

Mila stared, trying not to let her blood pressure get too high as she set her pad and pencil aside and slowly rose. She pulled in a deep breath and smoothed down her T-shirt. She certainly hadn't seen this coming...especially after their intimate conversation seconds ago. Did he think he could read her mind and then just roll right into something more permanent?

"Did you ask me if I wanted my stuff in your room?"

"Why would I do that? You're in here more than up there. It makes sense."

She took a step, then another as she kept her eyes on his. "What makes sense is you not assuming, but asking me."

"I didn't think you'd mind," he clarified.

Without another word, he moved into his bathroom and carefully set her bottles of lotions and face wash on the vanity. She did a double take when she realized he'd cleaned off a place for her already and all of his stuff was on the other vanity, on the opposite side of the bathroom.

"I figured you'd want closer to the window for the natural light." He rearranged the bottles, then turned to face her. "I heard Nora talk about that before with her makeup."

Mila rubbed her forehead, trying to be angry because he hadn't included her on this decision. But at the same time, he didn't have a malicious intent, nor had she ever noticed any control issues. His intentions weren't to impose his world on her. And he had a valid point of making things easier.

"Next time you make a decision regarding my personal life, maybe discuss it with me first," she told him.

Cruz closed the distance between them and rested his hands on her shoulders. "If you want me to take these back, I will."

That statement right there was nothing her father would have ever said to her mother. Mila had to move on. She had to see that not every man was like her dad, and Cruz sure as hell was a better guy in every way possible.

"We can leave them," she agreed. "But if we're moving that stuff, let's pack up my clothes, too. Might as well bring it all."

The grin he offered sent a curl of desire spiraling through her.

"Does that mean you're staying through the end of the month?"

They hadn't said those words out loud, but there

were things they needed to discuss. She supposed now was as good of a time as any, considering that passing day brought them closer to the end of the project—and their time together.

"I'll stay here," she agreed with a nod. "But I still want to be discreet. You know how important my career is, and a bad reputation could ruin all I've been working for."

Cruz nodded. "You know I'd do anything to keep you safe in every aspect of your life. I'm well aware of how hard you've worked and what's at stake."

Those dark eyes, framed by thick, black lashes, had the power to consume her. She'd thought twice now of leaving. The first time, she stayed because Mother Nature had given her no other option, and now, she simply couldn't bring herself to say goodbye just yet. She needed more time with Cruz. Whatever was going on here was tricky and brand-new territory for her.

Bottles of lotion on a counter didn't mean a commitment. She didn't have anything to worry about... she hoped.

He was going to just have to tell her the reasons he wanted her to stay.

Cruz rocked back in his leather desk chair and raked a hand over his jaw. The coarse stubble reminded him that he needed a trim. But there had been quite a few things he'd let go lately because of his tenant.

He'd gotten behind on his work, giving even more

than usual to his assistant. He'd never been in a position before where he cared about something—or someone—more than work.

Yet from the moment Mila had swept into his life, he'd been able to think of little else.

The whole one-month time frame had gone out the window since he and Zane had decided to have Cruz do the photos for the shoot. He'd yet to tell Mila since they wanted to make sure the other photographer could be shifted to another project with timing that worked for him.

So now that they could do the shoot anytime and then she could be free to go, he wasn't ready to get everything scheduled. But they had to. They were on an even tighter deadline than before.

Which is why he continued to stare at his computer monitor and the glaring email from Maddie trying to pin down a date and time. They had makeup and hair to bring in, plus wardrobe.

Cruz knew for a fact none of those extras was necessary. He could handle everything just fine, and so could Mila. She was more than capable of doing her own hair and makeup, but she also deserved to have the best experience as one of the models for *Opulence*. Besides, all of that had been written into her contract.

He fired off his reply and chose the first of the two dates Maddie mentioned. The sooner the better. He was more than ready to get Mila back on the other side of his lens.

Movement from the open doorway drew his attention from the screen to Mila. She rested her shoulder against the frame and stared across the room. Her soft smile never failed to calm him, to make him wonder if there could be more…or if this was it. If this was the best they could be and the only time in his life he'd ever have her.

"You've been working a long time," she told him, still remaining in the doorway. "Need something to eat or anything?"

His eyes darted to the time on his screen, and he had been in there for hours. He wasn't in the mood to eat. He had too much on his mind and too many things he needed to discuss with her.

"What is it?" she asked, moving farther into his office.

She stepped around the leather sofa and didn't stop until she stood on the other side of his large glass-and-chrome desk. When she crossed her arms and continued to stare at him, he shoved his chair back and came to his feet.

"You're scaring me," she stated.

"Nothing to be afraid of," he assured her as he circled the desk to be nearer to her. "The original photographer for your shoot is being moved to another project."

Her bright green eyes flared wider. "Are we postponing again?"

"Not exactly. We're actually moving the date up closer." He reached for her hands and laced their fingers together. "We're going for this week."

"This week?" She shook her head, then brought

her attention back to him. "I don't understand. Did you find another photographer?"

"Me."

Her brows jerked together in confusion. "You? But, what about the other guy? No offense, I'm just a little lost here."

"I was telling Zane and Nora about the mini shoot we did, and they saw one of the images," he explained. "We've decided on a new direction for the shoot."

"They were here days ago," she reminded him. "Why didn't you tell me before now?"

"I had no idea what we were going to do, and I didn't want to say anything until we were sure. If you don't want me to photograph you, then I understand. We can make other arrangements."

When she pulled her hands from his and took a step back, his gut clenched. But she held her palm up and wiggled her fingers.

"Let me see them," she demanded. "You never showed me these images and I want to know what I'm getting into. I looked a wreck that day."

She'd looked absolutely perfect, but he wasn't going to argue. Surely she'd be able to see for herself.

Cruz grabbed his cell from his desk and opened the folder of images before handing over his phone.

"If you want to see them on the computer, I can pull them up there."

She said nothing as she scrolled. She paused, then scrolled a bit more. She pursed her lips, then lifted her gaze to his.

"How did you do this?" she asked, still clutching his cell. "I looked haggard that day. My lipstick had faded, my hair was all over the place, but… These aren't terrible."

"Not terrible?" he scoffed, taking his phone and holding it up. "These are magical. You're captivating and breathtaking."

A corner of her mouth kicked up. "Maybe I'm not the one with the talent after all. Your little hobby should be front and center in your life."

He sat his cell back on the desk without looking away from her intense stare. Then he snaked an arm around her waist and pulled her closer.

"Or maybe we make one hell of a team, because I barely did any editing to those images."

Her hands flattened on his chest as she tipped her head back. "A team, huh? Is that what you're looking for?"

"Maybe I am," he admitted. Nora's advice kept rolling through his mind. "Maybe I want to see if we can be a team."

She stilled against him. "In business or personal?"

"Both."

Cruz didn't look away. He wanted to see every emotion passing through her eyes. Her feelings were unmistakable: confusion, fear, but then a sliver of interest. Silence enveloped them and his own heartbeat resounded in his ears. Moments seemed to tick by more slowly than usual as he waited for a response. He wasn't quite ready to fully admit or reveal his feelings, not while he was still figuring them out himself. But he had to give Mila at least a glimpse into his emotions. She deserved for him to be as transparent as possible since she was still making her own life choices. If she didn't have the facts, she couldn't make the best decisions.

Mila slid her hands up around his neck as she leaned in a bit closer. Perhaps she wasn't rejecting his idea, but embracing a possibility.

"I have a few prospects, but maybe I could stay here until I figure things out and find a place of my own," she suggested. "If that's okay with you."

If that was okay with him? Hell yes, that was more than okay. He didn't know where this whole situation was going or even could go, but he knew he didn't want to let her go just yet.

"So you're good with me being the photographer then?"

She grazed her lips over his. "There's no one I'd rather work with," she murmured against his mouth.

Ironically, Cruz had the exact same thought. There's no other person he wanted to see on the other side of his lens than the beauty in his arms. He just hoped his surprises panned out for her. He'd thrown a big one into the mix, and he couldn't wait to see her reaction. He wanted to give her the world…she deserved nothing less.

Fourteen

Mila's cell chimed from the desk in the corner of Cruz's bedroom as soon as she stepped in. The photo shoot had just wrapped up. They'd opted for a morning session because of the lighting, and with Cruz's encouragement and the team of experts at hand, she'd never felt so beautiful.

The experience had been amazing, but she was dead tired now. She hadn't realized just how much would be involved with this project, but she would be forever grateful. There wasn't a doubt in her mind that everything Cruz shot, with Maddie's direction and keen eye, would turn into something brilliant.

She padded across the room to get her cell from the charger. She had three voice mails and a few emails. The emails grabbed her attention. They were all from name-brand companies that had never reached out to her before. She scanned each one, her excitement growing by the moment.

Then she went to the voice mails and found more brands that were interested in discussing a partnership. Mila listened to each one again, then went back to the emails. No two were the same. All different companies and all amazing opportunities.

How did she get such an influx today? She didn't know what had happened, but she was grateful for these chances. This was exactly what she'd been waiting on. Oh, she didn't have the jobs yet, but she had every bit of confidence she was well on her way to her next big contract.

She didn't know who to reply to first, so she opted to answer the emails and set up future calls. Her hands were shaking, but more from excitement than fear. She paced the room as she reread each reply before hitting Send.

Then she pulled up her voice mails and took in a deep breath, trying to figure out who to call first. She decided to go in the order in which they came in. She wasn't sure where Cruz was, he'd still been talking to his employees when she came back to the house. Wait until she told him what happened while they'd been shooting all morning. He would be just as happy for her, she just knew it.

That was just one of the reasons she found him to be so perfect. He truly wanted to lift her up and see her shine. Yes, he was a powerful man, but he understood her need to stand on her own, and with the opportunity *Opulence* gave her, she knew she was destined for great things.

Those chances had just come sooner than she thought. She figured that something on her social media must had taken flight and made an impact somewhere for all of these messages to come in.

Mila's anxiety heightened when she ended up having to leave a voice mail at all three companies. Playing phone tag was not her idea of a good time, but at least she'd had a heads-up and could think of what she wanted to say when they returned her calls.

Mila looked down at the dress she'd worn for the shoot. She would have to change into something of her own...but not yet. She wanted to soak up this moment. Cruz told her he would get this stunning strapless, flowy piece of couture back to the wardrobe department next week.

Mila turned to the floor-length mirror in the corner and held out the skirt. She did a little spin, feeling all the excitement with the opportunities ahead of her. Never before had her future held so much hope.

While she could envision her career blossoming, she wasn't sure about where she and Cruz stood. He'd been the only person to ever hear about her past. Nobody in a beauty industry that thrived on perfection wanted to hear about an overweight child who had been borderline neglected and crawled through what felt like quicksand to get where she was today.

But Cruz had listened. He'd heard her, he'd *seen* her, and he'd still enveloped her in all the aspects of his life.

She'd agreed to stay at his estate until she had a better plan for her future. She'd taken a virtual tour of the home in Chicago, and while everything checked off those boxes she had, something had been missing. Ultimately, she hadn't put in an offer, and she wasn't going to.

"You were even more stunning today."

Mila's eyes lifted to the reflection in the mirror. Cruz stood in his doorway, his intense dark gaze meeting hers.

"I don't know how," he went on. "I have no idea how you could top what we did that day by the log, but you did."

"It's the hair and makeup team you have," she informed him with a shrug. "You have magicians at your fingertips."

"No, that's not it."

Cruz stepped into the room, those long legs eating up the distance between them until he came to stand just behind her. Strong hands came to rest on her shoulders. He eased her body back against his, all the while holding her gaze.

"What's at my fingertips is the most amazing lover, the most striking model, and the most kick-ass woman I've ever met."

Mila laughed. "Well, I'll be sure to put that on my next résumé."

But he wasn't smiling. He had such an intense stare when something was on his mind. It was little nuances like that she had come to notice and appreciate about him. Their bond had started forming on day one and became more and more secure as the days passed.

"What's on your mind?" she asked, reaching up to lay her hands over his. "Did something happen after I left?"

"Actually, yes."

Mila's breath caught in her throat, but she waited to hear what he had to say before she panicked. She had some news of her own to share with him, but she'd let him go first.

"I know you've been house hunting and trying to find the perfect place," he began. "I also know you've been stressed about the next steps with everything coming up, so I did something."

"I don't know if that's a warning I should be afraid of or excited for."

Regardless, nerves danced around in her belly as she waited.

"I hope you're excited," he explained, giving her a gentle squeeze. "I bought you a house here."

Mila blinked, confident that she'd misunderstood that last statement.

"Well, not *here*," he went on. "It's about ten minutes away, so close by. You can stay there while you're hunting or in between shoots. It's yours to do with as you want."

Mila's hands fell away as she tried to make sense of this unexpected, outlandish surprise. She took a step away and then another. She paced the room, rolling over every thought she had and how exactly she should reply.

"Are you out of your mind?" she demanded.

Okay, so maybe not the best approach.

Turning from the mirror to face her, he propped his hands on his narrow hips. Thick, dark brows drew in as he continued to stare at her as if he had no idea what she could be upset about.

"You can't just buy me a house, Cruz." She rubbed her forehead, still trying to gather her thoughts. "I mean, who does that?"

"I do."

Those two words summed him up. The power to do anything at a whim. She had to believe that his intentions were good, but she couldn't help but feel cornered.

"But I never said I wanted to stay in this area," she stated, trying to rein in her frustration. "In fact, I said the opposite."

"You also said you were unsure where you wanted to be," he reminded her. "You agreed to stay here so we could see where things went, and having your own place made sense in case you want space or a place to put all of your things from Miami."

"So you got me a house to store my things?"

She couldn't even wrap her mind around having enough money to just buy a house for the convenience. But he'd done just that for her so she could have a retreat and a place for all of her belongings. Or was there something else at play here?

Her gut clenched. "Cruz, I don't want to sound ungrateful—"

"Then don't. Just take the gift."

She lifted the flowy skirt and made her way back to him. His eyes remained fixed on her, and she saw a sliver of pain there. The very last thing she wanted to do was hurt him or reject his offer. But...

"I appreciate everything you've done for me." She dropped the skirt and offered a slight smile. "You've thrown me off here, and I'm regaining my footing. But you know where I came from, *who* I came from. So having you buy a house feels close to seeing my father always keep a controlling eye over my mother."

He opened his mouth, but Mila held up her hand. "I know," she admitted. "You're not him. I get it. I'm just still in shock. Not only that aspect, but you went from buying me pencils and paper to a home, so you have to understand my shock."

Cruz nodded and blew out a slow sigh. "I get it, Mila. I truly do. I want to give you everything, but if you're not ready for that, I can sell the house. I just didn't know if you'd be comfortable—"

Her cell chimed from the bed where she'd tossed it, cutting off his words.

"Let it ring," he told her.

But there were too many important calls she was waiting on.

"One minute." She held up her finger. "Don't go anywhere."

She moved to the bed and snatched her phone, recognizing the number on the screen. Mila pulled in a deep breath and tapped to answer. "Hello, this is Mila."

She kept her back to Cruz because she couldn't be distracted right now and every single thing about that man was a distraction.

"Hello, Mila. This is Edward Bevins. Is this a bad time?"

Well, it wasn't ideal, but no way would she tell a man of his standing and power such things.

"This is fine," she replied. "I'm sorry I missed your call earlier. I was working on a shoot."

"I imagine you were, considering you are in high demand now."

She was? Since when? Because nobody had contacted her, save for Arthur, who rejected her a couple weeks ago.

A thought popped into her head before Edward could even continue.

"After seeing a few of the images Cruz Westbrook sent over, I made a point to tell my assistant that we needed to…"

Whatever he said seemed to come out muffled as she slowly turned and locked eyes with Cruz. And from the look on his face, he knew damn well what this call was about.

"I hope we can come to an agreement about working together," Edward added. "I can send over more detailed ideas of the projects we have in mind for you, the pay for each one, and the travel allowance. I just wanted to speak to you before doing so and hopefully get you before you're committed somewhere else."

Her eyes continued to hold Cruz's.

"Oh, I'm definitely not committed to anyone," she replied. "I look forward to hearing more from you."

"It's my pleasure. My assistant will get you all of the information by midmorning."

Mila disconnected the call and clutched her cell at her side. Her entire world seemed to have spiraled out of control in the past few minutes. How in the hell had she gone from such a high to being completely gutted and feeling betrayed?

No. She felt controlled…which was worse.

"What have you done?" she whispered.

Cruz jerked. "What's that supposed to mean? Who was on the phone?"

"Edward Bevins."

A wide smile spread across his face. "That's great. What did he say?"

"*What did he say?* He said you sent him pictures and apparently, I wasn't in on that portion of my career, nor was there anything like that in my contract with *Opulence.* Since when do you leak your models before your own spread?"

He opened his mouth, then closed it as he ran a hand over that stubbled jawline. "Are you angry with me?"

"Hell yes, I'm angry with you," she confirmed. "You made a calculated career move regarding *my* career without telling me a thing. I assume all the other messages I got today were because of you."

When he continued to stare, her heart broke a little more. Maybe he wasn't too far removed from her father after all. How could she have been so blind?

Cruz was the most powerful man she'd ever encountered, both financially and mentally, and she'd tumbled right into bed with him in every sense of the term. Her business and personal life were now completely tied to him.

Hell, he'd bought her a damn house and had branches in all directions regarding the next steps of her career. Where did she go that he hadn't covered already?

"Why are you upset?" he asked. "Your project with the magazine would have propelled these calls anyway. I just sped up the process."

How could he not see the magnitude of his actions? Could he not comprehend how devastating this was for her?

Maybe, all this time, he hadn't known her at all. When she thought he'd been listening, he'd been plotting and leaving her out of the most important decisions of her life.

"When my spread comes out this fall, that's what I counted on people seeing," she explained. "That's what I would have gotten calls about. Not you asking for favors from your cronies."

"Did it matter if it was now or later?" he countered.

"Yes, it matters." The burn in her throat and sting in her eyes irritated her. The last thing she wanted to do was lose it now. "I want to get there on my own. I asked you not to intervene."

"You said that about your designs and I didn't," he volleyed back.

She pressed her fingertips to the bridge of her nose. "I can't be taken seriously in this industry with my lover trying to control my life."

In an instant, his lips thinned, his nostrils flared. "Is that how you think of me? A bedmate who wants to run your life? I thought we had gone well beyond the superficial."

"I thought so, too."

The uncomfortable, yawning silence settled heavily between them. She had no idea what to say next and there was no defense he could give her that would make her change her mind or ease her anger.

"I can't stay here."

"Mila—"

"I *won't* stay here," she corrected.

"I just finalized the house yesterday," he informed her. "I'll get you the keys and you can stay there."

"I'll be going to the B and B," she replied, crossing her arms over the dress she still had to give back. "Your assistant never canceled my reservation, and I called the business and had them hold my room in case I needed to stay longer."

Mila couldn't tell if that look in his deep brown eyes was anger, frustration, or sadness. Well, he might as well join the club, because she certainly had all three running through her.

"Then stay here and just take your room back upstairs," he suggested. "We can talk about this."

"What's there to talk about? You can't take back what you did, and I can't be under the thumb of a man who wants to run every part of my life. I just don't understand why you didn't discuss it with me. We've talked about this so much."

She'd shared her entire life with him and he'd failed to protect her heart. Maybe that wasn't his fault. Perhaps all of this was on her for being too trusting, for falling into bed so fast and for believing he might be genuine.

When he offered nothing else, Mila went to the walk-in closet.

"I need to change and pack my things."

He didn't budge, so she quickly added, "I'll take care of things from here, Cruz. We're done."

Fifteen

Cruz remained in his study, swirling the bourbon around in his tumbler.

He hadn't drunk a drop and really contemplated hurling the glass against the far wall.

He'd gotten out of Mila's way while she changed and packed. She didn't want his help—not in any way whatsoever, apparently. So he'd kept his distance.

She'd left two hours ago and he'd still been staring at the amber contents in this glass, trying to figure out where the hell he'd gone wrong. All he'd wanted to do was help, to give her all she deserved and had been working toward for years.

Nobody knew they were lovers, so nobody would think that's why she got the extra boost.

Cruz's cell vibrated on his desk and he glanced down to see Nora's name light up the screen. He was not in the mood to talk to anyone, not even his best friend. But he also knew that if he didn't answer, she'd harass him until he did, or have Zane call.

He swiped the screen and put the call on speaker.

"Hey, Nora."

"Hey. I wanted to see if you and Mila would come over tomorrow for dinner. Now, before you say no or come up with some excuse, you should know that Zane and I will just show up there if you don't come here. I just thought some family time with no talk of work—"

"She's gone."

Silence filled the room and Cruz set the glass down. He rested his elbows on the desktop and held his forehead in his hands as he stared down at the phone as if he could see his best friend.

"What do you mean, she's gone?"

"She left after the shoot," he explained. "Went to the bed-and-breakfast in town."

More silence, followed by, "What did you do?"

"What makes you think I did anything?" he snapped.

"Because I can tell by your tone that you're sulking, probably with a glass of bourbon or scotch nearby that you haven't touched."

Sometimes there was a downside to having Nora as his best friend.

"And I saw the way that woman looked at you,"

she went on. "There's no way in hell she'd just walk out because she didn't love you."

Cruz froze at how easily Nora tossed that word out.

"She doesn't love me. Don't be ridiculous."

"Men can be so naive," she muttered. "As a woman speaking on behalf of another woman, she does indeed love you. Maybe she hasn't said it, maybe she doesn't even realize it, but she does. So, what did you do?"

"It's not important, but we won't be coming tomorrow."

"Do you need me to come over?" she asked. "I don't like that sadness in your tone."

"I'm not too fond of my tone, either," he admitted. "But here we are."

"Cruz—"

"I need to go, Nora. Thanks for calling."

He didn't want to be rude, but at the same time, he didn't want pity or advice. He wanted to be left alone to wallow in his own misery and thoughts. He wanted to figure out where he'd let things get out of hand when he'd only been trying to help her.

Why couldn't she see that he would do absolutely anything for her? He wasn't sorry for what he'd done, because even if she never wanted to see him again, at least he knew her dreams would be fulfilled.

All that mattered now was her happiness…even if that meant sacrificing his own.

Mila had just stepped out of the shower when the knock sounded at her door. She stilled, wondering who would be at her B and B so late in the evening. The only person who knew she was here was Cruz, and after the way she'd left, she highly doubted he'd come chasing her.

Or maybe he would.

If that was him on the other side of the door, she really didn't know what to do. Did she want him to chase her?

No. She needed a clean break. She had to shift all of her focus to building the career she'd always wanted. She couldn't do that while playing mind games or bedroom romps.

The unexpected visitor pounded louder. Mila yanked the knot on her floral robe tighter as she padded across her plush suite. The moment she stepped up to the peephole, she cringed.

Maybe Cruz would have been a better option.

"I know you're in there," Nora called from the other side. "I just want five minutes."

There was no way in hell two women could have a conversation and be done in five minutes. That simply wasn't possible.

Mila flicked the antique lock and opened the door. "I just got out of the shower," she found herself explaining.

"And you're still stunning." Nora ushered her way inside. "I want to hate you for it, but I like you too much."

Mila assumed that was a compliment, so she let it pass.

"Have a seat." Mila motioned toward the plush

yellow sofa near the window. "I assume you're here on Cruz's behalf."

Nora laughed as she set her purse on the accent table near the door before crossing to the couch. "If Cruz knew I was here, he would not only be mortified, he'd give me the silent treatment for quite some time."

"Then why are you here?"

Nora took a seat at one end and Mila took the other. She adjusted her robe over her thighs to make sure she was completely covered before shifting to her guest.

"Because I want to know what Cruz did that had you leaving in such a hurry."

"Ask him."

"I did," Nora explained, adjusting her top over her adorable rounded belly. "He wouldn't tell me, and since I know the two of you are in love, I'm here to help. I know, it's not my place, but consider it a free service."

Damn it. Mila liked her. How could she not?

"Cruz tried setting up Zane and me not long ago," Nora started. "So I don't feel the least bit guilty about stepping in here."

"He mentioned that," Mila muttered.

Nora reached across and patted Mila's hand. "So what did he do?"

Mila had finally stopped crying in the shower, so she sincerely hoped she could get through this without losing it all over again.

"He bought me a house."

Nora squinted. "Okay, that's not where I thought this was going to go."

"He also sent my images to several brands before consulting with me. He just tried to take over every part of my life and he thought I would just be ever so grateful that he paved the way."

"And you wanted to do things on your own," Nora stated with an understanding nod.

Mila found herself opening to Nora and sharing a portion of her past, including the parts about her controlling father and submissive mother. How she'd been on her own for years and the importance of not relying on handouts.

"I mean, sure it's been rough," Mila went on. "Trying to shake that hold my past has had over me. Trying to prove to my father and to myself that I can be anything I want and be successful. So when I got the call from *Opulence,* I knew my big break was on the horizon. I got that far on my own and just needed the boost from this to launch bigger things. He didn't understand why I was upset when he sent out pictures early, and that's the problem."

"Did he say why he did that?" Nora asked. "Because I've been with this company since its conception and they've never done that before."

"He kept telling me that he wanted to give me everything, that I deserved nothing less."

Nora's soft smile spread across her face. "Cruz has such a big heart, and knowing him, he thought he was helping, I'm sure. He's always been the peacemaker and wanting everyone around him happy and safe."

"Is that what this is?" Mila countered. "Or is it him pushing his power front and center in my world?"

Nora rested her arm along the back of the sofa and glanced around the room, likely weighing her words. Mila waited, finding it refreshing to have a woman to talk to, even if Nora would likely take Cruz's side. They were best friends, after all, and soon to be family.

"That's not a characteristic of Cruz. He doesn't flaunt his power or his money," Nora started, her attention coming back to Mila. "For years, he tried to get Zane and their father, Barrett, on speaking terms. He doesn't like conflict, so if he has to put his strength to use, he will, but I assure you, his actions all come from a pure heart."

Mila thought back to every word he'd ever told her, every action he'd taken where she was concerned. In each instance, he'd never spoken about himself or his own needs. The conversations had been geared toward her and her goals, her future, her happiness.

"So he bought you a house?"

Mila snorted and shook her head. "Who the hell thinks buying a home is an appropriate gift?"

"Cruz and Zane are not like regular men, and that's why we love them."

Mila met Nora's knowing gaze and there was no denying how she felt. She'd tried and clearly failed.

"I don't want to love him—I'm trying to be angry."

Nora lifted her knee onto the couch and angled her body more toward Mila. She kept that sweet smile in place and Mila had a feeling she'd made a life-long friend.

"Maybe be angry at the way he went about things," Nora suggested. "But don't be angry with the man. He can't help that he acts before he thinks. It's just going to take the right woman to give him some guidance."

"And you think I'm that woman?"

"The fact that I'm here fighting for the two of you should tell you everything."

Mila replayed the entire day over and over in her head. Maybe she'd jumped to conclusions, but Nora was right. Cruz did need guidance. There had to be a middle ground for them. There had to be some way for them to be that team he'd mentioned, because she couldn't imagine her life without him.

Sixteen

The alarm on his driveway went off and Cruz jerked at the sudden sound echoing through the house. He'd never left his study. He'd tried to work but hadn't gotten very far. He'd started looking into that Hawaii trip next summer just so he could feel productive and try to have something to look forward to.

But he just kept thinking he didn't want to go without Mila.

He clicked on his computer screen and pulled up the exterior cameras lining the drive and the front of the house…and his gut clenched.

Cruz shoved his leather chair back and headed to the hallway toward the front of the house. He reached the door and threw it open just as Mila started up the steps. With her hand on the railing and one foot on the bottom stair, she glanced up and met his gaze.

He couldn't move. He just remained in the doorway, afraid to get too hopeful for her return. Maybe she'd just forgotten something.

"I should have called first," she began, but stayed in place.

He took in her fresh appearance. This wasn't the same Mila who'd shown up on that first day, fighting against the storm, striding right through it on her stilettos like a champ. Now she had on a pair of leggings, sneakers, an off-the-shoulder tee, her hair in a high ponytail, and a striking face devoid of any makeup—she looked as if she'd gone through a complete transformation.

But he truly believed he was the one who had been transformed by this beauty.

"Did you forget something?" he asked.

She mounted the stairs, one at a time, all the while keeping her eyes locked onto his. His heart sank at the thought that she'd only come to pick up a toiletry or something trivial.

"I forgot to tell you that I've fallen in love with you."

Cruz's breath caught in his throat and he took a step closer to her. "What?"

"That's not how I rehearsed my speech on the way over here." She laughed. "But I'm not sorry that that was my lead-in."

He raked a hand down his face, trying to clear

his thoughts, because just moments ago, he was still sulking in his office.

"I'm confused," he told her, clenching his fists at his sides to prevent himself from reaching for her until he had all the facts.

"We're both confused, but I think we can work on that." She came to stand within reaching distance, but she didn't touch him. "You see, you didn't communicate with me, which terrified me. I thought you were going to be like my father, and I couldn't get out of here fast enough."

"I never meant to—"

"I know that now," she confirmed.

"Sell the damn house if you want," he tacked on. "I just thought that would help put your mind at ease."

"Well, we can sell the house, but only because I'm living here."

Damn. That was the green light he needed to reach for her. He framed her face and stared into the expressive eyes he'd worried he wouldn't see again.

"You can't do that again," she told him, circling her arms around his neck. "We have to discuss everything. I have to be your equal in all things if this is going to work."

Relief spiraled through him as he covered her lips with his. Returning the kiss, she pressed her body to his, but Cruz eased back just enough to make his point. "I don't want you anywhere else but directly beside me. We're a team, remember? I love you too much to not have you as my partner."

She smiled, and that beautiful sight never failed to send a punch of lust to the gut.

"Is that wedding invitation still open?" she asked.

"Hell yes, it is. I'm not taking any other date."

"Nora will be so happy," Mila stated. "She told me—"

Cruz narrowed his eyes. "Nora came to see you?"

Mila curled her lips in as her eyes widened. "Pretend I didn't let that slip."

"I didn't need her to be a mediator," he grumbled.

"Yeah, well, we needed a little help," Mila retorted. "And she's the only girlfriend I have, so don't be too upset with her. She really loves you."

Cruz nodded. "I'm well aware. I won't say anything just yet."

"Never," Mila countered.

Cruz pressed a kiss to her lips and swept her up into his arms. "Let's argue later. I have better ideas."

He stepped into the house and kicked the door shut with his foot, more than ready to start his life with the woman he'd fallen for.

Epilogue

Cruz squeezed Mila's hand as they made their way beneath the draped white tent. With the sunset as its backdrop, the wedding between Zane and Nora had been stunning. Now the guests gathered for the reception near the pond. Chandeliers were suspended from the high points under the tent. Tables were draped with flowers in the wedding colors of lilac and white, and each cloth chair had a lilac ribbon tied around the back. The entire place exuded intimacy and elegance.

"I'm glad I came," Mila admitted as they crossed to the table with their names on the place cards. "This was a perfect evening."

Cruz released her hand and slid an arm behind her back. "Everything in my life is perfect right now."

As he spun her around, his eyes landed on hers and a smile spread across his face. Her heart did another flip, which seemed to be the norm with Cruz lately. She never thought she could fit so fluidly into someone else's world, but after seeing this close-knit family, she couldn't imagine her life without them.

"I hope you'll save a dance for me."

Mila and Cruz turned as Barrett came up beside them. The tall, broad-shouldered man had kind eyes and a smile like his twin sons'. She'd only met him right before the wedding, but he was just another puzzle piece of the many that were making up her new life.

"Of course," she agreed with a slight nod. "I'd love to have a dance with you."

"But the rest of them belong to me," Cruz joked as he tugged her closer to his side.

Mila swatted his chest. "You have me all of the time. I'd like to get to know your father better, and maybe I'll dance with Zane so he can fill me in on the stories you don't want me to hear about your wilder days."

"Did I hear my name?"

Zane and Nora came to complete their circle. The newlyweds held hands and looked like the happiest couple in the world. Not so long ago, Mila would have been jealous, but now she felt a special bond because she'd found her own joy and level of fulfillment. Not only with Cruz, but also with his family.

"My girl wants to dance with Dad and you, apparently," Cruz stated. "I think she's trying to find out if she made a mistake agreeing to stay with me."

"Oh, I'm right where I need to be," she countered. "But I wouldn't mind chatting with the rest of your family."

"Then let's get to it." Barrett held out his hand and Mila slid hers in. "The perfect song just got started."

Mila smiled over her shoulder to Cruz as she let Barrett lead her to the dance floor, but on her way, she overheard Cruz tell his brother how complete his life was now. And she couldn't agree more. Finally, after all the pain she'd endured trying to outrun her past, she'd come home. She'd truly found her forever home with her forever man.

* * * * *

Look for these other books from
USA TODAY *bestselling author Jules Bennett*

When the Lights Go Out…
Second Chance Vows
Snowed In Secrets